OUTLAW DRAGON

THE DRAGONS OF ESTERNES, BOOK 2

STEVE TURNBULL

TAU PRESS LTD

OUTLAW DRAGON by Steve Turnbull.

Ebook ISBN: 978-1-910342-96-1

Paperback ISBN: 978-1-910342-97-8

Hardback ISBN: 978-1-910342-98-5

Published by Tau Press Ltd.

Cover by Jeff Brown (jeffbrowngraphics.com).

Edited by Zoë Markham (markhamcorrect.com).

Continuity editing by Adriel Wiggins (www.adrielwiggins.com).

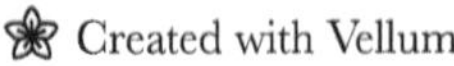

1

The white light of Lostimal shone across the undulating plains and the dim red glow of Colimar filled in the shadows. Beneath the bulk of the *tekrak*, they had made their camp a day's walk from the castle of Jakalain. Gally, Yenteel and Ulina had remained there with the patterner Tenical, and the two older *zirichasa*, Looesa and Shingul. Kantees carried the boy back to his home on Sheesha's back.

It had seemed strange going back there. The familiarity of the place on the one hand, balanced against the changes she had suffered. She had not promised Lord and Lady Jakalain she would return their abducted son but she felt responsible, and was glad she had done it.

However, in returning Jelamie to his parents, Kantees was careful not to give them any chance to apprehend her. They would have strung her up as an escaped slave and thief given a chance since she had flown off on their valuable property, taking another slave and an escaped prisoner with her.

She had given Jelamie the letter that Yenteel had written—Kantees could neither write nor read—and the boy had promised he would deliver it. He was certainly more subdued than he had been before his adventure. She had not liked the spoiled brat he had been, but she was not sure the new Jelamie was better. He had suffered badly at the hands of the mercenaries.

Letting Sheesha ride the winds at his own pace, Kantees had overridden the *ziri*'s desire to go to his own eyrie, and landed on the top of the Ziri Tower. She had slipped off Sheesha's back and knelt to give the boy a hug which he accepted willingly. The clattering of approaching armsmen drove her back into the sky immediately. She wondered if the boy would ever recover from his experiences; she hoped so, as long as he did not forget and go back to being the old, unpleasant, Jelamie.

The camp came into sight, the curve of the *tekrak* highlighted on one side by the fire. Sheesha went into his usual spiral descent to land. There was no need to guide him. There was no booming welcome from the other *ziri* at this time, unlike during the day. Perhaps they were just asleep, or perhaps at night the call might attract foes from the darkness.

Kantees dismounted and thanked Sheesha for letting her ride—neither she nor the others used any kind of saddle or even reins, so it really was up to the *zirichasa* whether they allowed people to fly them. But Sheesha seemed to enjoy it, and the others did not object.

"Any problems?" asked Yenteel, sounding barely awake.

"None."

He went silent and turned over. Kantees sat down by the fire and stared into its embers. Riding Sheesha, even in this mild weather, was not the warmest activity and she needed better clothing. She still wore what she had escaped in—rough trousers and a top that was long enough to be a smock. It was not that she wanted expensive clothes, which was fortunate given her circumstances, but just a linen undershirt would be nice to keep the roughness from her skin.

Or clothes like Daybian wore. She had lost the set she had stolen at Kurvin Port when that obnoxious Lord Hamalain had come to arrest and torture her.

She hesitated as she remembered Daybian's face in the cave. The serious Daybian. The man who had saluted her. Not the boy with the clever comments who thought the entire world revolved around him. And she remembered his words as his *ziri* had been killed. When he told her to save herself and the others.

Book design by Evelyn Fust and Emma Fust

Book Cover by Emma Fust

First edition 2024

For my cousin

-E

Prologue

An afternoon sun hung sleepily near the horizon, trying to decide whether to give in and melt into evening or freeze time forever. Its light spilled gracefully through the air, illuminating a giant airship sailing among the clouds. The *Freelander*, an enormous galleon-like vessel, gratefully lent its weight to 1,000 giant balloons bobbing faintly in the air. The wood of the ship was solid and worn, shining with the polish of the bare feet and bustle it often bore. People of every age, shape, size, and color swarmed the top deck and rooms below, all sharing an electric joy at their place in the annual Freely family reunion, and an ignorance of the disaster that was yet to come.

The Freelys were often described by others as magnificent, innovative, and ahead of their time. The Freelys were always described by themselves as *kind of big* and *weirdly popular*. The former statement was closer to the truth, despite the familial humility; most Freelys were inventors, scientists, artists, musicians, or pioneers, and dwelled in every corner of the globe, a turn of phrase which most of the family disliked considering its blatant contradiction. To be a Freely by blood was to be gifted a family of geniuses; to become a Freely through marriage, adoption, or mere friendship was to join a sort of club, albeit a very odd and exciting one.

"Uncle Leo! Uncle Leo!" Two little girls emerged from the chaos, faces beaming with identical grins as they launched themselves at a young man leaning against the railing. One girl was smiling, skin deep brown and glowing, her brilliant green eyes sparkling as her curled dark braids swung cheerfully. The other was around the same age, her skin light and freckled, her blond curls flying in every direction and giving her an impish, otherworldly halo of hair. Both were entirely failing to contain their excitement.

"Hey, Uncle Leo!" Arlyn Freely's dark skin glowed in the dying sunlight as she swam through the sea of legs. "Where are you?"

"There!" Graylin Freely pointed ahead, and the two cousins giggled their way to him, both quite literally bouncing.

The man in front of the girls looked up, eyes landing on them, a smile spreading across his face. Leo Freely, a mere twenty-seven, was one of those people destined to be a child forever. He scratched at the beard he couldn't really grow and scooped his two nieces into his arms with a laugh as they reached him.

"Well, hello there!" he grinned. "Boy, have you two grown since I last saw you?"

"Of course I have. I'm eight!" Arlyn gave her uncle a sideways look, as if he had slighted her age and status, while also attempting to subtly remind him of her recent birthday in the hope he had a gift for her.

"I'm *almost* eight," Graylin added, wounded that her cousin had brought up their age gap and poking her companion as compensation. After all, such an insult as discussing their whole *three months'* difference could hardly be ignored. With a laugh that only someone not yet a parent could make, Leo swung the girls around and up onto his shoulders, who screamed and clutched at his head.

"Did you two need something?" he questioned, reaching up to tickle them unceasingly. Immersed in a fit of giggles, the cousins were unable to answer. "Or do you just like my company?" Leo tickled harder, and their laughter turned to shrieks of mirth.

"No, no, we want to ask you something!" Arlyn gasped. Leo grinned and swung his nieces to the ground.

"Alright then, but you'd better be quick about it, because there is a cake downstairs in the kitchen with my name on it."

"We want . . . to go to the control room." Arlyn grabbed her uncle's hands, feet dancing as she proposed the tantalizing plan. Leo raised his eyebrows.

"The control room, eh? You'll be good?" he asked.

"We're *always* good," Graylin said, hands clasped behind her back, eyes shining. Leo made a face as if considering the proposition.

"Well, in that case . . . no." He smiled at his two very disappointed nieces. "But maybe later." Graylin folded her arms and dropped her head against her uncle's leg, Leo ruffling her hair as he gently pushed her away.

"Go on now," he told the two, "go cause trouble elsewhere. And *don't* go into the control room."

With resigned shrugs, both girls gave Leo hasty hugs, which due to their height really were more on his legs than anywhere else, before abandoning him and his disappointing adultness to dash into the maze of people around them. Arlyn sprinted ahead, feet flying with the freedom of the glowing sky. She let her eyes close, pretending for a moment that she was running on the puffs of clouds hanging like gentle white waves around the ship. She grinned, opening her eyes just in time to see a young woman directly in front of her.

"Ah! Sorry!" Arlyn cried, skidding and screeching while managing to stop right before barreling into the woman. "Oh, hi Aunt Rosie!"

"Shhhh, the baby is sleeping." Aunt Rosie lowered a bundle of blankets in front of Arlyn, who now had Graylin at her side.

"Oh, sorry!" Graylin whispered, her finger absentmindedly tracing an embroidered bee on the baby's blanket. The baby girl had sun-bleached blonde curls, very much like Graylin's, cradling her round face. Arlyn tucked one ringlet softly away from the baby's closed eyes, before turning and dashing away.

"Hey! Arlyn! Wait for me!" Graylin shouted after her, wincing as the young woman, who despite her title was definitely not their aunt, shushed her. "Sorry!" she whispered, before speeding after her cousin. She dodged and wove, squeezing between two men whom she knew she was related to, though not how, pausing to watch them fiddle with a strange invention until the thick smoke the little orb produced drove her away.

Just as the girls were about to reach the far end of the ship, both were swept up by pairs of powerful arms. Arlyn laughed and grinned up into her father's face, pressing her fresh cheek to his scratchy one. Benson Freely's dirty blond hair, just like his younger brother Leo's, was cut and trimmed, and his gray eyes shimmered.

"*There* you are, Bean," he chuckled, cradling Arlyn like the baby she most certainly was not. "Getting into trouble, I assume?"

"You bet!" Arlyn giggled, wrapping her arms around her dad's neck and fiddling with the rough collar of his shirt. It smelled strong and familiar, like engine oil and fresh air, and perhaps something a little sweet.

"Do you have my caramels?" Arlyn asked suspiciously, leaning close to her dad's ear and sniffing deeply.

"Caramels? I want some!" Graylin, perched on her own dad's shoulders, reached over precariously. Michelangelo, looking very much like his daughter, grinned and held up a hand to steady her. They both had Benson's characteristics, except somehow wilder: light blond hair which for Graylin fell in mounds of ringlets and unlike Benson's was neither brushed nor trimmed, gray eyes that didn't shimmer but burned, and scattered freckles that gave the entire trio a very trickster-ish aura.

"Here," Benson dug into his pocket and pulled out a handful of soft caramel candies, holding the stash out. "Don't tell your mom, and don't spoil your dinner."

"Spoil? No way," Arlyn grinned. "I have a special dessert stomach. It doesn't affect my real stomach."

"I see." Benson raised his eyebrows skeptically, and pressed a kiss to Arlyn's forehead before setting her down. "Well, you and your dessert stomach go have fun, but please stay out of trouble. I've already made several excuses for your behavior, and there's a point when telling our family that you've been poorly parented just doesn't work anymore."

"We'll be good," Arlyn grinned, tapping Graylin's arm as they moved to run away. "Promise."

Benson and Michaelangelo just shook their heads, both privately in awe at the two beautiful, extraordinary little girls who were their own daughters.

Benson removed a lighter from his pocket, flicked it open, and chuckled. "I feel terrible, you know?"

"Why?" His brother snatched it from his hand, pocketing it. "Also, you don't smoke."

Benson shrugged, his face spreading into a smile. "They're going to turn out just like us."

"Ha!" Michelangelo folded his arms, his smile mirroring his brother's, watching as the blonde little menace that was his daughter dashed away. He grinned. "Well, you're right about that."

The girls skidded to a halt as a large group of older kids ran past. They were chasing a small flying contraption across the deck screaming, "CATCH IT! CATCH IT! Don't let it fly off the deck!"

"Graylin! Get it!" an older cousin yelled as the device spun a sharp curve towards the girls. Graylin leapt up, maniacal in her attempt to catch the small machine. It zipped just out of her reach and into Arlyn's, who swatted at it, hitting it right into Graylin's hand. The crowd of older cousins triumphantly lifted them as they cheered. "Attaway girls!" High-fives were bestowed in giddy celebration, and as the crowd moved on to their next exciting game, the girls were left blissfully unnoticed.

"Control room?" Arlyn asked. Graylin just giggled and zipped ahead. The cousins wove and ducked through the crowd of friendly familial faces, bee-lining for the forbidden control room. It was one of those spaces which seems to exist in every childhood, a room which was very practically not meant for children and therefore was the goal of everyone under the age of twelve. While the pilot's chair on the top deck was for steering the ship and keeping a steady eye on other important functions, the control room was for managing them. It held access to the electric, the water tanks, the different air levels in the 1,000 balloons holding the ship afloat, and many other genuinely important facilities. However, this was not the draw for the cousins. For them, the tantalizing fact that they shouldn't be there was enough. They shared a look, a grin, and then pushed in.

A golden chandelier illuminated the room, shedding light on a long line of contraptions covering the walls, the wires and levers providing far greater temptation than the maps and papers scattered across the tables and floor. This was the brain of the *Freelander*. Every moving part could be seen and controlled from this room. While Graylin held a pen to her nose as a mustache and examined the results in a very reflective panel, Arlyn just breathed in the space, lungs filling with the atmosphere of light and beeps and blinks. Spotting the curve of windows at the far end of the room, she smiled and skipped toward it, beckoned by the expanse of sky visible through the glass. The air beyond was filled with sunset lit clouds, blushing puffs of orange and yellow shifting lazily in the evening breeze. Arlyn smiled, stretching out an arm, hand reaching for the cool glass, fingertips inches away from-

BOOM! A massive explosion shook the room. The chandelier rattled and swung, and the floor slanted under their feet.

"What's happening?" Graylin asked, her big eyes darting to her cousin. Arlyn began to answer, but was cut off as she tripped and stumbled into a wall. Graylin teetered herself, reaching for Arlyn's outstretched arm and instead falling to the floor. Arlyn grasped at the wall frantically as Graylin did the floor, both becoming increasingly frightened as wooden boards beneath their feet leaned even further. Maps rolled from the desk, and the wood all around them groaned. Faintly, just outside the cousin's formerly blissful bubble, someone screamed.

"GIRLS!" A desperate voice rang through the room, a voice which belonged to their Uncle Leo as he threw open the doors and flew in, eyes wild. Leo, so young, looked nearly fifty, his face transformed by panic. There was something gray that looked oddly like ashes strewn on his shirt and in his hair. When he spotted the girls, his face melted into momentary relief, his hands reaching out for them. "Come with me now- quickly!" Leo grabbed the confused girls by their arms and dragged them out of the room. The outside was bright, dazzling in a nightmarish way, the light much stronger and hotter than it should be, and the girls struggled to see. Perhaps, in the end this was a blessing, for it postponed the horror for at least a moment.

A section of balloons that held up the *Freelander* had caught aflame. Heat and smoke choked the girls, and they coughed. Graylin squinted through the dark billowing clouds.

Amid the flames, the expansive deck of the *Freelander* was filled with family members leaping off the sides of the airship, trying their best to escape. It was horrific, watching as the young and the old dropped out of sight in a panic, some fleeing the fire, some already being consumed. But even worse than the sight was the knowledge of the fate which awaited all those people when they reached the ground.

"Uncle Leo, what's happening?" Graylin shrank against him, eyes widening as family members screamed, sparks licking at their arms and legs as shrapnel flew through the air. Every second more of the *Freelander* broke, the wooden beams creaking as the deck tilted further. "Where's my mom? Where's Dad?" Her eyes were darting frantically from face to face, before squeezing shut as those faces began to disappear over the edge. Tears streaked down her face as sobs threatened to overtake her. "Please, Uncle Leo, where are they? We need to find them, I-"

"Graylin!" Leo took her face in his hands, forcing her frightened gaze to him. "We will find them!" He glanced up as a large shred of burning cloth tumbled past, and he grabbed his niece's shoulders. "But right now, we need to get off the ship." He grabbed their hands and pulled them across the deck, shielding them from the ashes and aiming for a hatch. He threw it open and dragged out a deflated balloon, glancing over his shoulder as the ship leaned further and further down. The girls, clutching to their uncle, suddenly caught a glimpse of a woman holding a wailing baby.

"Aunt Rosie!" Arlyn shouted, struggling to reach her. She was too late. Another explosion sent Rosie and her baby vanishing over the edge. Arlyn's stomach felt like it had fallen with them, and she stumbled back in shock.

"Arlyn!" Graylin grabbed onto her cousin's sleeve, yanking her back just as a piece of debris flew down in front of her. "Look out!" Though the flying chunk of twisted, melted metal missed the girls, there was no respite from the spitting embers that continued to rain down on them. Arlyn screeched in pain, rubbing her shin, and Graylin fell to her knees, frantically trying to rub off the small chunks of fire. Tears caused by smoke and confusion streamed down the cousin's cheeks, etching lines in their already dirty faces.

"Girls, come on, in, in, in!" Leo leapt forward and dragged both of the girls back to him by their shirts. "Hold on tight to me!" Leo heaved the basket of the half-inflated emergency balloon over the side of the airship, just managing to pull both himself and the girls inside of it. Arlyn now had her hands over her ears, the muffled terror echoing inside her brain and exiting as a scream as Leo struggled to untie the balloon.

BOOM! A second cluster of balloons holding up the *Freelander* exploded. Leo finally got the basket untied as the shockwave hit, and their vessel fell from the ship, spinning as if a vortex had surrounded it. They were too heavy, and the balloon not inflated enough, and the nightmare around Arlyn and Graylin bled into a rapidly rotating blur of fire and fear. The cousin's basket slammed into the hard, rocky ground with a shattering impact, and they were thrown away from the wrecked escape balloon as the newest cloud of flame lit up the darkening sky.

Arlyn's eyes flew open. The *Freelander* was falling, slowly, as if it was sinking underwater. Every second it came closer to hitting the ground.

Several feet away, Graylin struggled to stand. Her eyes drifted to her cousin, and then to the great airship, its orange aura fading to match the nearly set sun, all the sights hurting her pounding head and blurry eyes.

"Graylin!" Arlyn cried, rushing to her cousin as she teetered uncertainly. "Are you okay?"

"Yeah, I'm okay." Graylin bit her trembling lip and squeezed her eyes shut. She had a nasty cut above her eye; blood was running down the side of her face, matting her mounds of curls with sticky red. And yet, all she could do was watch the *Freelander* as it inevitably hit the ground, splintering with an earthshaking crash. Next to her, Arlyn dropped to the ground, green eyes reflecting only the burning light of the wreckage in front of them. A cloud of smoke billowed out, the fire that had started when the *Freelander* was airborne continuing mercilessly on the ground. The only movement was the dancing of the hungry flames, the only sounds the crackling of the embers and the weeping shifting of the burning boards.

"Uncle Leo . . ." Graylin said numbly. "Where's Uncle Leo?" Arlyn swallowed, and the girls glanced back at the wreckage of their escape balloon. Just behind it, still and dark, was a form. The girls were there in an instant, tearing away layers of fabric to reveal their uncle, lying still on the ground, his face ghostly in the firelight.

"Uncle Leo?" Graylin's throat tightened. "Uncle Leo, wake up!" She reached out to shake his shoulders, but couldn't make herself touch him. What if all she felt was cold?

"Uncle Leo! Come on, get up!" Arlyn had no such hesitations, shaking him back and forth, the tears running all the way down and collecting below her chin, falling softly on her uncle's shirt. "Please!" She shook him for a final time, then was stopped by Graylin.

"Stop," she choked. "I don't think he made it." She knelt down, trying not to sob.

The girls both turned away from their uncle because looking back at the burning *Freelander* couldn't hurt worse than seeing his lifeless face.

Arlyn shook her head and wiped her streaming nose with her hand. "We have to go see if anyone else is okay." Graylin's heart was screaming that she wasn't strong enough for that, but she stood up when Arlyn beckoned. After all, as far as she knew, Arlyn was all she had left.

The *Freelander* was splintered and mangled, pieces of the lives lost scattered all over the barren ground along with parts of the ship. Flames clung to the boards. The sand was littered with shards of glass and metal, wood was twisted and bent, and gears sparkled like glitter in the fire's light. Together, the girls began a trek through the wreckage of all that they had previously known.

All along the way, bodies were strewn around the detritus. A scorched baby blanket with an embroidered bee in the corner lay in front of Arlyn, who numbly shook it off and hugged it to her chest. Under Graylin's boot was a half-melted hairpin belonging to their great-aunt Josephine. Shoes, ribbons, clothes, some alone and some still attached to the humans to which they had belonged, were everywhere. The air which had so recently echoed with laughter was now consumed by the crackling of flames and rustling of wind, filling the girls with an unfamiliar yet overwhelming sense of hopelessness as they overturned body after body.

And then, as if exhaling for a final, violent time, the ship exploded. A ball of fire whooshed up into the night sky, a shock wave rippling out from the now-gone ship. Both girls flattened to the ground and curled up, hands over their ringing ears. Everything was sound and heat and fear, filling the cousins until they shook and trembled, huddled close together on the sand. Their shut eyes blocked out the flames, but not the fact that they were completely and totally alone.

That is, until somebody touched their shoulders.

"Girls. *Girls*." The voice faded slowly in. It was familiar, and comforting, and for just a second Graylin thought it was her father. Her eyes struggled open, everything blurry as she wiped away the tears to see, not Michaelangelo Freely, but Uncle Leo leaning over them. His leg was bent where it definitely shouldn't be, and the girls could just make out the white tip of bone piercing outwardly through the skin. Blood trickled from the wound, but in a forced, broken way. Their uncle's face was pale, and stiff with pain. "Come on," he wheezed, "we have to make sure no one else is alive."

"Uncle Leo, we already checked, and there's no one-" Graylin started, terrified to finish her words for fear it would make the nightmare a reality.

"We'll check again." Leo's voice was hard and fierce. He held out his hands, and the girls took them, standing up. They were silent as they passed back over the bodies, Leo beside them, boots crunching in the wreckage.

Hours passed, and by the end, the girls were silent, drawn, and utterly devoid of hope. Graylin's observation had been true. Nobody had survived the *Freelander* Disaster. Minutes turned into hours, which turned into a day. The three remaining Freelys stood together, watching in grieving silence, as the fires burned on.

1

Eight years later

"ALRIGHT ARLYN, A BIT to the left, I think." A scruffy shock of blond hair emerged from behind a fan blade, followed quickly by the face of Leo Freely. "Arlyn?"

"Would that be my left or Graylin's left?" Arlyn Freely was sixteen and hanging upside down above a thick tangle of machinery, tossing various small and easily lost parts to her cousin who sat upright on the floor.

"Who did I ask to move it?" Leo asked tiredly.

"Forget already, old man?" Graylin said from her new position under the belt. "Perhaps we need to make the nursing home a priority."

"I'll just assume it's my left then," Arlyn grinned, having already swung to the belt before her uncle had asked. "Hand me a wrench, will you, cousin?"

Leo Freely was only thirty-five, but his blond hair had already started to gray. The cousins considered this one of their finest accomplishments, alongside the rebuilding of the *Freelander* 2.0, which at the moment was in need of its monthly repairs. The ship on which the three Freelys were now working was a third of the size of the vessel lost eight years previously, but that did very little to diminish its magnificence, nor reduce the level of upkeep needed. Instead of 1,000 balloons the ship now had 350, the actual ship shrunk to reflect this condensed number. Even so, it had taken five years of planning, salvaging, and assembling to fully finish the current *Freelander*. Besides being a very educational project on the engineering front, the task of reconstructing their familial airship had been one of the greatest distractions for eight-year-old Arlyn and Graylin as they mourned the loss of their parents and past lives. Piece by piece, Leo had guided his nieces as they struggled to rebuild their ship and their family.

"Lunch!" A bright voice, muffled by the floors above, called to the three inventors from the *Freelander*'s kitchen.

"Coming, Lil!" Leo shouted back, squeezing through some machinery to the ladder where her voice had come from. He turned to the girls. "We'll bother with this later."

"You heard the man, cousin." Arlyn dropped down from her mechanical treetop. "Time for eats!"

The girls rushed ahead of their uncle, barreling through the halls of the *Freelander* as if followed by something far more sinister than responsibility. As usual, Graylin was slightly faster, leaving Arlyn to leap over furniture in a ploy to get ahead. A mighty crash shook the hall as Graylin tripped over nothing in particular and landed firmly on her face, letting Arlyn gain the lead. Scrambling and slipping, Graylin leaped after her cousin, slamming into her just as Arlyn was about to enter the kitchen. Glowing with her triumph, the girl hopped across the threshold with pride.

"Ha! In your face cousin, in your smug little face." Graylin helped her cousin off of the floor, dusting off her pants in Arlyn's direction.

"You two act like this is the first time we've ever fed you." A kind-faced woman with copper hair turned from the stove, the source of that siren song which caused the cousin's mad dash in the first place.

"You serve such fine cuisine that we simply *must* fight for the right to taste it, Lily," Arlyn said with an aristocratic bow.

Lily Duncan had been Leo's best friend since childhood, and now, well, Arlyn wasn't quite sure what to call her now. She wasn't Arlyn and Graylin's aunt, for she and Leo weren't married, or, as far as the girls knew, even romantically involved. However, 'My Uncle's Best Friend' didn't seem like enough to describe her, after all she had done for them. After the Freelander Disaster, having been made a parent with no prior notice, Leo had appealed to his best friend for help and Lily had provided it with kindness and warmth. In the Freely family, which was one which both disliked rules and enjoyed shouting, Lily was often the only calm voice of reason.

Well, except for one other person: Lewis Maynewin. Lewis was the Freely cousin's first friend, and remained one of six people who could handle the cousins in their entirety. She was generally calm, collected, confident, and, the girls had established, a bunch of other c-words, like cool, and cheerful. The cousins had spent many hours making a list of Lewis-descriptors starting only with 'c' and had been delighted to learn that she practically embodied the letter. Lewis's skin was a light, golden brown, which complimented her hair, dark and curling in zigzags. When she was with the girls, this mane was usually twisted up into a bun where it was safely out of her way and out of her uncommonly pretty face.

She also had an eyepatch.

Lewis was curvy, and shorter than Arlyn, which sufficiently negated the cousin's theory that taller people were smarter simply because they had more space to store their good ideas. This she did by being the cousins' only friend with consistent common sense.

When it came to friends lacking good decision-making skills, the cousins had multiple, and all three of them came stumbling over each other into the kitchen just moments after the cousins arrived. The first of these was River, entering the room with a shoved somersault. A well-built boy with short fiery orange hair and a personality that was irritatingly easy to deal with, everyone loved River, and River loved everyone. He was genial in the way that a rock wasn't, and smart in the way that a rock was.

The one who had shoved him was Teddy. His full name was Theodore, but he, along with everyone else in the world, agreed that it was dumb, so no one ever called him that. The kind of words that came to mind when describing Teddy were the same one might use to describe a particularly anxious giraffe. He was tall, avoidant of most interactive situations be they uncomfortable or friendly, and had a skill for bamboozling his friends into presuming him innocent with his big brown eyes. The biggest difference between Teddy and a giraffe is that giraffes rarely have curly brown hair and dimples, and Teddy didn't have hooves.

Coming in third to the kitchen and first in overall sensibility between the boys was Enland. Enland liked three things: maps, Lewis, and being just a little bit older than everyone else. The slight reddish tinge in his sandy hair was the only thing which kept it from matching his skin tone, unless he was particularly hot or blushing, in which case they were very similar. Thankfully, neither of these things were very common. His hair was usually pulled back into a ponytail to keep it from getting stuck in his thin circular glasses, which together gave him a well-deserved scholarly look. Often unsure when it came to functioning outside his group of friends, what Enland lacked in street smarts he made up for with pure book smarts, which did absolutely nothing to protect him from the cousin's relentless teasing.

"Don't you even think about it." Lewis, who had been helping Lily prepare lunch, pulled out a spatula from her belt and smacked Graylin's hand with it. "Your fingers are disgusting, go wash your hands immediately."

"But I'm starving," Graylin sighed, running her hand under the faucet for roughly two seconds before shaking it off directly in Lewis's face. "There. Happy?"

"No," Lewis said darkly, turning to wield her kitchen utensil vengeance on River as well. "If you even touch those biscuits so help me River-"

"What's all this ruckus then?" Leo finally entered the kitchen, relying heavily on his right leg as the left one limped behind. He'd walked like this ever since the *Freelander* wreck, his broken leg having never healed properly. For Leo, his limp was a reminder of the family he had lost, and the responsibility he held for his nieces. For Arlyn and Graylin, the limp was an excuse to call their uncle old.

"Ah ah ah, it's not us," Arlyn tutted, waving her finger at her uncle. "It's the elephants."

One day, not long after the girls had begun settling into their new lives, the cousins had been making significant amounts of noise doing nothing in particular, as eight-year-olds tend to do. However, it was not so loud that Arlyn and Graylin missed Leo's comment to Lily that described them as being, "as loud as elephants." From then on, whenever reprimanded for the frankly confusing amount of noise they were making, the cousins had taken to blaming said elephants. It was a running joke, though the humor was frequently lost on Leo, as elephants would likely cause half the damage the girls did.

"Oh, of course." Leo shook his head, sitting heavily at the table, the crinkles next to his eyes revealing his amusement even if his tone didn't. "Silly me."

"Boys, sit down, for goodness' sake." Lily pushed River towards the table, and fixed Teddy's collar as she handed him a tray of roasted carrots. Arlyn watched the woman's long braid, just in case she could catch the gray hairs growing in real time, but alas, no such luck.

"How'd your maintenance go?" Lily asked, tucking her long skirt under her legs as she sank into her chair. "Well, I hope?"

"Yes, actually," Leo nodded. "The girls were shockingly helpful."

"We do our best," Graylin bowed, stabbing her fork into her chicken, turning it upside down, and nibbling off it like a savory carnivore popsicle.

"In any case," Leo continued, using the same chicken technique and disgusting Lily thoroughly, "I think the ship's in reasonably good condition if you lot want to go to town later, though I *will* have to ask you to spare some of your wild teenage nefariousness-time to grab me a few new fan blade."

"I think we could manage that," Arlyn nodded with a grin. "We're dropping Lew off at her house anyway."

'House' was not really the right word to describe where Lewis lived. In fact, 'house' hardly even described the small building *next* to her home, the one used to store carriages or automobiles or small air balloons. No, Lewis Maynewin lived in a mansion, and her last name was the reason. Put simply, the Maynewins were rich- very rich. Mr. Maynewin had inherited an enormous fortune from a cold and distant father and then married a woman with an astronomical dowry. Why they'd settled in Odios of all places no one really knew, but it was a great blessing for the cousins that they had.

"Your parents finally want you home then, eh Lew?" Leo asked, slurping a noodle so fast it hit his left eyebrow.

Lewis smiled graciously. "Yes, it seems I've worried them long enough. Also, I think they're nervous that if I spend over two days with Arlyn and Graylin, I'll pick up some of their habits."

"A reasonable concern," Graylin conceded, wiping her mouth with the sleeve of her shirt. "We are extremely untrustworthy individuals."

"So why aren't you coming with us?" River asked Leo, leaning back in his chair a bit too far and teetering for just a moment.

"The plan is," Leo sighed, scratching behind his ear as he often did when thinking, "to take a nap."

Arlyn rolled her eyes. One pro of having Leo as their primary parental figure was that he had never outgrown most of his teenage habits. These included keeping an extremely messy room, eating far more than the girls thought possible, and sleeping a ridiculous amount. After turning thirty he'd discovered the right to nap, and it was a power he greatly overused.

"Right then," Lily smiled. "You'll go to town after lunch, grab whatever you need, drop Lewis off *nicely* with *no comments about the Maynewin's wealth*, and come home."

"I like two of those ideas," Graylin agreed.

Graylin Freely found the very idea of wealthy people to be pompous. What was the point of having so much money when you could be perfectly happy with much less? This ideal had been completely ignored when considering Lewis herself, but that didn't stop both cousins from commenting on the uselessness of wealth. They easily forgot the fact that they themselves owned a very large airship and lived in a fairly grand house.

This house was where the *Freelander* was docked now. It had been a nice house when Leo first bought it, the very epitome of architecture of the day, with many tall windows, two large brick chimneys, and all the wooden swirls and decorations a house might need. It had been big, too. Big, at least, for one young bachelor, the space filled with quiet rooms and silent halls. But that had been before Leo Freely had informally adopted his two rambunctious nieces. To find a still moment was a rarity now, for every second was filled with the sounds of various machines, explosions, laughter, shouting, or whatever new animal Arlyn had brought home as a pet that day.

"There won't be any comments, Lily," Arlyn assured her, skipping her usual disciplinary kick in the leg. There would most definitely be comments.

In the days before the Freelander Disaster, starting up the ship took roughly twenty highly skilled people, as whichever Freely had originally built it had left little instruction, feeling that it was a fairly intuitive task that anyone could figure out without them. It was not. When the *Freelander* had been rebuilt, Leo had specifically designed it to be easily started up by one to two Freelys, or a small crew of not-Freelys given detailed instructions.

It was just plain luck the cousins held the perfect number of close friends to form a crew, and un-plain luck that they all had skills suited to the task. Lewis, much to her parents' displeasure, had not only a knack but a passion for cooking and baking, and had accepted with enthusiasm when offered the position of the *Freelander* cook. Enland's admittedly strange propensity for maps and fantastic sense of direction made him the obvious choice for cartographer, Teddy had a skill for piloting the great ship which even Leo could hardly match, and River's basic personality and skill set made him the ideal handyman. Lewis the cousins had met randomly, when they and Leo had been hired to install a cooling system in the Maynewin's kitchen. However, the addition of the boys into the Freely's crew was a far more unusual story.

For centuries, the Freely family had held a tradition of randomly choosing an orphanage in whichever town they inhabited, and taking as many family-less children as possible under their wings, teaching them inventing, mechanics, etc. Leo and his three brothers had been raised with four such kids, giving them automatic friends to grow up and learn with. And so, when the girls were eleven, Leo had decided to follow the tradition, heading to Odios's only boys' orphanage. These pupils did not necessarily *have* to be male, but at that point in his parenting career, Leo simply couldn't handle any more preteen girls. And so, he had found the three boys, Enland, Teddy, and River.

Leo never revealed to the girls why he had chosen these three boys in particular. In truth, it had been because, at the time, all three of them had been engaging in mildly illegal activities. Eleven-year-old Enland was a known thief, River a common vandal, and local police had hauled Teddy in for loitering among the abandoned buildings and hanging out with a rather unsavory crowd. The master of the orphanage was a lazy man with patience shorter than his hair, which by chance was non-existent. Thanks to his remarkably low tolerance for inconvenience, the orphanage master had informed Leo early on that he was *this close* (holding his fingers extremely close together) to kicking all three boys out. This was not to be borne, and so Leo chose those three. Leo had rented a flat for them, though this was really only used as a place to sleep since they spent most of their days learning with Leo in the shop and letting three eleven-year-olds live alone was frowned upon. It was during these inventing lessons that their respective talents began to shine and before long, the cousins had gained a tight-knit, well-rounded crew of six.

"Fans are good!" Arlyn called, stepping away from her post in the underbelly of the ship towards the ascending ladder. Her cousin, blonde curls flying in several directions they shouldn't be, shot her the thumbs up and turned to relay the call.

"We're good down here!" she shouted. "River?"

"Got it!" River, who had been waiting for the confirmation on the level above Graylin, sprinted away, pounding down the hall, up two flights of stairs, and onto the top deck. "We're ready to go Teddy boy! Hit it!"

“Oh, it’s you, is it?” Teddy raised his eyebrows, pressing several buttons in quick succession, flipping a lever, and cranking a little wheel below his control panel. “I thought it was a rhinoceros, with that noise you made, or maybe a large cow.”

“Just because I’m not a skinny little twig like you,” retorted River, who definitely could be considered the broadest of the boys, “doesn’t mean I deserve this ridicule. *Ridicule* I say.”

“Be back by nine!” Leo called up from the ground, as the fans whirred to life and the ship slowly awoke.

“Ten?” Graylin asked, poking her head out a window on the side with a grin.

“Nine! And I mean it this time!” Leo shouted, folding his arms and trying not to be amused. Thankfully, the *Freelander* was already lifting into the air, or the smiling lines beside his eyes would have given him away.

“What a narc,” Graylin muttered, ducking back inside after her misused insult. Lily, standing next to Leo on the ground, laughed.

“They love you, you know,” she smiled at Leo, resting a hand on his arm.

“I don’t know what Freely girls you’ve been helping to raise,” Leo sighed, “but I don’t think it’s Arlyn and Graylin.”

"Mr. Denloy."

“Ah, Thaddius, you’re back.”

“The people of Odios know you’re on your way, sir.”

Wilmot Denloy, the blond-haired businessman, stood up from his desk and shook Thaddius’ offered hand. “Thank you for doing that for me. Are they receiving the news well?”

“Yes indeed, sir,” the heavily built man said, ensconcing himself into an open chair. “Some saying the program reminds them of something the Freelys used to run-”

"The Freelys are dead," Denloy's voice froze over, harsh and cold, his palm suddenly clammy. He drew it back quickly, reaching for his handkerchief and grasping it as he turned away, hurrying to repair his lapse. He took a deep breath, and when he once again faced Thaddius he was smiling genially. "My program is meant for talented young inventors without the means or recognition to launch their own careers. It's hard, at that age, to maintain confidence in your talents, especially when you compare yourself to inventors like the Freelys." Denloy leaned against his desk, hands resting in the pockets of his perfectly tailored suit pants. "As a country, Osden needs to stop living in the past with the Freelys, and let ourselves move into the future. There will be plenty of talent waiting there for us."

"Well said Mr. Denloy." Thaddius raised his hand, toasting with the cigar wedged between his fingers. "And so very true. Why, even in Odios alone you've already found some hidden talent. A Mr. Hooper, no?"

"Ah yes, John Hooper," Denloy smiled, heart rate slowed down to normal, adjusting his round wire-frame glasses on his nose. "I've invited him in, I thought it would be useful for the two of you to meet. With a bit of luck, he could be the next big thing in Odios, that crane of his is seriously impressive." Denloy moved his hand to a small button on his desk and pressed it. Somewhere in the hall outside, a ball rang.

"Sir?" The door opened uncertainly, letting in the speaker. He was older, with a gray handlebar mustache, and an extremely asymmetrical body type when viewed from the side. "You wanted to see me?"

"Yes, indeed Mr. Hooper, we were just talking about you," Denloy strode to the door to shake John Hooper's hand amicably. "I wanted to formally introduce you to Thaddius Morrow, though I suspect you are more familiar with him than I."

"I've certainly seen him 'round sir," Hooper smiled, shaking a less than enthusiastic Thaddius's hand as well. "You were the one who brought that circus to Odios, right?"

"Yes, yes," Thaddius sighed. "I was also the one who had to deal with the damage when they turned out to do less performing and more pilfering."

"As Odios's sole member of media management," Denloy smiled at Hooper, "Thaddius here has been assigned to helping me with whatever outreach I have planned. You are Pekin Co.'s first sponsorship here in Odios, and as such you too will have Thaddius's full support and resources."

"Oh, thank you sir," Hooper beamed, hooking his thumbs in his suspenders. "I can' tell you what this means to me, gettin' to build my inventions like this."

"It's about time someone recognized your talent," Denloy said. "Your crane adaptation is genius, and just in time to help build the water tower, too." He set a hand on Hooper's shoulder, patting it before offering him a cigar. "Now, you'd best get back to your crane, go let people know you made it." He winked, and smiled as John Hooper beamed his way from the room.

"You've certainly chosen a unique first sponsor," Thaddius commented, as Denloy leaned back against his desk. "Mr. Hooper wouldn't know a tailored suit from a burlap sack."

"I've had all the education in the world, and I still don't have an eye for fashion," Denloy said lightly, turning to look out his window. A small posse of workers bustled below, trimming hedges, raking gravel, planting flowers. They were at his beck and call. They respected him. Loved him.

How he hated it.

2

"FANS ARE SHUTTING DOWN in three," Graylin shouted, ". . . two . . . one . . ." She reached for the huge master lever to stop all the blades and yanked down. The engine room echoed with a final dying whir, the rumble and hum replaced by a suffocating inky silence. Silence which was quickly broken by the arrival of her cousin.

"Oh, cousin mine! Ready to go?" Arlyn dropped down the ladder, tossing Graylin a caramel as she skipped in a circle.

"Just about. Ship's stalled?" Graylin caught the candy, and popped it directly into her mouth before being abruptly reminded of the wrapper.

"Yes indeed, we're all set," Arlyn swung back up the way she'd arrived, eating a caramel herself, followed by her cousin and the disgusted spitting sound she was making. "You alright back there?" Arlyn grinned, peeking back down the ladder.

Graylin grimaced. "Paper," she said, "is not for eating."

"It most definitely is," Arlyn held out another caramel. "And it is delicious. Waste not, that's what I say. Reduce, reuse, recycle."

Paper-eating habits aside, the similarities between the Freely cousins were so great that their friends and uncle occasionally confused the two, despite the fact that they looked just about as different as two people could. Arlyn's skin was deep brown and warm, her round face framed by long black hair which actually was quite curly, but was so consistently done into two thick braids that everyone, Arlyn included, forgot this. Her general posture and vibe could only be described as waterfall-like: bright, bubbly, and often quite loud.

Graylin, on the other hand, consistently had the stance and demeanor of a jaded old detective, albeit one who was always either tapping her feet or rocking on them. While Arlyn generally took after her mother when it came to looks, Graylin looked very much like her father, and by extension Arlyn's dad and Leo. Her skin was pale, and slightly freckled, her hair light blonde, very curly, and falling in a wild tangle just past her chin.

Despite these differences, anyone who saw the cousins side by side would quickly deduce their familial connection, and this was because of their eyes. Though different in color, Arlyn's being green and Graylin's gray, the cousin's eyes were quite identical in shape. This, and their constant use of 'cousin mine' in reference to each other tended to give away their relationship.

The *Freelander* drifted to a stop above a particularly tall apartment, the balloons holding it afloat bobbing slightly as Arlyn tossed a rope ladder over the side. Air travel, be it by balloon, ship, or the ever elusive blimp, was very popular in Osden, and had been for nearly three decades. As such, many air-ship specific features had been added to the infrastructure of Odios, such as parking spaces in air and on ground, quick-filling gas tanks near the parking to prevent vessels from becoming stranded in the sky, and even tall, thin towers scattered around the city leading to boarding platforms. However, the crew had been banned by Leo from using such accommodations, for though Teddy was actually a superb pilot, the cousins were not the most trustworthy landing personnel, and Leo could only afford to replace so much. So, the *Freelander* was stopped in the air, just above the outdated apartment building in which the three boys lived. It was the sky equivalent of jaywalking: technically not allowed, rarely punished, and a regular habit of the girls.

The crew descended the dangling rope ladder, some (meaning Lewis) with elegant grace, and some (meaning Graylin) with a nail-biting clumsiness. All of them muttered an instinctual 'be good' to the ship, which floated inanimately in response, before jumping onto the roof below them. With a swiftness attesting to the regularity of their actions, the six friends scrambled to the street below them, tripping down rattling fire escapes, leaping to balconies, and sliding down gutters.

Arlyn pushed off the metal pipe she'd just shimmied down, landing with a pleasant crunch on the crumbling bricks of the street. It was a nice day, too warm for any sort of sleeve, unless you were River and insisted your biceps be covered 'lest the ladies become distracted'. A friendly breeze gave a bounce to the air that made the whole world seem friendly and ready for the taking. But, as the whole world wasn't readily available to the crew, Odios suited them all just fine.

Odios had been the cousins' home ever since the Freelander disaster. Why Leo had chosen this city over any others to raise his two nieces, the girls neither knew nor cared. However, it had served them well over the years, providing them with experience, friends (at least for Arlyn), and most importantly, ample opportunities to get into and or cause trouble.

"Right," River spun around to face the crew as they walked, "so I've had an idea."

"Oh no," Graylin groaned, "not again."

"An idea, River, really?" Teddy poked his red-haired brother from behind. "Punching a bit over our weight here, aren't we?"

"Aw, let the man speak!" Arlyn said, picking a bug off Enland's shoulder. "Look, even this little dude wants to hear."

"Oh no," Lewis protested, brushing the bug away, causing it to flutter off Arlyn's hand and directly into Teddy's face. "We need to buy that fan blade for Leo, and if we put it off you know we'll forget. Don't even try to argue," she said, holding up a hand to confront Graylin's objections. "You know I'm right." That was precisely the problem with Lewis, in Graylin's opinion. She was *always* right.

The crew maneuvered through the streets, slipping through the most crowded areas as they traveled to the less popular ones. The warmth of the spring sun rose as the six friends struggled against the ever shifting tides of people. When they finally arrived at their favorite mechanic's stall, the relatively empty area was like a breath of fresh air.

A figurative breath of fresh air, of course; there was enough smoke and exhaust in the air to knock out a large horse. Set off in a little side market which sold roughly half the things a person could want, the raised wooden platform of the inventor's stall was open air, with casual strips of canvas hanging overhead, dappling the products in shade. The light was tinted by the dull yellow and slight green of the fabric, the colors dancing in the breeze. There were hooks, barrels, and crates, boxes and bags, all full of an unorganized collection of vaguely useful inventing items. There were wrenches, nuts, screws, chains, gears, ropes, wires, and everything in between. The wooden floor was bedecked with an eclectic collection of rugs, most of which sparkled in the light thanks to the spilled bits of metal that could be found across most of the stall.

The crew split up. Arlyn and Lewis were assigned with purchasing Leo's fan blades while the remaining four searched for amusement. The boys instantly opted to test and rank random objects on their functionality as a grappling hook, while Graylin dug through a barrel of random bits until she found a small leather pouch full of old typewriter keys. From all appearances several typewriters had been disassembled to create the collection, for the fonts and sizes were all different. Settling herself on the floor, Graylin dumped the sack out and began to rearrange the keys, making words which she tried to fit into some sort of poem. So far, she had only the line "I like cheese", which was both unpoetic and hard to rhyme with.

A thundering crash interrupted this literary endeavor, a faint cloud of dust rising around a groaning Teddy sprawled on the bricks just outside the stall. It seemed the grappling hooking was not going very well. Graylin just shook her head. Enland she could relate to and therefore constantly fought with, River she couldn't relate to and therefore constantly fought with, but Teddy? Teddy she just avoided, which worked fine because she was pretty certain he avoided her in return. He was quiet and good and boring, while she was quiet and troublesome and tedious. Far too different, in Graylin's opinion.

Arlyn, in the meantime, was trying to fit the purchased fan blade in her satchel when she caught sight of a shaggy blond head peeking out from behind a crate. This could mean one of two things; her cousin had grown several inches in the last fifteen minutes, or she had a friendly stalker.

"We meet again!" she crowed at the crates. At her words, her 'stalker' revealed himself to be, as she suspected, a boy her age, Finnigan Larken. He stepped out, bedecked in a waistcoat, ascot, and dress pants, all made of colors and patterns which definitely shouldn't be together. "Finn, you painting of a boy! What are you doing here?"

"I just can't stay away from you, Arlyn Freely," Finn said with an attempt at flirtatious slyness, which, as Graylin had observed before, was not really something he could pull off. "May I say, you're looking quite fresh this morning?"

"Fresh? Like produce?"

"Like a daisy," Finn corrected with a wink. "Like a spring rain."

"What delightfully environmental compliments," Arlyn smiled. "Though I think I may prefer the produce. At least carrots and berries are useful."

Graylin glanced up from her poem writing, saw her cousin's current companion, and rolled her eyes. Out of all Arlyn's admirers, and there were many, Finnigan Larken was Graylin's least favorite, due only to his complete devotion for her cousin. Arlyn Freely was electric, Graylin thought, in the way that she attracted people to her like a magnet. All people, really, but teenage boys especially. These teenage boys generally found Arlyn to be entirely captivating, what with her bright, pretty eyes, her penchant for trouble, and her abilities to relate, comfort, and charm. She was also hilarious, and intelligent, and in general all the things which attracted the boys of Odios.

While Graylin was slightly bitter about this arrangement, the soreness of the subject was far outweighed by the many teasing opportunities it offered. Even the simple mention of her cousin's name drew all the boys in, like moths to a flame, and watching Arlyn become overwhelmed with teenage affections, especially ones she didn't want, was very entertaining.

"You're very useful, of course," Finn continued, struggling to regain his slick tone. "I simply meant, in regard to beauty-"

"Care for a challenge?" Arlyn interrupted, blatantly ignoring the boy's attempts to charm her. They weren't working anyway. She pulled a deck of playing cards from her back pocket and held it up for Finn to see.

"Of course, my liege." Finn made a movement between a curtsy and a bow, which was both confusing and awkward to watch. "I was hoping you'd say that."

Arlyn had been playing cards with Finn for years now. At every meeting, he became slightly more obvious in his interest, and subsequently *she* became intentionally less perceptive. She enjoyed Finn, despite his atrocious fashion sense and awful pick up lines, but she was nearly certain she didn't enjoy *him* the way *he* did *her*. But she preferred to ignore this, as he was nice, occasionally funny, and the only one around who could nearly match her skill with cards.

"See that crate over there?" Arlyn gestured, laying a random chain in a line on the ground. "That's our target, and you gotta stay behind this line."

"First to ten?" Finn asked, shuffling his cards and leaning against a pole like the responsible person he most certainly wasn't. Arlyn agreed to the terms, and Finn stepped forward to make the first throw. They didn't play cards in the normal sense, but threw them instead. Arlyn preferred this, because it was harder for Finn to flirt when he kept having to chase after poor throws.

Finn drew his arm back, then stopped. "If I win, I get to buy you a treat."

Arlyn sighed inwardly, because she wasn't sure how to reject the idea without being rude. She'd just have to make sure she won, she supposed. It wouldn't be *that* hard. Finn's throwing skills were generally several levels below her own.

"You've got yourself a deal," she said finally, and Finn beamed. He drew his arm back, flicked his wrist, and the card was quivering in the wood of the crate, just in the upper left-hand corner.

"Nice one," Arlyn said approvingly, pulling out her own card. Arm up, hand back, wrist forward and- *thwick*, the card was in the wood. Back and forth they went, Finn doing reasonably well, but Arlyn doing better. Finnigan stepped away from his last turn with a satisfied smile, his newest card sitting firmly in the center of the box. He had hit every throw but one, so all Arlyn needed was a good final card to win. She shuffled her deck, fingers flying, and stepped up to the line. Plucking out a card, she kept her eyes on the crate, hand moving back, wrist winding up, and-

"Cousin! Cousin mine!" The call startled Arlyn, and her card flashed through the air . . . and into the floor.

"Beans!" Arlyn said irritably, turning as her cousin skipped towards her. "This better be important."

"Important? Probably not. Interesting? Absolutely." Graylin plucked the cards from her cousin's hand and dropped them in Arlyn's satchel, lifting the bag from where it'd been set and shoving it into her cousin's arms. The huge fan blade, fitting just about as well in the satchel as a watermelon might in a sock, wobbled precariously, nearly hitting Arlyn in the face.

"I'm really sorry Finn," Arlyn told her opponent, gathering all her thrown cards and tucking them into her bag as Graylin snatched Lewis and the boys. "Maybe another time?"

"I shall hold you to that!" Finn smiled forlornly, looking just disheartened enough to make Arlyn feel bad. She waved apologetically, starting to run as Graylin pulled at her arm.

"You, cousin, are a lifesaver," she muttered as they dashed out of the stall. Graylin shrugged.

"I do what I can," she said, before grimacing. "But out of all your choices, why Finn? He's just the worst."

"He's not so bad," Arlyn said, defensive of both herself and her friend. "And we made a deal. I thought I was pretty safe, betting that

I would beat him, because let's be honest, his card throwing skills are usually mediocre at best."

"Speaking of mediocre," Graylin spun around, making a quick head-count of their little group, "where's Enland?"

"Here! I'm here!" Enland ran up as an automobile drove by haphazardly. "I got distracted at the candle stall."

"Dude," Teddy sighed as the six dashed off, "you can't just say that sort of stuff out loud. It's secondhand embarrassing. To me. Stop it."

"So, where is it we're going?" Arlyn asked no one in particular, skidding to a stop and narrowly avoiding being trampled by River behind her.

"There's something very interesting going on by that new water tower they're putting up." Graylin hopped in a puddle, the iridescent film of oil on top splashing. "It looks to me like some giant crane of sorts, and personally, I would like a closer look."

"Right you are, cousin," Arlyn grinned, glancing at Lewis and River before gesturing to Graylin. "Lead the way."

The city of Odios was in the cliffs that lined the far northwest part of Osden. It was small by Osden standards, it being the large, industrial country that it was. However, thanks to its size and general detachment from most other cities nearby, Odios had retained much of the wildlife, relatively clean air, and fair tax laws the rest of Osden had lost. Nevertheless, Odios was quite average in one way, and that was its constant and undeniable state of change. Buildings were constantly being built up or redone or added on to as new machines and innovations were discovered. This left many buildings abandoned, and many alleys to be invaded by people of the shady sort who had created inconspicuous pathways off the ground through boards stretching over alleys and rope bridges connecting to whole floors of neglected buildings. It had been the crew's good luck that they had stumbled upon this literal *high*way, because it provided not only interaction with people of an interesting and relatable demeanor, but also a quick way to move across the city.

Graylin darted over a thin board leading to the top of the next building, the makeshift bridge bouncing as Arlyn followed close behind. Six sets of shoes bounded across the plank and onto the roof, and then through a shattered window as the cousins led the way into a disreputable building smelling strongly of gasoline.

"There!" Arlyn pointed through a gaping hole in a wall, beckoning to the crew. "Boy howdy, if that isn't uptown."

Above the buildings, stretching into the sky with towering magnitude, was a crane. One mechanical arm, braided with chains and wires and supports, held up a large load of bricks with one simple rope. Arlyn smiled. It was gorgeous.

"See what I'm saying?" Graylin grinned, leaning out the break in the bricks. "We've got to get a closer look at this thing. I've never seen a machine so big, and I thought all cranes were gas powered."

"It's in the river," Arlyn breathed, eyes beginning to sparkle like the sun against the machine. "It's hydraulic!"

"It runs on water?" River asked, standing on his tiptoes and peeking over Teddy's shoulder.

"That's right," Arlyn said, before Graylin could interject something sarcastic. "But I'm not sure how. There's no mill wheel, no gears down in the river that I can see. Cousin?"

Receiving no response, Arlyn glanced up to see her cousin heaving herself onto the roof of a building several alleys away, the intrigue of the crane drawing her in. Arlyn grinned and bounded after her.

When Arlyn finally caught up to her cousin, it was to find her snooping around the machine, examining it from the shore with her hands clasped behind her back. Graylin climbed on a small stack of crates, squinting down into the river as the water flashed reflections of light into her eyes, before jumping down and sprinting around to study it from a new angle. As Teddy and River threw their heads back to stare up at the gargantuan invention, and Enland had Lewis sniff test his new candles, Arlyn bee-lined for an older man sitting happily on the stone sidewalk next to the river. Though seemingly occupied by the sandwich in his hands, and the crumbs of which that had taken up residence in his mustache, he glanced up happily as she approached, kind eyes crinkling.

"Excuse me," Arlyn called, waving as she neared, "but is this your crane?"

"That it is little miss!" the man beamed, wiping his fingers against his trouser leg and standing. "My pride and joy, she is."

"It's incredible!" Arlyn beamed, shaking his hand. Out of the corner of her eyes, she saw Graylin shove River into the river, just to be yanked in after him. "Is it hydraulic?"

"She is, at that," the man turned around to stare at his invention, pride glowing in his worn features. "I'm John, John Hooper."

"Arlyn," the girl smiled, shrugging her satchel higher on her shoulder as the massive fan blade weighed it down.

"Well, Miss Arlyn," John Hooper lifted his cloth cap to scratch his mostly bald head, "you seem pretty keen. You don't happen to be interested in engineering and inventing and such, do you?"

"As a matter of fact, I am." Arlyn flipped her left braid back over her shoulder into its rightful place, trying to ignore the commotion behind Mr. Hooper as a sopping wet and very disgruntled Graylin drug herself onto the sidewalk. "My cousin and I both, actually." She leaned against one of the canopy poles, staring up at the looming contraption. "So, how long did it take you to design this beast?"

"I've had the idea for 'bout ten years now," Mr. Hooper studied the crane as well, arms folded across his ample belly. "but, well, I'm not the most educated of sorts. Couldn't really seem to get a good footin' with the city. Besides, a project like this would've cost me more than I'm worth."

"Would have?" Arlyn asked curiously, watching Graylin shake herself like a dog before grabbing the front of River's shirt and holding her fist threateningly to his face while the boy just grinned. "You mean you got funding from someone?"

"That's right," Mr. Hooper nodded, "from a Mr. Wilmot Denloy. Have you heard of 'im?"

"No, I haven't," Arlyn said, "though I don't leave Odios very often." Leo's biggest rule, and the only truly enforced one, was that the girls stay close to home. Arlyn had never really asked for an explanation regarding this regulation, but suspected that it was easier to make excuses for the girls' behavior to people he knew.

"Apparently he's a pretty big name out there, sponsoring inventors and such." Mr. Hooper waved his hand vaguely. "But hold a second- you said you were an inventor yourself? You and your . . . cousin, was it?"

"Yep," Arlyn grinned, "though we've never made anything near as impressive as your crane."

"Say, you wouldn't be interested in joining a program for young inventors, would you?" John Hooper was rummaging around a tool belt draped over the back of his chair, tossing out spare screws and bolts.

"Would we!" Arlyn chirped, taking the pamphlet Mr. Hooper withdrew from the belt. It was crinkled and dusty, but smoothed out well enough to reveal the letters YIP. "Yip?" she asked, as Graylin slopped her way over, face drawn into a sulk. "What's yip?"

"It's an acronym," Mr. Hooper said proudly, and Arlyn got the feeling the word was outside his regular vocabulary. "Kid Engineer Workshop or summat."

Ignoring the fact that this name did not align with its acronym whatsoever, Arlyn flipped open the pamphlet, scanning the pages as Graylin peeked over her shoulder and dripped water on the paper.

"What's all this then?" she asked, reading along with Arlyn. "*Youth Inventing Program, for bright young engineers who want to make their way in the ever expanding world of machines. A two-year program, in which participants will learn from some of Osden's top inventors, travel to see the most inspiring of the country's inventions*, bla bla bla etc etc. *Run by Mr. Wilmot Denloy*. Who's Wilmot Denloy?"

"Apparently he funds inventors all across the country," Arlyn said, smoothing at a few more of the wrinkles. "*Two-year program, Osden's top inventors, travel* . . . hmm."

"*Wilmot Denloy*," Graylin was repeating the words, rolling the names around her mouth and grimacing. "Wilmot Denloy. He sounds rich, or royal maybe. I hate royalty."

How Graylin had developed this dislike of royals, Arlyn didn't know, as Osden did not in fact have a monarchy. So, she just rolled her eyes and shook the pamphlet.

"Well, of course he's rich, cousin. How else could he afford to do all this, sponsoring kids and Mr. Hooper?"

"Oh, it's not just me," Mr. Hooper assured them, hooking his thumbs in his suspenders. "He's been runnin' programs like this all over the country for round about a decade now, maybe a bit less."

"And we've never heard of him?" Graylin asked skeptically. "Seems shady."

"Graylin, you haven't heard of lots of things," Lewis sighed, stepping up to investigate their little group. "Like manners, for example, or a hairbrush."

"Odios *is* pretty small," River added, slopping a fresh splash of water over Arlyn and her pamphlet as he approached. "I mean, there's a reason it's taken this Denloy guy so long to extend his program here."

"Cousin," Arlyn tucked the pamphlet away, and grabbed Graylin's shoulders, thus grabbing her attention, "Cousin cousin cousin cousin. Think about it." She waited until Graylin had met her gaze before continuing. "Travel. Mentorship. Free money. Probably some snacks. That's what this program would mean. What's not to like?"

Graylin stared at Arlyn, a smile slowly creeping onto her face. "What *is* not to like?" she mused, coming quickly to the conclusion that there was nothing. In fact, the more she thought about it, the more fantastic the idea sounded. The girls turned around, the crew having gathered behind them. After so many years, the four friends had cultivated quite an acute sense of when the cousins were developing an idea, and everyone realized the Freelys were doing so now. The almost gear-like churning behind their eyes and the mischievous quirk of their mouths, and the looks they kept giving each other filled the air as the cousins stared at each other.

"Ask Leo?" Arlyn asked.

"Immediately," Graylin nodded. With a shared thought, they thanked Mr. Hooper profusely before shoving the pamphlet in Arlyn's pocket and sprinting away.

"So you'll be taking us on this inventor-ing jaunt of yours, right?" Teddy asked Arlyn as they ran towards nowhere in particular.

"Were you not also trained by the one and only Leo Freely?" Arlyn's braids hit her in the face as they whipped around a corner. "We could all go, probably even Lewis!"

"Definitely Lewis!" Enland said from behind them. "And remind me again where are we going?"

"Wherever Graylin is going!" Arlyn declared, taking an unnecessary leap over a crate in the road.

Graylin was sprinting ahead of the group, her head buzzing with dozens of thoughts. Too many thoughts. She had to run to get them all out, and since she didn't know nor care where at the moment, she simply turned down the road which led back to the *Freelander*. Her feet flew with the buzz of their new opportunity. A chance to travel, to see things, to learn! Was this not what she had been preparing for her whole life? The boys could come! Lewis could come! This mentorship could change everything.

The office was bathed in the soft amber of lamplight, painting stacks of contracts and blueprints and documents in a golden glow. Denloy frowned at them. What right did they have to look so glorious and important anyhow? But, he supposed, as long as everything else was illuminated he looked just as bright. Just as clean. Just as good.

His eyes came to rest on his desk, drifting to a jar there. It was filled to the brim with caramels, the only candy he could stand anymore, and he pulled one out. He was careful as he unwrapped it, trying not to drop any sweet on the papers beneath him. It reminded him of his childhood, he and his brothers being scolded for messes they made on the furniture as they rumbled through the house. They thought they could take on the world back then, and Denloy had gone out and done it.

I'm a fraud, he thought, *a damn fraud.* He'd spent seven years building Pekin Industries from the ground up, sponsoring inventor after inventor, making connections and meeting smart and interesting people, but what was he? Wilmot Denloy was no inventor, not an artist or some talented writer. All he knew was how to talk to people, but what good does that do for a man with no friends?

A knock at the door announced the arrival of an assistant. "Meeting in ten minutes, Mr. Denloy," the voice came through the door.

"Right."

3

"ALMOST FINISHED!" LEWIS ANNOUNCED, staring at the ticking stop watch in her palm. "One minute left!"

Graylin flicked her eyes up, and spotted a particularly useful vial of liquid peeking out from the pile of junk between her and her cousin, and dove for it. Standing opposite one another, the two Freely's movements reflected the other's, both snatching and grinding and screwing and building with lightning, frantic speed. Their hands, different though they may be in color, were equal in speed and skill.

"Thirty seconds!" Lewis called.

"Oh, come off it! It's not been thirty seconds," Graylin shouted irritably, testing the liquid of the vial on her wrist. A quick sniff, and the delightful smell of gasoline (the cousins had a thing for chemical scents) met her nose. Perfect.

After sprinting all the way back to the *Freelander*, and then neglecting to drop Lewis off at her mansion, Arlyn, Graylin, and the boys had arrived home to find Leo buried in a pile of papers in his workshop. While the girls weren't sure if this meant he had finally learnt how to do his taxes, or if he'd simply been bullied into organization by Lily, they *did* know that they didn't want to interrupt him. What if he decided to rope them into it? That was a horrific thought to say the least, so the crew had started up a round of the cousin's favorite game: Partsy. Partsy was a competition that gave the participants five minutes to make the most impressive invention out of a pile of various scraps and whatever ingenuity they happened to possess.

It was also a game which Arlyn was pretty sure she was currently losing. The chain of gears she'd just assembled was slightly too big, much to her intense frustration, and her hands shook ever so slightly as she examined the issue. A slip of the pliers in her belt, and the chain was fixed.

"Five!" Lewis called. Graylin pushed back her hair and bent a few wires into place.

"Four!" This time it wasn't just Lewis, but River who called out the number.

"Three!" Enland joined in the chant, as Arlyn punched a hole in a metal panel with her screwdriver.

"Two!" Teddy threw his quiet call into the mix.

"One! Step away!" Lewis cried. Arlyn tugged on her braid; Graylin ran her hands through her hair.

"Arlyn, please introduce your item!" Lewis declared with the dignified bravado only she could manage. There was a reason, after all, why she alone of the crew was the designated announcer for Partsy. Arlyn held up her machine and beamed.

"Gladly. This, my friends, is the world's first food transporting hot air balloon!" In her hands rested a small basket made of bits of wood and metal panels. Above it, a rounded square of cloth, filled with hot air so that it resembled a balloon, floated merrily in the air. "As you can see," Arlyn announced, "the basket of this hot-air balloon has two compartments. One for ice, and one for your delightfully cooled food."

"That," Graylin said with a grin, "is truly brilliant, cousin mine." For anyone else, Graylin would have kept her praise to herself, if she even had any, but just as the cousins had soft spots for Leo, Graylin had one for Arlyn. There was not a thing her cousin could do which would not awe and inspire Graylin, and vice versa.

"Thank you cousin, thank you. Now, if I may demonstrate. River, be so kind as to toss me that orange, please!" Arlyn gestured grandly to River, who was standing next to a fruit basket.

"Ah, yes!" River scrambled to match Arlyn's gusto and failed miserably. "The orange!" He tossed it to her, the fruit sailing through the air and into Arlyn's hand. She slipped the orange into the slot, shut the compartment, and pushed the hot air balloon so it began to travel towards Graylin. It floated fairly smoothly all the way to her, bobbing in the air. When Graylin scooped it into her hands, she flung open the tiny door and pulled out the orange.

"It remains chilled!" she announced grandly. Everyone cheered and clapped, while Arlyn pretended to reject the praise.

"Oh, no, please," she said, holding a hand out dramatically. "I couldn't possibly, I mean, thank you folks, thank you kindly . . ."

"Well, that was a fine showing indeed," said Lewis, her refined language shining through as she held a pretend monocle to her eye (Graylin found this amusing, considering the other eye was covered in an eyepatch, but no one else did). "Graylin, it looks like it's up to you to produce something even *more* spectacular."

"Oh, I shall," Graylin said. She pulled from behind her back a glove of sorts, and slid her arm in. "This, esteemed ladies and less esteemed gentlemen," she gave River a pointed look at this, to which Arlyn rolled her eyes, "this is the world's first message glove, name pending. If you have a better idea, let me know."

"Anything would be better than *message glove*," Arlyn said, flipping a braid over her shoulder.

"Alright, communication finger sweater, is that better?" Graylin asked, and then laughed inwardly at the phrase 'finger sweater'. Arlyn nodded her approval, so Graylin continued. "This is the world's first communication finger sweater." It was a Partsy tradition to title one's inventions 'the world's first . . .' Arlyn had the world's first self constructing hose, Graylin had the world's first self *detonating* hose, and so on and so forth.

Graylin held up her left arm, the one covered by her invention, and turned so the whole crew could see.

"If you pay close attention, you will notice that the top of this finger sweater is covered in typewriter keys." These keys were placed close together, stretching the full length of the glove all the way to her elbow, while the underside of the machine was adorned with a complicated mess of gears and wires and a small phial of gasoline. Graylin gestured to her arm.

"Say, perhaps, you have a bad cold, and are unable to speak. Say the joke you wish to tell only makes sense when written. Say you are trying to be stealthily quiet. Say, perhaps, you are simply tired of talking. Well, my friends, the solution to all of these problems is the communication finger sweater." Graylin moved her right hand over to the machine and began to type. Every click sent a small burst of black smoke into the air, and made a small ding like a typewriter would, though Arlyn realized with amusement that this was actually just her cousin tapping a bell on the floor for effect.

Graylin ripped off the slip of paper that had been gradually growing from the machine with a flourish. She handed it to Arlyn, who saw typed there the insightful and poetic words:

RIvEr SucKS

"Must you be so antagonistic all the time, cousin?" Arlyn asked, trying to hold back her laughter for River's sake.

"Antagonism is my specialty," Graylin said grandly, grinning proudly as she passed the message around.

"Oh, come on!" River groaned, reading the message. "I do *not*."

"Okay, okay, I accept that River's suckiness is not a definable fact," Graylin said. "But consider my invention, my *vastly impressive* invention, which spits truths whether you like to hear it or not."

"Graylin," a tired voice called from downstairs, "are you tormenting River? Again?"

"No Uncle Leo," Graylin shouted back, just as Arlyn and River shouted, "Yes!".

"I'm getting mixed signals here," Leo called, voice tilting in that way which told Arlyn he was grinning. Nothing made Leo Freely as benevolent as ending a boring task, which clearly meant he had finished with his papers. "Yes or no?" he asked. Arlyn smiled and leaped for the stairs.

"Uncle Leo, you won't believe who we met in town today!" She hopped onto the banister and slid down, a method she'd taken so many times as to make it second nature. Down she sailed, both braids flying behind her as she flew towards her uncle waiting at the bottom of the steps.

"If you say the police . . ." Leo was sighing, as one by one the crew coasted down. "That's where this is going, isn't it? Someone was arrested?"

"Pshaw. Of course not." Arlyn waved her hand as if that was a crazy accusation, when in fact it was reasonably plausible. "No, we met a nice old inventor man, roughly your age, who invented the sickest crane ever. It's in the middle of the river, it's hydraulic, and they're using it to build the new water tower! I think his name was like John Cooper or Mooper or something."

"Ah, John Hooper!" Leo nodded, helping River to his feet. He was not as skilled at banister surfing as Arlyn was. "Yes, I've run into him before, he's very intuitive in his inventing. I wonder how he got the money to-wait a second," his face screwed up, "did you say roughly my age? *My age*? John Hooper's at least fifty-five!"

"And you are . . . not?" Graylin asked, leaning against the banister.

"No," Leo said incredulously. "I'm like thirty-five."

"My bad," Arlyn shrugged, just to annoy him. "Anyway, Mr. Hooper told us about this amazing young inventor's program, it's called yip or yap or something, and-"

"Yip?" Leo shook his head, rubbing his eyes. "That sounds so legit."

"It *is*," Arlyn rummaged in her pocket, pulling out a thimble, a marble, a dog treat (the Freelys did not have a dog) and a screw before finding the pamphlet. Now quite creased, the paper was shaken out and read with true Arlyn moxie. "*Youth Inventing Program, for bright young engineers who want to make their way in the ever expanding world of machines*. It's two years long, and they take the participants all over Osden to see stuff and get inspiration. *And* they bring in all the best inventors in the country to teach."

"Oh ho!" Leo chuckled, leading the crew to the kitchen and sitting heavily at the table. "Am I not good enough anymore? Looking to leave old Uncle Leo behind?"

"No," Graylin assured him, suddenly feeling guilty after realizing how her uncle might be offended by their request. It could be argued she had an unhealthy relationship with this particular emotion. "No, of course not. We just . . . it seemed like a great opportunity, and that it would be fun to go see places, and-"

"And we would cause you a lot less trouble!" Arlyn interjected eagerly. "You could nap all day every day, your dreams filled with daisies and rainbows and definitely *not* worries about us!"

"I like how you think you are the focus of *all* my worries," Leo snorted, pouring himself a cup of coffee and sipping it. "Maybe I'm actually really stressed out over the boys." He gestured to the three brothers, all of whom were in various states of pantry raiding.

"But they could come too!" Arlyn beamed, stealing a swallow of her uncle's beverage and immediately regretting it. As far as Arlyn was concerned, coffee was just a socially acceptable way to eat cream and sugar, and yet Leo's cup was completely undoctored and therefore disgusting. "You'd get rid of us all in one fell swoop."

"This idea is becoming more and more appealing." Leo scratched behind his ear, at the same time stealing his coffee back and poking Arlyn. He caught the look on Graylin's face and laughed. "I was just kidding about the 'leaving me behind' thing. In fact," he folded his arms on the table and looked around at the crew. "I think this whole program thing is a fantastic idea."

"Really?" Arlyn asked excitedly.

"Really." Leo drained the last of his drink. He rubbed his chin, as smooth and fresh as it had been eight years ago aboard the *Freelander*. It was one of Leo's greatest burdens that he simply couldn't grow a beard. "We'd need to figure out a few details of course, and to be completely honest you probably wouldn't be able to start until at least next year, but beyond that . . ." He caught the glowing expressions on his nieces' faces and grinned. "Yes, I think it is a very good idea."

"Boy howdy!" Arlyn hollered, throwing her arms around Leo's neck as the room erupted in shouts. "Uncle Leo, you are the absolute best!"

"I'm going to remind you of that next time you're mad at me," Leo chuckled, kissing Arlyn's forehead as she danced away.

"C'mon fellas, let's go finish Partsy! We'll all need the practice to prepare for the program anyway!" Arlyn laughed, skipping to the door, the leader of a pack of grinning faces. They jostled out of the room, making it all the way to the stairs before being stopped.

"Wait a second."

The crew filed back into the kitchen to find Leo watching them suspiciously.

"How much does this thing cost?" he asked, narrowing his eyes and leaning on his elbow. Arlyn beamed and waved the pamphlet.

"Well, that's the best part- didn't we tell you?" She was almost giggling, braids swinging. "It's free!"

"It can not be fre-" Leo was shaking his head, but Arlyn hurried to correct him.

"No no, it is! See here," she read from the pamphlet, "*All expenses of the program will be covered by Mr. Wilmot Denloy, originator of the YIP. Room, board, travel fees, and specialty tools will all be provided. Program participants must only bring clothing, a tool belt,* etc, etc." Arlyn laughed, giddy with the prospect of change. Just imagine it, two years of travel and learning and fun with her cousin and friends! What could be better?

"What?" Leo's voice had lost its sunshiny quality. Arlyn looked at him, shocked to find that his face was no longer lit and laughing. Rather, his expression had faded to one of confusion, an emotion which was quickly darkening into something else.

"What do you mean, *what*?" Arlyn asked, the arm holding the pamphlet falling.

"I mean what did you say?" Leo was watching the girls carefully now. "Who is running the program?"

"Some random rich dude, I don't know." Arlyn checked the paper. "Wilmot Denloy, that's right." There was silence.

"I'm sorry girls," Leo's voice could have cut ice. "I should never have said yes before learning who was putting it on."

"What are you talking about?" Graylin folded her arms, eyebrows lowering. "You mean you're not going to let us do it?"

"No." Leo stood, chair screeching against the floor, and he limped to the counter.

"I don't understa-"

"End of discussion Graylin," Leo said tersely, beginning to unload pots and pans from the cupboard.

"But-" Arlyn stepped toward her uncle, holding a hand out, and was shocked when he slammed down the skillet he was holding.

"I said end of discussion!" he snapped, his very gray Freely eyes flashing as he spun to face his nieces and the crew. "I recognize you guys are used to doing whatever you want all the time, but the fact is that I am the adult here, and I will be making the decisions, and I say no." Leo turned away, shutting the girls and their friends out of his view.

"Take Lewis to her house," he said gruffly, waving his hand. "She was supposed to be home hours ago."

"C'mon," Arlyn said softly, gently ushering her friends out of the kitchen, still watching her uncle out of the corner of her eyes. He was still standing at the counter, head slightly bowed, pots and pans forgotten.

"What the heck was that?" Graylin muttered to Arlyn as the six donned their shoes and hurried out the front door.

"I have no idea." Arlyn rubbed her forehead, remembering the way Leo's brow darkened and his hands had paled. She sighed. "Let's just get Lewis to her house. I'm sure he'll be back to normal when we get home."

"I don't know." Graylin tugged on a curl as they climbed the *Freelander* ladder, the ship already rumbling to life as Teddy and River started it. "He's never acted like this before."

"Maybe he realized we used all his medicinal wine in the explosion contraption last week," Arlyn offered, hauling herself onto the deck with a groan. Graylin shook her head, beginning to pull up the ladder behind her. She was hungry, and had been expecting to grab a snack and or lunch after Partsy. However, Leo's uncharacteristic outburst had scared her off, and she resolved to go bother Lewis and hoped the *Freelander* kitchen was well stocked.

Musing on her now broken hopes and dreams, Graylin plodded down one flight of stairs, stepping into the hall leading to Lily and Leo's rooms, and alighting down the set of steps leading to the main cabins, kitchen, map room, and meeting area. She had just stepped toward the kitchen in pursuit of her snacky stomach but was distracted by a very jarring *squawk*. Graylin paused for just a second to mentally rate how much trouble she thought her cousin had caused (she guessed about a six), before opening the door.

Arlyn's room was not normally pristine by any means, but the disaster which lay before Graylin was far more chaos than even Arlyn could normally achieve. Papers were scattered wildly over her desk, her lamp was tipped over, and three pencils lay on her floor. Shreds of something that looked oddly like leather were scattered around as well. It didn't take long for Graylin to find the culprit; a dark, excitable looking crow perched on Arlyn's windowsill. Graylin raised an eyebrow. It appeared Arlyn had acquired a pet, and hidden it on the *Freelander*. She briefly considered the possibility that this crow was the reason Leo had snapped so shockingly, but no, that wouldn't make sense. This was only like a level three bit of trouble. He was accustomed to far worse.

Graylin had never had any desire for a pet, but her cousin found animals to dote on just as often as she found friends. Luckily, the 'pets' rarely stuck around as long as the people. If they did, there would be so many by this point, Leo would be faced with an amateur zoo. Graylin supposed this was true for the friends as well, if such a thing as a people zoo existed.

A people zoo. Hm. What a very disturbing thought.

As Wilmot Denloy entered his third meeting of the day, it occurred to him just how many people he knew. People of all shapes and sizes, of every sort one could wish. It came with the job, he supposed.

However, as he entered the stuffy, smoke-filled room, he imagined every member around the table behind their own pane of glass as if in a zoo. *The Businessman*, a plaque would read, resting in front of the round man with the pristine suit and expensive cigar sitting to his left. *The Genius* would be the name of the woman to his right, *often found conning unknowing men of their riches and dignity*. The older man across from him, hair thin with age, hands spotted, would be *The Elder. Wise as his years denote.*

What, he wondered, settling in his chair, would be *his* title? *The Outcast? The Charmer? The Loner? The smart one, the nice one, the friendly one?*

"Ah, there he is!" called a man from down the table, chuckling. "I wondered when Mr. Moneybags would arrive!"

The Rich One, Denloy realized, heart sinking a little. That's how he would be viewed. That's what his plaque would say. It would say nothing about his family, or what he cared about. It would say nothing of his talents or skills. It would mention only his money, for what else was he anymore?

What he truly was, Denloy didn't want to think about.

4

Arlyn Freely pulled her deck of cards from her back pocket, shuffling them with practiced movements before flicking one into the ceiling. It quivered, but stuck. Laying next to her on the floor of her cabin was Graylin, sketching irritably.

"I just don't understand," Graylin said, her pencil denting her sketchbook page. There was one last drag of the graphite before the tip of the pencil snapped clean off. "I wish he would just explain."

"Explain what?" Arlyn asked, the sharp movement of her arm and card stirring up stray black feathers the crow left behind before being re-homed. After dropping a freshly dolled-up Lewis off at the Maynewin mansion, the *Freelander* had stopped in town to dump off the boys before sailing back to Leo's house where it remained hovering in the sky, harboring the two frustrated Freely cousins, too irritated to go inside. Every second that ticked by, these being very obvious thanks to the obnoxiously loud alterations Arlyn had added to the clock on her desk, brought the girls further from confused and closer to fuming.

"Don't you think he has a reason for saying no?" Graylin was now sharpening her pencil aggressively, the shavings dropping to Arlyn's eccentrically patterned rug.

"No, I don't," Arlyn threw another card into her ceiling. "I think he just decided he ought to tell us no, because we wanted to go so bad."

"Leo's not like that, and you know it," Graylin said fiercely, as strong in her defense of her uncle as she was in her anger at him. "He was all for it until he learned who was putting it on. Maybe this Denloy guy is like a real weirdo, you know, a creeper."

"Okay first off gross, second," Arlyn tossed a card at Graylin's head, "If that were true, why wouldn't he have told us?" She examined the remaining cards in her hand before tossing them roughly across the room. "He *would* have told us *if* he had a proper reason. He's just . . . he's just so . . ." She let out a frustrated breath and hopped to her feet. "That's enough of this sitting around stuff. We just need to go inside and make him explain himself."

"And how are we going to do that?" Graylin asked skeptically, flipping shut her sketchbook. She had been drawing ideas based on Mr. Hooper's crane, his hydraulic system running circles in her brain and begging to be put to other uses. So far, she'd been quite unsuccessful.

"We are going to march inside and tell him that if he doesn't let us go, we are going to hate him forever," Arlyn announced, tossing a braid over her shoulder and beginning to lace up her boots.

"Why do I feel like that isn't going to work?" Graylin muttered, considering the donning of footwear and deciding against it.

"Because you, cousin, are a pessimist," Arlyn said, quite truthfully, before skipping from the cabin.

The cousins found their uncle in his workshop, once again shuffling through papers. Arlyn grimaced, hoping his irritation had vanished the way her and Graylin's certainly hadn't. She reached out a hand, hesitating just a moment, before rapping gently on the door frame.

"Come in," the man called, squinting at a page. Arlyn glanced back at Graylin, who shrugged, before entering.

"Hey, Uncle Leo," Arlyn smiled nervously, beckoning to her cousin and holding her hands behind her back. "Uh, is it alright if we . . . talk?"

"Well, I suppose we'll have to," Leo said, sighing and dropping his papers. He leaned against his workbench. Arlyn nodded and sat herself on a side table.

"Great. First off . . . can we do the program?" She pulled a screw from her pocket and popped it in her mouth to roll around.

"No." Leo's mouth was nothing more than a line.

"Wonderful," Graylin said. "Great. Great start."

"Would it change your mind if, in the event you continue to say no, we promise to hate you forever?" Arlyn asked cautiously. Leo was not amused.

"As that is an empty promise," he said firmly, "no, it does not."

"Then can you tell us *why* we can't do the program?" Arlyn questioned. Once again, Leo's face remained stoney.

"No, I can't."

"Can you tell us why you've suddenly become an absolute loser?" Graylin asked, raising her eyebrows.

"You know what Graylin, I actually can," Leo said, folding his arms. "I've suddenly become an absolute loser because I want what's best for you, and in my opinion the best thing is for you two to not join the inventing program."

"But why?" Arlyn cried as Graylin let out a string of mild vulgarities, thus suitably disguising them.

"You don't always need to know why," Leo said loudly. "Why can't it be enough that I think it's best? Don't you trust me?"

"Don't *you* trust *us*?" Arlyn asked, pulling the screw from her mouth in frustration. "No, don't answer that," she waved her hand, as Leo started to respond. "We *know* you don't trust us."

"Of course I trust you," Leo said wearily, rolling his eyes. "I just don't trust other people, or that you'll make good decisions in the presence of other people."

"Who are you talking about," Graylin interjected, frowning as she often did, "what other people? Like the crew?"

"No, no, I love the boys, and I love Lewis, they're wonderful! I mean-"

"You mean you don't trust *us*, Arlyn and me," Graylin snapped. "Because if you trusted us and you trusted the crew then you would let us travel with them, to go explore or go camping, but you don't!"

"You want to go camping?" Leo cried. "Go camping! Camp your hearts out, I don't care."

"What?" Arlyn popped the screw back in her mouth, rolling it around furiously. This conversation was not going as smoothly as she'd hoped. "Really? You're okay with us going alone?"

"Yes." Leo hesitated, before his shoulders sagged slightly. "Yes, I'm okay with you going alone. Just drop the inventor's program idea, please."

"Are you buying us off?" Graylin asked sharply. Arlyn held up her hand.

"No, no, let him keep going, cousin. I'm okay being bought off."

"Well I'm not!" Graylin kicked the air. "Just because Leo's an adult doesn't mean he should get to boss us around without explanation and tell us to deal with it."

"The best explanation I can give," Leo said, re-catching both girls' attention, "is that I don't trust Wilmot Denloy."

"Why?" Arlyn asked.

"I can't tell you," Leo said, "and please don't ask anymore because it will just make us all more frustrated. All you need to know is that I don't trust Mr. Denloy, and because of this neither you nor the boys will be participating in his program."

"Is there anything you can do which would improve your opinion of this Denloy guy?" Arlyn asked. "Research or interviews or something?"

"I said don't ask any-" Leo's voice stopped, his hand moving to his chin. "Hang on, that might be an idea. He'll be in town looking for program recruits, won't he?"

"I think so," Arlyn nodded encouragingly. "You could go grill him, make sure you think he's legit."

Leo was silent, which made Arlyn slightly nervous as it gave Graylin a great deal of room if she decided to butt in. Thankfully, Arlyn's cousin remained quiet as well, simply watching as Leo mulled over the proposal.

"Alright," he said finally, glancing down at the papers next to him. "Deal. I will talk to him, but if after doing so I still find him untrustworthy, you two will accept my decision without argument."

"Deal," Arlyn grinned, bouncing off her perch and shaking her uncle's hand. "And while you do that, us and the crew will go on that camping trip you just promised us."

Leo tilted his head, opened his mouth, and then shrugged.

"Fine," he said. "I can live with that."

All three broke out into grins, which after an argument was quite normal. They could never stay mad at each other for long. The cousins gave their uncle a long hug and sprinted out of the house to inform the boys of the news.

The flat in which Enland, Teddy, and River all lived was fairly old, fairly large, and had several leaking windows as well as a busted door. There were many ways in which this busting could have happened, and no one seemed quite certain which was the culprit. Teddy and River's roughhousing, Enland's poor attempts at Freely-like machines, or even a freak and totally accidental firework set off inside were viable options on which to lay the blame. Now added to the list was Arlyn Freely's foot kicking it open with much more force than was needed, scaring Enland half to death in the process.

"Pack your bags idiots, we're going camping tomorrow!" Graylin announced proudly.

"Say what?!" A loud crash rang down the single hall as River, Teddy, and Teddy's chair came tumbling down it.

"We're going where?" Enland asked, his scowl slightly less scowly than normal. "Explain."

"Camping," Arlyn clarified. "Out in the woods where we can hit each other with big sticks and not get yelled at."

"Sounds great, I'm in. When do we leave?" River dusted himself and Teddy's chair off.

Teddy himself remained on the ground, now propping his head up with an elbow. "And who gets the biggest stick? How many times do I get to hit River with it?"

"Do we get armor or other defenses?" Enland asked, already trying to strategize his way out of getting hit with sticks.

"To each his own, and armor to the cowards," Graylin said, already starting out the door. "Get packed! We're going to tell Lewis!"

Lewis's parents turned out to be far more against the idea than Leo had been, even after learning he had condoned it. To be fair, Leo had just recently and uncharacteristically agreed, and also Lewis was currently under 'voluntary home confinement'. This was not to be confused with 'house arrest', though Mr. and Mrs. Maynewin promised this would be the next level of punishment if Lewis were to disobey again.

"Come on Mama, it's just for a few days," Lewis had said, as the Maynewin's butler Jarno carried in a tray of little sandwiches. He set them carefully on the little table the group was sitting at, glancing once at the cousins before sliding the tray ever so slightly further away from them. This, Arlyn supposed, was only to be expected, considering how she, Graylin, and Lewis had used such platters the last time they were over. Stair surfing, it turned out, was not Graylin Freely's strong suit.

"I don't care Lewis, darling, I simply can't allow it," Mrs. Maynewin said primly, cupping her hand delicately under the bite-sized sandwich she lifted to her mouth. "You must have a punishment of some sort. You came home several hours after you were supposed to, earlier today, I might add. The least you could do is give it some time."

"We won't leave until tomorrow," Graylin offered, stacking two finger sandwiches on top of each other and popping them in her mouth. "If that helps."

"To be honest, my dear," Mrs. Maynewin smiled at the Freelys, of whom she was quite fond despite their negative influence on her daughter, "it doesn't. I'm sorry, but you'll either have to postpone your trip or go without Lewis."

"Mrs. Maynewin," Arlyn tried to sit properly, "all due respect, but we *need* your daughter to come with us. We'll starve otherwise. Uncle Leo said it was alright, remember?"

"Yes, you keep saying, and I'm still shocked by it," Mrs. Maynewin shook her head. "I'm afraid I'm putting my foot down on this. Lewis will not be going." She reached out to pat her daughter's hand, looking sympathetically at the face which looked so much like her own. "I'm sorry, darling."

"I'll walk the Freelys to the door," was all Lewis responded with, rising from the table and striding from the room.

"I'm sorry Lew," Arlyn said, pausing at the ornate double doors leading out the house. "We can go a different time."

"Are you kidding me?" Lewis said, raising her eyebrows. "We're leaving tomorrow, and I'm coming. Just be here at eight-thirty on the dot, and I'll be ready."

"I always forget you know how to break rules," Arlyn grinned, fist bumping her friend.

"And I always forget just how poor of an influence the two of you are." Lewis shook her head, but she was smiling as she waved the cousins away.

Arlyn and Graylin spent the rest of the night planning their trip, shuffling through papers and knick-knacks and food, running between house and ship, and then back to the house again. It was close to midnight when the last supplies were loaded onto the *Freelander*, these being an entire crate of marshmallows which Teddy and River together had to finagle up the rope ladder. This was very amusing to watch, and Graylin, leaning against the front door frame, was actually pleased they had brought the boys in to help. Not only could she watch the two brothers struggle their way up to the ship repeatedly, but also she could listen to Leo coach Enland on chart coursing.

"See this line here?" Leo drug a finger along the map laid out before himself, Arlyn, and their cartographer. "This is the average wind current for this time of year, you'll want to factor that in."

"So we should sail a bit more this way?" Enland asked, taking his pencil and sketching a perfectly curved line along the map. When using his artistic skills toward map making Enland was quite adept, drawing nary a shaky line or lopsided circle. This, however, was the extent and limit of his abilities, and he had actually been banned from sketching anything beyond plain lines, mostly in the prevention of others' nightmares.

"Just like that!" Leo smiled proudly, resting an arm on his semi-adoptive son's shoulder. It was strange, the relationship the boys had with Leo. Arlyn had mused it over many times, and still wasn't entirely sure how to categorize it. If the three boys' adoption had really been legal, no one knew, and Leo never intended to reveal the truth, which just made distinguishing the connection Leo had with Enland, Teddy, and River even harder. It wasn't really father-son, though Leo loved the boys and they respected him. It wasn't really brotherly either, for their connection was slightly more distanced than that. Really, Arlyn decided, Leo was like an uncle to the brothers, and like an older brother to the cousins.

"What are *you* doing?" Leo asked, yanking on one of Arlyn's braids as he limped by. *Older brother my left foot*, Arlyn thought, aiming a playful kick at her uncle. *Annoying younger brother more like.*

"I am just relaxing," Arlyn told him, slumping on the couch as Graylin, Teddy, and River entered the room. "Mentally preparing for freedom, you know."

"I can't believe I agreed to this." Leo shook his head, hobbling back over to Enland and lowering himself into a chair. His leg seemed to be bothering him more than normal, though this happened sometimes. The cousins had noticed a correlation between Leo's leg stiffness and the rain, which was both hilarious and oddly useful.

"You're not considering backing out, are you?" Arlyn asked, narrowing her eyes and propping her legs up on a few pillows.

"No, no, I'm just regretting my life choices," Leo shrugged, waving a hand as he peeked over Enland's shoulder. "Ah, no, that destination mark is a little too far south. Try it a little more like . . . here." Leo reached down and drew a quick X on the map.

"Mr. Denloy! Mr. Denloy!"

Wilmot Denloy hurried through the sprawling hall of his house, trying to listen to all the words directed at him at once. It was not an easy task.

"Mr. Denloy, what is the best date for the ball?" A young woman with pale eyes and paler hair scurried up to him, holding a clipboard.

"Whichever is best for you, Louisa."

"But sir-" The poor girl was cut off by an older gentleman with a thinning mustache.

"I say, Denloy, this is quite the madhouse you've got here. It's a wonder you stay sane in all this racket," the man said, struggling to keep up with Denloy's long strides, surveying the bustling hall. People were running up to each other, slamming in and out of doors, and hurriedly scrambling about their duties.

"Whether I *am* indeed sane is debatable," Denloy flashed him a grin, before being overtaken by another employee.

"Mr. Denloy! *Mr. Denloy!*"

"What is it now, Higgins?" Wilmot asked, finally stopping to face the young lawyer bounding up to him. "I have places to be, you know. A meeting with Mr. Hooper-"

"Yes, sir, but-"

"If this is about a will again . . ." Denloy said, shaking his head, and resumed his rushed pace. "Then forget it." He had a ribbon, an old bookmark he believed, that he was twisting around his fingers, the stress of the day getting to him.

"Sir, you can't keep putting it off. You *must* write a will. Your fortune is large enough that you are running quite the risk by neglecting it further."

"Tell me, Higgins," Denloy said, smiling, "how old do I look to you?" Poor Higgins reddened.

"Not old, sir, I mean, very young." Not near as young as Higgins, but young enough.

"And I think we can both agree that my job is not exactly rife with danger," Denloy said pointedly, gesturing to the velvet carpets and cushioned chairs around them as they entered his study.

"No, sir, but listen," Higgins drew himself up to his full height as they stopped, his boyish face and thatched head looking out of place with his professional suit. "As your lawyer, as your *friend*, I must strongly recommend that you write a will. Anything can happen sir. Even the unexpected."

Too true, Denloy thought. He stared at Higgins for a moment before patting his shoulder.

"I appreciate the concern, Higgins, but I have more pressing matters to attend to. Now, Mr. Hooper." Denloy turned to the round man sitting awkwardly in a velvet chair, a material which clashed magnificently with the inventor's dusty suspenders. "Doing well, I hope? How is fame?"

"Oh, I wouldn't say fame, sir," Hooper said bashfully, standing hurriedly to shake Denloy's hand. "But I will say it's fun, havin' people come up an' talk to me an' all.

"I'm glad to hear it," Denloy said, gesturing for Hooper to sit back down as Denloy himself took his seat. "And I'm glad you could spare the time to meet us here. Don't worry," he chuckled, catching the nervous shift in the engineer's expression, "nothing has changed. Mr. Higgins here, my lawyer, has just finished up those papers we were waiting on, so now we can finalize your introduction to the Pekin Construction team."

"Oh, sir, I-" Hooper hesitated, before taking the papers slid to him and lifting his pen. His eyes roved the page, his large hand shaking slightly.

"Er, Mr. Hooper?" Denloy said kindly. "The page is upside down."

"Oh, right, I mean, I'm sorry," blustered the poor Mr. Hooper. He clearly could neither read nor write.

"It's quite alright," Denloy fixed the paper, smiling at the old inventor. "Just put an X here."

5

ARLYN SAT ALONE AT the kitchen table, head buried in her arms. This was her thinking pose, most often assumed in the morning when everything was quiet. She could think, or she could not. She could hum, or she could not. It was entirely up to her. No sounds, no light, no feelings, just stillness. On bad days, she needed this time. But, on good days, like this one, it was merely a bonus, a bit of time for her to have to herself.

However, the silence predictably was soon to be disturbed, as Arlyn's cousin entered the room. Graylin walked right to the counter to retrieve what she considered the most important meal of the day: ice cubes. Or, as Arlyn referred to it, chilled water with a side of drama.

"Shhm-morning." Arlyn raised one arm sleepily, greeting her cousin.

"Mmph." Graylin grunted in reply, yawning, and dropping the ice tray. The cubes spilled all over the wooden floor, instantly starting their slow melt onto the kitchen rug. Graylin made an irritated sound and bent to pick them up. After finishing their course plotting, Leo, the cousins, and the brothers had played a rousing few rounds of Partsy, and the gathering hadn't dispersed until well into the dim morning hours. This was obvious by the way Graylin was fumbling the ice cubes, dropping just as many as she picked up. She even started dropping the rescued cubes into a saucepan before remembering they were destined for her jar, not the stove.

Finally giving up on most of the ice, Graylin reached for a banana, quickly peeling it, and throwing away the unwanted bits . . . but when she looked down, she found the peel still in her hand, and the edible part in the trash can.

The cousins made eye contact.

"Listen, I'm tired," Graylin said dully, throwing away the peel as well. Arlyn started laughing, and was still doing so when they heard their uncle hurry down the stairs from his room.

"Morning, girls!" Leo cheerfully waved to them from down the hallway. He'd clearly been up for a while as well, and relished his awakeness. "Sleepy?"

"I'm not sleepy," Graylin yawned contradictorily, pulling a new ice tray from the freezer. "I'm completely awake." She turned away from her uncle, who was still smirking as he leaned against the doorway.

"Hoh!" There was a tremendous thud, and a pained wince.

"Uncle Leo?" Graylin dropped the ice tray, which spilled once again as she started at the thump. Arlyn was already helping Leo up, holding his arm and watching his face.

"Are you okay?" She asked him while Graylin drug a chair over.

"I'm fine," Leo winced, breath catching slightly. "Just knocked my air out, I'm alright." He drew himself into the chair, carefully keeping off his bad leg. He bent it slightly, face flashing with pain as he straightened it again.

"You want a bandage or something?" Arlyn asked, watching the bloody streak on the front of her uncle's shin. The place of the injury seemed familiar, as did the deep, sickening bruise blossoming beneath it.

"No no, it's barely even bleeding," Leo waved his hand, his breathing returning to something more normal. "I just banged it up, that's all." He grabbed at the table, using it like a crutch to stand. As the weight shifted to the now injured leg, his face turned gray. It was an ashen color that took Arlyn straight back to that moment after the *Freelander* crash, when Leo had stood after breaking his leg. She didn't like that color anymore than she liked the sudden weakness in her uncle's voice. *He's not as young as he used to be*, she reminded herself. Despite her and Graylin's jokes, Arlyn always thought of Leo as very young, but she supposed at some point a person's body would start reacting more harshly to injury.

"There we are," Leo said cheerfully, moving his shoulders and leaning against the table. "I reckon I'll have a nice bruise tomorrow, but not much else. Now, aren't you two supposed to be out of here, exploring your teenage freedom and making me regret my choices?"

"Oh, yeah," Arlyn reached for an apple, deciding that some breakfast would fix the strange anxious feeling in her stomach. "We've got to pick up Lewis at eight-thirty, and then grab the boys. Apparently they still needed to pack, surprise surprise."

Graylin caught the apple her cousin tossed her, holding it in one hand as the other fiddled with a little chain. She wasn't sure why she felt so nervous, but something about Leo's instant expression of worry, something in the very pit of Graylin's self, told her that something about this injury was not normal. But she was being silly, of course; pessimistic, as always.

"Eight-thirty?" Leo asked, walking firmly, if slowly, to the cupboard. "You'd best hurry up then, it's already nearly eight."

"Eight?!" Graylin choked on her apple, spraying juice all over her cousin. "Crap!"

"You two go make sure you have everything ready, and I'll take a final glance at the fan," Leo chuckled. "I don't think it should give you any trouble on this short of a trip, but I want to give it a once over all the same." The girls watched as he paused in the hall, considering the coat rack before drawing out an umbrella and using it as a crutch.

"Do you think we ought to help him?" Graylin watched uncertainly, grimacing as the umbrella, and Leo's elbow, caught the front door.

"Nah," Arlyn said, trying to act nonchalant even though she didn't feel so. "Nah, he's fine."

As Leo lowered himself into the bowels of the *Freelander*, he allowed himself to feel everything he'd been hiding from the girls. He took a deep breath, inhaling air through his nose for five seconds and then releasing it for five, trying to push through the nausea-inducing pain in his shin. He sat on a nearby machine, sucking air through his clenched teeth, and yanked up his right pant leg. His shin was rapidly swelling, much larger than was normal, and the tender skin around his slight scrape was a sick yellow green, with bursts of purple blossoming in the center. Leo let his pant leg drop and leaned back against the wall. He was thirty-five. He knew, deep down inside, that something was wrong. And he was pretty sure he was dying.

He didn't know how long it would take, or if it would be painful. His still childish imagination had always whispered in his ear that dying would be the most excruciating moment of his life- the part of it, in fact, where he was saying goodbye. What could be more painful than that?

But, surely, he had *some* time. He would let the girls take their trip, and when they got back, they would settle everything. He would say goodbye then.

Leo grabbed at a panel on the wall, and pulled himself to his feet, using oxygen to quell the pain and glancing around the dark chamber. His eyes landed on the machines, but didn't really take them in. He had spent so much time with his nieces here, and he couldn't help but smile as certain memories resurfaced. All those years of instruction, teaching, and laughter. All the hours of inventing and fixing. Playing tag with them, racing around machines when they were still little. Urgently calling in Lily when a young Graylin had gotten her hair stuck in a bundle of gears, resulting in an impromptu and very distressing haircut (Graylin had stuck with the look ever since.) Then of course there had been that one time, maybe a year back, when he had found a pet duck hidden down there, quacking loudly as one Arlyn Freely hurriedly tried to shush it. And even that moment, not even a full day ago, when his nieces had smiled and laughed and called him an old man as they fixed the engine with him.

If only he had known how close the end really was. If he had known, if he had just seen a few hours into the future, maybe he would have savored it more.

Arlyn smiled and waved at Lily as the *Freelander* slowly rumbled awake. Leo had taken a few painkillers, wrapped up his leg, and danced a small jig for the girls to prove his fitness before Arlyn and Graylin had agreed to go through with their trip plans. As his footwork seemed only slightly hindered, their remaining fears were dispelled, and Leo helped his two nieces ready-up quickly lest they be late rescuing Lewis from her mansion. The *Freelander* held ten cabins, eight of which were assigned and four which were in regular use. Every crew member had one, plus Leo and Lily, and all eight rooms were packed with each person's traveling essentials thanks to the cousins and their friends' efforts the night before. After stepping heavily off the ladder, Leo pulled his nieces to him, giving them both hugs and kisses on their foreheads.

"I love you, Arlyn," he said brightly as he embraced her. "Take care of Graylin, and yourself too."

"Well, look who is acting like a sentimental old man," Arlyn said teasingly, hugging him back. "I love you, too."

Leo turned to Graylin and hugged her tight. "I love you, Graylin. Stay safe."

"Yeah, yeah," Graylin said, ignoring the embarrassing urge within her to say 'I love you' back. Leo ruffled her hair and grinned.

"Okay okay, get out of here."

Graylin bounded to the pilot chair, both girls' fingers flying as they smooshed into the single seat and raised the ship. The flight to the Maynewin Mansion was reasonably quick as well as trouble free. Leo's final tune-up had taken longer than expected, and it was well past the instructed time when the *Freelander* finally drifted to a stop over the sprawling house.

“I said on the dot!” Lewis hissed as she dashed to the ladder, her one eye glaring as she started up it. An ornate leather satchel hung from her shoulder, swinging with the momentum of the ladder as the morning breeze loosened her dark waves. “What sort of time do you call this?”

“The best one you can expect from the Freely cousins,” Graylin shrugged as their friend climbed aboard. “Since when has timeliness been our forte?”

“I had a plan, which worked flawlessly, by the way,” Lewis told them, following the cousins to the pilot chair as they began their getaway. “I got both my parents out of the house by reminding them it was almost their anniversary, and busied Jarno by giving him some new silver polish. But because I foolishly assumed you’d be here on time, I only set my distractions to last until just after eight-thirty.”

“So then how’d you get away?” Arlyn asked, punching the button to turn on the second fan.

“Snuck out,” Lewis shrugged, before narrowing her eye. “I won’t be making a habit of it, mind. This is a unique situation, and only because we’ve been waiting for so long am I willing to do this.”

“Yes ma’am,” Graylin grinned. “Understood.”

“Yes, yes, I understand.”

Denloy shut the book in his hands, a children’s story about a duck he’d been perusing, and turned to face the man in front of him. Ashton De Saturnius, the closest friend Denloy had developed over the last eight years, was standing by his library door. Kind, passionate, and skilled, Ashton was developing a similar sort of program as Denloy was, just over in the more populated cities of Osden.

“I would suggest some sort of outreach project, beyond Mr. Hooper and his crane,” Ashton said, watching Denloy carefully. “How many teens would willingly go chat with a middle-aged engineer just sitting by the river?”

"Alright," Denloy smiled, "I see your point. What do *you* do?"

"Well, I put up posters, banners, small bits of graffiti . . ." Ashton grinned, "though if anyone asks, I don't condone vandalism." He chuckled, leaning against the wall. "However, I'm operating in cities with a large population of wild kids, running around doing rebellious whatnot. *They're* the ones who will see the messages I'm sending. But for you, well, Soamtin isn't that big, and Odios isn't any better. You might need to try something more . . . quaint."

Denloy nodded, fingers absently tracing the cloth cover of the book in his hands.

"What are you thinking about?" Ashton asked kindly, unfolding his arms. Denloy sorted through answers in his mind, stopping briefly on several lies before settling with the truth.

"My family," he said. He lifted his eyes, caught Ashton's confused expression, and hurried to explain. "I was just thinking about what would have drawn my brothers and I in, if we were still kids looking for an inventing program." Denloy slid the book back on the shelf, turning his back and shoving it from his mind. "I think we would have liked a festival of some sort, or a competition. It will have to wait, though. I have a ball coming up in a few months that's taking most of my efforts to plan."

Ashton nodded, smiling as he reached for the doorknob.

"Of course. I hope I'm invited."

"Always, my friend," Denloy grinned, adjusting his glasses on his nose. Ashton waved and swung from the room, and Denloy settled back against his desk. It occurred to him that he sat on his desk far more than at it. He closed his eyes. That made him think about his family, too, but now that Ashton was gone, Denloy didn't have to pretend they were happy thoughts.

6

Doctor Bannler pulled the stethoscope out of his ears and sighed. He hated when this happened. When he got to a patient too late.

Leo was watching the doctor with a sad smile.

"Well? How soon will I die?" Leo's voice was cheerful, but Bannler heard the pain behind it.

"Don't say that," Lily said sharply from behind the doctor. She was standing against the wall, her arms knotted tightly. "You'll be fine. Won't he?" She looked to Bannler. He rubbed his forehead.

"You . . . *could* recover."

Leo laughed. "But it's not likely." He saw the doctor open his mouth. "Don't lie to me, Bannler," Leo commanded. The man shut his mouth and sighed again.

"It would have been easier to stop if you'd come to me earlier. I know this kind of injury, Freely. It doesn't just *happen*. This is a blood clot, probably caused because of your fall from the Freelander. And blood clots take a while to build up. Your fall today just re-fractured your bone, and let the clot in your bloodstream. When it gets to your heart . . . well, I wish you'd have come to me after the first fracture." Bannler looked up from the floor. He saw Leo and Lily exchange looks.

"I'll give you two a moment," he said, before ducking from the room. He'd been a doctor for nearly thirty years now, and he could always tell when the fatal diagnosis was sinking in. He could see it, in the eyes of the loved ones, when their hearts were breaking, and all they wanted was a promise of more time. *That* he could never give them, but he *could* leave them alone.

Lily turned to Leo as the door shut, tears in her eyes. She sniffed and blinked a few times.

"I don't care what he says. You'll get better." The way she said this, salty tears threatening to spill over, was as if trying to convince both herself and Leo. Leo just smiled and took Lily's hand as she sat on the end of the bed.

"The girls left?" he asked quietly. Lily sniffed.

"Yes," she said, voice altered by her stuffy nose.

"Good. That's good," Leo said, smiling a little and squeezing her hand. Lily's lower lip trembled, just like it had always done when she was about to cry. Leo smiled at that lip quiver, it reminded him of their childhood, when a very young Lily had cried over a scraped knee, or a dead bird, or a trampled flower.

"You know," Lily wiped her nose with the back of her hand, "It will destroy the girls if you . . . you know . . ."

"Die?" Leo asked, a grin tugging at the corner of his mouth. "Come on Lil, it's not a curse word." Lily glared at him.

"It's not funny. Don't you see what I'm trying to tell you? You're all the girls have left," she said. *You're all I have left*, was what she thought. Leo laughed again.

"If you think that my death will break them, you're kidding yourself. You've met them. They probably won't even notice for a week, and then it'll just be like a pet died." Lily got teary again, but Leo realized they were tears of anger, not sadness. This he realized when she slapped him.

"Don't *say* that!" Lily's eyes were blazing, the tears looking like angry flood waters. "You are so *selfish*." She hunched and pulled her knees close to herself, like a child pouting. This took Leo aback.

"Selfish? *Selfish*? I'm dying, Lil! How am I being selfish?" Lily shook her head.

"You're only thinking about yourself."

"I don't understand," Leo said, watching as Lily struggled with her composure.

"Because you are just dismissing the girls' feelings. Losing you will *devastate* the girls, and that's not to mention the boys! You're like their older brother, don't try to deny it. You know you've been more of a friend than a father figure to them. And they'll be losing the only family member they have left."

Leo smiled.

"That's not true. They'll have you," He said. Lily shot him a withering glare.

"I don't count."

"Why not?" He asked, squeezing her hand. Lily sniffed.

"Because I'm not part of the family, not really," she said. Leo smiled again, but this smile was neither jovial nor sad. It was gentle.

"Oh, yes you are. This family wouldn't have survived without you, Lily."

"You'd have managed."

Leo barked a laugh. "You've seen us. We'd have torn each other apart." Lily laughed sadly.

"Well, yes," she said, "You would have." She was watching Leo. She had known that their friendship would have to end eventually, when one of them died, but she had never expected it to be so soon. Leo had been her closest companion since they were three, and Lily could barely even imagine day-to-day life without him at her side. But the small part of life she could imagine was melancholy and dark.

Lily stood and wiped her sweaty hands on her pants.

"I'd better go after the girls. Tell them to come home. I doubt they've even gotten the boys yet."

"No," Leo said sharply. "Let them have fun." Lily bit her lip.

"But what if," she took a deep breath, "What if you . . ."

"Die before they get back?" Leo asked. He smiled. "I won't." Lily nodded. Leo grinned at her and closed his eyes. For a dying man, he truly didn't feel *that* awful; his leg hurt a bit, and he was filled with a sort of chill. But he was exhausted, and sleep felt like the best thing in the world.

Lily pulled down the thin window covers so that the light that shone in dimmed. She set a glass of water next to Leo's bed, and then just watched him. Watched him breathe, watched the way his chest rose with each breath. With each one, she thought she saw the even rhythm stop, *this was too early.*

With that thought, Lily swept herself from the room before she burst out crying.

Arlyn yanked a lever to her left and flicked a switch to her right. The thrum of the engine stopped. Graylin, sitting next to her, was frantically pressing buttons with one hand and turning the wheel with the other. When they had maneuvered the *Freelander* to its desired position, Arlyn pulled a huge lever down on the control panel. This cooled down the air in the balloons just enough so that, while the ship would stay floating, it would not continue to gain altitude.

"There," Graylin said, exhausted. This was the process needed to stop the ship, and neither girl could do it without the other. Graylin simply didn't understand how her uncle and Teddy could do it so deftly by themselves. Or deftly *at all*. The girls' method could be called haphazard at best.

They had flown all the way to the center of Odios, and were hovering over a tall brick tenement building, built nearly fifty years previously. It was tall, old, and not entirely structurally sound, but this was practically a given in Odios, whose safety and integrity committee had openly declared their motto to be 'If it hasn't fallen yet, it's fine'.

A figure poked their head from a window, which Arlyn estimated to be on roughly the fourth. This would make sense, as the fourth was the floor on which the boys lived. Arlyn could just make out River's spiky red hair blowing in the wind as he waved.

"Stopped the ship alright then?" He shouted. Arlyn laughed.

"Well, it went better than the last time!" she shouted back. River chuckled and ducked back in the window. Graylin pressed a button, suddenly cutting both fans, and Arlyn flew forward so her ribs smacked into the ship's railing.

"*Ow*," she cursed, earning her a look from Graylin. "Oh, don't pretend I haven't heard you say a few unnecessary words."

"Uh, my words are *very* necessary," Graylin muttered. She flicked one last lever on the control panel, backing away from it like one might from a dangerous animal, before knocking the rope ladder off the edge so the brothers could board.

"Where's Lew?" Enland asked, the first to reach the top, eyes scanning the deck behind his round glasses.

"Here," Lewis waved from where she was helping Graylin tie down the balloon ropes, shortening them ever so slightly as they ran through their pre-journey routine. This was the first time they'd prepared for such a lengthy trip alone, and both cousins were having a hard time remembering exactly what they were supposed to do.

"This rope?" Graylin asked, winding in a line as the wind plucked at it. The morning breeze was picking up, rusting the balloons, the crew's clothing, and Graylin hair in a most triggering way. Graylin's feelings for the wind changed nearly as often and as quickly as the weather did itself, these emotions ranging from pure adrenaline and bliss as a stormy gust pushed at her to nagging irritation when it swirled at her curls.

"That's right cousin, tie it up!" Arlyn called, gesturing to River and Teddy to help her knot the thick rope she was pulling in. "I want to be out of here before Leo can change his mind about all this, so let's hurry!" The crew quickly finished the remainder of the tasks they remembered to be essential, and several extra just a precaution. Once this was completed, the individual members set about their specific roles. Teddy slid into his spinning pilot's chair, Enland stationed himself next to him burdened with maps, and Lewis escaped to her post below decks.

"I'll be in the kitchen, do not bother me, I *will* smack you," she called, waving mostly to Enland and descending below. In general, Lewis's spatula threats were merely verbal- until it came to River. He was constantly sneaking food, a habit which drove Lewis absolutely crazy. One time she had caught him eating flour straight out of the bag. He had claimed it was a dare from Teddy, but no one believed him, and Teddy had publicly denied the fact.

River, in the meantime, was tasked with unpacking the small bags the boys had brought, starting by situating Enland's room. Though, admittedly, most of the ship could be considered Enland's room. He was often found asleep under tables, on tables, near big windows, on rugs, on his maps, under his maps using them like blankets, next to the wall opposite Lewis's oven (his excuse being, "It's warm over here!"), or really any mildly flat surface he could curl up on. Graylin often thought of him like a cat, but not a disappointing cat that eats all your food and then hates you, more like a cat that sometimes helps out and does your dishes. A dish-cat.

The cousins themselves were left on the deck, watching the city skyline fade into the haze of the morning as they sailed away. Arlyn glanced at her cousin, and grinned.

"Wanna go bother River?" she asked, knowing full well the answer.

"Always, cousin mine," Graylin beamed at her, and they dashed away to fulfill their duty.

The lights on stage were hazy with prop smoke, the illuminated stage reflecting the light and laughter of the production. The golden hue lit the faces of the crowd, most of which were shining with smiles, a very amusing bit having just been played out. Wilmot Denloy, sitting toward the front among other well-off colleagues, folded his hands, a small smile settled on his mouth. He loved the theater and had since he was young. He and his brothers had spent countless hours writing and performing, the fact that their entire audience was made up by themselves diminishing none of the thrill.

The actor on stage waved his hand, a sleek top hat wobbling on his head before toppling off with a gust of artificial wind. The dark ocean of faces rippled with laughter, the sound filling Denloy's row and spreading to him. He hadn't realized this play he'd agreed to attend with some business associates was a comedy, but he was glad it was. Comedies had always been his brother's favorites.

"Enjoying the show?" the man next to Denloy whispered, leaning over the arm of the padded red seats toward the businessman. Denloy smiled.

"Oh yes. I always thought it would be fun to be an actor," he whispered back. The man, whose face and voice Denloy knew but name he didn't, chuckled, the sound just a bit too loud for the silent audience.

"Ah, haven't we all?" he said. "Some people have a natural gift for it, you know? Bringing out that kind of emotion on stage and making you believe with all your heart that it's really the character on stage. I just saw *Elbus Loode* here last week, beautiful production, nearly as good as the original cast. When it first ran they had Barleone Saks and Imelda Freely in the leads. Goodness me, they were incredible. Absolutely incredible."

Denloy nodded, taking in the curious head-turns and interested whispers and trying to ignore both. It wasn't his job to entertain those intrigued by the Freelys. It may have been once, but it wasn't anymore. However, there would be a cocktail party after, and perhaps he could play on their curiosity and use it to his advantage. He may no longer be associated with the Freelys, but that didn't mean he didn't remember how to mimic that part of his past.

7

"IT JUST DIDN'T HAVE to be like this!" River cried, standing in the middle of the deck, raising a sword. The sun settling along the horizon set quite the backdrop for the scene unfolding. "Do you not recall our friendship o' Bernard? The many years we spent together in this very place? Those people have done you no good, I tell you!"

"Gideon, please. Those days are but faint in my memory, for actions speak louder than words. No man in his right mind could miss the treachery behind your eyes. Take the honest man's word, but beware, for the snake is waiting behind him." Enland's hair, loose and straight, floated majestically in the breeze.

Graylin watched from her seat on the deck as River strode solemnly to his opponent. "You may be an honest man, but I live in a world of truth."

"I love that part," Teddy whispered. His part in the production, acting as a now-killed brother to Bernard, had already played out. His roughly tucked white shirt was stained with what was supposed to be blood, but actually smelled more like paint. The nearly eight hour flight to the campground was one the crew was well accustomed to, having taken small trips to the location many times with Leo. As such, the six friends held no qualms about letting the *Freelander* do its thing as it hummed along in the sky, leaving them to fill their time in other, more imaginative ways. Currently, this meant rehearsing one of their favorite plays, a production they had put on many times and knew by heart.

"The truth is," River said solemnly from on stage, "there is no one in the world that could've stopped this. No man nor woman, for there will always be us, won't there Bernard?"

"That's debatable." Enland hopped down from his box and circled around River. "There is a place for but one of us, and if greed be to my name, so be it. For what is a man but a measure of his place?"

River laughed. "I truly have sorrow for you. You've become lost in their mazes and riches. I pitied you, friend. Truly. But now I see it is my job to fix this!" He ended with a shout, knocking Enland down with his sword, which was really several cardboard rolls taped together.

"Gideon, you mustn't do this!" Enland cried dramatically, drawing his own dagger. "Have you no shame in killing a man?"

"Not for one who is already dead," River bent over his friend and ran his blade over Enland's throat. Enland closed his eyes and went limp on the deck of the ship.

"Bernard!" Lewis charged from behind some stacked crates, rushing to Enland's side. "Bernard, my sweet husband, what has he done to you?!" She burst into tears and threw herself over him, Arlyn barely catching her snicker as she landed awkwardly on top of him.

The girls rose and cheered for the performance, and soon after Enland and Lewis stood up as well. The actors took their bows and hurriedly ran off to change out of costume.

"That was even better than last time!" Graylin shook each of the cast's hands. "Very impressive murder, River." Graylin was, in contrast to her normally gruff manner, an avid lover of the *Freelander* theater performances. River took another bow in face of the compliment.

"Natural talent, I guess," he said, elbowing Enland, who still had flowers from the wedding scene stuck in his hair. "How come when I was Bernard we had to use leaves?"

"Underpropped," Arlyn said through a mouthful of strawberry biscuit.

"Hey!" Lewis chased her across the deck. "I told you those were off limits!" She pulled out her spatula threateningly, upon which was clearly written River's name. This made sense, as he was the most frequent victim of it. Suddenly the ship lurch downward, and Arlyn stumbled, glancing up at the pilot's chair. Teddy was standing at the control panel, hands flying, a very concentrated look on his face. If

Arlyn didn't know better, or if it had been someone else at the wheel, she would have said that the jumble of words coming from the pilot's chair was a very fluent string of vulgarities.

"Oi, Ted! Bit of a warning next time, eh?" she called, rubbing her ribs where she smacked against a crate.

"Oh, of course. My bad. We're landing now," he said pointedly, his tone and sass a reflection of his thoughts on the nickname 'Ted'.

As the *Freelander* lowered, a thick cloud cover folded over the ship, and Graylin covered her head as they went through the mist, freezing cold water droplets clinging to her skin. Though the sun was still in the sky, it was close enough to the horizon that it seemed to have given up on supplying warmth, and the chilly fog folded over the ship as it descended.

"Land ho!" Arlyn cried, the entire ship shaking as the belly of the *Freelander* sunk into the ground.

The little meadow clearing in which the airship settled was just as it had been during their first trip; the grass was soft and downy, sprinkled with spring flowers, and surrounded by the large towering oaks. The trees here had always been fascinating to Graylin. With trunks that were dark and twisted, they looked almost like chunks of metal thrown into a fire. The dark fluttering leaves were constantly moving, as if alive, and now even the grass was rustling, blown by the breeze and the air expelled from the *Freelander*'s fans.

Everything thing the crew might need, as well as several supplies they most certainly *didn't*, was tossed off the ship. The crew members themselves followed, though they were not tossed, they climbed down the ladder, mostly because Lewis's tentative nursing abilities ended at broken bones. A fire was lit, tents pitched, and a dangerous and unwise game quickly started by Teddy and River, before being hijacked by one blonde Freely cousin. Now, River and Graylin were having a competition to see who could get closest to shoving another in the fire, taking turns rushing forward and pushing the other. It was most certainly a recipe for disaster, but it was the only recipe Graylin could actually follow.

"Why you . . . !" Graylin shrieked as she tumbled backwards after a particularly hard shove from River. Flame licked at the edge of her shirt and she scrambled away before rounding on her rival and bestowing a blow of her own.

"It's like danger is attracted to her," Arlyn said, shaking her head and trying not to join in. Leo had said to watch after Graylin, after all. "Every time Graylin gets close to anything that explodes, destroys, cuts or burns, it's like her mere presence spurs the dangerous thing on."

"Like gasoline," Teddy said, watching the girl with a peculiar expression that Arlyn didn't recognize. "Put her by fire and it jumps to her, and she fuels it on."

"Exactly like gasoline," Lewis said from Arlyn's other side. "She spurs on danger, she gets all sorts of places she shouldn't be, you keep her as far from fire as possible, and she smells bad."

"Woah woah woah!" Arlyn cried indignantly. "Gasoline smells *great*. I could sniff it all day."

"That explains some things," Lewis teased. Suddenly, Graylin gave a cry, and the three looked up just in time to see the girl tripping back, her curls flying. Lewis and Arlyn were there in a second, grabbing her arms and pulling her to safety. She was entirely uninjured, save her pride, of course, which had been mortally wounded by River's win, but Arlyn tossed a large bucket of water on the two just to make sure. Then, satisfied with the sopping scowl on her cousin's face, Arlyn turned back to her two friends.

"So, how did you and Graylin convince Leo to let us take this trip alone, anyway?" Lewis asked, raising a skeptical eyebrow at Arlyn. "He *did* say yes, didn't he? It's not going to be a huge disaster when we get home, right?"

"Oh yeah, he was great with it. In fact, it was his idea," Arlyn assured her, kicking Teddy from his chair and flopping in his vacated seat. "We made a deal, we and him. Him and us. Leo and his nieces. Nieci?" Arlyn considered her phrasing, and then shrugged. "Whatever. The point is, Graylin and I just wanted to ask him if we could do the inventor's program after all, and it sort of spiraled into this argument." Arlyn waved her hand. "It was this whole thing. Long story short, Leo told us he'd let us take a trip if we dropped the inventor's program thing."

"What?" River exclaimed, plopping directly in the lap of Teddy, who had settled himself on the ground. "You gave up? You agreed to drop the yip?"

"I really don't think that's how you say it," Lewis shook her head. "It's the YIP."

"Yes, we agreed," Arlyn ignored Lewis's correction. "But only on the condition that he interview this Denloy guy first, to make sure he really doesn't trust him."

"Doesn't trust him?" Lewis asked. "Why? I've met him, and he's very nice."

"You've met him?" Arlyn and Graylin asked, astonished.

"Of course," Lewis said. "He's rich. Obviously I've met him. He holds balls and galas and stuff all the time."

"Ewwwww," Graylin groaned. "Disgusting rich people events."

"And you said he's nice?" Arlyn asked Lewis as Enland sat himself in the chair next to her. "He's not . . . a creeper?"

"What?" Lewis laughed. "No! No, he's very nice. I mean, at least as nice as most of my parents' friends. He's a businessman, all charm and politeness and handshakes."

"Does he serve good food?" River asked. "Can you bring us sometime?"

"Over my dead body," Lewis snorted. "You lot, at a formal ball? What a nightmare. I mean, Graylin is still smoking, and River picks his nose in public!"

"Do not!" River protested. "I'm not the embarrassing one! Look at Enland!"

Enland was sitting in his canvas folding chair, apparently trying to . . . crochet? Arlyn couldn't be sure, but that was what the activity closest resembled. "Pull it through the loop. Through the loop," he was muttering to himself.

"Yeah that's true," Graylin commented, absently grinding out the bit of glowing char on her shirt that Lewis had pointed out. "I don't know what Enland's making, but it *is* pretty embarrassing."

"I'm trying my best," Enland protested. "I just can't get the hang of this crochet stick."

"I'm sorry what?" Arlyn laughed. "You mean the hook?"

"No, the crochet stick," Enland lifted it up to show her. "Isn't that what it's called? I'm trying to make a scarf."

"That definitely isn't what it's called," River laughed. "Just like that *definitely* isn't a scarf."

"Oh, it's not that bad," Arlyn assured the cartographer, motioning for everyone to stop their ridicule. Their amusement now taken away, River and Teddy scurried off. "Just imagine that it's supposed to look like that."

"Like a mangled heap of string? Like a broken bird's nest?" Enland asked, sighing. "It's a wreck."

"No, not a wreck, and not a bird's nest. More like . . . a rat nest! Think of it like a rat-scarf," Arlyn patted his shoulder while Lewis kissed his cheek. "Enland buddy, I don't think you're listening to me. A *rat scarf*."

Enland just sighed, though he looked a bit more cheerful. "Well, I certainly won't be the one wearing this rat-scarf. You want it when it's done?" Arlyn grinned.

"I would absolutely love it."

Enland nodded and turned back to his work, a look of disgust on his face.

"Guys!" An excited yell came from the thicket next to their camp. "Guys, look at this giant stick!" A gloriously muddy Teddy emerged from the brush, triumphantly hoisting a decently sized tree limb above his head.

A few moments later, an equally triumphant River emerged with an even larger stick. "Stick fight!"

Within a minute, five out of six crew members had equipped themselves with their own arboreal weapon. Arlyn, wielding dual branches, extended a large piece of shield-ish bark to Enland. He stared at her disapprovingly. "Stick fight?" she asked hopefully.

Enland sighed, accepting the bark. "Stick fight."

She grinned and pulled him out of his chair into the ongoing battle. "STICK FIGHT!"

Lewis just sighed. "And you wonder why I don't want to take you places," she said.

Teddy, curled into a ball in one of the folding chairs, yawned. There were some abnormally loud crickets making a lot of noise behind the tents, and the flying embers of the fire mixed with the stars in the sky. Snoring rumbled from the boys' shelter, while Lewis and the cousins' canvas canopy was completely silent. But only one cousin was asleep.

Graylin was still up, lying silently. She knew Teddy was awake, but she didn't want to go out there and talk to him. It sounded mean she knew, but to be honest, Teddy sometimes made her feel guilty that she didn't have an electric personality, one that might encourage the boy to speak, and guilt made her irritable. Besides, she was too quiet. *He* was too quiet. In those rare moments they were together, there was just too much quiet to go around, and that left a whole lot of space for Graylin's thoughts, which was never a good thing.

After another ten minutes of stillness which dragged on like an hour, Graylin told herself that boredom was worse than guilt. She grabbed her tool belt and pushed out the tent.

Teddy was still in his chair, just staring at the fire. He glanced up when she came out, before returning his gaze to the flames. It was just as she thought, then; Teddy disliked her just as much as she disliked him. Grand. Now she didn't need to feign politeness. Graylin fumbled in the pouches of her belt until she pulled out a small trinket in the shape of a square. There was a hole in the side, and a panel on top which she removed. The machine was small, maybe three times smaller than Graylin's hand.

"Can't sleep?" Graylin asked finally. The words came across gruffer than she had intended. Teddy shrugged and made a sound. Graylin had expected little else, so she just fiddled with her machine.

"Well, maybe I could sleep if I wanted to, but I'm thinking," Teddy said suddenly. Graylin was quickly regretting going out to the fire. Why hadn't she just stayed in the tent and dealt with the silence? And she couldn't leave now, it would seem rude. Her impulsive decisions had, once again, gotten her into an uncomfortable situation.

"Sorry, I shouldn't have said anything," Graylin said quickly, wondering why she was still talking.

"Don't be. It's fine," was all Teddy said in response. Graylin felt so awkward, she could have been sick. *This* was why she didn't talk to Teddy, this sort of interaction exactly. And now, to make things worse, the boy seemed mad at her. Wonderful.

"Well, um, I feel like you're maybe a little irritated right now, so I'm just going to go back . . ." Graylin started to get up, her bones screaming with the uncomfortableness of the moment. Teddy sat up, a line forming between his eyebrows.

"No, no I'm not irritated. You should stay, if you want," he said, fingers dancing over the arm of his chair. Graylin considered her options. After a few seconds she sat back down, and hugged her blanket around her. Teddy too relaxed.

"Do I really seem irritated?" he asked. "Sorry."

"Oh, I . . ." Graylin scratched her nose. "I don't know. Not really, I guess. It's just, River says stuff like that a lot, that you're angry or mad, and I guess he knows you a lot better than I do, so I thought maybe . . ." Graylin was rambling, and she knew it.

"No, I'm not mad," Teddy said quietly. The fire crackled, the crickets chirped, and then he turned in his chair to face Graylin. "River assumes I'm mad because I'm quiet when really I just . . ." He cut off and rubbed his eyes. "I don't know. I guess most of the time I'm not irritated, but once River jokes that I am, I *am*, and so I can't even defend myself.

It's just this endless cycle where either people think I'm irritated, or I really am irritated, or I'm frustrated that those seem to be my only two options. You know?" Teddy glanced at her and then focused back on the fire. "Sorry, that wasn't-"

"No, I get it," Graylin said, surprised that it was true. "It's like when Arlyn makes all these jokes about how antisocial I am, or how I hate people. But I'm not antisocial, I just don't know . . . what to do, I guess. Sometimes it feels really easy, and then other times it's like I've suddenly forgotten how to speak or move."

"I know," Teddy said, smiling a little. "I'm not antisocial either, but sometimes I wish I was, because sometimes it's just easier to not say anything than find the right thing." He laughed. "Besides, being antisocial really irritates socialites, and personally, I find irritating socialites endlessly fulfilling."

Graylin laughed, and Teddy smiled. More fire. More crickets.

"Arlyn says you're antisocial?" Teddy asked suddenly, face still lit with laughter. Graylin shrugged.

"Yeah. It doesn't help that when I finally work up the courage to speak, I can't seem to hold my tongue and just," Graylin made a barfing gesture with her hands, "say whatever comes to mind. Leo says I don't have a filter, but I *do*. I'm filtering all the time. It's just, sometimes stuff gets past the filter, and I don't realize until after I've said it." Graylin pulled a panel off her little invention. "They're right though, Leo and Arlyn and River. I am rude, and awkward, and-"

"No, you're not," Teddy said, watching her seriously. "I don't think you're any of those things."

"Clearly you haven't spent enough time with me," Graylin said with a small smile. Teddy laughed. As the fire died a little so did his smile, and his expression grew serious.

"You're right though. I haven't spent much time with you at all. I really don't know anything about you besides that you like inventing," he said, actually meeting her eyes. Graylin felt a smile tugging at the corner of her mouth, so she turned back to her work.

"Well, what do you like to do besides pilot an airship?" Graylin asked, inexplicably unable to keep her eyes down. Teddy smiled.

"I like music," he said, twisting in his chair, folding his arms over the edge and resting his head on them.

"Music?" Graylin asked, wrinkling her nose. Lily liked music too, but Graylin wasn't a huge fan. The slow, whiny strings and the distant wood winds always put Graylin on edge whenever Lily took them to shows.

"Yeah. Piano, guitar, drums, singing." He stretched in his chair.

"Why?" Graylin asked, trying not to sound too disappointed. Teddy lifted his eyes to her, and then the sky.

"I guess . . . because I can say so much more in music than I can in talking. And I like music because it makes me feel happy, and it's nice to know that I can be happy. I want to be reminded that I can feel happy, sometimes," Teddy said.

It was the truth, but not the full truth. If he were to speak completely honestly, Teddy would have told the girl in front of him that his whole life, he'd been afraid of becoming trapped, and music helped him escape. Ever since he was young, Teddy had been afraid of growing up, starting a family, and becoming a man who simply had a life but didn't really live. He was terrified at the idea of becoming dull, sad, and detached. Truthfully, Teddy just wasn't built like that; he was destined to be a feeler, a dreamer, a lover. But he didn't know that.

"I like to feel happy," Teddy continued quietly. "That's why I like music."

"Huh," Graylin said, thinking about this. All Lily's music ever made her feel was irritable, but to each his own, she supposed. "Why don't you ever play for us?" She asked. Teddy shrugged, smiling.

"You don't want to hear it. Trust me."

"We might want to hear it. Do you have any instruments?"

Teddy nodded. "Leo got me a guitar, but I'm not particularly good. I'm better with a piano."

"You could sing for us," Graylin said, imagining Teddy, hands clasped, singing a very soft opera tune. Teddy laughed. Graylin didn't know if she'd heard Teddy laugh before tonight. Certainly not his laugh alone, when it wasn't lost in everyone else's. It was nice, really; his eyebrows went up when he laughed, and his smile brightened.

"If you convince everyone else to listen," Teddy said, smiling, "I'll play for you."

"Good."

Silence.

"So what else do you like doing, besides inventing and yelling at people?" Teddy asked, his expression almost too innocent. Graylin thought for a moment.

"I like reading, and just wandering the streets, and going into town when there's something big going on. I really like watching the plays you guys put on. I could never be in one, I'd feel silly, but I think I'd like to try writing one."

"That'd be great," Teddy grinned. "You write the plays, I compose the music, and the rest of them act. We'd have a regular acting troupe."

"Would you two shut up?" Arlyn's muffled voice yelled from the cousin's tent. "I am trying to get some sleep."

"Well sorry, I didn't realize you sucked, cousin!" Graylin shouted back. Teddy was laughing.

He yawned again and closed his eyes. Graylin watched him for several moments before standing. The cool air blew pleasantly, and anyway, Arlyn was a blanket hog. So, Graylin retrieved her covers and settled in her own chair. She pulled it over her shoulder, tucked in her feet, and as the edge of the eastern sky was tinged with gray, fell asleep.

Wilmot Denloy rubbed his eyes. It was late, far too late to work with any coherent thought, and yet he was still up. Things needed done; there were papers to be signed, documents to be read, and letters to be written. Plus, there was that charity ball coming up in three months, and he was supposed to be deciding on the details, like the flower arrangements and color themes and menu. He remembered, smiling a little, all those years he and his brothers had laughed and fantasized about being rich. What would it be like, they had wondered, to be a famous inventor, to have so much money you could do whatever you pleased? To live alone, be the sole owner and occupant of a giant mansion, a house so big you could get lost just trying to use the bathroom? Wouldn't it be cool, they'd thought, to live like that? Have maids and butlers and advisors who did all the proper work and left you to your own devices.

Yes, he and his brothers had certainly imagined the life he lived now. If only they had foreseen the loneliness that filled the giant house, or the distrust seeping into every relationship, or the hours and hours spent writing and reading and chatting, all to maintain a facade of a life Denloy wasn't even sure he wanted anymore.

But this was the life he'd chosen for himself, the hole he'd dug himself into to escape everything that came before. There was no getting out now.

So, as the eastern sky slowly faded from black to gray, Wilmot Denloy pushed up his glasses, rubbed his eyes, and got back to work.

8

ARLYN WOKE UP AND sat bolt upright. She had been dreaming that someone had kidnapped Graylin, and that her cousin had been so annoying they had given her back and kidnapped Arlyn instead. And the weirdest part was, the kidnapper looked like a mix of River and Finn. At least, he had at the end. Arlyn had the vague thought that at the beginning of the dream, he had looked like Teddy.

Arlyn shook her head to clear it and looked over. Her cousin and her blanket were both missing. Perhaps Graylin really *had* been kidnapped; wouldn't *that* be a nice surprise? Leo would be disappointed, but disappointment could be dealt with. Oftentimes Graylin could not be.

Arlyn ducked out of her tent. The fire was practically out and her cousin was asleep in a chair next to it, as was Teddy. Arlyn rolled her eyes. She vaguely remembered being woken up by their chatter the night before. Of *course* her cousin chose the dead of night to be friendly.

Arlyn had woken early, but not without reason. She ducked into the boys' tent and found the mound of blankets she suspected was River. She knelt down, grabbing handfuls of covers and shaking. "River, hey River, wake up." The red-haired boy snuffled, rolled onto Enland, was shoved off by his groggy brother, and settled back into his original position. Rolling her eyes, Arlyn employed her favorite friend waking technique: a Wet Willy. With much pawing and squirming, River awoke while Arlyn hurried away lest he retaliate.

"Wake up sleepyhead, and be quiet about it," she commanded, opening the tent flap to shine in River's eyes as he blinked and yawned. "We have places to be."

The two made their way through the thick woods to a stream sparkling in the early spring sun. Arlyn had always liked spring in the woods best- the new foliage was bright, and the air fresh. The canopies of the rustling oaks created enough shade that only a bit of undergrowth grew, mostly ferns and moss, scattered across the rocks around the creek. Next to the water sat a small, extremely rudimentary hut, constructed out of sticks and mud. Arlyn had built it some time before River found it, building the little shelter bit by bit on each trip. If the campground had been any less secluded and sheltered by trees, Arlyn was convinced the hut would have fallen by now. However, once her red-haired friend found her refuge, she invited him to help her make additions. Now, in the mornings after camping, they had made it a tradition to hike and hang out there. This morning, the two had decided to fish, as Lewis always made an excellent breakfast out of bass.

"You know, it's nice having something nobody knows about," River said, casting his line into the bubbling water.

"Yeah." Arlyn worked a small fish off her line and tossed it back in the water. "I wish I was better at keeping secrets, but I just seem to give up all the stuff I'd like to keep close to the cuff as soon as I meet anyone."

"Secrets are hard when you have brothers," River agreed. "They're not *intentionally* nosy- well, Lander is, but mostly just their general vibe kills secrets. Even if I had things I should keep quiet, I just feel like saying it." He reeled in a completely empty line.

"Never change, River," Arlyn told him, privately thinking that even if just one of the two learned to hold their tongues now and then, River and Graylin's disagreements would greatly decrease.

"How are you catching so many?" River snagged his line on a rock. "You've caught like fifteen already!"

Arlyn laughed. "Well, how often do you practice stealing hats off of people with a fishing pole?"

"Never?"

"Well, that's your problem right there." Arlyn tugged on her line and, feeling resistance, reeled it in. Something in the water flashed, and there was a glittering spray of water as she pulled out yet another glistening catfish.

"Well," Arlyn grinned, laughing at River's look of shock, "This will do nicely."

As the two hurried back to the campsite, they found the rest of the crew awake, though Teddy and Graylin looked distinctly tired.

"Where've you been?" Graylin mumbled through a mouthful of apple. Arlyn smiled and held up her fish.

"Shopping," she said, handing her catch over to Lewis. "Will these do?"

"Oh yes, they'll do wonderfully," Lewis announced sweetly.

Arlyn just caught the gagging gesture Graylin made to Teddy, and the smile said boy tried to hide.

"Yes darling, they'll do *wonderfully*," Graylin said mockingly, voice stiff and refined. "Oh, Enland my dear, I know you wanted to chat tonight, but I'm busy cooking these delectable aquatic animals, so would you please kiss my rich-"

"Graylin!" Lewis shrieked, loud enough to cover Teddy's laughter. "Language *please!*"

"Oh, my monetarily well off ears!" Graylin cried, still walking with peacock levels of mockery.

"If you don't behave, I'll put you on kitchen duty with me," Lewis threatened

"I take it all back," Graylin quickly announced, skipping out of reach of Lewis's spatula, before a very large lime suddenly smacked into the back of her head, and she spun around to face the incandescently innocent Lewis.

"Alright, alright, let's stop this before someone gets injured," Arlyn declared, stepping between them. "Speaking of injured, I wonder how Leo's doing."

"Why? What happened?" Lewis asked.

"He fell yesterday," Graylin said, eating a handful of blueberries. She was a snacker of the highest order.

"Dang. He's getting a bit old to do that, eh?" River said jokingly, as Enland finally left his tent, looking like he'd had an intense fistfight with sleep, and sleep had won.

"That's what we said," Arlyn grinned, knowing how irritated her uncle would be to hear how they were talking about him.

"We should probably pack up and head home soon. I've got a formal dinner to attend at noon, and my mom will be extremely displeased if I'm late," Lewis announced from her place by the fire, turning the fish on a spit.

"Righto!" River said. "I'll take care of our tent." As he moved off to disassemble the shelter, the rest of the crew folded blankets, re-packed supplies, and ate the breakfast Lewis provided. The sun, above the trees now, was drying the dewy grass as Graylin and Lewis attached the packed bundles to a rope hanging from the *Freelander*. It was a pulley system, which made lifting the supplies up into the air much easier. Up on the ship, Arlyn pulled the stuff off the rope and piled it on the deck.

Teddy kicked out the fire, River sneakily replaced his and Arlyn's fishing poles at their stream, and Enland, already back on the *Freelander*, started to plan their route home.

"Ready?" Teddy asked once at the top. Every crew member turned and looked down over the edge at their campsite. Graylin hoped they'd come back soon. She liked it here.

"Yep. Start it up, Teddy," she said, and the boy took his place at the pilot spot. He flipped the switch and turned the wheel, and then cranked back the lever. The engine rolled over twice, the back fan blades emitting a dark cloud. The *Freelander* coughed, groaned, and rose into the air. Golden early light shone on the deck, glinting brightly off the polished boards. Lewis was downstairs in her cabin, preening for her party, while Enland and River were arguing rather loudly over who had won a recent staring contest, with brief input from Teddy.

As they flew away, Arlyn could sense the light feeling of the trip leaving and the regular weight of her small bit of responsibility coming back. Also returning was the memory of Leo's interview with Denloy, and his impending decision regarding their involvement with the inventor's program. Arlyn hoped it had gone well; this little trip had left her itching for more.

The ship glided over Odios. The trip home had been fairly smooth, especially when compared with flights taken in the past. Graylin had gotten bored about an hour in, and started some very intentional and mildly hurtful teasing of River, which Teddy and Arlyn had found amusing and the handyman most certainly hadn't. Lewis was still miffed with the blonde Freely for her early morning teasings, and together she and River brought up a fine collection of Graylin's past mistakes from memory, which set her into quite an irritable mood for the remainder of the trip. That is, until she caught a few of the unsavory words Teddy was muttering to himself at the pilot's chair, which honestly surprised Graylin out of her irritation.

They had dropped Lewis off at her house roughly on time, which had also helped Graylin feel a little better. Lewis's hair had been brushed silky smooth, and she had donned a fancy dress that dragged on the floor, lace gloves that were impeccably white, and dainty black boots with so many hooks that Graylin got impatient just thinking about lacing them up. Enland, however, had been enchanted, so enchanted that when Lewis had invited him to stay for the dinner, he had accepted with uncharacteristic grace.

"I'll drop you two off, park the ship, and then River and I can walk home," Teddy had offered.

"Sounds good to me," Graylin answered, leaning over the edge. The sun was bright enough that she had to squint as she looked over the town. The metal pipes on the outside of many houses gleamed in the light, as did the corrugated tin bolted to roofs and the glass of the windows.

The sun was still in her eyes when they got home. The house, expansive and tall, looked just like normal. Everything was just as the girls had left it. Through the windows, two silhouettes waited for them.

Arlyn strode up to the door, her 'please let us do the program' speech formulating in her head. Leo had come to his senses, she just knew he had. She raised her fist to knock in case her uncle was busy, but the door swung in before she even made contact. Standing in the doorway, eyes red and cheeks pale, was Lily. She sniffed once, her voice fragile like it had broken days ago.

"I'm sorry."

Three months later

"Girls, I, uh . . . I made some breakfast." Lily set a plate of scones on the table.

"I'm not hungry," Arlyn said quietly. "Thanks."

"Graylin?" Lily asked hopelessly. No answer.

It had been three months since Leo died. Lily had stopped them at the door, eyes red and tear-filled. Upon seeing the girls, she had been driven into such a state of misery that she'd been unable to speak. So, it had not been Lily who had explained Leo's cause of death to the girls. It had been the doctor, standing behind Leo's friend. He had sat the cousins down at the kitchen table and told them how, when Leo had fallen down the stair, he had re-broken the bone in his leg that had fractured after the fall from the *Freelander*. He had explained how this had released a blood clot, encased in Leo's bone all these years, which had slowly but surely reached their uncle's heart. He'd told them how they hadn't expected it to travel so quickly; that if they had, Lily never would have sent them off on the trip. The girls had remained silent, still, and unresponsive. Doctor Bannler had asked them gently if they wanted to see the body before the funeral, and Arlyn had nodded, standing with him. Graylin watched her cousin go, refusing to even consider looking at her uncle. Arlyn had returned, pale and trembling, and they had sat in silence all night.

The quiet had stretched on to the next day, and then the next, until weeks had gone by without a single word from either cousin. Lily had shouldered most of the work: organizing the funeral, accepting condolences, consoling those who came crying, and striving to care for the now-distant girls. She had even made the dreaded trip to the little apartment where Enland, River, and Teddy lived to break the news to them. Arlyn supposed their continued absence from Leo's house meant they were grieving just as deeply as she and Graylin were. Maybe they, too, hadn't left their house. Maybe they, too, didn't want to wake up and couldn't make themselves sleep. Arlyn didn't really care either way.

For once in her life, Arlyn allowed herself to feel all the feelings and do nothing about them. She didn't try to mask, or pretend, or conceal. She didn't even try to protect her cousin. She just floated from day to day, drifting in stifling silence because Leo was dead. She ate a few meals a day, trying to swallow the food as it stuck in her throat like sandpaper. When night fell, Arlyn dropped into her nest of blankets, and she dragged herself out of it in the morning. Because Leo was dead, and Arlyn didn't know how to go on. All she could think was that Leo was gone, and that he would never come back. Sometimes it got too much, and she would hurry into her room, shut the door, and explode, just to get it out. She would cry and scream and shout at no one in particular, holding a pillow up so Lily might not have to hear. Her heart burned with despair and ached with anger and sobbed with loss.

As for Graylin, the bags under eyes were darker than they ever had been. A sickly greenish blue, they made her gray eyes look dim and angry. A combination of sleep deprivation and little food had made her cheeks thin, and she had a bruise on her finger the color of the bags under her eyes where she had twisted her chain too hard. And yet she kept doing it, over and over and over, never stopping even when it dug into her skin. She spent her days pretending to read or draw or invent, when really all she saw were the thoughts in her head. At night, she sat in her room, tinkering and fiddling and crying. Anything but sleeping. Her shirt hung a little looser every day as each morning brought another cycle without her uncle there. Sometimes Graylin felt so sick at heart, and cried so hard, she actually drove herself to throw up the little food in her stomach. Other days, she just floated numbly, listening to her cousin's frustrated shouting and the screaming inside her head.

Lily had tried to reach the girls in the beginning. She had felt guilty for sending the girls off without letting them know just how much danger Leo had been in. But after a month of muteness, she'd given up. It was just too hard.

Arlyn would respond sporadically with muttered thank you's or mumbled good nights, but Graylin had consigned herself to occasional nods or grunts and nothing more. So Lily had stopped the trickle of comforting words and focused on keeping the cousins alive. She fed them and made them tea to help them sleep, and hated herself every day for being the reason Arlyn and Graylin had never seen their uncle again.

Without Leo, everything the girls had based their lives on felt shattered. It's how they'd felt after losing their parents, but at least then, it could be chalked up to a tragedy; a disaster, a freak accident which, undoubtedly, would change Arlyn and Graylin's lives forever, but would never happen again.

Except, Arlyn thought desperately as she stared at her breakfast, it *had* happened again. Once more, they had lost their guardian and parent figure, the person who was supposed to always be there, but wasn't.

"I'm not sure when it's going to be the right time for you two," Lily said softly, setting a box on the table next to the untouched scones, "but I think you two should really consider looking through some of Leo's old things."

Arlyn looked up at her and then glanced at her cousin. Graylin was staring at Lily, her mouth shaped into her signature frown, the one which made her look like she was about to cry.

"I know it's hard," Lily added gently, "but it has to be done, and I don't know if . . ." she cut off, taking a deep breath, "I don't think I can do it alone. Besides, it could bring you some comfort."

"You think it's hard for *you*?" Graylin asked, voice scratchy and quiet. Lily's mouth trembled.

"Yes, it *is* hard for me," the woman said, her voice quavering. "I know you cared about Leo. I know you loved him, but guess what? So did I, and I . . ." Lily stopped and closed her eyes. Her fists clenched. The cousins watched her blankly.

"It's just unfair," Lily finished, tears welling up. Arlyn felt her mouth twitch in anger, and her arms went rigid. She stood, and even though she'd regret the words about to spill out, she continued. She'd held it in for too long.

"No. What's *unfair* is that we never got to see our uncle again. What's *unfair* is that the only family member I have left in the world is Graylin. You lost your friend?" Arlyn hated how she said the word *friend*; it came out in a nasty, twisted sneer, but she couldn't stop it. "You lost your friend? I lost my *uncle*."

Lily looked like she'd been slapped, and her expression twisted into a sob.

"I know," she cried, "and I'm sorry. I'm sorry that Leo is dead, and that you never got to see him again, and that I can't do this alone and spare you the trouble. But the truth is, girls, that I'm as lost as you." Tears were streaming down her face, her words hindered with hiccups. "I wish I could do it alone, but I can't. You two are all I have left."

Arlyn's heart dropped, and she could tell by the slightly sickened look on her cousin's face that Graylin was experiencing the same feeling. She'd never thought of it that way, that Lily was also alone now. She'd never really thought to consider Lily's family and friends. Were her parents alive? Did she have friends beyond Leo and the girls? Siblings, maybe? Arlyn didn't know. She'd never asked. How was it possible, she thought sadly, that she had never asked?

There was an acid burning inside of Graylin, bubbling and rising. It was guilt, singeing her heart and the thoughts in her head.

"I'm sorry," Graylin murmured. "I want to help."

Lily tried to blink back her crying, thoroughly unsuccessfully, and gave the cousins watery smiles. This set Arlyn off, the tears springing to her green eyes, which in turn made Graylin rub her eyes and sniff quickly. The three sat down without a word, though the silence was a different sort now. It seemed to soothe and calm the three mourning young women as they ate the scones, appetites finally returning after so long an absence.

Breakfast was eaten quickly, if not completely. After so long eating so little, neither of the cousins could stomach their usual amount of food. However, the sustenance did pull Arlyn and Graylin somewhat out of their lethargy, and they followed Lily to Leo's workshop with firm footsteps.

As they entered, Arlyn had to shake her head and smile at the disaster which was Leo's work space. Papers were strewn every which way, and half-made inventions were lying on chairs, shelves, and the floor, hiding several crumb ridden plates from Leo's frequent snacking. Stacked all around were pots and bouquets of sympathy flowers, all of which Lily had piled in the workshop, unsure of where else to put them.

For the past three months, smiling had felt like an impossible task to Arlyn, as if the act would use up every bit of energy left inside her. But now, grinning felt natural as she breathed in Leo's presence. The thought of finding what he had left them gave Arlyn a sad sort of happiness, like her uncle, young and carefree, was smiling next to her. Scratch that, Arlyn thought with a grin. He wouldn't have been smiling. Probably scowling at something she'd done. But still.

The three spread out, opening drawers and sorting through papers. Dust swirled and pages rustled at the movement they made, the little particles whirling up into the air and dancing in the sunlight streaming through the window. Graylin fiddled with her chain, wrapping the metallic coolness around her fingers as she sifted through a stack of papers she'd removed from a drawer. The tips of her fingers brushed over the uneven edges, stopping every now and again on anomalies in the pile. There was a thick envelope, which when opened revealed the title, deed, and insurance for the *Freelander*. Soon after, she found a packet of patents under several people's names, including Leo and her father's.

Just as she was about to peruse the next drawer, another envelope presented itself. Pulling it out from the pile, Graylin noticed the words on the front, faded, but legible.

"*To Arlyn and Graylin.* Cousin?" Graylin glanced curiously over as Arlyn dropped the blueprints she'd been examining and hurried over.

Sliding her nail under the edge, Graylin broke the seal, and Arlyn went to her side as she unfolded the letter inside.

The writing was square and blocky, much akin to Leo's, but it wasn't quite his. There was something more mature about it. It was vaguely familiar as well, like a picture Arlyn might have seen a long time ago.

Dearest Arlyn and Graylin, began the note (Arlyn read this aloud).

We love you. Know that, please, and remember it. We loved you when we last saw you, and we love you now, wherever you are and wherever we are.

If you are reading this, it means that two terrible things have happened, and that the two of you have had to live through them. Firstly, it means that, despite our precautions, the family reunion did not stay as safe as we had hoped, and that your Uncle Will had to get you off the Freelander. Secondly, it means that the situation after we escaped the Freelander was as dangerous as we had imagined, and we could not come back for you. Both situations are terrible on their own, but combined must surely have been a nightmare for the two of you. However, your Uncle Will loves you very much, perhaps almost as much as we do, and we know you'll grow up happy and loved and safe. Happy and loved we could have given you, but safe *we could not, and we're sorry for that.*

Alternatively, our plan with the Freelander went off without a hitch, we are still together and thriving, and now as the two of you are adults we are showing you this letter as proof of your dear old parent's sketchy pasts.

As your mothers insist this is unlikely, we are going to assume that is not the case, and that our previous joke was both untimely and probably not appreciated.

We knew the risks of using the family reunion as means of our escape, and while we cannot know just how terrible the situation turned out to be, there is no doubt it will have marred your young lives. Dearest children, if you must blame anyone, blame us. It is our fault. You cannot blame the dead, but you can blame the living. In the event that we have not made contact with you within the last years, consider this confirmation of the fact that we are indeed alive. Just as we had precautions set up for you two, we had precautions set up for ourselves. The fact that you are reading this means that they were necessary, and probably that those whom we didn't give fail-safes are gone. If this is true, know that it kills us every day, and that only the knowledge of the life you two are now living helps us live through the pain.

We love you with all our hearts. We will see each other again.

Your parents,

Benson and Delilah, Michelangelo and Juliet Freely

Dated the fifth of August

Lily had stopped shuffling papers to listen and was now as still as the girls. She watched them with wide eyes as they re-read the letter, dated just before the *Freelander* disaster.

"Uncle Will? Our parents?" Arlyn read over the letter again. "*If you must blame anyone, blame us . . . we knew the risks*, what does that mean?" Arlyn's thoughts were racing frantically, looping circles in her mind around the only answer rising to plausibility. It was such an outlandish thought, though, impossible really. It *couldn't* be true.

"And they are *alive*?" Graylin added, sinking into a chair and playing with her chain.

"Lily?" Arlyn looked up from the letter to see Lily, looking almost haunted. "Lily, who's Uncle Will?"

Lily paused and gave Arlyn a funny look, almost like she thought she was joking, which was entirely fair because this sort of tense, world-changing moment was exactly the sort Arlyn would choose to joke in. However, Lily just kept watching the girls, seeming to realize they were serious. Her mouth just barely opened.

"You don't remember him?"

9

WILMOT DENLOY WAS STARING at flowers and had been doing so for the last twenty minutes. He had conferred with his housekeeper, Mrs. Wren, his cook, Mrs. Roylen, and every other female member of his staff when he first had set the date for his upcoming ball. However, that had been several weeks ago now, and he just couldn't remember what they'd all said. The pink bouquet or the yellow? He wasn't sure.

He stepped back from the flower arrangements, turning instead to the sample place settings and food. Among the dessert samples was a plate featuring his favorite sticky caramel rolls. With a small smile, Denloy reached out and tagged the dessert, signifying that it was his choice. Mrs. Roylen knew him well.

As he reached out with the tag, a tremble ran through his hand. Denloy paused, considering it.

"Sir? Are you quite well?" An older man with wild hair and tired eyes stepped forward, one of his white-gloved hands offered to Denloy.

"Yes, March, I am just fine," Denloy smiled at his butler, taking a deep breath. "I just have the strangest feeling that I'm missing something."

"You've been saying that for nearly three months, sir," March said, producing a caramel from his sleeve and offering it to his boss. Denloy took it gratefully; March was quite the amateur magician.

"Yes, I know," Denloy said, popping the candy in his mouth. "I've probably forgotten something, or lost something. If only I knew what."

"A business deal, maybe?" March offered. "Have you forgotten to follow up with something?"

Denloy considered this, scratching behind his ear as he thought. He was still working on launching the YIP in Soamtin and surrounding small cities, like Odios, so that wasn't it. He was currently planning the ball meant to launch the YIP, so *that* wasn't it. John Hooper continued to do well, his water tower having been finished several weeks previously. Ashton DeSaturnius's own program in Belhaven was growing nicely. With no obvious sources of the deep, empty feeling in his stomach, Denloy glanced around his library. There, on the desk, was his jar of caramels, next to a paperweight he thought might have once belonged to his younger brother. Underneath it were several papers, sketches of airships and the will Denloy had drawn up at Higgins's repeated request. Sighing, the businessman reached into his pocket and pulled out his ribbon, twisting it around his fingers as he mused.

"Well, it looks like I shall have to deal with this another day," Denloy sighed, clapping his butler on the back and heading for the door. "I simply don't remember."

"You guys are messing with me, aren't you?" Lily stared at the girls, eyes narrowed in pure confusion. "You remember him. You *have* to."

Graylin caught her cousin's eye. The last thing they needed right now was for Lily to act certifiable, talking about people who didn't exist, and then being surprised that the girls didn't remember him. Whoever he was.

"Remember who, exactly?" Graylin asked, hooking one foot over her leg.

"Your Uncle Will. William Freely?" Lily blinked at the blank looks on Arlyn and Graylin's faces. "You actually don't remember him?"

"No, we're pretending for the fun of it," Graylin said sarcastically, before getting hit in the head with a disciplinary paper airplane sent from her cousin. It was what Leo would have done.

"Who was he?" Arlyn asked, sitting on a stool. Lily sighed, but the lines between her eyebrows deepened with something other than lament.

"William was Mike and Ben's younger brother. They were quite the crew, the four of them. I am, no, *was* older than Leo," her voice caught just a little, "by about three years, so that would make Will two years my senior. He was an inventor too, just like your dads."

"Why don't we remember him?" Arlyn asked quietly. Everything was moving a bit too fast for the cousins' taste.

"I don't know," Lily said simply. "I suppose you wouldn't have seen him as much as you saw Leo. He had a job with a small engineering firm, but I do think he worked with your parents a lot, especially in those years before the disaster."

"Did he die on the Freelander?" Graylin asked, though she suspected she knew the answer.

"Yes," Lily said. The placid rustling of shrubs outside the window was the only sound as the cousins processed this information, and all the questions that came with it.

"So why was Will supposed to get us off the Freelander?" Arlyn asked, tapping her chin.

Lily shrugged. "Maybe it was just a precaution, in case something went wrong. I know Leo mentioned something at the time, worried about a propeller or something." Lily started to braid her hair, biting her lip and thinking.

"Will . . . well, he was the most responsible brother. He was very sweet, very kind, and was the quietest and the least talented in inventing. But he was always looking out for the others. Maybe that's why they asked him, just in case."

"Or," Graylin said quietly, looking back at the letter, "maybe it *wasn't* just a precaution. Maybe they *knew* something bad was going to happen." She scanned the page until she found what she was looking for.

"*We knew the risks of using the family reunion as means of our escape, and while we cannot know just how terrible the situation turned out to be, there is no doubt it will have marred your young lives. Dearest children, if you must blame anyone, blame us. It is our fault. You cannot blame the dead, but you can blame us, the living.*" Graylin met her cousin's eyes.

"That doesn't sound like an accident to me." Arlyn's voice was soft.

"What do you mean?" Lily's words were almost a dare, warning the girls not to voice the thought sinking into all their minds. Graylin had to disobey.

"It means," she said roughly, "that it's our parent's fault the Freelander caught on fire." What else could it suggest? Their parents had set up a safety system to ensure their children got off the airship, and then wrote a letter apologizing for what they had done. It had to mean that the *Freelander* disaster, the fire and subsequent crash which had claimed the lives of nearly all Graylin's family members, had been her parent's doing. Graylin buried her face in her hands and shut her eyes, trying to sort through the tangled net inside her head. This was heavy.

"No, no, no," Lily stood up and began to pace, tugging her long braid in a way very reminiscent of Arlyn. Whether the Freely cousin had copied Lily, or Leo's friend had mimicked Arlyn, no one seemed quite sure. "You're wrong. Your parents were good people."

"But it says, right here, that it was their fault," Graylin said quietly. "All of it. Their deaths. Our family's deaths. Even Uncle Leo's death."

"But it also said they *aren't* dead, that they had precautions set up for themselves," Arlyn said, brain fuzzy with the idea that her parents were responsible for Leo's death. The idea that they had killed all the Freelys was horrible, of course, but there was something heart-wrenchingly tangible about Leo's death over the others.

"The way I see it, cousin," Arlyn continued finally, tugging on a braid, "is that we have three separate issues here. Issue one: Our parents seem to have been the cause of death for most of our family members. Issue two: Our parents claim to still be alive, and simply aren't here for unknown reasons. Issue three: We appear to have an uncle whom we completely forgot about, and who was supposed to save us, but didn't."

"One of those is certainly easier to investigate than the others," Graylin commented, raising her head. She glanced at her cousin, and seeing the same determined look reflected there as was in her own mind, shifted her gaze to the room, taking in all the boxes and safes and drawers brimming with papers, all of whom could give them information which they needed. She sat a little straighter; Graylin Freely *loved* having something to do.

"Are you thinking what I'm thinking?" Arlyn asked.

"I dare say I am, cousin," Graylin nodded.

"Well, I'm not thinking what *either* of you are thinking. What are we doing?" Lily asked.

"We're going to re-remember our Uncle Will," Arlyn said.

The hours between breakfast and dinner flew by faster than Graylin knew hours could fly. Light from the windows quickly turned from morning bright to afternoon warm before disappearing completely and coating the outdoors in inky darkness. But the cousins saw none of this. They had firmly glued their eyes to the slew of papers they were sorting through, looking for answers among their dead uncle's belongings. So far, there had been nothing particularly enlightening; a few photographs here, sketches there, newspaper clippings and pages upon pages of notes. Lily had sat in a chair, blanket on her lap, telling them stories of their forgotten Uncle Will and his brothers.

"Oh, you might remember this one!" she said, smiling. The relaying of tales regarding both Leo and Will had brought some color back into her cheeks, and slowly, the memory of her beloved friend began to comfort her in the wake of his death. "Once, I was probably twenty-five, your dads were asked to act in a silent film."

"Really?" Arlyn asked, grinning. Lily laughed.

"Yes! One, Benson I think, was cast as a backstreet gangster, and Michaelangelo was a shop owner who got shot within seconds. The movie studio asked Leo to help with some mechanics behind the scenes, but he got stuck on how to make the puff of smoke from the gun meant to shoot Mike," Lily smiled. "Leo always went to Will for help on everything, especially since the twins were busy. Leo thought he was so wise. Anyway, Will got dragged into it, and they were *all* obsessed with that movie. You two five-year-olds wreaked havoc on that set."

"Is there somewhere we can watch this movie?" Graylin asked eagerly. Lily shook her head, grinning.

"No, it was never finished. The director abandoned it maybe a year into production."

"So weird," Arlyn shook her head.

Lily raised her eyebrows. "What is? That they stopped the movie? From what I've heard, that's quite common."

"No, no, that we don't remember him. Uncle Will, I mean." Arlyn sighed. "Like it makes no sense. We obviously remember Uncle Leo, and we remember our parents. Not very well, I'm going to be honest, but well enough."

"They haven't been erased completely," Graylin nodded. "So why has Will?"

"It was a traumatic experience, for the both of you," Lily said softly. "I wouldn't be surprised if you've forgotten more people than just Will."

A few hours later, as Lily regaled the girls with yet another tale of their fathers and uncles, a particular paper caught Arlyn's eyes. Solemn, she held it out to Lily, whose voice choked to a stop. It was Leo's will, though of course being Leo he had titled it *Leo Freely's Last William Billiam and Testamilliam.* Lily held it with trembling hands and tear-filled eyes, a small smile remaining on her face as she whisked herself from the room to read it. As soon as she left, Graylin set down the packet in her hands and crossed her legs.

"Cousin, have you noticed that Leo has a suspiciously large number of papers regarding Wilmot Denloy in here?" she asked, pushing back the curls that had fallen into her eyes. They were frizzy and limp after so many weeks of neglect.

"As a matter of fact, I have," Arlyn said. She picked up a pile of papers she'd been collecting, all relating to the businessman. "He's all over. Newspaper clippings, Leo's notes, even an invitation addressed to the Maynewins from him. *Please join me for a charity ball, August seventeenth,* blah blah blah. I wonder if he collected this stuff to prepare for his interview thing."

"Within two days?" Graylin asked, shifting through some notes of her own. "You're forgetting how little time Leo had after we left. There's no way he could have built up this much info within two days. I doubt he even felt well enough to do much of anything."

"Well, Leo *did* act like he'd had prior experience with Denloy. Maybe he wanted a sponsorship himself at some point?" Arlyn suggested.

"Don't you think he would have told us?" Graylin asked. "No, there's something else, and I feel like it's connected with his telling us we couldn't do Denloy's program. For some reason unknown, Leo has been researching this guy for years, and the conclusion of all this research was that he didn't like him."

"Maybe he *did* want a sponsorship at some point, but while looking into it, he learned something about this Denloy," Arlyn wondered. "He's probably like a money launderer or something, or a plagiarism . . . er. Someone who plagiarizes. A plagiarist."

"Or a creep," Graylin said. "My vote's still on creep."

"We asked Lewis, and she said he was nice," Arlyn reminded her cousin, starting on a new stack.

"Eh, what does Lewis know?" Graylin shrugged, stretching her arms above her head and resuming her sorting. "She may be cool, but she's still rich. Speaking of Lewis, I'm just now realizing we haven't seen her or the boys in like three months, and I feel like maybe we should be concerned . . ." Graylin caught the expression on Arlyn's face, one which told her that her cousin hadn't heard anything she had just said. "Cousin?"

"Look," Arlyn's voice was almost a whisper as she lifted a paper she'd just spotted. On it, scrawled in Leo's familiar handwriting, was what resembled a timeline, starting with the *Freelander* crash. There were lots of question marks scattered along the line, but interspersed were phrases like *First title under Denloy name, August twenty-seventh. Changed name, or beginning of career?* and *started Pekin Co., October* ???. Next to Pekin Co. was the scrawled note *Named for Arlyn? Or does he just like ducks?*

Arlyn beckoned Graylin over to examine the page, and her cousin's forehead wrinkled as she read the words.

"Pekin Co.? Named for you?"

The cousins glanced at each other, the same thought reaching both brains at the same time. But the very idea . . . no, it was so far-fetched, so asinine, that neither Arlyn nor Graylin wanted to voice it. Finally, Arlyn cleared her throat and held up the page.

"Cousin," she said hesitantly, "I may be wrong, but I think that Uncle Leo might have thought this Wilmot Denloy fellow is our Uncle Will."

"I think Uncle Leo might have been right," Graylin said quietly. She suddenly felt very light at the thought that there was still an adult out there who cared about her and was related to her. It was like a single drop of deep blue relief floating into a jar of water. But at the same time, that water represented dread and grief that there was another family member out there whom she could grow close to, just for them to die.

"And I think *you're* right," Arlyn said finally, nodding. She took in a deep breath, and then stretched. There was a split second during which both girls just sat, trying to understand, and failing miserably. Arlyn turned the Maynewin's invitation over and over in her hands, thinking.

"We need Lewis for this," she said. "Maybe this Denloy guy *is* our uncle, but no matter what, he's rich."

"Blegh." Graylin got to her feet, straightening all four of her lanky limbs, and pulling her chain out. She passed it from hand to hand, letting the coolness fill her palms.

"Which *means*," Arlyn said pointedly, "that we'll need someone who's also rich to get us some more info on him."

The Freely cousins may or may not have had an unrealistic view of the upper class, such as they were all uptight, all snooty, and all in a secret rich person club. However, in this specific instance, Arlyn's logic was fairly sound, as Lewis had previously mentioned knowing Wilmot Denloy.

Graylin nodded. "It's pretty late. Think Lew will be up still?" The sky outside the window was solid darkness, the kind of impenetrable black that only came after midnight.

"We'll grab the boys first." Arlyn dashed from the room, snatching up her satchel from a chair in the kitchen. She swung it over her head, and was about to speed out of the room, when she spotted a shape slumped at the kitchen table. It was Lily, fast asleep, a slightly tear-stained will under her face. Arlyn gently lifted her head, pulling the paper off her cheek where it stuck, and resting Lily's head back down. She thought back to the morning, when Lily had admitted that Arlyn and Graylin were all she had left. Heart aching, Arlyn scrawled her a note:

Gone to find Uncle Will (maybe). Will be back soon. Love you- Arlyn

When she reached the door, Arlyn was met with the sight of her cousin, hopping around on one foot, attempting to pull her boot on. Watching in amusement and disappointment, Arlyn sighed as Graylin was forced to sit down and pull it on, and then had to bury her face into her hands as her cousin tried to remember how to tie her shoe.

"It's been a while, okay?" Graylin said defensively as the two strode out into the night. "I just psyched myself out trying to remember which way the rabbit goes."

"And you were pretending to be said rabbit as you hopped around the entryway?" Arlyn asked, raising her eyebrows as the girls headed towards the parked *Freelander.*

"You know my balance sucks," Graylin insisted, as she climbed the ladder to the land-stranded airship. "And it's been a rough few months."

"No kidding," Arlyn said, following.

10

As the apartment where the three boys lived was in the relative center of Odios, the girls had rather no place to park the *Freelander*. Because Graylin had been banned from operating the *Freelander* alone, *and* because Arlyn wanted to respect her uncle's memory by honoring said ban, it was decided that Arlyn would keep the ship hovering above the building while Graylin shimmied down a ladder to fetch the boys. The city was as quiet as it had ever been, which in reality wasn't very quiet at all. Dogs barked, cars screeched and rumbled, metal fire escapes rattled, and people sang and shouted. Graylin hurried down the ladder, as fast as her nervousness around heights would let her, and then dropped to the ground. Her boots clacked as she ran across cobblestones and into the boys' apartment building.

Enland, River, and Teddy lived on the fourth floor, and by the time Graylin reached the top, she was thoroughly out of breath. Three months of rarely eating, sleeping, or exercising had done little good for her physical well-being. Graylin pounded on the door before bending over, hands on knees to regain some air. She sucked in a deep breath, and then knocked again, even louder.

"Sshhhh!" An old woman with rollers in her hair stuck her head out a neighboring door. "It's three in the morning, you lunatic!"

Graylin maintained malicious eye contact with the lady and pounded even louder. She was just about ready to kick down the bloody door when it swung open, revealing an exhausted looking boy with shadows around his eyes and wild hair.

"Teddy?" Graylin asked in surprise. "Why are you still up?"

"Why am I still up? Why are *you* still up, or here, for that matter?" he asked, ushering her inside and shutting the door behind her. Slightly taken aback by how talkative he was being, Graylin opened her mouth to respond, before noticing Teddy's appearance even more fully.

"Dang, are you okay? You don't look so good," she said, taking in his sad eyes and worn expression. She folded her arms. "I won't tell you why I'm here until you tell me why you are up."

"I-" Teddy started, glancing back at his room and thinking of the poems and songs he'd been writing, and about how glad he was Graylin wouldn't see them. "I was just . . . thinking."

"Graylin?" Another voice shoved its way into their conversation, and Graylin turned to see a very disheveled River squinting at her from his doorway. "Graylin, is that you?"

"No, it's my identical twin," Graylin said sarcastically. River beamed, and rushed out of his room, throwing his arms around her, hugging her tight. River was a very *huggy* person.

"I'm sorry about Leo," he said. His tone was one of a nice, tender moment, where two opposites bonded over a common sorrow. This effect was slightly ruined by Graylin karate-chopping River all over until he let go.

"Would you- get away- *please*?" She pushed him back, holding her hands up defensively. "No hugs. No. Never."

"Wow," River said, flicking on the kitchen light and watching Graylin. "You look *terrible*."

"I look terrible?" Graylin asked, seriously miffed by River. Already. "What about Teddy, huh? He's the one who looks terrible."

This conversation was not doing much for Teddy's abysmal self-esteem regarding his appearance.

"Teddy hasn't been sleeping very well," River said quietly. "Not since Leo died."

Well, Graylin thought, *I've been there.* She gave Teddy a small smile, which he tried to reflect. River just stood there, unusually quiet, and Graylin was feeling a little bad about her outburst regarding Teddy's looks. He really didn't look *bad*, and certainly not off-putting; his shadowed gaze and set mouth had just surprised her. She'd never seen someone look so sad, or make her feel such sympathy.

"So, why are you here? Is Arlyn with you?" River asked eagerly.

"She's on the ship, and we're heading to Lewis's next. There's a lot to explain, but the basics are we, meaning Arlyn and I, seem to have a secret rich uncle whom we've completely forgotten about and he's Wilmot Denloy, and our parents are alive, and it *appears* to be their fault that the Freelander burned."

River blinked at her, wearing his 'deer in the headlights' look that he always wore whenever anyone imparted knowledge to him, like these new ideas were just too overwhelming.

"You know what?" Graylin amended, grabbing Teddy's arm, "River, get Enland. We'll explain on the ship."

Back on said ship, Arlyn was paying less attention to the controls than she ought. In fact, she wasn't even in the pilot's chair; she was below deck, flipping through Leo's old photos. She was searching, waiting to find one face that was different.

"Mom and Dad, Grandma, uh . . ." She knew the lady in the picture, but she couldn't place her name. She flipped to the back of the book, to a picture of the entire Freely family from the fatal last reunion. Arlyn realized she recognized almost nobody in the picture. It was sad, the way her memory had wiped out all those faces she had once known as well as her own.

Wow, she thought, as she spotted a small girl with mounds of curly hair so blonde, it showed up as white in the gray-toned photo. *Is that really Graylin eight years ago?*

She couldn't help but snicker at her cousin's face. "Still looking annoyed at life, good for you, cousin."

The thunking of boots and chatter of voices from above her informed Arlyn that her cousin and friends had returned, and she bounded up the stairs to greet them. Graylin was looking particularly irritated, and kept throwing the beaming River dirty looks.

"What, did he offend you already?" Arlyn asked her cousin, as Teddy hurried to the pilot's chair.

"He *hugged* me cousin," Graylin spat, throwing a very nasty gesture towards the red-haired boy. He, still smiling, walked up to Arlyn as Graylin fled, lest more comforting gestures be bestowed.

"Hey," he said. "How are you guys doing?"

"Us?" Arlyn asked. How *were* they doing? "Yesterday, not so good. But today . . . today it's getting better." She glanced at her friend. "What about you guys?"

"We've been better," River said honestly. He sat on a crate, and Arlyn was surprised by how serious he suddenly looked. "Enland's been with Lewis most days, but she says he doesn't say much. Teddy's barely slept, I don't know if he's been eating much . . ."

"And you?" Arlyn asked. River shrugged.

"It's hard, you know, to lose your parents the first time. Leo was like a mix between an uncle, a brother, and a dad, and it turns out that losing your father the second time isn't any easier than the first."

With Teddy piloting, the *Freelander* made it to the Maynewin's sprawling mansion in record time. It was roughly four in the morning as the five crew members hurried up the long, uphill cobblestone driveway and corralled themselves in front of the grand double doors. It amused Arlyn how much longer it took them to organize themselves without Lewis there to command them.

Arlyn glanced around their group, got nods of approval from everyone, and knocked.

Only she didn't knock. The door seemed to avoid her fist and swung in to reveal . . . Lewis.

"Are you guys *insane*?" she hissed, clamping a hand over Arlyn's mouth. "Do you realize what time it is? You are going to get me grounded for life!"

"I-" Arlyn started, but Lewis glared at her.

"No, no words from any of you until we are in my room. Silence, *please*." Lewis creaked the door open a little more and let them in, shushing them aggressively as they tiptoed across the marble floors, over thick gold-braided rugs, and up stairs so shiny, Arlyn could see her reflection.

"You guys are lucky," Lewis whispered. "I thought you'd come to see me at some point, most likely at an outrageous hour, so I've been waking up every few hours, to check."

"For how long?" Arlyn whispered back, impressed with her friend's dedication.

"Nearly a week," Lewis muttered, pushing open the door to her room. The crew filed silently inside. Lewis shut the door carefully and spun around.

"Toss me that pillow, Enland, so I can shove it under the door. Then I want to hear what this is all about."

Soon the shades were drawn, the lights on, and the pillow stuffed in the crack under the door. Arms and legs folded, Graylin had settled herself into Lewis's desk chair, pillow hugged to her lap. She *always* had pillows on her lap. Conversely, Arlyn was stretched out on Lewis's bed, leaning against the headboard.

"First," Lewis said, sitting primly in a high back chair (her room was *massive*), "I'm sorry. About Leo. And I'm sorry that I didn't come visit you guys. My parents weren't exactly pleased with the whole 'sneaking out of the house for our trip' thing. But I really am sorry. Leo was a wonderful person."

Arlyn swallowed. Graylin fiddled. Both avoided eye-contact.

"Second," Lewis added finally, "why, exactly, are you at my house at four in the morning?"

Arlyn then launched into an explanation, covering the events of the day, including rifling through Leo's papers, hearing Lily's stories, and finding papers regarding Wilmot Denloy.

"There was even an invitation to a dance thing for your family, from him," Arlyn said. Lewis was watching her.

"So Leo did what you asked him to," she shrugged. "He researched Denloy, maybe even talked to him."

"In the space of two days?" Graylin asked quietly. "We were hardly gone Lew, and Lily said he was in bed pretty much as soon as we left."

"I feel like you have some sort of wild theory you're trying to get me to guess, and that I definitely won't ever be able to," Lewis said, re-positioning her legs. "Why do *you* guys think Leo collected all this stuff on Mr. Denloy?"

"We believe that Wilmot Denloy is our uncle," Arlyn said. Teddy dropped the music box he'd been examining and it twinkled to the floor, the sound a backing track for everyone else's shock.

"Your *uncle*?" River asked, mouth gaping like a stranded fish. "Wilmot Denloy is your *uncle*?"

"We think," Graylin said, nodding. "And we think Leo knew, or at the very least suspected."

"Why?" Lewis asked, standing, and taking a seat next to Enland.

Arlyn then dove into her and Graylin's discoverance of the timeline, and papers after. The more she talked about it, the more far-fetched this idea felt.

"That's not a lot to go on," Enland said, rubbing his eyes tiredly.

"But what other explanation is there?" Graylin asked, voice ringing with something resembling desperation.

"Oh, Graylin," Lewis's tone was calm, sympathetic and gentle. "There could be countless reasons Leo was interested in him. Maybe he knew him a long time ago, maybe they used to work together, maybe they were old schoolmates. There are a dozen possibilities that aren't 'I think this guy is my brother'."

"But Leo said he didn't trust Denloy, and wouldn't tell us why. If they just used to be friends, why wouldn't he explain his reason for disliking him?" Graylin asked.

"If they were brothers, why wouldn't Leo trust Denloy?" Lewis protested. "Or know he was alive? You two and Leo were the only Freelys left. If this Denloy really was one of you, wouldn't he have found you guys? Wouldn't people have found *him*? Before the Disaster, your family wasn't exactly unknown. Surely we would have heard if another Freely was alive."

"Well, obviously he's not calling himself a Freely," Arlyn interjected. "He's going by Wilmot Denloy, for whatever reason."

"Exactly! *What* reason? There is none!" Lewis cried, catching herself and lowering her voice to a whisper with an anxious glance at the door.

"Listen," she said, tone hushed, "I understand why the idea is appealing. It's all part of grief. You lost your parents, and just lost your uncle. The concept that there is another . . . *replacement* is bound to be nice."

"*Replacement*?" Graylin's voice was like shattering ice, cold and broken. "Will could *never* be a replacement for Leo. No one could be."

"I understand," Lewis continued. "But it just doesn't make any sense. You know that, right? Why would Denloy have stopped being a Freely? Everyone loved the Freelys."

"Maybe it has something to do with what our parents did," Arlyn said softly. "They left us a letter before the Disaster that we found in Leo's workshop. It was sealed, so I don't think he ever read it, but it said that it was our parent's fault that the Freelander burned."

"What?" Enland asked, eyebrows lowering. "How?"

"We don't know," Arlyn said. "But maybe whatever it was, our Uncle Will was also involved. And afterward, he was ashamed."

"Okay okay, back up," Lewis held up a hand. "Wilmot Denloy is not your uncle, and all of this speculation is getting way out of hand."

"But what if he is?" Graylin asked, squeezing her pillow.

"He isn't," Lewis said firmly. "Now, I don't know what your parents meant in their letter, but I suspect it was something far more benign than you're imagining. Probably they forgot to check a fan, or filled the tanks too full or something."

"But-"

"No buts," Lewis said, "and shut up. I hear something."

The crew stilled, listening as muffled footsteps grew louder and louder before ceasing. A sharp knock shot through the room, making everyone jump. Lewis stood instantly.

"Lewis?" A female voice came from the other side of the door. "Lewis, darling, are you awake?"

"Yes, Mother!" Lewis called, holding up a hand to shush the crew.

"Is there someone in there? I heard voices," Lewis's mom asked. Mrs. Maynewin had an exceedingly proper voice, her words sharpened by an accent, inherited from her home country of Howlevird, far south of Osden.

"No Mother! I've just woken up!" Lewis said.

"Could you please open the door, darling? It's quite tiresome, shouting through like this."

Lewis walked to the door, intentionally stepping heavily to disguise the sound of her friends' footsteps as they silently shifted to the other side of the room.

The door opened just a crack, Lewis poking her head around.

"I'm not dressed Mother, so please, make this quick," she said. Mrs. Maynewin ticked her tongue, but didn't reprimand her daughter for her rudeness.

"I was simply coming to remind you that today is Mr. Denloy's ball, and that I'll be out purchasing my new gown." The voice of Lewis's mom floated to the crew, and the two cousins stared at each other.

"Tonight," Lewis said, blinking her one eye.

"*Yes*, darling, we've been talking about this for weeks. The seventeenth, I've been telling you, August seventeenth," Mrs. Maynewin said tiredly. "I swear you don't even bother listening to me speak, I really do." With that, she patted her daughter's face, and turned away.

Lewis shut the door quickly and spun to face the crew.

"Here's the plan," she whispered. "We will go to Denloy's ball tonight. There, you will either learn that he *is* your uncle or, and I suspect this is more likely, you will realize that he is not, and simply used to know Leo when they were kids or something."

"Ah, an infiltration," Graylin sat a little straighter, a light in her eyes. "I like this idea."

"What happened to taking us to a ball only over your dead body?" River grinned. Lewis shot him a glare.

"This is a unique situation. Besides," Lewis began to smile, "maybe it'll be fun. After all, we'll have a lot of dressing up to do." Lewis was an avid lover of fashion.

Graylin sighed. "I no longer like this idea."

11

LEWIS HAD THE FIVE other crew members climb out her window and down the side of the house. Arlyn and River and Enland all made the trip with ease, but then it came to Graylin's turn.

Teddy watched, torn between offering help and letting her be, as Graylin repeatedly put a foot out the window and drew it back in.

"I can do it," she told him firmly as he offered a hand. "I can do it," she repeated to herself, swinging her body out the window and sitting on the ledge. Already on the ground, her cousin waved, and River seemed to be smiling. Embarrassment flooded Graylin's head. "I can't do it." She hurried back into the room. Every time she got out there, on the ledge, it was like her whole body froze, and she couldn't even force herself to move anywhere but backwards.

"What if I go first?" Teddy asked gently.

Graylin scratched her nose. Not only was she embarrassed over her trepidation, but now Teddy, of all people, was offering to help.

"Alright," she said, because getting down the side of the house and out of Teddy's singular presence was quickly becoming a top priority. Teddy hurried to the window, swinging out and grabbing hold of the vines twisting down the side of the house.

"Come on, it's perfectly steady." Teddy turned to look out over the Maynewin's front gardens, and then further all the way to the tall buildings of Odios. He smiled, watching the city as the sky to the east turned progressively lighter.

When Graylin finally made it to the bottom, her friends most wisely chose not to speak of her fear. Instead, they did just as Lewis had commanded and hurried to the front doors where a suspiciously frowning Jarno greeted them with a sigh.

"Ah, the Miss Freelys," he said dully. "We are thrilled to see you- one moment, please." He strode away before returning with a smiling Mrs. Maynewin.

"Oh, I am so glad to see you girls!" she said, pulling them both into a hug. Graylin, face still red from her embarrassment, squirmed. "I am so sorry, girls. We looked for you at the funeral, but we couldn't find you."

"We didn't go," Arlyn choked, unable to breathe due to the affection of Mrs. Maynewin's hug. The woman did not seem to notice. "It just felt too . . . real."

"I understand completely," Mrs. Maynewin wiped a tear from her eye. "Oh, my darling Lewis will be so thrilled to see you. Jarno!" Mrs. Maynewin turned to her butler. "Please escort these delightful children to my daughter's room."

"*Children*?" Graylin hissed to her cousin, who pushed her away absently. With the most forced of smiles plastered on his face, Jarno complied with the lady's orders. It wasn't long before the crew was reunited with Lewis, and plans for attending the ball were set into action.

The first assignment, Lewis said, was to 'dress the crew to the nines', as Arlyn would put it. Enland was in charge of the boys as, being Lewis's frequent companion to fancy events, he knew basic dressing etiquette and the layout of the Maynewin's sprawling home. Luckily, Lewis had, in fact, had an older brother, long moved out now, who had left behind quite the collection of suits. Enland tried to channel his inner Lewis and paced up and down in front of his brothers, trying to decide which suits fit them best. He had been informed, very seriously, by Lewis that this was a *formal* event, and that *formal* attire was needed. No twill trousers here, no sir. Evening suits and dinner jackets would be the motif of the night. Teddy and River were both found suitable options within the untouched closet of Damien Maynewin. The waistcoats, cutaway coats, and trousers were slightly outdated, but by only a few years, and Lewis assured the boys that no one would notice or care. Teddy's three-piece was a dark gray, while River's was a deep brown, and both looked extremely uncomfortable.

The real trouble came when they sought clothing for Enland. None of Damien's suits fit him (Teddy's outfit hung loose around the shoulders and showed at least an inch of ankle, while River's bunched comically around his shoes). Luckily, Mr. Maynewin was a generous soul, especially with the boy who would undoubtedly one day be his son-in-law, and Enland was easily granted the use of one of his tuxedos. The difference between the boys' attires lied mainly in the cut of the vest, and the silkiness of the fabric. Also, unlike his brothers, Enland was used to moderate dolling up, and while he had never attended quite so formal an event, he tried to help River and Teddy come to terms with the richness of their dress with sympathy.

As for the girls, Lewis escorted them to her special sewing studio, filled with fabrics and thread and mostly-finished projects. She tended to stick with her ideas with more commitment than the Freelys did, and proof of this lay in a few completed dresses which Lewis had designed for the three girls for such a time as this. Lewis, as the cousins had thought before, had a remarkable skill for thinking ahead.

Dressing the Freelys took multiple hours, and it gave the girls quite a while to talk. As always, the girls were very long winded and contemplative.

"So, we have a secret uncle," Arlyn said. "And Leo probably knew about him."

"And it's our parents' fault the Freelander burned," Graylin mused.

"*And* they are still alive. Somewhere," Arlyn added. Lewis stayed silent as they talked, simply pinning and sewing and brushing.

"Yes," Graylin sighed. "They are alive somewhere. They claim." There was stillness for a moment.

"We've got to find them," Arlyn said softly. "If they're alive."

"Wouldn't it feel a little wrong?" Graylin asked, staring at her hands. "Trying to find them, I mean. It's just . . . I can barely even remember my parents. Leo did so much of the parenting, and he's *been* there. The most I remember of my parents is when they were gone, and busy. Leo was always there for us, and now that Leo's dead, it feels like finding our parents would be like, I don't know . . . replacing him."

"I know," Arlyn said. She knew how attached Graylin had been to their uncle. She understood a bit of what her cousin was saying, but she also wanted to see her parents again. They were her *parents*. "But if we stay away, knowing they're alive, we'll be no better than they are."

Unless, of course, the whole note was completely irrelevant, and her parents were just as dead as Arlyn had believed them to be for the last eight years. If they were dead, she could ignore their note and file it away with other things she didn't understand but also didn't care about. If they were alive, she would have to give credence to the other things the note claimed, which in turn would change her perception of her parents entirely and shake those few memories she still had left. But instead of saying this, she just smiled reassuringly at Graylin.

"I suppose it doesn't really matter, anyway. That's like step seven, and we're on step one and a half."

"Which is?" Lewis asked, as she used a fancy hook to button Graylin's dress.

"Learning if Wilmot Denloy is our uncle," she responded. "And if he is, why didn't we know, and why didn't Leo trust him?" Within the next three hours, all the girls were bedecked, bedazzled, and becoming increasingly nervous for the event.

Lewis' dress was a soft, light yellow, decorated with loops of pearls and intricately sewn floral designs. The neckline was deep, and swooped up to connect to short, puffy capped sleeves that pooled on the top of her shoulders, made in the most current fashions. Of course, Lewis needed little to be breathtakingly beautiful, but this dress took her to the next level. It was light, flowy, and fairy-like, the fabric swooped in ruffles and bustles around the waist, and seemed to dance in even the slightest breeze, the bottom ruffles dragging on the ground. Lewis had brushed her hair silky smooth, and piled the dark curls towards the back of her head, letting a few hang down near her face and at the base of her neck. Woven into her hair were strings of pearls, shining like her eye and smile.

Graylin's attire was nothing short of stunning, and even she had to admit the dress was wonderful. The deep cool green of the stiff fabric brought out her gray eyes excellently, and just barely skimmed the floor when she walked. Osden was such a melting pot of eras and fashions that keeping up with the times was far less important than in other countries. The neckline was very wide, leaving her shoulders and most of her arms bare, but not for long. Lewis had given the two girls a *very* stern talk regarding the etiquette of gloves, and Graylin had been handed lacy silk ones of a light green, which extended halfway up her forearm. Lewis's own pure white kid gloves stretched to her puffed cap sleeves, with nearly twenty buttons. Besides the main dress, the corset underneath, and stockings, Lewis also made Graylin put on three different cream petticoats, which swirled every time she moved. Her hair had been wetted, brushed, dried, run through with one of Lewis's gels, and re-curled, her cheeks splashed with color, and her feet shoved into a pair of Lewis's dainty boots. Lastly, a black ribbon had been fastened around her slim neck. The experience was uncomfortable, but when Graylin looked in the mirror, she felt a strange sense of satisfaction.

As for Arlyn, her gown was the product of a fit of wild motivation to make *something* while sleeping over at Lewis's, and the young female heiress had been happy to help her friend with the project. It had taken quite some time, but there was no doubt that the result was worth it. Made of a light ochre muslin, the fabric pulled tight around the bodice and spread fluidly out upon the floor like a puddle of color. Sewn dark red roses filled the neckline and hem, stitched vines of the same color tumbled down the whole thing. The heart shaped bodice spread into short little sleeves, the color shining gorgeously against Arlyn's skin tone. The skirt was slimmer than Graylin's, but slightly fuller than Lewis's, just puffy enough to make Arlyn feel princess-like. The silver earrings dangling in delicate vines from her earlobes and the simple necklace of a similar color around her neck added to this effect. Lewis was extremely proud of this dress, giving Arlyn every warning of what not to do in it.

"Remember, don't bend over, don't sit down too fast, don't run, don't laugh too hard, don't dance like a crazy person, and, please, don't get into any fights. You'll completely ruin the dress." She pulled firmly on a strand of Arlyn's hair, which she was currently trying to mangle into place. Lewis had a large magazine of popular hairstyles, categorized from occasion to occasion. Most of them looked impractical, painful, and frankly unattractive, but Lewis had insisted that they were necessary.

"Do you *want* to stick out like a sore thumb? Now choose one."

"Graylin got a good hairstyle," Arlyn complained, flipping a few pages.

"Graylin has too short of hair to do anything reasonable with," Lewis said. Finally, Arlyn landed on a design, with hair pulled back at the sides and pinned on the top of her head with some flowers, leaving the rest of her hair to be tightly curled and hanging loose around her shoulders. Lewis pulled her new-fangled curling iron away, letting the last ringlet drop against Arlyn's neck. She smiled and grabbed the cousin's hands, ignoring Graylin's squirming.

"I think we're good to go," she said, nodding.

Enland beamed at Lewis as she glided into the entranceway of the Maynewin's home. He took her hand, kissed it, and spun Lewis around. Graylin grimaced, but said nothing. Inside, she tried to calm her breathing and ignore the pounding headache seeping into her brain. She was hungry, she was tired, and she'd been riding an emotional rollercoaster all day. She was *exhausted*. Both she and Arlyn hadn't slept since the morning before, and in the space of time since, they had gone through Leo's papers, discovered a secret uncle, left their house in the middle of the night, snuck into the Maynewin's mansion, and spent hours being preened. But instead of speaking, she pulled out her chain from a little pocket in the skirt, and passed it from hand to hand. Best not to bother her cousin with this, she decided. Arlyn had taken the burden of too much before Leo's death, and Graylin did not intend to do that again.

"Is everyone ready?" Mrs. Maynewin asked sweetly, gliding into the room. She was glittering, jewels swirled in her hair and around her neck. Lewis glanced around at the crew and nodded.

"Ready."

12

THE TIRES OF THE Maynewin's car were silent as the vehicle climbed up the clean brick driveway of Wilmot Denloy's mansion. It was a shame the automobile was so quiet, for Graylin thought it might have helped break the unbearably stiff silence within the vehicle. She was squished between River and her cousin, and there was a bit of embroidery on her left arm that was itchy and very close to driving her insane. The three-hour drive to Soamtin, the city south of Odios where Wilmot Denloy made his home, had been unbearably awkward, with the two cousins and River stuck with Lewis's parents and one chauffeur, while Enland, Teddy, and Lewis were in the second car.

The house, Arlyn thought as they pulled up, could barely be called a house. Rather, it was an enormous structure that fit what Lewis described as "Chateau Architecture". The car rolled up to a grand set of double doors that were medieval in appearance with large door knockers that resembled the head of a duck. Graylin could hardly think of a more frivolous way to spend money, excepting, of course, the equally duck shaped fountains in the gardens in front of the house. Personally, Graylin wondered why the guy hadn't just gotten a real duck.

An attendant in an expensive-looking green uniform took the car away, his clothing shining just a moment in the afternoon sun as he slid into the seat.. When asked, Lewis confirmed it was, in fact, silk. Teddy whispered something to River which made his red-haired brother break into a fit of laughter, a noise which died after one shot of Lewis's specialized 'River' glare. Besides answering questions for the wide eyed crew, Lewis was also in charge of keeping them proper, at least until they got inside. Thus far it had been a full time job.

"We haven't been to one of these parties in over a month," she said as her parents spoke with the doorman. "Mr. Denloy-"

"You mean our uncle," Arlyn interrupted. Lewis rolled her eye, but Graylin stopped in her tracks.

"Don't call him that," she said stiffly. Arlyn scanned her cousin's face, the frown which pulled at her mouth and the set of her eyebrows, and nodded.

"As I was saying," Lewis continued gracefully. "Until we can get him alone, you guys have to act . . ." She looked at the group, noticeably excluding Enland. "How can I put this? Like you go to parties like this often."

"Don't be hobos, got it," River nodded.

The doorman approached Lewis. "Your party can come in, Miss Maynewin."

"Thank you, Demitrius," Lewis shook his hand delicately before turning back to the crew. "Behave yourselves."

As they entered, each boy moved to take a girl by the arm, Lewis gliding elegantly as ever next to Enland, Arlyn skipping through the entrance and taking River with her, and Graylin giving a very suspicious glare to Teddy before walking in on her own. The effect of her very pointed independence was rather lost when she tripped on the entrance rug, stumbling grandly.

"Fine. I'm fine," she muttered, trying not to catch the eyes of her smirking cousin or the struggling stone-faced guards. Her dignity having fallen with her, she focused on her surroundings, her eyes drifting from the white and gray checked marble floors, reflecting the smooth pillars, to the intricate plaster molding on the ceiling.

Past the hallway was a grand ballroom where the party itself was centered, lit by several crystal chandeliers. The papered walls were bedecked with a fancy pattern in a deep shade of emerald, occasionally broken up by a wooden pillar. An enormous mosaic mural cut from smooth marble made up the floor, the constant clicking of shoes making the space sound similar to a room full of clocks, a noise which neither Arlyn nor Enland were fond of. Even worse, for Graylin at least, was the mixture of the chatter, the strong fragrance of many dancers' perfumes, and the slight stuffiness of the air.

A grand staircase stood as the centerpiece of the room, connecting to the rest of the house. Crafted of fine, dark wood, any part that wasn't a stair was part of an extensive, intricate relief sculpture carved into the wood. The banisters were lined with thick garlands of yellow flowers of numerous shapes and sizes, all fresh and smiley. A slightly more acceptable way to use money, Graylin figured. Still pompous, though.

The part of the room that grabbed the crew's attention was a long table lined with expensive-looking party food. Finger sandwiches, vegetables cut to resemble flowers, and what Lewis introduced as caviar was spread on trays across the silky tablecloth. All were disgusted.

"Why wouldn't you just wait until they're full fish?" Arlyn asked, cautiously spooning some onto a stiff bread. "That has to be better than egg paste."

"The full fish is much better," River agreed, holding up a cracker topped with salmon dip. "How expensive did you say caviar was again, Lew?"

The number made the entire crew uneasy.

"Have you considered having no fish at all because it's gross?" Graylin said, eating her own bread plain. "I don't know how you guys can tolerate that stuff, fish is nasty."

"Graylin," River said, blue eyes going wide, "do you realize how many enemies you've just made? Fish is delicious!"

"You know what else is delicious? Sauerkraut." Enland chimed in.

"And because you've said that, you have no credibility in this conversation, Lander," River said.

"What?" Enland folded his arms. "It's good."

Lewis set a hand on his shoulder and shook her head. "It's fermented cabbage, Enland. It's disgusting, like one would expect."

The tall cartographer sighed in defeat, deciding instead to walk his partner onto the dance floor. Lewis floated out, the yellow fabric of her dress swishing around like sunshine colored waves, Enland holding her hand. That left the cousins and their respective boys to their own devices.

Graylin turned back to examine the table of food, avoiding anything that slightly resembled fish, trying to find something reasonable. She wasn't good at dancing, and frankly, there was zero chance of River asking her. Clearly Arlyn would be his first choice, and Teddy's too likely. So, she focused on the food. There were a couple of sandwiches, cut into tiny shapes, such as triangles, circles, and . . . an octagon maybe? Graylin didn't really feel like counting the sides to make sure. She shifted her gaze to the drinks. There was a selection of very round glasses with something crystally on the rim, and bright purple liquid. Next to them was a collection of tall, skinny glasses, with something clear bubbling up, and three different citrus slices inside. Sighing, Graylin tried to ignore the embroidered leaf still touching her arm. She turned around, planning to find her cousin, but saw Teddy instead. He was not, as she'd assumed, vying for Arlyn as a dance partner. He was walking up to her, holding out a plate.

"Instead of seafood, I offer this delicious, er," he looked at the item on the small glass plate, and seemed to decide he couldn't quite describe it. "Uh, this dessert. Of some kind, I'm not sure what *kind* of dessert it is." Then he pulled out a small white crinkly flower. "And this paper flower. I found it on that table."

The gesture strangely touched Graylin, and she tucked the paper flower behind her ear. She wasn't entirely sure what she would do with it later, but the desire to keep it was too strong. She was a known collector of items, so it would likely end up on a random shelf somewhere in the *Freelander*.

"Thanks, Teddy." Graylin took the plate, and Teddy was forced to turn away so that Graylin couldn't see his grin. Graylin popped the dessert in her mouth (it was, indeed, delicious) and then realized she probably should have shared with him.

"So, do you wanna dance?" she asked, turning to him. "I mean, we probably look pretty suspicious, just standing here." Teddy seemed to consider this.

"You know, you're right. We probably do." He took her hand and led her onto the dance floor.

"You can copy me, if you like. I am a practiced dancer," Teddy told her dryly.

"Are you really, or are you teasing me?" Graylin asked, raising an eyebrow, trying not to focus on the fact that she was on a dance floor, in a dress, surrounded by many pairs of eyes.

"I'm serious. I practice with River," Teddy said, pressing his hand to hers, holding the other behind his back, and stepping like the others. It was a melodic, graceful dance, all the heads slowly rising and falling as they stepped and spun. This was unfortunate, as Graylin had a track record of being extremely un-graceful.

"River?" Graylin asked, wrinkling her nose. Then she sighed. "You know, I think maybe I'm too hard on him sometimes." Graylin turned her head to watch River, swirling around with her cousin, a ridiculous grin on his face. "What do you think?" she turned back to Teddy, smiling a little. "What are your thoughts on River?"

"River is in surprisingly good shape, considering he has no back-bone," Teddy said. Graylin grinned. Having rarely been privy to his jokes, she wondered if he was trying to be funny, or just naturally was.

"What do you think of Enland?" she asked, still smiling.

"Enland is the scourge of the stars, and ought to be ashamed of himself, what with his blatant infatuation with Lewis Maynewin," he said, mouth quirking.

"And what about Teddy?" Graylin asked her dance partner with another grin. Teddy scoffed.

"Teddy? Screw him, he is far too sensitive for his own good," he said, stretching his arm out and spinning Graylin. She swirled in a circle, a few more curls falling out from her do.

Graylin was pulled back in after the spin and they continued dancing, Teddy remarkably well, and Graylin trying her best to keep up.

She looked to the side, searching the crowd for anyone somewhat Freely-ish. Teddy could feel it when she froze.

"What? Do you see Denloy?" Teddy asked, stopping. Graylin stared at the space where she'd seen him; not Wilmot Denloy, but Leo. It *had* to have been him. The tall frame, the blond hair, the expressive eyebrows . . . but no, Leo was dead. She had probably just seen someone who resembled him, and her mind had inferred the rest. Or perhaps there had never been anyone there at all, and she'd imagined it.

"No, no. I just thought I saw . . . no one. Nevermind." Feeling slightly shaken, Graylin tried to focus her mind on dancing, in an attempt at sparing Teddy's toes. As Graylin's focusing abilities were subpar at best, this wasn't entirely effective. But she did try.

Arlyn smiled, watching her cousin and Teddy move around the mosaic floor in time with the other dancers. Occasionally she would see Graylin slip, but pull herself back together in time for the next swing in the dance. It was an extreme relief to see Graylin and Teddy actually getting along, but the sculptural carving on the wall was where her attention was focused. She and River had made their way to the center of the staircase, between the two carpet covered wings of stairs, and were inspecting the art piece.

The three-dimensional mural showcased the story of a duckling starting off in a small pond and exploring the world. Skillfully carved scenery followed the little duck on its journey, eventually ending up at the lagoon it started in, but now as a full grown duck.

"I think Denloy likes ducks," River said, petting the wooden bird at the end of the relief. "Just a hunch."

"The only thing he and I have in common," Arlyn said, her favorite animal famously being a duck. "Although you'd think as a grown man he would have something more majestic than Huey's Journey on his staircase."

"Huey's Journey?" River asked.

She nodded. "It's a kids' book, Graylin and I used to know it by heart, about a duck named Huey who travels the world, and eventually goes back home to visit his parents. It was my favorite, and he's got every page on this wall."

"Except for the parents," River noted, pointing to the last 'page', which featured only Huey.

"Huh," Arlyn felt over the empty space as if expecting the wooden foul to suddenly appear. "I always remembered him going back to see his parents. Why aren't they there?"

"Ah," a voice said from behind them, "are you two familiar with Huey's Journey?"

"Actually, yes!" Arlyn turned around to face the voice. "It was my . . ." her voice rose in her throat and froze there, "favorite."

The man that stood in front of them was a ghost. There was no other explanation. A young yet tired face with inquisitive gray eyes. A well-kept beard and mustache paired with styled but casually kept dirty blond hair. Over the stiff, pointed nose rested a pair of wireframe silver glasses. There was a sparkle to his eyes that felt honest and jovial. Arlyn's previous hesitation, that perhaps the businessman they were looking for wasn't really her lost, forgotten uncle, suddenly seemed insane. How could she have ever wondered about the truth? It seemed so obvious now. Wilmot Denloy looked exactly like his brother.

He looked down at her in bewilderment for a moment before blinking away the shock. "You'll have to, to excuse me," he stammered. "For a moment, I thought you were someone else. Did I see you with Miss Maynewin?"

Arlyn nodded.

"She's a wonderful young woman, I'm glad to see she's bringing along friends." He extended a cordial hand. "I'm Wilmot Denloy."

"Pleasure to meet you," Arlyn shook his hand, studying it as she did so. His middle finger was bent outwards, a trait notably found in the Freelys. Graylin's bend was slightly less noticeable than her own, and to the left, but still very much present. "What I was saying to my friend was, in the last page of Huey's Journey, Huey goes home to visit his parents. But in your mural, he's in the pond alone."

The wealthy businessman studied the mural for a moment before giving the two a puzzled look. "Hm . . . I could have sworn they were in the book. I had the carpenter follow it to the letter." He clasped his hands together with a genial smile. "I have the book in my library, and we can figure this out once and for all. That is, if you two are alright leaving your group."

Arlyn glanced at River, and then back at her cousin, who had now exited the dance floor. Seeing that she was watching them, she gave a nod that meant 'follow me'. Graylin took the hint. Sending Teddy to fetch Lewis and Enland, she carefully tailed her cousin through the crowd.

Arlyn and River followed Denloy to an enormous study. Ornate shelves of meticulously bound volumes snaked through the room like an enormous beehive, not a single one dusty. Denloy led them back to a small corner closed off from the rest of the room. The walls were covered with paintings and drawings, all of them noticeably done by a single artist. Intricate details combined with areas of rubbed graphite or color, like the artist had both gotten bored halfway through. Graylin's signature style, especially when she was young, had been just the same. The painting above the desk was a duck, a Pekin to be exact, with a ladybug on its bill.

From a specially made cabinet, Denloy removed an old book with the spine noticeably worn. *Huey's Journey*. "It's funny this came up," he said, opening it to the first page. "I was just reading this a few months ago." On the opening page there was a spot for a dedication, and Arlyn caught her and her cousin's names before Denloy flipped to the closing of the tale.

"And Huey waddled down the road, across the bridge, under the willow tree," Denloy began to read. "And through the daisy field." As Arlyn heard the words, she felt something in her heart pop.

13

GRAYLIN QUIETLY SLIPPED INTO the room she'd watched her cousin enter, and froze. There, standing by some bookshelves, was a man, the man she'd seen before. Leo, but slightly different. His nose was longer, he had round glasses over his gray eyes, and he had a mustache and beard that matched his blond hair. Wilmot Denloy, no, William Freely. Their uncle. And standing across from him was Arlyn, as still as Graylin was.

It was then that Graylin noticed the words and the voice reading them. It was Denloy, reading from the children's book in his hand. Graylin couldn't have said what it was immediately, as Arlyn had, but as Denloy continued to read, it was like her mind caught on, snatching at memories so far in the back of her mind, she'd forgotten she'd had them. It was like hearing a lullaby she'd listened to as a baby, her brain filling in the next word, the next inflection, just slightly before it was read.

"Huey stopped to smell the lilacs and said hi to the ladybug. He paddled across the stream and hopped over stones in the river," Denloy read. *The vines. The vines are next*, Graylin thought. "He waddled through the vines, into the sunshine, and down the dirt path, back to his pond. The water was still, and blue, and empty, and Huey slid into the water. He was glad his journey was over. He was glad to be home."

Denloy swallowed, and looked up, face frozen in an attempt at a genial smile he directed toward Arlyn.

"Well, would you look at that? It seems we were both wrong, young lady. There were no parents after all. I-" Denloy's gaze flicked up, and he saw Graylin. It was as if everything in him changed in an instant. His posture slumped, his eyes widened, and the book fell from his hands.

"No," he whispered, taking a step back. He shut his eyes, his fists clenching. He was breathing in and out, trying to calm himself. Graylin glanced at her cousin, who was looking both worried and a little confused.

"It's not them, it's not them," Denloy was saying, as Graylin hurried over to her cousin.

"What do you mean, it's not them?" Arlyn asked gently.

"It's not . . . you're not . . . *them*. Not really. They're dead, they're dead, they're dead." Denloy kept repeating the words. He was almost rocking, leaning away from the girls.

"But, uh, Mr. Will, Denloy, Freely guy," Graylin said cautiously, not entirely sure how to help. "It *is* us."

"No, no!" Denloy opened his eyes and then shut them again. His breathing was getting faster. "It's getting worse. I'll have to tell Augustus."

"What do you mean, worse?" Arlyn asked, a little loudly. "You are seriously freaking us out now."

"I've seen you before," Denloy said, his voice softening, his breathing slowly. "Both of you. I've seen you before, but never . . . never have you *talked* to me. You've never interacted with me. Usually you just run around, or laugh, or look up at me when I enter a room." He opened his bright eyes again, and this time he kept them open. "I'd thought the visions had stopped, but now you're back. And you're still here. Why are you still here? Usually you leave right away."

He lifted his eyes, very gray and very Freely, his knees giving out ever so slightly as he stared at the girls. His hand moved to his pocket, pulling out a ripped bookmark and clutching it until his knuckles turned white.

"Because we're real this time," Arlyn said. "See?" She touched his arm, and he shrunk back before relaxing. His eyes finally lifted from the ground, and he studied each girls' face. Then he reached forward and pulled them both into an enormous hug, like the big bear ones that Leo used to give. Graylin squirmed.

"Real or not real, I am going to hug you while I have the chance," Denloy said quietly. "I'm so sorry. Girls I'm so, so sorry."

"What if I swear I'm real, and you can let me go?" Graylin asked breathlessly. "You are like seriously crushing my lungs." If he'd heard Graylin, Arlyn didn't know, but Denloy did release them, stepping back and watching them with a hand on each girls' arm.

"Girls, I . . ." Denloy's eyes moved between each of them. "I was young, and stupid and, and I was angry. Your dads, they sent me a letter, they told me what they were going to do. They asked me to save you. I didn't read it until it was too late." He spoke between sharp, staggering breaths, a well-rehearsed speech he had never expected to say aloud. "I was so stupid. I tried, I swear I tried! I went back to the wreckage and no one was there. I looked for days and you . . . you were gone and I . . ." He buried his face in his hands. "I'm so sorry."

Watching this man, her supposed uncle, shattering in front of her made Arlyn's heart sink. She silently cursed herself in Graylin's voice for being so soft for a man she'd despised not an hour earlier. But if he had actually tried to go back for them, could he really be all that bad? She stepped closer, side eyeing Graylin to stay behind as she did. "Uncle Leo would have been proud of you," she said. "He was the one who got us off the Freelander."

Denloy's head shot up from his hands. "Leo?" he stammered. "He's alive?" He looked at the rest of the crew, all now gathered in the library. The boys looked to the floor; Lewis simply shook her head. The room suffocated in its silence.

"Uncle Leo died three months ago," Graylin mumbled softly.

"I'm sorry," Arlyn said. "He was a good man."

"A good man?" Denloy stood up, not with authority or poise, but slowly. He looked old. "He was the best I ever knew. Better than me in every right."

Better than everyone, Graylin thought. *Better than you, Denloy. He didn't like you.*

"How did he die?" Denloy asked, looking back at Arlyn, the rims of his eyes a pale red.

Arlyn took a deep breath. She could feel her throat tightening. "When he got us off the Freelander, he broke his leg. It . . . it never properly healed, and when he broke it again . . ."

"Blood clot. All the way to his heart," Graylin finished, her own voice cracking. "That's what Dr. Bannler said."

Arlyn's breaths were quick. Her throat was tight, her vision was blurring. It was too much. The world was closing in around her, and she hated it. She hated being overwhelmed. She felt a thin, bony hand grab her own. Enland. The silent gesture gave her room to breathe. "I'm sorry," she mumbled again. "I'm sorry."

The library fell back into silence, a moment of mourning for the man who connected everyone in the room. But it wasn't a warm, loving kind of remembrance. It felt cold, awkward, and somewhat lonely. The stillness was only broken by the opening of the library door.

"Mr. Denloy?" A round man, clearly unfamiliar with fancy attire, peered into the room. Seeing the small crowd, he stepped behind the door. "Oh, I'm sorry."

Arlyn recognized the man, and apparently so did Denloy. "Ah, Mr. Hooper," he said, his professionalism returning in his voice. His posture was no longer worried and worn. He stood confidently. "Very nice to see you again. I was just chatting with this group of bright young things, who come from Odios just like yourself." Denloy gestured to the crew.

"Nice to see you again, Mr. Hooper!" Arlyn said automatically, her improvisation kicking into high gear. She walked over and shook his hand. "We met a few months ago at your crane."

"It's a genius invention, truly," Denloy went to join the two at the door, his step noticeably quaking. He motioned for Graylin to follow. She did. "It's a right shame it has to come down once the water tower is completed," he said. "I was actually hoping to get you three together to brainstorm some ideas on what else it could be used for."

"In fact, I have an idea for it right now," Graylin said, jumping into the conversation. "Have you ever been to the market back in Odios, Mr. Hooper?"

"He's a Freely all right," River whispered to Teddy as the conversation at the door became animated with ideas. "Nobody but a true blooded Freely could come up with a story that fast and have the cousins roll with it."

"I'm pretty sure they're all psychic," Teddy whispered back. "Ever notice how they know what the other is thinking before they even say anything? It's creepy, man."

"I'll tell you who's a creepy man- Mr. Maynewin. He must be seven feet tall!"

"I heard that, River!" Lewis snapped as they hurriedly followed the group from the room.

Denloy and the girls smiled and chatted with Mr. Hooper for nearly four hours, all three putting on very convincing fronts of calm coolness, the very pictures of sanity, peace, and normalcy. However skillful their acting was, though, what was undeniable was that on the inside, every Freely was exhausted. Throughout the course of the night, Graylin had slowly drawn into herself, becoming more quiet, her false smiles growing dimmer. Denloy, too, was pale when the last of his guests left his house, his hands trembling as he pushed his glasses up his nose. Only Arlyn had maintained her facade firmly, refusing to let it slide even a little. But, as they bid Mr. Hooper their final goodbyes, she turned to Lewis and grabbed her hand desperately. She'd kept her panic down, but now she was buzzing with a nagging feeling of unsettlement. She met her cousin's eyes and knew that Graylin was just as worried for her as she was for Graylin.

"Mr. Denloy?" Arlyn said cautiously, turning to the man who looked so like her Uncle Leo. "Would it be alright if we stayed here a little longer, just to settle some things?"

Wilmot Denloy nodded, and then seemed to force himself to wake up from his trance of exhausted memories. "Yes," he said, standing, "Yes, of course. In fact, I'll go have the cook whip up something to keep us all awake." He hurried off, and Arlyn recognized the slump of his shoulders. It was the shape Graylin's made when she was feeling overwhelmed and needed to be alone.

The six crew members headed back to the library, all falling in step behind the Freely cousins, their finery still glimmering in the golden lights hanging from the embossed ceiling. Lewis's parents had left already, both unusually uninformed regarding Lewis's location and oddly okay with that. However, Enland had given them his word to stay by her side, and for some reason that Graylin couldn't puzzle out, the Maynewins had decided to trust the tall, lanky map boy. He settled himself next to Lewis, who gently tugged the ribbon holding his hair back out and re-did his ponytail. Arlyn also sat next to Lewis, perching on the edge of a navy velvet chair. Graylin slumped to the ground, pulling a pillow off of a nearby couch and hugging it to her lap. She wished she wasn't still in the dress, it made her feel very self-conscious, with the wide neckline and tight bodice. She both looked and felt very small, and her love for the deep green hue of the fabric didn't really make up for it.

"Is he what *you* expected, cousin?" Arlyn asked finally, adding her voice to the metronome that was a ticking clock.

"You mean did I expect the secret rich uncle to actually be mentally unstable and look just like Uncle Leo?" Graylin asked, pulling at a tassel on the pillow. "No, I didn't. Speaking of unstable, does it not seem even a *little* creepy that this guy who we don't remember at all has all this stuff of ours, like your copy of Huey's Journey, and my drawings? 'Cause I'm kinda creeped out."

"Not to mention the fact that he's been having visions of you guys," River said, perching himself on a small velvet stool that Graylin thought was a footrest. The silence wove itself back together as Teddy settled himself on the floor, resting his arms over his knees. Graylin chewed her lip and pulled at the pillow, scanning the room they were in for the first time. The walls were wooden panels painted a dark, cool green. The bookshelves and plaster ceiling featured swirls of gold embossing, which matched the delicate chains from which the lights hung. On the walls were a scattering of oil wall sconces, as if the building had been built before electricity was readily available for home lighting. This was not unlikely, as even five years ago most houses were still lit by whale oil, gasoline, or candles.

The bookshelves were packed to the brim with books, cloth covers both worn and brand new. As Graylin scanned the room, she noticed telltale signs of a hastily tidied space which was usually a disaster. There were drawers almost bursting with papers, corners of pages sticking out from seams. Half the novels on the shelf nearest Denloy's desk were either upside down or inside out. The pen and quill jars on the side tables were all stuffed to the bursting point, pillows were stacked on chairs to cover the papers resting there, and the hat tree in the corner was covered in various outer-wears. The only part of the room that looked like it had been paid extensive attention were the higher book shelves, the ones only reached by a rolling ladder. The books were dusted and lined up beautifully, and several dried flowers, cool rocks, and little wooden boxes rested between them. Graylin could practically *see* herself cleaning this room, getting excited to tidy and starting in the hardest place, ready to do everything all the way. She would have taken out every book, skimmed them, wiped them, and placed them back. She would have re-organized the little knick-knacks collected throughout the years, putting them in an order she liked best . . . and then she would have gotten sick of cleaning and did the rest of it as quickly as possible. Thank *goodness* she didn't have such a fancy house with guests all the time.

The door of the study swung open, the knob biting into the wall as Wilmot Denloy entered, holding a tray of food. He stepped in, watching the delectables on the plate, which appeared to be a slightly teetering stack of . . .

"Are those cinnamon rolls?" Arlyn asked eagerly, hopping to her feet and rushing toward the food.

"Caramel-pecan rolls, actually," Denloy said, his so very Freely eyes locked on what he was carrying, as if trying to keep it straight through telepathy. "They're some of my favorites. Oh, and the cook is going to bring us some tea."

Denloy set the tray on a footstool and wiped his hands on his pants. He glanced around nervously at the room. Eyes catching on each of them, he seemed to take in their faces for the first time, and sat himself stiffly in a slick, dark red leather chair. Sliding up his glasses, he rubbed his eyes with one hand, the other automatically cleaning off his lenses.

"So," Arlyn asked, taking a roll, "can we . . . start at the beginning?"

"Yes, yes." Denloy sighed heavily. "I was born about five years before . . ."

"Not *that* early," Graylin interrupted hurriedly. She was holding a roll of her own, and the caramel frosting was making her fingers irritatingly syrupy. She tried to lick some of the stickiness off, but it didn't seem to be working very well, and her rich, secret uncle was staring at her. Graylin cleared her throat and wiped her fingers (*not* very sneakily) on her skirt. "Um, what if we begin just after the Freelander crashed?"

Denloy nodded twice.

"After the Freelander . . . well I guess I just wanted to restart." He hesitated, unsure how much to say. "We, well, your parents and I didn't exactly see eye to eye on a few things, towards the end. And you probably wouldn't remember, but the Freelys were well known for a while. Still are, to be honest. Your parents . . ." Denloy looked away from the crew's ever-present stares and smiled a little. "They were *brilliant*. There was nothing they couldn't solve, and their reputations proved it."

"Lily said you helped them with inventing," Arlyn said. The tired man snapped his head up sharply.

"Lily? *Leo's* Lily?" he asked.

"Yes! Yes, she helped raise us," Arlyn smiled.

"You mean she's here? In Soamtin?" Denloy asked.

"No, back home in Odios," Graylin told him. Wilmot Denloy leaned back in his chair, smiling.

"I'll have to see her. After the Freelander, well, when I wasn't a Freely anymore, I tried to stay as far away from anyone I knew before as possible. Even Lily." he glanced at his feet. "And as far as I knew, she was on the Freelander when it crashed."

"What do you mean?" Graylin asked, trying to get the rest of the stickiness off her fingers. Now bits of lint and dust were stuck as well, and she rubbed at the pads of her fingers mercilessly. "You *weren't* on the Freelander?"

Denloy looked like a man very much regretting his words. He jiggled his legs.

"Ah, I mean, no," he gave the girls a sad, lopsided smile. "No, you two and Leo were the only ones lucky enough to make it off that ship alive."

"Not exactly," Arlyn said. She reached into a slim pocket sewn into her corset and pulled out a slip of paper. Graylin recognized the creases- it was the letter from their parents. Arlyn leaned and handed the page to her uncle. He seemed to scan it quickly, his forehead wrinkling in the same way Arlyn's did. He glanced up at the girls, and then pushed his glasses up his nose, starting the letter over.

"I . . ." he cleared his throat, the page fluttering in his trembling hand. "I didn't know they had a plan to escape." He wiped his eyes and pulled a handkerchief from his breast pocket. Graylin was currently wiping her nose with the back of her hand, and stopped self-consciously. "I didn't know until after that they had wanted me to get you two off the ship, if something happened." His shoulders sagged. "I'm so sorry. You can't imagine . . . after I heard what happened, I read the letter, and when I knew I was supposed to be the one to get you guys off, and that I hadn't been there . . ."

"Letter?" Arlyn asked gently.

"Your parents gave me a letter, right before the reunion. At the time, I assumed it regarded our disagreement and didn't bother opening it.

But really . . . they were asking me to get you off, in case something happened." Denloy tucked his handkerchief away. He held the letter from Arlyn and Graylin's parents tightly.

"We want to find them," Arlyn spoke into the silence. No one asked who she was talking about. Denloy's gray Freely eyes scanned the six teenagers watching him. Arlyn let him mull over the words before continuing.

"Will you help us?"

Graylin gave her cousin a look, a '*what the heck cousin, we didn't discuss this*' look. But Arlyn didn't notice. She was focused on her uncle. It was strange, as she hardly knew the man, and just hours ago she had felt quite firmly opposed to him, but she desperately wanted him to say yes. It would be almost like having Leo there.

"I-" Denloy started finally, when the library door swung open. A round, older woman with bright eyes, mounds of red hair, and a cook's apron bustled in, holding a tray of cups and a teapot.

"I'm terribly sorry, sir," she said, "but I've got your tea, as requested."

"Ah, thank you Mrs. Roylen." Denloy stood quickly, smiling at his cook. He took the tray and nodded graciously to his employee. "Please, Mrs. Roylen, go to bed now. You've had a long day, and, may I say, your delicious food was *greatly* admired tonight. I heard rave reviews from all of my guests."

"Oh, thank you, sir." The slightly flustered Mrs. Roylen bowed and hurried from the room, swinging the door shut behind her. Denloy busied himself by pouring all the crew members tea, handing the cups out before sitting heavily into his chair.

"Will you give me the night to think about joining you?" he asked finally. "I want to . . . consider all the sides, before I make a decision."

What is there to think about? Graylin thought, hugging the pillow. *You want to help, or you don't. You care, or you don't.* Personally, she didn't *want* to like this man, who had, for some reason or another, been erased from her current life, her childhood, and her memory. Besides, Leo hadn't wanted her and Arlyn to meet Denloy. In a way, it has been his dying wish.

"Of course you can think about it," Arlyn said. "But we want to leave soon."

"I'll have your answer by tomorrow morning," her uncle said firmly. His hands were folded, and he watched his nieces earnestly. "Likewise, I have a proposition for you. Please, stay here tonight? I've kept you guys up far too late for you to make the trip back home. I'll have beds made up in one of the sitting rooms, and Mrs. Roylen will be delighted to have someone other than myself attend breakfast."

Graylin was watching her cousin, trying to tell her through her gaze just how little she liked the idea. *Don't do it cousin,* she thought urgently, *don't say yes. I don't want him to come, and I don't want to stay.*

Arlyn seemed to miss her cousin's mental messages, and she smiled at Denloy.

"We'd love to stay," she said emphatically.

Graylin sighed and turned to Teddy.

"I hate her," she muttered, and while the boy's mouth quirked into a smile, no one else noticed the exchange. Denloy was smiling, a real genuine smile that further irritated Graylin, as it seemed to prove his genuine affection for her and Arlyn. And, as Graylin had noted to herself on previous occasions, it's much harder to dislike someone who cares for you. *Remember Leo,* she reminded herself. *Leo suspected Denloy's identity, and still didn't want us to meet him.*

"I'll fetch the housekeeper to find you girls some clothes to sleep in, and I'm sure the maids will set up some beds. The butler can handle the boys' pajamas- hang on." Denloy hurried from the room.

Within minutes a cheerful housekeeper entered the room, holding a large stack of clothes. The girls were led away to change, the boys left in the library, and it wasn't long before all six members, freshly clad in their borrowed pajamas, were settled in a sitting room which could only be described as extravagant. The three couches were wide and low to the ground, with rich wood so dark it looked almost black, carved into swirls for the arms and legs of the chair. Here alone was the floor carpeted, a true expense in Osden. It was emerald green and gold patterned with a wide border around the edges.

Graylin pulled anxiously at her nightgown, which she'd been informed used to belong to a maid no longer in employment at Denloy's manor. She hated it. There was a reason she never wore nightgowns to bed; they were far too loose and flowy for comfort when standing, and tended to wrap around her legs when sleeping. Besides, the former maid had clearly been larger than Graylin in several specific areas of the body, and she kept clutching the neckline upwards to her throat.

As a baggy-eyed butler, whose hair suggested he'd been woken up to fulfill this task brought in mounds of blankets and pillows, the boys of the crew looked no less awkward. Enland had his arms folded, standing protectively next to Lewis, wearing pajama pants which showed a comical amount of ankle. Teddy, alternatively, was teetering nervously by the wall, hands in the pockets of his baggy borrowed pants, torn between joining the crew and blending into the shadows.

Arlyn and River had no such reservations, and were engaging in a very violent game of Rock, Paper, Scissors, Foot. It was a game of the Freely's invention and was just normal Rock, Paper, Scissors, with the added element of danger that the winner of the previous round had full rights to kick their opponent randomly.

"I see you are all settled," Denloy hurried into the room, wearing one of those floppy night-caps that looked so silly, Graylin actually forgot to be awkward. She caught Teddy's eye, saw him trying not to laugh, and had to cover her mouth to resist the temptation herself.

"Yeah, it's great here!" Arlyn said, narrowly dodging a kick from River, and stumbling back into Lewis. Lewis shoved Arlyn back with a pillow she was holding, and River used the same weapon to smack her from behind. Graylin couldn't just stand there and watch her cousin be double-teamed, and she bounded into the fight, snatching up a pillow and thwacking River with so much force, his head whipped forward.

"Ow!" he cried, rubbing his neck. Gripping his pillow tighter, he swung heartily at Graylin, who ducked, letting the blow smash into Enland.

"Ack- watch it!" the tall boy cried, clutching his circular glasses to his face. Lewis calmly chose her weapon from the stack of pillows, examined it as a master marksman might his sword, and swung at River with all her might. Lewis was small, the shortest of the crew. But her muscles? They were prodigious, famed, and feared, especially by River. His arms flew up as he attempted to protect himself, but too slowly, and he caught a faceful of Lewis's pillow.

Teddy, laughing, caught the pillow Graylin tossed him (she felt bad for the dude, just standing there), and joined the fray. He swung for his red-haired brother, or at least tried, but River was taken out by Enland and Lewis's conjoined force before he could make contact. So, instead, his blow hit upon Graylin, who had never felt so betrayed in her entire life.

"You!" she cried, actually sending feathers flying as she smacked Teddy straight across the face. He went down, laughing so hard that his rudimentary shield, involving his arms and legs, was weak indeed, and he kept catching Graylin's blows. Graylin, for one, had never heard so contagious a laugh in her life as Teddy's, and was doubled over herself before long. This left her open and completely defenseless to the vicious double attack Arlyn and River pulled on her, beating her mercilessly with the downy, freshly starched pillows.

Denloy watched the fray, smiling. All he could think, watching his nieces, that they're alive, they're alive, *they are alive!* The businessman could have cried from joy and exhaustion. He turned from the group, ready to head to bed, when a thought hit him. He was the girls' uncle, and they were mere teenagers. Should he tell them to go to bed? Was this now expected of him? Denloy wavered by the door, watching the crew's fun, and struggling with how much responsibility and authority he now possessed. On the one hand, Arlyn and Graylin may have been *expecting* him to act as a father figure of sorts now, someone to guide and teach them. This made the poor Mr. Denloy nearly freeze in panic-he didn't know how to *parent*, especially not two girls he hadn't seen for eight years. On the other hand, it might seem like an imposition, if he were to start parenting them so soon.

Finally, driven mostly by his fear of messing up, Denloy decided to simply wait for a lull in the shrieks of laughter coming from the pile of people and pillows, and then say good night.

"I'm going to bed now," he said, waving a little to catch Arlyn's attention. She smiled and gave him the thumbs up.

"Awesome! Good night!"

"Good night." Denloy gave an awkward sort of nod/bow thing, unsure of what to do, and then hurried off to bed.

"And now," Arlyn cried, picking her pillow back up and holding it like a long sword. The dropping of the squashed pillow weakened the metaphor. "We duel, cousin mine."

"Oh no you don't." Lewis stepped in between the cousins, catching both of their blows simultaneously, one pillow in each hand. "*Now* we go to bed. It's late, it's been an insanely long day, and we're probably keeping the staff up with our racket." She tossed the pillows to the ground. Sighing, and muttering variations of 'yes *mom*', the crew chose their blankets and pillows and settled in for the night.

Arlyn picked two small woven blankets, which seemed both light, comfortable, and too small for her body. However, Arlyn wasn't a huge fan of using blankets for their intended purpose, and usually just scrunched hers up in a ball and hugged them. Plopping her pillow on one of the cloth sofas, she laid down and watched the room until Lewis turned out the light.

As for her cousin, Graylin has chosen two blankets as well. One was very light and large, and the other unusually heavy, as if there were tiny beads inside. Graylin curled up on the floor next to Arlyn's couch, arranging her blankets until they were perfect, before clutching her pillow tightly. Graylin's sleeping habits were a conundrum; she couldn't stand anything on her feet, and *had* to have them sticking out from the blankets to sleep. However, she also loved the feeling of weight on her, and would often pile extra blankets around her head and on her body. It made her feel more peaceful and comforted. Graylin settled herself, wiggling her toes until all the 'wiggle' was gone. But unlike Arlyn, Graylin didn't close her eyes when the light went out. She stared into the darkness, waiting until she could see again. She watched the shapes of Teddy and River, lying opposite directions on the same couch, pushing and shoving until one would silently slide from the sofa and have to climb back up. She didn't want to sleep, just yet, and she knew that if she closed her eyes she would. She was *exhausted.* But there was so much to think about, so much to imagine, so much to dream of. Like this trip, this trip their new uncle might come on. Maybe they would travel to a new city and find all sorts of fun stuff there . . . like a circus. Arlyn was pretty balanced. Arlyn should join the circus. Then Graylin could draw the promotional stuff, and Lewis could make costumes, and Teddy could play the music (here, Graylin's eyes finally closed). Hm, Teddy. Teddy, Teddy should laugh more. If Teddy laughed more, Graylin was certain *everyone* would laugh more. Laughing was a funny sort of thing . . .

And with that, Graylin's drowsy thoughts drifted into her dreams as she fell asleep.

14

WILMOT DENLOY STOOD IN his office, suitcases wedged under his arms and filling his hands. He wasn't ready for this; he wasn't ready to see his nieces again, or leave his home, or embark on this trip. After the girls had gone to sleep, he'd spent all night fiddling with the ring on his finger, trying to decide what to do. He had sworn, after that argument eight years ago, that he would never get involved with his brothers' affairs again. However, ever since the disaster, he had also promised himself every day that if he had just one more minute with the girls, if there was any sort of opportunity to be with them, that he would *have* to take it. So which promise should he break?

There was also the matter of the girls' intentions for the trip to be considered. They were hoping to find their parents, and Denloy really couldn't blame them. After all, they didn't know the truth. All his nieces remembered were two good, kind fathers and their smart, loving wives.

Sighing, Denloy looked one last time around his office. It represented eight years during which he had distanced himself from the name Freely and all emotions associated with it. It felt strange to so quickly be pulled back into his birth name. He'd tried so hard to be Wilmot Denloy, rich philanthropist and engineer sponsor, that now becoming Will Freely, inventor, brother, and uncle was the difficult task.

Somewhere downstairs, he heard his nieces laughing, and he smiled. They laughed like his brothers, untainted and joyfully wild. Right then and there, Denloy decided. He *would* go with Arlyn and Graylin, to protect them, if nothing else, to stop them from finding the truth, and to get to know the girls that, until last night, he'd been convinced that he'd killed.

Denloy joined the girls for breakfast, which the crew downed with a speed that did not do fair credit to the magnificence of the cooking. Only Lewis had truly appreciated the meal, eating slowly and carefully the pastries, the hard-boiled eggs rolled in sausage, and slices of potato. Denloy watched his nieces inhale their food and thought of his brothers' prodigious appetites and general lack of manners. Clearly, Arlyn and Graylin had inherited both traits.

As the food disappeared, Denloy folded his napkin in his lap, and cleared his throat. He was ready to speak his piece.

"Girls," he said, pushing his hair back into its perfect place. "I've thought about it, and I've decided I *will* join you on your trip to find my brothers."

Arlyn dropped the grape she'd been about to chuck at her cousin. "Really?" she asked excitedly. "You mean it?" She smiled. How much easier this all would be with Wilmot Denloy there! And besides, remembering his actions the night before, the fear and hurt in his eyes, Arlyn felt bad for the man. He was their uncle, after all, and clearly torturing himself over her and her cousin's supposed deaths.

"Yes. I mean it," Denloy said, giving his niece a smile.

"Well then, let's get going!" Arlyn threw down her fork and hopped up. "Come on, cousin. Mr. Denloy, you don't happen to have a car, do you?"

Dcnloy's chauffcurs (hc had multiplc) drovc thc crcw, Dcnloy him self, and all of his luggage back to Leo's house, where the *Freelander* still floated. While Lewis and the boys ushered the rich gentlemen up the ladder, the girls having insisted that he not come in the house and slow down their departure with sentiment and sadness, the cousins hurried inside the house. Running to their separate rooms, they began to pack frantically, grabbing clothes, blankets, pillows, drawings, tools, and anything else they could get their hands on. Graylin had an intense fear of leaving necessary items behind and had to check multiple places multiple times.

"Come on cousin, almost done?" Arlyn poked her head in. Graylin nodded.

"Just a second, I need to check under my bed." She bent down and glanced under before straightening.

"All good?" Arlyn asked. Graylin's answer hesitated in her throat.

"Actually I can't remember. Hang on." She crouched down and looked again.

"Good?" Arlyn asked once more, tapping her foot impatiently.

"I-" Graylin couldn't remember if there'd been anything she needed under there. "Uh, give me a second."

"*Cousin*," Arlyn sighed, shaking her head. Graylin bent down, thinking very hard about looking. *Look for stuff, look for stuff, is there anything under there, make sure it's all good.*

She stood up again and buried her face in her hands.

"I'm sorry cousin," she said, voice muffled. "I was thinking so hard about looking, I forgot to look."

"Here," Arlyn shook her head and looked for herself- it was completely barren. "It's shockingly spotless, not a thing under there. We're good to go." The girls rushed from the room, and had just returned from their third trip out to the *Freelander* when they were confronted.

"Girls!" A woman with loose copper colored hair, a set mouth, and blazing eyes was standing, hands on hips, glaring at the cousins sharply. "Where have you two *been*?" Graylin gulped and ducked behind her cousin.

"There's a lot to tell you, and not much time to say it," Arlyn said, rushing up to Lily, "But we're going after our parents. I don't know how long we'll be gone, or where we'll even be going, but I do think we'll be fine."

"What?" Lily stepped away, confused.

"Our parents are alive, right? And we're gonna find them," Arlyn said soothingly.

"No!" Lily said, looking as close to outraged as the girls had ever seen her. "Absolutely not!"

"But, Lily," Arlyn said urgently, "They're our parents! We *have* to find them."

"No way." Lily shook her head. "You two are not leaving to find your parents. You are not traveling across the country, and you most certainly aren't doing it alone. We don't even know if they're alive! That letter you read is nearly a decade old!"

"I'm sorry, Lily," Arlyn said, grabbing her friend's hand. "But we are going. You stay here and watch over the house. Settle Leo's stuff, take care of the money, the will."

"Wait wait wait, no," Lily said, going pale, voice cracking. "I can't do it alone. *You* can't do it alone." She clutched at Arlyn's hands, squeezing them tight.

"You don't need us," Arlyn told her sincerely. "We'll just get in the way. Get yourself settled, learn to live without Leo." She smiled gently. "I'm truly sorry. But we have to do this."

"And we won't be alone," Graylin put in. "We found our Uncle Will, he's actually alive and super rich."

"*What*?!" Lily dropped Arlyn's hands.

"Okay, bye!" The girls tore off, out the door, running from their friend, and the questions she undoubtedly had.

"Wait!" Lily called from behind them, rushing to the door. When the girls most certainly did *not* wait, she leaned against the doorframe, thoroughly overcome. "I love you!" she called helplessly.

"Love you too!" Arlyn shouted back.

A flurry of movement greeted the cousins when they reached the *Freelander* deck. Lewis was chasing River with a spatula in hand, holding her skirt up with the other as she ran after him. Enland was standing next to Teddy in the pilot's chair, holding up several maps, pointing in vague directions. And, in the center of the deck, Wilmot Denloy was standing, turning in slow circles.

"You like it?" Arlyn bounded up to him, gesturing to the ship around them. Denloy nodded, his mouth firmly clenched shut.

"It's . . . smaller than I remember," he said. Arlyn saw through this cardboard guise and knew that this size observation was the only one the man could make without bursting into emotion.

"We downsized, when we rebuilt it," Arlyn nodded. "Three hundred and fifty balloons, instead of one thousand. Much easier to fly, I've been told."

"It's beautiful," Denloy said quietly. "I worked on the original, you know. It was . . . it was our favorite project, me, Mike, Ben and Leo. We'd had the idea since we were kids- imagine, an airship large enough to hold our whole family. When we were growing up, air transportation was just starting to be explored, hot-air balloons and blimps mostly, and it seemed like such a fantastical idea." Denloy took off his glasses and cleaned them on his shirt, smiling at his niece. "But clearly, it's not fantasy anymore."

"Nope," Arlyn said, noting how Denloy reached into his pocket, fiddling with something inside. What a very *Graylin* thing to do. "One hundred percent real, just like us."

Denloy glanced away. Arlyn hesitated for a moment (her cousin would *hate* her for this) but plowed ahead anyway.

"Hey, uh, since you're embarking on this illustrious adventure with us," she started, "I figure you'll need a room."

"Ah, yes," Denloy said. "Miss Maynewin moved all my suitcases, single-handedly, to just by the stairs, I believe." He smiled a little embarrassedly. "Just between you and me, that girl sort of scares me."

"Fear is the right reaction when faced with Lewis Maynewin," Arlyn agreed, listening to River's terrified shrieks in the background. "Anyway, it seems only right that you get Leo's old room. It's the biggest, anyway, and still has a bed and desk in it."

Denloy watched his niece, his smiling, brilliant, cheerful, and very much alive niece, and smiled.

"I would like that," he said.

"Well, come on then." Arlyn motioned for him to follow her. "Let's get you settled in. We'll stop at Lewis's and the boys' to grab stuff, and then we'll be on our way."

Denloy stood for just a moment, filled with a lightness as he hadn't felt in years. Behind him, he could feel the eyes of his inner demons blinking, but decided, just for now, to ignore them.

"As I am obviously in charge of the logistics of this trip," Lewis announced as they flew away from the boys' apartment, "I'm gonna need a solid list of our sources of income."

"Sources of income?" Arlyn asked, disgusted. Money words turned the cousins off, completely and totally.

"Wait wait wait," Graylin held up a hand, leaning against the kitchen counter. "Who put *you* in charge of logistics?"

"Why, do you want to do it?" Lewis asked, rolling her eye. "You know, organizing when and where we're stopping for fuel, how we're gonna get money to buy said fuel, plus food, clothing, personal hygiene supplies? Where are we going to stop and refill our water tanks- how much water will we even use, living on the ship full time, counting in drinking, showering, washing clothes, using the bathroom? You really want to figure all that out, Graylin?"

Graylin, completely stunned that someone could think ahead so well, shook her head. One step into planning and she was lost.

"That's what I thought," Lewis said. "Now, this trip will take money, and I need to know where we're going to get it. I have savings of my own, but I don't think I can provide for all of it."

"Lucky for us," Arlyn said, "we recently acquired a very rich uncle."

Denloy was in his room, slowly unpacking, when Arlyn found him. He had all three suitcases open, but very few things seemed to be put away.

"Overwhelmed?" Arlyn asked from the doorway. Denloy spun around to look at her, and then nodded. "It's okay. It happens to Graylin too." She moved to a suitcase and clicked it open, noting the well-organized packing job. "But *you* clearly don't pack like she does."

"I'm sorry," Denloy said, moving to flick on a light. "I guess I just got distracted, thinking about Leo, and then by the time I remembered what I was supposed to be doing . . ."

"You felt guilty for wasting so much time, and then panicked, unsure where to start." Arlyn finished. "Like I said, it happens to Graylin too. The key, for her, is to just give her something to start with, something small. For example," Arlyn pulled a waistcoat from the suitcase. Her cousin would have despised the velvety texture, but Arlyn didn't mind it. "Start with the clothes. Don't put it in the chest yet, don't worry about organizing the drawers, just get it out of the case and put it in piles."

"Thank you," Denloy said, embarrassed.

"No problem," Arlyn told him, setting the vest on the bed. She glanced back at the suitcase, a rectangular box catching her eye. "Hey, do you know any good card games?" She grabbed the box, pulling the deck of cards out and shuffling them.

"A few," Denloy said. "Often, people I meet with enjoy playing cards. It's like an icebreaker, of sorts. Play a round of poker, drink a few glasses of wine, and settle some business dealings."

"Ew," Arlyn said, flicking through the pack.

"I'm not a huge fan of it myself, or at least, I wasn't." Denloy sighed. "I suppose I spent so long trying to like it, I just convinced myself I did." Then he smiled. "But, truthfully, I use those cards for throwing."

"No way, really?" Arlyn handed the box to him, tossing a braid over her shoulder. "I'm something of a card-thrower myself."

"Yeah, like that time you totally lost to Finn and I had to rescue you from his date," Graylin added, peeking her head into the room. She'd clearly been eavesdropping.

"This is an A B conversation cousin." Arlyn now turned her gaze to Graylin. "C your way out of it."

Denloy, smiling, pulled out a card and positioned himself perpendicular to the wall, holding the card between his fingers. He lined up his shot and flicked it towards the wall.

The card stuck into the door frame. Denloy turned to his niece, giving her a smile which Arlyn returned as she handed him another card. This was a challenge.

"I actually came to ask you something," Arlyn said, flicking a card of her own.

"Oh?" Denloy tossed a card casually, his card hitting so close to Arlyn's, you could barely tell there were two cards there.

"Well, it's just that Lewis has recently brought up that we're gonna need some money for this trip," Arlyn said, throwing one from behind her back. It bounced against the wall and fell to the ground. "Ah, gosh darn it."

"That was a good move," the businessman nodded, trying to ignore the sinking in his stomach. *Money*. That's all he ever was to people anymore.

"What I'm trying to say," Arlyn told him, trying the behind the back throw once more, "Is that we need your help. Monetarily." This time, the card stuck, quivering in the wood.

Denloy threw his own card, and then nodded.

"Is this *all* you need me for?" he asked quietly. "Because I can just send the cash with you and stay here. I'm sure Graylin would prefer that."

"What? No! We *want* you here," Arlyn said, dropping her arm. She took a deep breath and sighed. "Just give Graylin some time. She needs time with things." She fiddled with the card in her hand. "Listen, I've lived with my cousin for a long time now, through losing our parents even, and I've never seen her shut down like she did after Leo died. She's always had a problem with loss, because it brings extra guilt, and fear, and anxiety, all things which Graylin deals with on any given day."

Arlyn lifted her hand and flicked, sending the card snicking into the ceiling. "Besides, Graylin tends to hold on to emotions. If you asked her what caused them, she probably couldn't remember even the day after, but emotions sort of lodge themselves inside and resurface all the time. And that abandonment she felt when our parents died only resurfaced after Leo's death, and when she learned *you* were supposed to be there the whole time, but weren't? That *you* were supposed to save us, and raise us, and that if you had Leo might still be alive? That hurt Graylin even worse. She'll work through it, but she needs time."

Denloy fired another card, this one aimed at a model airship hanging from the ceiling. The card hit the ship squarely in the side, wobbling it from side to side. He was silent until Arlyn jabbed an elbow into his arm.

"Oh, cheer up. Graylin is my best friend, but let me tell you, you're not missing much." Arlyn smiled up at her uncle.

"You, cousin, are the worst!" Graylin shouted from several rooms away. Denloy smiled and threw one last card.

"Alright, you're not a horrible card thrower," Arlyn said, tugging a blue card out from the wall. "Who agrees we clean this up later? Say aye!"

"Aye," the uncle and niece said in unison, before leaving the card-scattered room together.

Lewis's house was quickly raided, with Denloy most happily staying on the ship. The thought of meeting Mr. and Mrs. Maynewin in their own house while several teens rushed around taking their things was a situation so awkward it completely exceeded Denloy's mental awkwardness meter. Besides, then he'd have to explain things, which was another impossible task. So he stayed in his room, taking his niece's advice and slowly unpacking his possessions. However, it took him so long, night had fallen by the time all his clothes were put away. The crew, under Lewis's direction, had agreed that they would simply fly to the edge of Odios, and park for the night.

Lewis was on a high of sorts, having stood up to her parents for the first time in several months. She told them, in no uncertain terms, that she would be leaving with the Freely cousins for an extended amount of time, that she would be completely safe, and that she loved her mom and dad dearly. They had spluttered, and raised their arched eyebrows, and wrung their gloved hands, but ultimately let her go, her disobedience regarding the camping trip proof that she could just leave, and she would too. So, to put her departure on their terms, and to ease their consciences, her father had forced Lewis to take several thousands of dollars in 'back-up funds', and her mother had overseen the packing of most of Lewis's wardrobe.

Thus, it was rather late when the ship finally took off, ready to start the first leg of their journey. The plan was to fly for a mere two hours, and then stop, so the whole crew could get a full night of sleep. There was one person aboard the ship, however, who drifted off soon after they departed. Wilmot Denloy, thoroughly and understandably exhausted from the past day's events, had collapsed on his bed, sleep hitting him before his own head hit the pillow.

The rest of the crew had flown the distance with ease, all six members excited at the prospect of this adventure. Dinner, funded by the Maynewin's kitchen, was a joyous affair, and only Arlyn noted her uncle's absence. She had peeked into his room, seen him fast asleep, and decided to leave him well alone. And yet, she wondered if perhaps it would have been good for him to witness this side of the crew- the joy, the laughter, and the fun. She got the feeling that Denloy hadn't had the happiest of lives. But the very things Arlyn wished her uncle were experiencing eventually drove him from her thoughts, and she left dinner with only the faintest worry in the back of her mind.

The boards of the *Freelander's* deck creaked and settled under Denloy's footsteps. All around the ship was a vast ocean of clouds, the only thing giving them depth being the cold light of the moon above. He paced and paced, unsure of quite what was on his mind. He looked up as he passed through the shadow of an enormous balloon. There were 1,000 of them, just like he remembered. He counted them using the method his brothers had taught him. *Remember*, Benson's voice echoed in his head, *if you want to make sure all 1,000 are there.*

"Multiply the bundles by the number of ropes looped down," three voices said behind him. He turned to see his brothers smiling at him.

"A little late for you to be awake, isn't it, Will?" Leo chuckled, his eyes sparkling. He looked older than Denloy remembered.

"I thought you always went to bed at 10 o'clock sharp," Michaelangelo punched him in the shoulder. "Suppose you fell asleep with your work clothes on again?"

"Lay off him, you two," Benson commanded. "He's had a long couple of days, and he doesn't do well away from home too long." He pushed his twin away to put an arm around his brother. "You know, you passed your homebody-ness onto Arlyn. How's my little girl, anyway?"

"She's intelligent, kind, and still so imaginative." Denloy paused for a second and grinned. "Everything you're not."

"And to think I was having the boys be nice to you!" Benson pushed him away, laughing. "If I didn't know better, I'd say you were *enjoying* the idea of a trip. You never insult me when you're miserable."

"That's because *you* can't see over your quote unquote, 'comforting' hero complex enough to realize people are insulting you," Leo grinned. "Although as blind as you two are, you wouldn't be able to see an insult coming until it hit you in the nose!"

The four burst into laughter, the boards underneath them rumbling as they did. The four were often lovingly referred to as 'The Parade', as their presence could be compared to a parade of elephants tramping about. This boisterous way of conversation was unique to the four, as outside of this, all of the brothers were quiet and pragmatic in their speech.

"I'm dying to see Graylin again," Michaelangelo said as the laughter and rebuttals finally died down. "To see her, and Arlyn, and you, Will."

"To be a family again," Benson chuckled. "I've missed that."

"To be a family?" Denloy looked between the twins. Leo was missing. He would always be missing. "No, no no no, this isn't right," he said.

"Not right?" Benson asked. "Will, are you okay?"

"I'm *fine!*" he shouted suddenly. "But this isn't right! None of this is! No, you two are *murderers!*"

"Murderers?" Each twin set a hand on his shoulder, Michelangelo trying to calm him down. "Will, what are you talking about? We're not murderers, we're your brothers!"

"No no no," Denloy stepped back. "You're trying to *trick me!* I'm not stupid! I know when you're lying! You *burned* the Freelander! And because of that, you'll never see Arlyn and Graylin again! You hurt my family!"

"*Your* family?!" Benson raised his voice, making Denloy wince. "You don't *have* a family! You have yourself and your company, and *that's it.*

Arlyn is *my* daughter, and it was my choice to leave her behind, and you know why? Because I trusted *you*, and you failed me."

The sky around had turned a dim orange, and only looking down did he realize the ship was on fire. "Denloy?" A girl's voice said from behind him. Arlyn, teenage Arlyn, the real Arlyn, was watching with wide eyes.

"Arlyn! You have to get off the ship!" he cried, trying to run towards her. The smoke was choking him, whatever fear his brothers' posed was gone. He had to save her.

"Denloy, are you okay?" she asked, seemingly not noticing the fire around her. "What's going on?"

"We have to get off of the ship, *now*!" he grabbed her arm, only to be met with Michaelangelo's face.

"Will, we just want you home again," he said. "We're *family*, Will."

"YOU'RE NOT MY FAMILY!" he yelled, waking with a start. Sweat glued his shirt to his back and his hair to his forehead, and he found Arlyn and Lewis standing at the side of his bed. He looked around wildly; where was he? This wasn't his room.

"Bad dream," Lewis stated flatly, offering him a cup full of something warm. "Drink."

Only when he took the cup did he realize his hands were shaking. Almost as quickly as he got it, Arlyn took it away. "You'll spill it on yourself," she said. "Nightmares plus first-degree burns never did someone well."

"Did I wake you up?" He asked, straightening himself on the bed. Lewis shook her head.

"You and Graylin have nightmares the same way," Arlyn explained. "Every night she has a nightmare, she goes to bed in working clothes with textures I know she doesn't like. You're still wearing that velvet vest, and ever since yesterday, I've noticed you avoiding touching it. Lewis and I set alarms, just to make sure we could wake you up if it got too bad."

"Your hands aren't shaking as much now," Lewis said, motioning for Arlyn to give him the cup back. "Now drink, it's good for you."

Taking her word, he did as told. He had expected tea, but was surprised to find it was instead hot chocolate. Lewis sensed an upcoming comment and interjected. "It would be apple cider, but that makes your dreams more vivid, and I don't think we can trust your dreams right now. Now, I'm going to bed, I still haven't journaled yet, so take care of yourselves, alright?"

"Goodnight, Lew," Arlyn said as she left. She turned to her uncle. "Whatever you do, don't tell Graylin what happened. As much as she'll complain about it, she takes the fact we know when each other is going to have a nightmare very pridefully, and would be miffed to know that I figured out you were going to have one first, let alone without her."

"She seemed exhausted tonight. Are you sure she would have stayed up for me?" he asked.

"Never underestimate how far pride alone can drive Graylin Freely," Arlyn chuckled. "Now I love you, I'm going to bed. Hopefully no more nightmares."

"You what?" Denloy spluttered as Arlyn reached the door.

"I love you?" she said as if she said it every night. "It's what you say to people you care about when you tell them goodnight?" She rolled her eyes. "Adults."

The morning dawned bright, but clouds quickly curtained the light. When Denloy arrived at breakfast, Arlyn was pleased to see him looking rested.

"How are you feeling?" she asked, munching on a breakfast burrito. Everyone else was eating an egg casserole thing, but both Freely cousins despised the texture of spongy eggs.

"Much better, thank you. That hot chocolate worked wonders." He straightened his tie. "I would like to thank Miss Maynewin as well."

"Call her Lewis," Arlyn said. "She tends to smack people when they use her rich person name." She handed him a burrito, taking another bite of her own. "Now come on, Enland needs your help with the maps."

The crew filed into Enland's map room, standing around the largest table in the center. Cartographed papers and sketches stretched over the dented wood, lit by the many lamps hanging from the ceiling, and large windows.

"So, any starting ideas for where we should head?" Arlyn asked Denloy, standing next to Lewis. Graylin was fiddling with her chain, and looked up at her uncle. He thought for several seconds, struggling with the sudden question. He needed somewhere interesting, somewhere they could find information, but not too much. Just enough to keep the girls going while he figured out what to do.

"They were in Belhaven often," Denloy said finally. "Especially towards the end. We could start there." *Gives me more time*, he thought.

"Belhaven?" River asked. "What were they doing there?"

"It's the capital," Denloy said, deftly avoiding River's question. "Have you ever been there?" His gaze shifted to his nieces.

"No," Arlyn and Graylin answered together. The boys shook their heads as well, but Lewis raised her hand.

"I have. It was a while ago, on a vacation with my parents, but I *have* been there. Isn't it a fairly long trip? It felt like it took ages to get there."

"By airship, it's probably two weeks away. Maybe a bit more, this is quite a large vessel," Denloy told them. "I send representatives there fairly often, looking out for new program recruits."

"Belhaven, Belhaven . . ." Enland traced a line on his map, one that he'd bought. "That's south of here. Pretty simple route- no mountains, a few cities, several towns."

"Will we make it that far without fueling up?" Lewis asked.

"We will, but it'll be close," Graylin said. "But the more we hover, the more gas we use, so we'd better get moving. Teddy?"

The boy nodded and hurried from the room, followed quickly by Enland. The map room was directly above the engines, and Arlyn could feel the floor vibrate and rattle as Teddy started the *Freelander* up, and the ship rose slightly. They were off.

15

OUT ON THE TOP deck, dark storm clouds were rolling in over the *Freelander*. The balloons, all 350 of them, were beige, but not like a nice beige, more like a dirty beige. The original *Freelander*'s 1,000 balloons had been much nicer, made of either white, cream, or gray fabric. However, when Leo had rebuilt the ship with the girls, both the number and physical appearance of the balloons had been diminished.

Graylin scrambled up a rope and stretched out on a net the girls had hung from a few balloons. It was like a large hammock of sorts, and it swayed as the ship's engine whirred and the breeze spat mist. Graylin was feeling particularly inspired to do something, but she wasn't sure what.

Below her, Teddy was sitting in his pilot's chair, tapping his hand on his knee, humming a little to himself. She wondered what song he was singing, and if he had written it himself. *I should ask*, she thought, staring up at the balloons. But he was so far away, and she'd have to shout at the top of her lungs, and that was an awful lot of work.

I wish I could just, like, send him a message somehow, she thought, tossing a rubber ball from her pocket and tossing it in the air. Suddenly she sat up, as an idea, an absolutely, positively, unaccountably exciting idea, hit her. She would *build* a message system that ran around the *Freelander*.

Every once in a while, Graylin Freely would get totally and completely overtaken with an idea or new interest that she *needed* to act upon. Arlyn called them obsessions, and they sort of were. These fixations were unpredictable in the way that Graylin couldn't control when they came on or how long they lasted. However, she had learned by this point that when a new interest hit her, she needed to use the momentum. And this message system idea? It was a fixation. Graylin flew off the net, down the rope, and across the deck, hurrying to find her cousin.

Arlyn studied the contraption in front of her with great interest. Four rows of keys with various letters attached to them made up the front of the typewriter she had "borrowed" from Denloy's room, and a spinning cylinder to hold the paper made up the back. This was nothing unusual. The cousins had many typewriters at home, most of them broken, but what had piqued Arlyn's interest was the small bulb and quiet humming coming inside the machine. It was electric.

"COUSIN!" Graylin slammed open the door, adding another dent to the well-worn hole in the wall. "I have an idea." She jumped onto Arlyn's bed and folded her legs in, ignoring her cousin's disgruntled look as she glanced up from her desk. "Okay, so what if we built a message system that ran around the *whole* ship, and I mean mostly everywhere. The map room, the bedrooms, the kitchen, the pilot chair, the engine room-everywhere!" She was practically bouncing with eagerness. There was a look in her eyes that both excited Arlyn and made her very nervous. Graylin snatched at a sheet of paper and began to sketch quickly. "We'll build these little tube sort of things, which run all over the ship. You know that suction mechanic in the engine downstairs? We use that concept, so that the suctioning is happening to our messages. You write the note, roll it up, and away it goes!"

Arlyn stared, both surprised at this sudden outburst and impressed with her cousin. How did she come up with these ideas?

"So," she started slowly, "each room can send messages to every other room?"

"Yes."

Arlyn thought for a few seconds. Graylin's wild, spur-of-the-moment ideas always had at least one major flaw, and she was usually very good at finding them. She could practically *smell* one close by now, and sure enough, it showed itself almost instantly.

"Hang on, that doesn't make sense." Arlyn spun around in her desk chair. "To do that, you'd need to have, what," Arlyn made a quick mental count, "at least *ten* pipes in each room, one for each destination."

Graylin, quite out of character, had come prepared.

"Yes cousin, *unless* we rig it so each room has one pipe, and they just branch off of each other," she said, kicking her feet. Once again, Arlyn considered her cousin's idea. That 'Graylin definitely didn't think this through,' smell had mostly disappeared.

"That, cousin," Arlyn said, grinning, "Is actually a *brilliant* idea." She was getting excited now. Then, glancing at her desk, a thought hit her like a bolt of lightning. She beamed with that same manic energy Graylin was radiating, and pulled her cousin off the bed to stare at the strange machine she had "found", and which she had been examining until Graylin had burst in.

"What if, instead of handwriting these messages, we *type them!*" she exclaimed. "Look at this thing. It's just like a regular typewriter, but it puts itself back when you finish a row," she explained as she typed. "I found it in Denloy's room. Honestly, it's really fun to finish a line, because-" she was cut off by a little *ding* as the typewriter automatically slid back to the right. Arlyn grinned and did it again. "Ding! Ding!" It was quite addicting.

Graylin's eyes lit up as she inspected the electric typewriter. It was a *brilliant* idea; she really didn't know how her cousin came up with them. "Say cousin, if this is all connected to power, you could rig up all sorts of things on here. Like something that puts it in an envelope for you."

"Or ties it in a little roll when you want to be fancy," Arlyn said, taking the paper off of the carriage and tying it with a spare strip of ribbon left on her desk. She pulled a chair up to the corner of the room and stood on it, slipping the roll of paper through a small hole in the corner of the wall into Enland's room, as a small acoustic demonstration, which did its job perfectly. The cousins glanced at each other, shared one last thrilled grin, and raced to the engine room.

"First things first, cousin." Arlyn surveyed the 'spare parts' pile in the deepest parts of the *Freelander*. "We need some tubing."

"No problemo cousin mine." Graylin popped up from behind the pile, tossing a few random parts out of the way, producing a few lengths of clear tubing. "This do?"

The cousins sorted surprisingly quickly through the pile, considering both had abysmal concentration skills. However, great lengths of tubing were found, and the cousins shoved armfuls of it up through the trapdoor, wiping sweat from their brows.

"Goodness, it is hot down here," Graylin said, pulling off her waistcoat and unclipping her suspenders. She stripped off her white button up, and then pulled the suspenders back on. Osden's undergarments were relatively comfortable and easy to deal with when compared to other countries' fashion guidelines. However, they were far too revealing for both societal standards and Graylin's preferences to be worn alone . . . normally. Even Graylin's modesty could be overruled by heat.

"Good news is I think this is all we need from down here, for now," Arlyn told Graylin, helping her shove the last of the tubing up out of the engine room. "Now hurry up and get out, you'll catch asthma staying down here too long."

River, Enland, and Teddy all looked up from where they'd been 'chilling' in River's room, their attention drawn by sudden wood shavings and a whirring mechanical noise. One, two, three seconds, and then a perfect little circle of wood fell out of River's wall, from where the wall and ceiling met. Graylin's eye appeared in the hole, then her fingers to brush out the extra sawdust.

"Uh, what are you doing?" River asked, setting down the chess piece he'd been about to throw at Enland. There was no answer from either cousin, so Teddy set down his notebook, Enland removed the protective pillow from his head, and all three boys peeked curiously out the door.

Standing just outside it, holding some sort of drill-looking machine, was Graylin Freely, lifted to the necessary height on Arlyn's shoulders as the girl staggered and strained. She had drawn the short straw, again, and holding her cousin up was no simple task.

"Cousin, next time we are just finding the step-stool," Arlyn gritted through her teeth.

"But that's so much work," Graylin said, pushing the drill into the hole and clicking it. The blades whirred, sending more sawdust into Graylin's hair and Arlyn's face. Arlyn coughed and blinked her eyes rapidly as Graylin scrunched her nose. "This is *much* easier."

"For you, maybe!" Arlyn said, moving to the left to keep her cousin balanced. "Are you almost finished?" She tilted and leaned precariously. "Because I'm dropping you in three, two . . ."

"Hang on, one more thing!" Graylin shoved a length of pipe through the hole, twisting it until it fit snuggly.

"One." Arlyn let go of her cousin's feet, and Graylin tumbled from her shoulders to the floor. She rolled onto her back, groaning. Arlyn ignored her melodramatic cousin and focused on the three boys still watching them.

"What are we doing, you ask?" Arlyn said, reaching into her belt and pulling out a roll of paper. "We are installing the Freelander's very own messaging system. These tubes here," she gestured to the ones they'd just installed, "will run all around the ship, and we'll send notes through them."

"How will it work?" Teddy asked from behind his hair, helping the still wincing Graylin up from the ground. Graylin stood next to him, arms folded, not because she felt like being by Teddy, but to prove her irritation with her cousin.

Arlyn, trying so very hard to ignore her cousin's disappointment (this was *not* difficult), unrolled the sheet of paper covered in her writing and Graylin's drawings. Teddy studied it for a moment, rubbed his nose, and then shook his head.

"I have no clue what any of this means."

"How did you get to be the pilot without any basic engineering knowledge?" Arlyn asked, flipping a braid over her shoulder. Teddy started to make a gesture, but River smacked his hand down.

"Alright, look." Graylin stepped forward, feeling unusually irritated at her cousin for teasing Teddy and not just explaining how it worked. So, she began to point at the 'Ideas Sheet', which Arlyn held smooth. Graylin's cousin, it turned out, made a fairly proficient easel. "This box looking thing is the suction mechanic. It's just like the one which runs inside the engine, taking the hot air, cooling it, and spreading it to the rest of the ship for AC. In these tubes, though, the air moves our little message rolls." She pointed to the specific parts with one hand, fiddling with a pencil in the other. She was constantly tapping pencils against her leg, so often in fact, that by the end of nearly every day there were gray lead marks on her pants.

Teddy looked at her, and gave her a rare, genuine Teddy smile. Graylin grinned back, and then wondered why the people who smiled the least had the best and brightest smiles.

"That's pretty smart," River nodded, "but wouldn't it make more sense to crunch the messages into little balls so that they rounded the corners?"

"Shove off River, no one cares," Graylin said absently. What a stupid question, honestly.

"*Rude*," huffed River, but he threw his arms around his brothers (he couldn't reach Enland's shoulders, so he consigned himself to the waist, which made Enland most seriously displeased) and directed the three away.

"Really, cousin?" Arlyn smirked as the boys left. Graylin was piling various books on top of a chair, and straightened.

"What do you mean, *really, cousin*?" she asked, stepping precariously onto the teetering pile, reaching up to the ceiling for support. Arlyn shoved her hands in her pockets and rocked on the balls of her feet, an adequate imitation of Graylin.

"Oh, Teddy, you have a question? Let me explain that to you in full detail, and give you as much information as possible!" she said, eyebrows raised in exaggerated earnesty.

"I would feel bad if he was confused," Graylin said, ignoring what her cousin was hinting at.

"Yeah, 'cause you're in love," Arlyn teased. Graylin whipped her head around to snap back indignantly at her cousin, to shoot down the blatant lies she was so freely spreading. Arlyn liked to exaggerate every friendship Graylin formed, which frustrated and embarrassed her so much it actually encouraged her *not* to talk to people. However, Graylin was unable to explain just how wrong Arlyn was concerning Teddy, as the movement was too much for her unsteady perch. The books she was standing on flew out from under feet, sending her toppling to the ground once again.

"Ow," she groaned, rolling to her side and rubbing her elbow. Arlyn rolled her eyes.

"You ready for that step-stool yet?" she asked.

It took the cousins three hours, five snack breaks, and two disagreements to finish installing the pipe. Finally, Arlyn had gotten sick of her cousin returning with yet another treat to keep herself occupied, and had brought out a jar of ice cubes from the *Freelander* freezer to give to her cousin. Graylin then crunched happily on the ice for the next hour, pushing the pieces into her cheek whenever she needed to speak. The cousins decided to use the tubing as efficiently as possible, running one main line from Arlyn and River's rooms (they were parallel across the hall) and a secondary line branching off to the kitchen. Then, they added all the extras, based off those main tubes, branching to every bedroom, the map room and winding all the way up to the pilot's chair.

"I don't get those two," Lewis muttered to Enland, watching the cousins sprawled on the floor, both staring at the ceiling and kicking their feet. "They set up hundreds of feet of tubing in a matter of hours, taking multiple breaks, mind you, but they both take at least two days to tidy their rooms."

"They're Freelys," Enland said through a mouthful of cornbread. "I don't think we're *supposed* to get them."

Back in the hall, Graylin rolled to her stomach and jumped to her feet. "Come on cousin, we're almost done. All we have left is Leo's room."

Leo's room, which wasn't Leo's room anymore. The thought hung in the air, mixing with the smell of whatever Lewis was making for lunch. The room which had belonged to their cheerful uncle was now occupied by a different one: Wilmot Denloy. The girls glanced at each other, and decided it was best not to discuss feelings that may or may not have arisen based on this arrangement. So, scooping up their tubing, shoving bolts and gears into their pockets, they headed to Leo's room.

"Hey, uh, Denloy? We're gonna drill a few holes in your wall, just a heads up." Arlyn poked her head into the room, gave him a thumbs up, and then ducked back. Denloy glanced up from his desk, took roughly three seconds to process the information, and then hurried out of his seat.

"Hang on, what-" he stepped out of his room, to see his nieces, both glancing up at him. It was like someone punched him in the chest as their eyes turned to him- they looked so much like his visions. Graylin was sitting criss-cross on the ground, fitting two pieces of tubing together with a metal connector, and Arlyn was tightening the drill head. *They're real,* he had to tell himself, shutting his eyes. *They're alive, and they're here. And they're drilling holes in my wall.* It was such a Mike and Ben move that Denloy had to smile.

"Uh, Mr. Uncle Denloy?" Graylin asked, watching the man smile to himself with his eyes still squeezed shut. "You okay? Is this gonna be a regular thing, these weird attacks, because they kinda freak me-" Arlyn kicked her cousin in the leg, trying to get her to shut up. Clearly, whatever Denloy was seeing now wasn't like what he'd experienced the night before. This was less of a panic attack, and more of a flashback. Arlyn had to sigh inwardly, wondering why Graylin, who was quite experienced in the world of panic attacks and complete breakdowns herself, was so terrible at spotting them.

"No, no, I'm okay," Denloy said suddenly, opening his eyes, and smiling slightly at his nieces. "I was just thinking. Now, what did you say about my wall?"

Arlyn launched into their explanation, gesturing to papers and supplies, while Graylin used the finally found footstool, and installed the pipe. Denloy nodded and asked questions, just like Leo might have, and every time Graylin caught sight of him out of the corner of her eye, her stomach gave a little flop as her brain told her it was Leo standing there. But of course it never was, and by the time Arlyn had finished giving Denloy the rundown, Graylin was feeling decidedly and unfairly irritated at him for raising her hopes so many times.

"It's a great idea," Denloy told Arlyn, nodding at the drawings. Then he glanced at Graylin. "You drew all these?"

Graylin nodded, then turned back to her task of tightening the rivets connecting the tubing.

"You really are talented," Denloy said admiringly, studying the drawings. "Do you mostly just draw machines?"

Graylin shrugged. Denloy glanced at Arlyn, wondering what he'd done to make his niece so silent, but not wanting to ask. Arlyn decided to smooth out the situation and gave her uncle a smile.

"Graylin draws a lot of people, but she never lets us see them. I have no doubt she's good, though," Arlyn told him. "Her handwriting is hardly legible, so I write all the notes."

"And the words are quite beautiful as well," Denloy said teasingly. He examined the paper again, and then pointed to a sketch of the tubes, where two of them joined perpendicularly. "How do you two plan to get the messages around these corners here?"

"Won't they just be sucked around?" Arlyn asked. There was a disappointed feeling growing in her stomach, the one she'd always gotten whenever Leo had pointed out faults in her and Graylin's plans. It was like when Graylin couldn't find something; she would search for hours, and as soon as she pulled Arlyn in, her cousin would find it in seconds. "I *swear* that wasn't there before," she always said. Similarly, Arlyn and Graylin would spend ages pouring over ideas, and the second they told their uncle, he would laugh, shake his head, and point out exactly why it wouldn't work.

"Ah, no, I don't think so," Denloy said, studying the blueprints. "I think you have two options here, really. Either you add in little doors, which open and shut to block off and reveal certain tubes, or you add extra systems which emit puffs of air to push the notes along."

Graylin and Arlyn glanced at each other. Now that they thought about it, getting the messages around the corners *would* be a problem, which irritated Graylin even further because River of all people had foreseen it. Arlyn, however, was more open-minded, and to her, Denloy's ideas seemed like pretty good options. Except . . .

"Uh, we don't really know how to build either of those," Arlyn said hesitantly. "I mean, we could figure it out, I'm sure, but it will take us a long time."

"I can help you," Denloy offered. "I'm out of practice, but I *do* have a bit of inventing under my belt."

The cousins looked at each other again, having one of their silent conversations. Arlyn raised her eyebrows, *do we let him help?* Graylin pursed her lips and scrunched her nose, *if we have to.* Arlyn shrugged, *it could be nice, having his help.* Graylin thought, bit her lip, and then shrugged too. *Fine. But I'm not happy about it.*

"Okay, thanks," Arlyn said, turning to her uncle. "We'd love your help, actually."

Wilmot Denloy smiled, a real, Leo-esque smile, that somehow reminded Arlyn not only of her beloved uncle but her dad, too.

"Great," he beamed, voice warm. "Let me pop in and see if I've packed my tool belt, I'll be right back."

Denloy flung open a chest, tossing out multiple items before deciding the tool belt was not hiding in there. Clicking open the locks, he unlatched all four of his suitcases, the spring loaded lids flying up. He threw out waistcoats, cravats, a three-piece suit, and five pairs of socks before spotting the worn leather pouches sewn to the thick belt. He pulled it out with satisfaction, breathing in the brackish aroma hanging around the suitcase of ragged leather and expensive cologne. He examined the tool belt and reached into a pocket, pulling out a few screws and scraps of paper. The words were faded and smudged, but he thought he knew which project they regarded. The memory of it was faded too.

"Wow," Denloy spun around to see Arlyn, standing in the doorway, looking at him with a laughing smile. "You look for stuff *just* like Graylin. Filthy animals, both of you."

Denloy glanced around sheepishly at the mess he'd created, and hurriedly began to shove stuff back into his suitcases.

"I'll be just a moment," he muttered, but Arlyn just laughed.

"You can clean it later. Come on, Graylin will get impatient if we wait much longer."

The three Freelys decided that the best, easiest solution to their problem was to employ Denloy's idea of extra bursts of air to get the messages around the corners. They discussed their options, the girls doing the majority of the talking as Wilmot Denloy listened in wonder.

"So first we have to install the suction system," Graylin said, counting on her finger unnecessarily considering she only remembered the one step.

"First, we have to *build* the suction system," Denloy corrected. "Then we can install all the puffers at the corners, install the gates that let the air out, and hook the whole thing up to the air compressor that's running the rest of the system."

The cousins shared a glance, then looked back at Denloy, who was fitting a few parts together already. He worked methodically, already knowing what parts needed to go where on this contraption. His hand didn't hover over pieces to consider a new thought or idea. It only took what was needed and made it work. He tested every lever exactly once. It was all he needed. Denloy was a trained professional.

The Freely cousins stood in awe as Denloy set the first of the twelve puffers they needed aside and began to construct a second. He looked up at them with a content smile, simply saying, "You learn how to assemble things pretty fast when everyone around you has a new idea every five minutes."

Arlyn raised her eyebrows at her cousin, *impressed?* Graylin had to admit that she was. But rather than silently convey the idea back to Arlyn, she sat herself on the ground and got to work. Both girls watched Denloy's hands like hawks, taking in every movement he made, and every part he picked up. Soon they had mastered the movements, building the fans even quicker than Denloy himself. In fact, after the first few puffers were made, the cousins turned their area into a sort of assembly line, with Graylin building the basic mechanics, and Arlyn adding in the extra detail work. They moved so quickly that when their uncle turned around to check on them, he actually dropped the puffer he himself was working on.

"My goodness, you two are fast," he said, shaking his head. "I imagine you work well together, after all these years."

"We work better than *well*," Arlyn told him, handing Graylin the pliers she knew her cousin wanted. "We are practically in sync, Graylin and I."

"Is that so?" Denloy asked, actually curious.

"Yep," his niece told him, flipping a braid over her shoulder. Half a second later, both girls were wincing and rubbing their heads where they'd smashed into the others as they both snatched for a wire at the same time. Denloy smiled to himself; in sync indeed.

"Mike and Ben were always like that, with the mind reading stuff," he said after a few moments. "I was so envious of it too. It seemed like it would be so gratifying to have someone who knew what you were feeling, and understood, all the time. Of course, there was Leo, but it wasn't the same. We just didn't have the same relationship as the twins, and we didn't have close bonds with *them*. I mean, when the twins entered their apprenticeships, Leo was still a toddler."

Graylin laughed a little to herself. It seemed so funny to think of Leo as a toddler, bouncing after an eight-year-old Denloy, with her and Arlyn's teenage dads cooking up a prank behind them. The image of her father and uncles as children amused her for a moment, but the joy was quickly drowned by sadness.

Graylin never understood why, but while she tended to be judgemental and cold towards some people, she also had an innate empathy that showed itself towards the strangest things. For example, just after she'd moved in with Leo, Graylin had lost her favorite stuffed animal. It had been a little ragged dog named Philippe, though since she'd gotten it when she was roughly three, Graylin's brain always imagined the name pronounced and spelled 'Flepe'. Eight-year-old Graylin had played with Flepe outside the day she'd lost him, sitting outside in the grass with a book and an apple. Later that night, a proper summer storm had rolled in, pounding the windows and grass, the wind snatching at tree branches and shingles. And poor Flepe, with his warm brown embroidered eyes always covered in fur, was nowhere to be found. Graylin had searched for hours, looking everywhere three times, and even braving the storm to search the yard. The thought of her little Flepe, battered by the rain and wind, outside at night, all alone, was enough to drive the girl to tears, and the sobs continued until she fell asleep.

Flepe was in fact eventually found under a tree, battered but as alive and well as a stuffed animal could be considered.

But that same sort of heart wrenching sadness was filling Graylin now, as she envisioned the four brothers together. Who would have thought, as the siblings played and laughed and argued, that thirty years later, that little laughing five-year-old Leo would be dead? Who could have guessed that the fifteen-year-old twins, Mike and Ben, would be missing? And who could have imagined that ten-year-old Will would have ended up a sad, broken man, with lots of money and no friends? It was so sad, this unrelenting and cruel twisting of time, that Graylin had to remind herself of all the things she was irritated about to snap her out of it. What was she angry with currently? Oh, yes, Denloy kept reminding her of Leo, he was supposed to have rescued them from the *Freelander*, but didn't, and the very fact that Denloy was with them now was against Leo's last wish.

Having successfully dropped herself back into the pit of irritation, Graylin silently resumed her work, neglecting to answer her uncle when he asked her to hand him a screw. The simple building was soon finished, however, and it wasn't long before the three Freelys were starting their next task: construction.

"So," Denloy asked Arlyn, trying to fill space. "How did you find your crew?" He climbed up the stepladder and took the puffer contraption

Arlyn was handing him to install. Several feet away, Graylin was doing the same thing, having once again refused the use of a stool. This time, she opted for a small side table.

"Well, you know that tradition the Freelys have had, finding orphans and taking them in?" Arlyn asked, watching as Denloy sliced a hole in the clear plastic tubing. "Leo did that with us, too. The boys all came from an orphanage in town, in Odios. Uncle Leo claimed he adopted them, and we all acted like he did, but he never told us if it was official or not."

"I'm afraid I'm not very good with names. Will you remind me of the boys'?" Denloy said, twisting the puffer into place. "Also, could you hand me that red wire, please?"

Arlyn plucked one from her tool belt and held it up to him. He held it between his teeth, lowered his glasses to the end of his nose, and clicked it into the adapter.

"The red-haired one is River," Arlyn told him, stepping to hand a wire to her cousin. "He's our handyman, and honestly, the nicest. Except for maybe Lewis."

"He definitely seems the most outgoing," Denloy agreed.

"Oh, he's great. Definitely my favorite." Arlyn said, rolling her eyes when Graylin gave her an incredulous look. "Wait, that's right, Graylin doesn't like him, she has a *different* favorite. Her *darling* Teddy."

"He's not *my* Teddy, nor my darling, nor my favorite. I hardly know the dude," Graylin muttered, twisting wires into place. She quickly attached a battery to the opposing ends of the wires, making sure the system worked, before detaching it.

"Teddy's got brown hair, and hardly ever speaks. He's the pilot," Arlyn said. "When he talks, he's usually saying something which is both pretty funny, and goes completely over River's head."

"Ah, I see," Denloy nodded. He stepped off the ladder, moved it forward to the next junction, and climbed back up.

"He also likes music," Graylin added. Arlyn wasn't sure if this was true, or how her cousin acquired such info, but decided not to argue the point.

"Last but not least we have Enland," she said instead, handing both workers new puffers. "He's basically a cat. He's got a ponytail, glasses, and likes maps and sleeping and Lewis."

"He's your cartographer?" Denloy asked, spinning the fan blade manually to check it was operating.

"Yep," Arlyn tossed Graylin a wire she knew on instinct she was about to ask for, and then handed Denloy some pliers. "When Uncle Leo first took them out of the orphanage, he mostly just taught them what he was teaching us. Basic mechanics, a bit of electric work, that sort of thing. We were . . . how old would you say we were, cousin?"

"Dunno," Graylin said. She twisted two wires together, and used some rubbery medical wrap from Lewis's cabinet to cover the live ends. Wiping her hands on her pants, she started the next puffer. "Maybe . . . ? Thirteen, mayhaps?"

"That sounds right," Arlyn nodded. "So we were about thirteen when Leo took the boys in, and he was just starting to teach us how to drive the Freelander. With assistance, of course."

"I should hope so," Denloy said, giving his niece a look.

"Well, it turned out Graylin and I *suck* at piloting," Arlyn said. Graylin snorted with laughter.

"That's an understatement. We *phenomenally* and *royally* suck. We suck with a capital S. Rabid campground raccoons could drive better than us," she said.

"After testing us several times," Arlyn continued, "Uncle Leo quickly lost hope in Graylin and I, so he started trying the rest of the crew. Lewis could manage, but we needed her to cook, Enland kept falling asleep at the wheel, and River was hardly better than we were. Teddy, though, he was pretty good, so Uncle Leo shoved him in the pilot chair, and banned the rest of us."

"And does he do a good job?" Denloy asked.

"Oh yeah. He's never crashed us once," Arlyn said.

Denloy was silent for a few moments, moving the step ladder once again. Arlyn handed him a third puffer, and he installed it, before turning to the cousins, as if to speak. *I'm sorry*, he wanted to say, *for everything. I'm sorry Leo's gone, and that I'm here instead. I'm sorry I wasn't there for you.*

But no, he couldn't, not yet. Arlyn had said to give Graylin space, and time, and that's what he would do. So instead, he turned back to his work, hands moving slightly stiffly.

"Can you hand me that tape?" Graylin asked sharply, looking at her uncle. He glanced over at her, surprised. "Please?" his niece relented, holding out her hand but staring at the ground.

"Of course," Denloy handed her the requested tool, and it had been used and put aside before Graylin added,

"Thank you."

Over the next few hours, the three's silence slowly turned from stiff to amiable. Arlyn Freely, Graylin thought, truly was a miracle worker. Despite Graylin's ardent wish to stay unsociable and taciturn, her cousin knew every trick in the book to get her to relax, and she deployed them with pleasure. This included but was not limited to teasing various crew members, an attempt that was much helped when they heard Enland say the phrase 'Hamnurger' to Lewis in the kitchen.

"Ham*nurger*?" Arlyn asked, raising her eyebrows.

"I didn't say that!" Enland called irritably.

"You totally did," Arlyn chuckled. "Nurger."

"Hot bog," Graylin said, grinning.

"Spagwetti and geet malls," Arlyn giggled back.

"Macanoni and knees," Graylin laughed, bending over, hands on said knees.

"Sloppy woes," Arlyn had to lean against a wall, shaken by laughter. Graylin pretended to stumble and drop something.

"Ahh," she cried, "My woes!"

"*My woes*," wheezed Arlyn, putting a hand to her face.

"It was not that funny!" Enland poked his head from the kitchen.

"Enland help, I've dropped my woes!" Arlyn cried dramatically. "They're getting everywhere!"

"I hate you guys."

It wasn't long after this that Denloy stepped back, having attached the last bit of wire, and rubbed his hands together.

"I think that's it!" he declared. The windows outside were curtained with darkness and splattered with drops of the pounding rain. Denloy turned to the yawning girls, whose energy after dinner had long worn off, and held out a paper. "Shall we test it?"

The three hurried to Denloy's room, the tube path to which was undoubtedly the most complicated. His room was also the only space with the typewriter feature hooked up- everyone else's was still manual.

"Care to do the honors, cousin?" Graylin asked grandly, gesturing to the machine. Arlyn bowed, stepped forward, and typed a small message on the typewriter.

If this doesn't work, it read, *I'm going to cry*

"Truer words have never been spoken," Graylin declared, ignoring the fact that those words had not, in fact, been *spoken*. Arlyn flicked a lever in the typewriter, and the paper sprung into a tight little roll, sealed by a ball of wax. A mechanical arm grabbed the message and lifted it to the base of the vacuum tube. On the wall next to the tubing were twelve little buttons in two rows of six, and Arlyn pressed the one with her name printed on it. Denloy had described them as being similar to those of an elevator, to which the girls had stared blankly at him, completely lost. They had never seen 'a giant dumbwaiter for people', as their uncle described it, but it sounded *awesome*. Just like the elevator had buttons in it, to control which floor the platform traveled to, these buttons next to the tubing signified which room the message was to travel to. When the button to Arlyn's room was pushed, the puffers along that specific path would be powered. Once the system had been activated all along the tubing, a little green light would turn on. And, within seconds of Arlyn pushing her button, the small light bulb lit up. It was ready to test.

"Here goes," Arlyn said. She flicked a switch, and the mechanical arm placed the message inside the tubing. Instantly, the roll of paper was sucked away, up through the tubing and out of the room.

"Come on!" Graylin called as she tore out the door, following the message like a dog would a frisbee. Arlyn pounded after her, and they raced through the hall, down the stairs, and around the corner, all the way to Arlyn's room. They shoved each other inside, and sure enough, in a little basket they had placed under the exit of the tubing, sat the small roll of paper. Graylin lunged for it, rolled it open, and gave a whoop.

"It worked!" she cried, tossing the message to her cousin. Arlyn scanned the page and shouted herself.

"Yes, cousin! *Yes!*" They performed their signature high-five (a regular high-five except they wiggled their fingers) and then locked arms and danced around the room. From outside, Wilmot Denloy watched his nieces cheer over their creation, and he smiled. The eyes behind him, the ones belonging to the brothers in his head, blinked and turned away.

16

LATER THAT NIGHT, GRAYLIN sat at her desk, too wound up to sleep. The girls had spent nearly an hour sending messages to and fro from room to room, including the engine room and the pilot chair. This final test, the one to Teddy, had reminded Graylin of two things. First, she was aghast to find the poor boy was sitting up there, soaked to the bone in the pounding rain and darkness, insistent on piloting the ship a bit longer. Second, she remembered the conversation she had held with Teddy that night by the campfire, before Leo had died. They had talked about music, and how much Teddy loved it. She didn't want to go up to the top deck and tell him to get out of the rain (she wasn't the dude's mom, after all, and he'd already come down) but, maybe, she could talk to him about music again, to cheer him up. He'd seemed sad.

Graylin padded out of her room and crossed the hall to Teddy's cabin. She raised her hand to knock . . . and then stopped. Three realizations, that she was *not* friends with Teddy, that they *didn't* really speak, and that she was *not* at all someone people usually enjoyed, all hit her at once. She hesitated as a deep chasm inside her chest reopened, so wide she wanted to just crawl in. She hadn't tried making friends in so long, she'd forgotten it existed, but it'd shown up before. It slithered in when she was in a crowd full of watching eyes, or a group of adults judging her every move, or with kids her age all doing better than her. It appeared when she tried to order food, or buy something at a store, or make small talk. Every time, the chasm, stretching strings of a sort in her mind, let loose whispers of thoughts always chasing around her head.

And they all told her she absolutely *sucked*.

Through Teddy's door, Graylin could hear music, low and soft. Teddy had mentioned a guitar from Leo; surely, that was what she was hearing. But no, that wasn't the only sound- there was singing too. It was quiet, and sad, and heartbreaking, and didn't sound remotely like soft spoken Teddy. However, it didn't even cross Graylin's mind to wonder who was singing, for just as quickly as the chasm had suddenly opened, exhaustion slammed into her in the blink of an eye. She hadn't realized what was happening until she was sitting on the floor, knees drawn up to her chest, leaning against the wall by Teddy's door, lungs rising and falling quickly, eyes squeezed shut. As she had heard the music, all the happenings of the past days, the past *years* really, seemed to catch up to her.

Her parents had been dead. Her parents were no longer dead. Her parents had been good, trustworthy people, whose morals and kindness she had never questioned.

And now her parents weren't that, either.

Graylin tried to take deep breaths as waves of exhaustion rolled over her, threatening to shut her eyes. She wanted to cry, to curl up into a ball and shut everything out. She bit her lip as it trembled and her breathing turned into gasps. She wanted to cry, but she would not. She *could* not. She needed to stay strong, for Arlyn, for her friends. She *could not* break down. Things needed done. They needed to find their parents and learn the truth. Everything would be okay if they could learn the truth.

Graylin was still thinking about the truth when she fell asleep, arms hugging herself, leaning against Teddy's wall.

Denloy sat at his desk, taking deep breaths. Going on this trip had been the right decision, he knew that now. Seeing his nieces today, watching them work and laugh and live, had filled him with such joy as he hadn't felt for nearly ten years. Arlyn . . . Arlyn was a wonder. She was bright, cheerful, and so strong. He could practically see her holding up the worries and emotions of the entire crew, and yet she just kept smiling and laughing. And she was smart, goodness was she smart. He'd watched her glance at the puffer design, and copy it instantly, and then understand the completely foreign button concept in mere minutes. Then of course there was Graylin, Graylin who was intelligent and . . . well, honestly, he knew little else about Graylin yet. She was guarded, and serious. But then again, Arlyn had said Graylin was like *him*, and hadn't he always been the most guarded brother? The one who stayed back and worried and tried to hold everything in? Perhaps Graylin was a bit like that, too.

Learning the truth about his brothers had nearly broken Denloy, and he had even been involved. He had seen it coming. If Arlyn and Graylin, now, were to discover what their parents had truly been doing . . . it would destroy them. He knew, beyond a shadow of a doubt, that he could not let them learn the truth.

Now Denloy's only question was how long he could wait before throwing his nieces toward the wrong trail. After Belhaven, at least. They had a few weeks before they reached the capital city, in which he could get to know the girls and their friends, and relive the life which he'd been certain he'd lost. Until Belhaven, he didn't need to worry. He would figure out how to hide the truth later.

Much like her cousin and uncle, Arlyn was not asleep. However, unlike the others Freely's, her mind was not concerned with the discoverance or disguising of truth. She was sitting in her room, sorting through a collection of old typewriter parts she'd found downstairs, organizing keyboards for each crewmember. The only issue? She didn't know how typewriters were supposed to be set up. So, she had started by marking out six alphabets, sorting the keys and their corresponding arm and letter stamps into piles, and then pulling one from each pile, resulting in roughly eight and a half piles of twenty-six letters. Unfortunately, there were ten message system stops which needed typewriters . . . so Arlyn decided to improvise, something she was, coincidentally, quite good at. First, she took away all but a few letters from River's pile, as he couldn't be trusted to say much. He got only enough letters to say the most basic of things, O and K. This gave Arlyn enough letters to finish Teddy's pilot chair keyboard, as well as the one for Enland's room.

However, she simply could not scrounge up enough keys to give the map room a full alphabet.

Sighing, Arlyn looked out her window. The rain was pounding against the glass, small drips running down the inside, and Arlyn smiled. It had been a good day. Their message system had been a success; Graylin had been semi-responsive to their uncle, and Denloy was fairly enjoyable. Like a more serious, slightly distant Leo. Or her father.

Arlyn rested her head on her desk and sighed again. Sighing was a delightful way to push out emotions, she had found, especially when the emotions were ones she didn't particularly want to address. For example, all the feelings associated with her parents, and their aliveness, and Leo and his death, and this journey they had, quite impulsively, thrown themselves into. High on her list of emotions were fear, excitement, and several others equally hard to deal with.

Good thing I've got something to distract me then, she thought, lifting her head and refocusing on the typewriter parts. The map room was the only one which still needed letters, and, honestly, there were none left. She'd already had to give Graylin and herself only capital letters out of necessity.

Perhaps, she thought suddenly, the map room didn't *need* letters. There were quite a few unused symbols she'd decided not to give everyone: semi-colons, commas, parenthesis, slashes and dashes, the little stars and squiggly lines. Maybe she could give the map room *these*, and Enland could use the typewriter to make maps with the symbols. The kitchen was right next to him anyway, so if something was urgent he could send a message through there.

Pleased with her problem solving abilities, Arlyn gathered all the symbols into a pile, pulling out a few to give herself. One never knew if one might need them.

Over the next week, as the *Freelander* flew across the Osden summer sky, the crew slowly settled into a routine of sorts. Every morning, Lewis would wake the crew up, starting with Enland, then Teddy, the girls, and then River, who, admittedly, was the least important when it came to moving the ship. As Lewis whipped up breakfast, one cousin would check the airship's mechanics (the generator, engine, tubing, fans, etc.) and the other would manage the fluid levels, such as the water tanks, gas levels, oil in the engines, and cooling fluid. Arlyn both relished in and needed routine, and loved having a set task in the morning. Conversely, Graylin despised it. In her mind, if she woke up at say 7:30, her chores would take her probably an hour, meaning she wouldn't be done until 8:30, which was practically 9:00, which was basically 10:00, and 10:00 was pretty much noon, in which case half of her day was already gone.

But, no matter how true this felt in Graylin's mind, the fact was that her tasks only took her an hour, after which the day would continue in a fairly regular fashion. Denloy would arrive for breakfast, everyone would eat, and Teddy would disappear upstairs. Usually around this time, River and Graylin would start arguing over something, often ending with Graylin being told off by Lewis and River nursing a fresh bruise. Irritated, Graylin would stalk upstairs and hide in the net hammock. Her thoughts would wander, landing often on Teddy despite her frustrated attempts to direct them elsewhere. She was not at all sure why their pilot had recently started stirring her sympathies, but she didn't not like it at all. So, her hammock musings would turn to the things about Teddy which she *didn't* like, as she hurriedly tried to convince herself that she was *not* growing soft, and she still had the ability to aimlessly dislike people. She would list off Teddy's shortcomings (a list which seemed to miraculously shorten every day, but always included shyness, boringness, sweetness, and goodness), and thinking about shortcomings would then remind her first of herself and then Denloy, whom she would stew on before turning to her parents. If Graylin could possibly have managed her mind, and controlled where it jumped to during its never ending thinking, she would have stayed as far away from the topic of her parental figures as possible.

Unfortunately for the rest of the crew she could not, and when she finally left the hammock for lunch, she was always in an irritable mood, thanks to her musings and the fact that she had wasted so much day on said musings.

As for Arlyn, she spent most of her day moving from crew member to crew member, teasing Enland, chatting with Lewis, and hanging out with River, who was often unemployed. After lunch, she and Graylin would wander the ship, trying to find the best way to encourage good ideas to hit them. Two weeks into the trip, they had tried everything from hanging upside down off the couch to drinking a whole jug of chocolate milk. The latter attempt had done little for the sparking of genius, but it *did* make Graylin feel terrible.

Thus flowed the days on the *Freelander*. The summer evenings were breezy and calm, and most nights Lewis dragged everyone to the top deck for dinner. As they sat down to eat at the end of the third week, Arlyn couldn't help but smile at the shining faces of her friends. Even Denloy looked happy, sitting next to Enland as the two discussed a map the cartographer had just made. Lewis had started a game of poker with Teddy and Graylin, but ducked out to bring up the food, leaving the two to finish their game, both oscillating from feeling awkward to laughing. Teddy would say something, Graylin would laugh and then feel awkward and stop, making Teddy self-conscious. Then it would wear away, and Graylin would say something, to which Teddy would *want* to laugh, but be too afraid of coming on too strong, and simply smile. Arlyn shook her head and grinned at River. Watching the two most socially awkward and opposite personality crewmembers try to interact with each other, and utterly fail, was very amusing.

"Well, thanks to Enland's masterful navigation and Theodore's skillful piloting," Denloy announced, "I think we'll reach Belhaven by tomorrow night." Wilmot Denloy had slowly gotten used to calling the crew members by their names, save Lewis, whom he still called Miss Maynewin out of habit.

"We should make a list of what we need to buy when we stop," Lewis said, placing a serving platter filled with roasted potatoes on the table. The inky sky glittered with stars as she sat down, tucking her apron around her skirt. "We need more flour, and some fresh stuff, fruits and vegetables and the like."

"We'll need gas too," Graylin said, laying down her hand. "Royal flush, Teddy. Eat it." Teddy made an extremely unsavory gesture, which made Graylin snort so hard, the water she'd been drinking came out of her nose.

"Ack cousin! Your nose juice!" Arlyn cried, throwing some napkins at her cousin.

"Speaking of water," Lewis said. "I wouldn't mind filling up the water tanks when we stop. Who knows when we'll land next?"

Arlyn, still wrinkling her nose at her cousin, spoke up. "I need a few more parts to finish up our typewriters."

"Can we get some gummies?" River asked, using his spoon to catapult a pea at Enland. "I want gummies."

"What sort?" Lewis asked, raising an eyebrow.

"I don't know, just some gummies. We'll stop at a general store or something, grab one of those little stripey bags," he said, ducking to avoid Enland's retaliation pea. Lewis gave Arlyn a 'what is with this guy' look, but shrugged anyway.

"Okay, *fine*, we'll get some gummies. Any other requests?"

"I'll stop and buy some new guitar strings," Teddy said quietly, smiling, playing his own hand. "Two pair."

"Curse you, Teddy," Graylin sighed, laying down a pair of fours. "You are the worst."

"Ah, I'm sorry," Teddy said, trying to hold back a smile and looking extremely uninnocent, "but you officially owe me your dessert for the next week."

Graylin pushed over her brownie with a sigh, mentally adding *insufferably good at poker* and *unfortunately funny* to her list of Teddy's faults.

"River," Lewis sighed, voice icy with disappointment. "Is that your *fifth* brownie?"

"What? They're good," River said defensively, dropping a shower of chocolate crumbs on the table.

"You are disgusting." Lewis shook her head.

"If anything, take it as a compliment that I like them so much," River said, reaching to grab a sixth. He set it next to his plate, reaching for his glass of water, and completely missing Teddy stealing the dessert from behind his back. River turned around, blinked at the space where his brownie had been, and shrugged before grabbing another, which Teddy also deftly stole. It took four times of this happening before the red-haired handyman grew suspicious.

"Alright, that's it. Who's taking my dessert?" He glared around the table. "Lewis? Enland? *Teddy*?"

"What are you looking at me for?" Teddy asked innocently, holding a half eaten and very stolen brownie in his hand. "I would never touch another man's brownie."

"I don't believe you," River replied, grabbing the final treat from the tray. "And once I figure out who's behind this, you'd best believe we're gonna have some problems."

"What're you gonna do, change some lightbulbs at us?" Graylin snorted, laying down her cards. "Oh, wait, you can't *reach* the lightbulbs."

"Listen here!" River set his final brownie down, far away from Teddy this time, and shoveled some potatoes into his mouth. Why his basic instinct was to fill his mouth every time he talked, Graylin would never know. "Not last week I changed all the light bulbs in the kitchen."

"Yeah, standing on the counter," Graylin rolled her eyes, just glimpsing her cousin as she stole River's final dessert.

"I am still growing!" River cried, reaching desperately for his brownie to relieve some stress, only to see one Arlyn Freely finishing it happily.

"You?!" River spluttered, quite speechless. Metaphorically, of course, River was never truly speechless. "I hate you all!" he cried.

The next day flew by in a flurry of movement as the crew collectively prepared for their first landing of the journey. Half way through the day, River and Graylin got into a spat over the correct pronunciation of 'peninsula', a fight which Lewis and Enland had had before and which had nearly broken their relationship. River and Graylin's argument was just as fiery, and Graylin was very close to tackling the boy to the ground before Arlyn intervened, dragging her cousin away to help her calculate just how much gas they needed to purchase while in Belhaven.

By the time the sun had set, the *Freelander* had traveled all the way to the southwestern coast of Osden. Glowing out of the darkness was Belhaven, capital city of Osden, and a hot-spot for people with three major interests; inventing, thieving, and betting. Luckily, the Freely cousins deeply enjoyed all of these things, and a little excitement and adventure, Arlyn thought, leaning eagerly on the railing as Teddy steered closer to the grid of lights below, was precisely what they needed.

"Well, dang," Graylin muttered, awestruck. The city, so far below, was bright and chaotic. A mixture of smoke and fog blanketed the towering buildings that rose from the water, connected by hanging bridges, docks, and wooden terraces. Graylin felt her stomach squirm with excitement. Leo had always promised to bring them here, when they were older. She knew Belhaven's reputation; smoke, lies and cheating. Not the charming, upright capital that one might imagine for a country such as Osden, but then, the government wasn't all that stable, and this was, after all, the home of the government. Wars were common, and every few years a new idiot trying to be a dictator in a democracy was elected, each worse than the last. Back home, the government didn't have much control, which was probably, Graylin thought, smirking, why things went so smoothly. But here, in the heart of it all, the cityscape reflected the decency of the country's leaders.

If River, looking on in moral uncertainty, had hoped that this quite iffy reputation would take away from the crew's excitement, he was sadly mistaken. Everyone, even Teddy, was practically hanging over the railing as the airship hung over the city.

Arlyn watched her cousin's eager face. Graylin's eyes were shining as they neared the city, and she was biting her lip. She turned and caught Arlyn staring and nodded, grinning.

"This, cousin, is gonna be awesome."

"You can say that again," Arlyn said.

"Would you look at that?" Teddy leaned over the railing, smiling. He motioned to Graylin, who looked vaguely surprised, but then beamed and examined whatever it was Teddy was so eager to show her. "It's the Treble Club," he said. "It's the most famous music venue in all of Osden." He was pointing down at a large building, seemingly just like any other flat or apartment around, save the large, lit sign above it. That, and the vast crowd gathered outside, and the hammering beat floating up to them.

"Oh, it's Race!" Teddy beamed.

"Race? Who's that?" asked River.

"Who? You think it's a person?" Graylin scoffed. "What kind of name would Race be?" She caught River's expression, and it suddenly struck her that Race wasn't all that different a name than River. "Oh, wait."

"No, it's not a person. It's a style, brand new. Race music," Teddy explained. "It's got guitars hooked up to these wooden amplifiers to make them louder, and pianos sometimes, lots of drums, and bass guitar. It's generally louder, and faster than most music hall stuff. Not so bouncy, either."

"It doesn't sound very much like music. Not any I've heard, at least," Enland said, just stiff enough to signify that he didn't like what he was hearing.

"Well that's the point, isn't it? Race is *about* different. It didn't develop among the rich and well-to-do, like most music. It started with the rebels, the bar-goers and alley-dwellers. It's not easy to play either." Teddy was tapping his foot, still standing very close to Graylin. She, oddly, didn't seem to mind.

"See? I knew this was a good idea," Arlyn muttered to Lewis. "We haven't even landed yet, and look how good Graylin's behaving."

"You make her sound like a naughty child," Lewis murmured back with a smile.

"Isn't she?" The two glanced at Graylin, who was trying to hide her smile as Teddy and River danced wild circles around Enland. They looked at each other and grinned. They were *all* children.

"Out of all the people on board that Teddy decides to team up with-" Arlyn said, shaking her head. "Graylin?"

"Well, he's always had a soft spot for her, you know that," Lewis said, smiling happily.

"What? No, I very well don't know that," Arlyn shot back, indignant.

"Well, it's obvious Teddy adores her."

"But why *Graylin*?" Arlyn asked, scratching her head. "I mean, why not you?" Lewis shrugged and smiled.

"It's not like *you* need any more wanna-be lovers, anyway," Lewis said slyly. Arlyn smacked her on the arm.

"Shut up."

The ship was brought down quickly, the wood creaking as it settled against the brick streets. Graylin pulled on her favorite waistcoat, Lewis re-did her bun, and both cousins filled their pockets with fiddly items before the six crew members dropped to the street.

It was magnificent. There was no other word which could sum up the sight before the crew so well. Magnificent. The street stretched out before them with huge brick buildings lining the planked and cobbled streets, signs and lamps lighting the way, smoke and steam swirling everywhere. Overhead, long swinging bridges connected the upper level of the city, buildings built up multiple levels. Between some of the highest houses were small balloons with baskets, transportation through the airy streets above. Bright colors swirled in every direction, shining from over windows and on signs. There was no end to the sights to see or sounds to hear, and the cousins just stood in the street, breathing in the newness of this never ending world.

"Dang," Teddy muttered.

"Cool," Enland said, his usual monotone lit with enthrallment.

"Brilliant," River beamed.

"Alright, we need a game plan," Arlyn announced, hopping onto a nearby crate to gain the higher ground. "Lewis, our supply list, if you please?"

Their cook read off what they needed to buy in her crisp, clear voice, as Arlyn nodded along.

"Right then, let's split into groups and buy everything, and we'll tackle the whole 'figure out where our parents are' thing after. Deal?" she asked, hands on hips. Everyone nodded their approval. "Lewis and Enland, you grab the food and water we need. Graylin and Teddy, you guys get Teddy's guitar strings at that music club because honestly I don't trust you to do anything else."

"Right. Sounds good to me," Graylin said, lying to her cousin's face. Chatting with Teddy by the fire, playing poker over the dinner table, those were all manageable situations and interactions, ones where she could run to her cousin if needed. But wandering an enormous city, when she was already prone to losing herself and others, with only a boy whom she didn't know and spoke even less than she did? With *Teddy*, who was funny and intelligent and rebellious, and opened up the chasm of fear and insecurity in her chest faster than anyone else ever had? No, that did not sound even remotely like a situation she wanted to be in.

"Yeah, that'd be good," was how Graylin followed up.

"Lovely. That leaves River, Uncle Denloy, and me to get the gas. Ready?" Arlyn glanced around the group, returned everyone's nods, and clapped. "Okay, break."

17

"C'MON, IT'S THIS WAY," Teddy motioned for Graylin to follow before sticking his hands in his pockets and ducking his head. Graylin wanted to disappear, which in friendly group settings was a specialty of hers. She was the one who dropped behind when the path wasn't wide enough. She was the one who remained silent, just listening, as her friends chatted and smiled. She was the one who, when spotted, people remarked on how they'd forgotten she was there. That's what she was, she thought. Entirely unwanted, irritating, and forgotten.

Was that what had happened with her parents? Was that the real reason they hadn't returned after the disaster yo become a family again? Maybe they had forgotten her, or decided coming back just wasn't worth it. Perhaps they *had* remembered their eight-year-old daughter, remembered, indeed, the tears and the whining and the coldness and the harsh words. The idea that she had been forgotten and rejected by not only Denloy (and Leo, in a way) but also her parents was scary. More than scary, it was heartbreaking.

As the two crew mates hurried through the summer night towards the music club, that deep, unforgiving pit inside Graylin opened again. *Boy oh boy do I suck*, she thought, staring at the ground, trying to laugh off the words like her cousin might. But Graylin Freely was much more sensitive to criticism than her cousin, from others or herself. Another fault, she thought. Graylin suddenly had the urge to run away, or better yet, grab a blanket, wrap up in it, and sit in a corner. She wanted to hide, to surround herself with stuff until none of her could be seen. She wanted all the eyes off her, all the sounds to go away.

"Are you okay?" Teddy asked quietly. Graylin had stopped, and was blinking, trying to block out the sound for just a second. This was a bit of an odd approach, as one doesn't actually hear through one's eyes, but the brief darkness did help. At least, it was enough that she could compose herself, lest she become a burden to Teddy too. The two weren't even friends; she couldn't let him see her weakness, her forgetability.

"I'm fine," she said, smiling and giving him a thumbs up. A wave of heat rolled over her, and she tried to keep her breathing calm. *Come on, don't embarrass yourself. Do you want Teddy to dislike you, too?*

"I think we're almost there," Teddy said, giving her a small smile himself. A forced smile, Graylin thought. Like the one she was giving him. *Well great, you've already annoyed him.*

Turning away from everything wrong with herself, Graylin tried to focus on the city around them. It was a bit overwhelming, considering her current less-than-satisfactory mental state, but the more they walked, the further they moved from the towering buildings and bright lights of the main city. The streets narrowed, the buildings becoming skinnier and more rundown. The bouncing show music she'd heard before, filled with horns and dinging sounds, had disappeared, shifting into beats which were strong and fast and fun.

The building in front of them seemed to be the source of this music. It had at least four stories, with bridges and lights and signs hanging all over. Bright, circular bulbs encircled the sign that read "TREBLE CLUB", the light dancing over the heads of the crowd. The noise coming from it was phenomenal; how the band could hear themselves playing was a mystery to Graylin. The crowds inside were screaming and cheering, throwing bottles and whooping. Graylin could tell that she would normally love the place.

Graylin expected Teddy to rush to the center of the crowd, he had seemed so excited on the *Freelander*. But he just skulked at the edge, looking vaguely nervous, and staring at the performers. How unfortunate, her presence had ruined even Teddy's enjoyment.

There were four of them on the stage, all dressed in suits in a slight state of disarray, whether it was cuffed pants or a loose tie or an unbuttoned jacket. There was a man playing a huge upright piano, with words painted on the side facing the crowd. His hands were bouncing and sliding up and down the keys.

Next to him, another man with very long hair held in a ponytail was sitting, surrounded by what looked like barrels made of metal, cloth stretched over the top, two wooden sticks held in his hands. Graylin had never seen these before, but the sound coming from them could be felt inside her, in her chest and feet.

Then there were two more musicians, more towards the front, both holding what appeared to be guitars. Only, these seemed different to Teddy's guitar. They were slimmer, and lacked the hole that his had. In addition, one of the men's guitars had only four strings, which he was hitting one by one with the pads of his fingers. Emerging from the base of both instruments was a long, slender metal tube that ran into large wooden boxes open at the front. Graylin opened her mouth, and turned to ask Teddy what they were when she noticed the expression on his face. He was watching the stage still, but he looked miserable. Her question forgotten, Graylin just watched him. She felt like there were too many loose ends in her mind at the moment, and she couldn't tell what was supposed to be tied where, and it was messing with her emotions.

One string was still pulled tight with pain at the loss of her uncle, another twisted with a sense of being lost without his guiding reprimands. How she had hated being told off, but now, with no one to take the responsibility, she was starting to feel overwhelmed. Then there was a string, the one that had despised Teddy and his quiet perfection-it had been cut, which made her feel decidedly uncertain. In all honesty, that particular string had begun to weaken long ago, only she just noticed now. Even more confusing was the string that *enjoyed* Teddy, just starting to unravel. All she knew for certain was she felt intensely uncomfortable, like she just wanted to crawl out of her skin and run away. Teddy, coincidentally, was feeling precisely the same for slightly different reasons.

With the sharp movement of someone desperately regretting their motions, Teddy reached at out and tapped her arm, his skin seemingly as shocked at the contact as Graylin was.

"I'm going to get some air. I'll be back soon," he muttered, melting into the raucous crowd. Graylin hovered, torn between her options. Should she follow Teddy, whom she knew and felt awkward near, or should she stay in the bar, leaving Teddy well alone as she slowly descended into panicked madness? It truly was a difficult decision, which was why Graylin was genuinely surprised to find herself at the back door, pushing out and stepping into the alley. The brick corridor was dark and cold, and Graylin could hardly see Teddy in the shadows.

"Thought I'd join you," Graylin said, voice a little gruff. She felt distant, as if watching the alley from above, seeing herself shove her hands in her pockets and Teddy fiddle with his hair.

"Oh, yeah," Teddy nodded, one hand pressed to the opposite wall. Graylin was quite chagrined to realize she was doing the same on her side, letting the coolness course over her sweaty palms. Teddy sighed and looked to the street. "I feel like I need to apologize for bringing you here," he said quietly, avoiding her eyes.

"What, is it a trap? Are you selling me to someone?" Graylin asked dully, trying to ignore the tight tugging of the strings. They were distracting, those strings, like a nagging headache that wouldn't go away, or a thought that kept resurfacing.

Teddy shook his head.

"What? No, no, nothing like that. I just want you to know that . . . I feel like I'm pushing my friendship on you, and that you don't want it. And I hate that feeling."

Graylin wasn't spectating now. Every sensation was loud, like the way her heart was pounding in her throat, and the scraps of newspaper rustling in the alley breeze, and the vibrating brick wall shaking with the beat of the music inside. She noticed a strand of Teddy's dark, wavy hair which had fallen from its place, and the little bob his neck made as he swallowed, and the way he hesitated as if trying to decide to speak or not. He did speak, eventually, glancing up.

"I can't shake the idea that I'm being annoying by showing you stuff and asking you places," he said quietly. "It won't hurt my feelings, or anything, if you don't want to be, you know, friends. I just want to know the truth." He was trying to maintain eye contact with Graylin, but seemed to be having a hard time. He kept glancing away, touching his hair, putting his hands in his pockets, and then repeating the cycle. Graylin felt stunned. What in the world was this?

"You think . . . you feel . . . unwanted?" Graylin was trying to grapple with the fact that the sweet boy in front of her was experiencing dramatic teenage girl emotions. Not only that, but *her* dramatic teenage girl emotions. The very ones that had been singing the tips of all those loose ends in her head. *Unwanted*. First by her parents, who had pretended to die rather than raise her. Then Denloy, who hadn't cared if she survived enough to be on the *Freelander* the day it crashed. And then there was Leo, her last hope, her beloved uncle and friend, who had abandoned her to death.

"Well, yeah," Teddy said, cheeks flaring red.

"That's ridiculous Teddy. *Ridiculous*," she said the words in the nicest way she could. "Why *wouldn't* I want to be friends with you?"

"You used to hate me," he said.

"Intensely disliked," Graylin corrected.

"Is there a difference?"

"No, but one makes me sound better."

"Right." There was a long stretch of silence, and Graylin was getting the feeling that she wasn't handling this very well.

"Listen, Teddy-"

"No, uh, nevermind," Teddy's eyes refused to meet hers, and his cheeks and ears were glowing with embarrassment. "Yeah, I think I'll . . . actually, oh great I can't . . . nevermind, forget what I just said . . ." Graylin looked over her shoulder to make sure her cousin wasn't secretly spying on her, and then stepped forward . . . and gave Teddy a hug. She didn't hug, not ever. She didn't hug Leo, or Lily, or Arlyn, or anyone, if she could help it. But her words weren't working at the moment, and she had to do *something*.

Teddy stopped mid-sentence. He sort of stiffened, surprised.

"What are you doing?" he whispered.

"I'm hugging you," Graylin whispered back.

"But-"

"Teddy, stop talking now, or I'm gonna start crying," Graylin spoke very quickly, voice still hushed.

"Okay," Teddy said. Then he seemed to relax, leaning his head down on top of hers, breathing deep, and hugging her tight. Graylin hadn't realized that hugging someone could feel so . . . right? Healing? Like a thousand words couldn't have conveyed what they did through an embrace. Like a thousand little strings, vibrating with Teddy, had unwound themselves and wrapped around the two struggling-not-to-cry crewmates.

"Teddy, I know how that feels," Graylin said, stepping back, hoping that her common sense wouldn't return before she finished talking. The chasm would open soon, she could feel it, and she needed to get her thoughts out before that happened. "I know what it's like to feel like an extra. To feel like someday you'll just be forgotten, because no one really cared if you were there in the first place. To be afraid that you're unwanted. To feel like you are so . . . so ugly, so out of place, so weird and rude and awkward and twisted that you can't *possibly* be wanted."

Teddy was watching her, as if reading her mind. His face was drawn into an expression of pure pity. Weren't these feelings the reason she always was so protective of her cousin? Because, whether she wanted to admit it or not, Arlyn had always been the only one that Graylin trusted really wanted her.

"I never knew you thought that," Teddy said quietly. Graylin shrugged.

"I never knew *you* thought that," she said. What an odd interaction; first Teddy said he thought he was unwanted, and then Graylin decided to tell him all her secrets? Why was she here?

Because, Graylin heard a revolutionary voice in her head say, *Teddy needs you. At this moment, he needs Graylin to be Graylin.* And just like that, those loose ends that had been driving her mad started healing. The one that despised Teddy disappeared, and in its place, the ones that felt a strong kinship with the musician-turned-pilot tied itself up. Sealed. They were here to stay.

The ones that were spewing uncertainty and loneliness melted away, and the ones that tied her to her friends, yes, her friends, and cousin, strengthened. She didn't feel lost anymore- how could she? She had five good friends telling her where to go, and when they needed her, she would help. Like now. It was like her head had suddenly cleared. She knew what to do. Teddy, her friend, the boy who seemed to enjoy her despite her many faults, and whom she was realizing she enjoyed just as much, needed her help believing it.

"You *are* important, and wanted, and funny, and, and *wild*, and . . ." Graylin was searching for the right words. "And *amazing*. Pretty damn amazing." She wasn't entirely sure what to do with her hands, so she just wiggled her fingers together as Teddy brought his head up. Graylin looked him straight in the eye as he raised his gaze. "And you matter to me. You are *my* friend."

"You're sure?" Teddy asked hesitantly.

"Positive."

"You're not just saying it to make me feel better?"

"Am I really the sort of person who would do that?" Graylin asked, swinging the club door open. Teddy began to smile.

"No, I don't think you are." He moved past her to re-enter, but she stuck out an arm.

"One thing. We're not telling the crew about any of this, you hear me? If Arlyn learns I hugged you, I won't have a moment of peace for months." Teddy smiled even wider, a dimple tugging at his cheek.

"I wouldn't dare," he said. "Thank you."

"You are very welcome," Graylin nodded to him, feeling oddly light and comfortable.

"Ready to head back inside?" Teddy asked. Graylin smiled.

"After you."

Far down the street, Arlyn and River were confronted with a problem.

"I think we should go right," Arlyn said, folding her arms and looking toward the collection of fascinating shops tugging at her fancy.

"But the right is so dark and creepy. I think we should go left," River said, turning to look at the brightly lit square opposite the street.

"You know what they say, River- right is right," Arlyn raised her eyebrows.

"I've never heard anyone say that." River shook his head.

"It's a *very* common saying. A proverb. A word of wisdom, passed down for generations. Right is right, everyone knows that," Arlyn grinned.

"Well, what about 'left is best'? Ever heard that one?" River asked.

"Of course I haven't. That saying is peddled by liars and con men," Arlyn insisted, while Denloy shook his head. He'd been listening to the two argue for ten minutes, all the time thinking it was only a matter of time before they gave up and noticed the very obvious gasoline salesman directly in front of them. So far, the teens had entirely failed to meet his expectations.

"Come on," he said finally, tapping Arlyn's arm and grabbing River's shirt collar. "It's just up ahead."

"See? I told you," River muttered as he was dragged away.

"What? No, I told *you*," Arlyn argued.

"'Right is right' you said," River whispered. "The things straight up ahead!"

"Would you two stop?" Denloy sighed. He was beginning to wonder how his younger brother had stayed sane raising the Freely cousins and their friends for so many years. "We need this salesman to see three responsible, calm, collected individuals who he will feel obliged to sell gasoline to for a reasonable price."

"See? Calm," River said, pushing Arlyn away. She rolled her eyes.

"Personally, I don't think this guy really values responsible, collected buyers," she said, gesturing to the man they were approaching. The salesman had a very round, bald head, a very round, aproned belly, and a single eyebrow. It wasn't a unibrow, no, he simply had an eyebrow over his left eye, and no eyebrow over the right. It was an odd look, especially because his entire left arm was covered in tattoos. It gave the impression that someone had taken an eraser and just wiped off everything extra on his right side.

"I realize you don't trust me," Denloy smiled, "but I am a businessman. I know what people look for in a buyer."

Arlyn paused.

"I trust you," she said quietly. Her uncle, looking perhaps more like Leo than ever before, glanced at her.

"You do?" he asked softly.

"Of course I do," Arlyn told him. Denloy smiled, his stomach twisting just a little.

"Then I admire your optimism and trusting nature. I wouldn't trust me so soon," he said.

"Well, you are a jaded old man," Arlyn waved her hand. "I doubt you trust anybody."

She's right, Denloy thought. He didn't trust people anymore than a certain blonde-curled, bright-eyed niece of his.

"Old man?" he asked Arlyn as River approached the salesman's counter. "I'm not old."

"Well, comparatively . . ." Arlyn grinned. "Let's just say you add quite a few numbers to the average age of our crew."

The one eyebrowed man sold them the desired gas quite happily, and while the prices shocked Arlyn's cheapskate soul, Denloy assured her that they were only being *slightly* swindled. Besides, the salesman had agreed to help them wheel the huge metal barrels full of gasoline to the *Freelander*, where they would pump it into the tanks. This task was slow, sweaty, and repetitive, as they had to make multiple trips from shop to ship to fill the tanks to the brim. Needless to say, by the end of the venture Arlyn Freely was eager to explore Belhaven and forget about gas completely.

She waited while River stretched a muscle he'd pulled, and used the time to truly take in the surrounding city. Her eyes followed the bright tubes of lights lining the buildings around her, tracing the outlines of strangely shaped buildings that looked like something right out of a fantasy.

Puddles colored by the bright lights swirled and splashed as feet ran through them on the cobbled streets. All the feet crowded to the edge of the road as one of the most beautiful contraptions Arlyn had ever seen whizzed past. A bright, windowed box of colored tin and wood, its edges lined with those same colorful lights. It cruised down the street on a set of inlaid tracks, above which was a thick cable that ran down the entire street. The tin box had a long rod extending from its rear which clasped around the wire, powering the whole contraption. As soon as the first one had disappeared down a different street, another came by, stopping a short distance away from them. People began piling off the giant machine, some who had been hanging on to the poles that lined the outside. Arlyn, jaw dropping, looked back at Denloy and River, just to make sure they were seeing the same sight.

"What *is* that thing?" River asked, eyes wide.

Denloy chuckled. "Oh, that's right, you two have probably never seen a cable car before."

"I need on it. Immediately." Arlyn grabbed River's hand, starting for the neon wonder before stopping to look at Denloy. "You coming?"

Denloy looked at the two children in front of him. They were truly ready to just tear off into a city they didn't know without a care in the world. It was terrifying. He shook his head and smiled. "I suppose someone has to keep you out of trouble."

The three hopped on the colorful car, Arlyn and River taking two poles on the side, while Denloy took the seat between them. Once the car was full, the operator clicked a stick into place and it began to glide along the tracks. As it got to speed, Arlyn kept one hand on the pole and one foot on the floor before swinging the rest of herself out into the rushing air. The streets and crowds whizzed past them as the cable car buzzed through the city. For the first time in a long time, Arlyn felt small, but in a purely freeing way, small and filled with wonder. The city was enormous around her, and she wanted to see every last bit of it.

Denloy watched as the two teenagers excitedly pointed out everything that passed them on the cable car, their eyes shining with every color imaginable. To them it was a spectacle, brand new and shiny and fascinating in every way. He tried to remember the last time Belhaven had felt like that to him. Too many business trips, hours of investors, and recognizing his brothers' trademark on everything around him had spoiled it. Everywhere he looked he saw another building that he'd held a meeting in, another face he vaguely recognized, another alley to get robbed in. He sighed at the thought. *What sort of stuck-up rich fool have I become?*

He looked up to find the car slowing down. He recognized this part of town, and he had an idea. "This is our stop," he told the pair, who leapt off before the car had stopped moving. He followed them (once it was safe) and tipped the driver. The cable cars were free, but it was nice to tip when you could.

"Follow me, you two," Denloy led them through a maze of streets. The alleyways glowed with bright lights and colorful drawings. Down one, a young man stood on an older woman's shoulders, his hand around what looked like a can of sprayable paint. In short blasts of color, he put the finishing touches on a mosaic-like mural depicting a circle of children holding hands and dancing in a circle.

"That's beautiful!" Arlyn said, already detoured into the alley, gazing up at the painting in awe.

"Why, thank you!" The young artist winked down at them.

"Why draw it in a back alley though?" River asked. "Seems like not many people will see it all the way back here."

"Well, it's not exactly city commissioned," the painter admitted, leaping down from the woman's shoulders. "Gotta keep it out of the eyes of city council members. The law's good about it though. Belhaven could always use a little brightening."

"You know, that Ashton De Saturnius fellow is working to get it legalized," the woman said, ruffling the man's hair.

"De Saturnius?" Denloy asked. "He's a friend of mine. He was behind that lovely mural on City Hall."

The gleeful glances exchanged between the two artists told Arlyn the mural was *also* not city commissioned.

"And you're the one who got it framed, weren't you?" The young man stuck out a multicolored hand. "I thought I recognized you. It's a pleasure, Mr. Denloy."

Denloy awkwardly shook the man's hand. "Really, I can't take the credit. It was Ashton who funded the painting, after all. I just framed it."

"And made sure it stayed up," the woman chuckled. "*And* 'anonymously' gathered the funds to save the university's art program."

"Well, I *tried* to be anonymous," Denloy stumbled over his words. He glanced at Arlyn, nervous she would recognize this new information for what it really was, his attempts to cure his own guilt by giving away money. "Just didn't try hard enough, apparently," he said, looking away from his niece. "But it really wasn't about me. Ashton has been a good friend to me. I couldn't just let his program fall apart or his art be demolished."

"So when you, Mr. Denloy, saved De Saturnius's youth program, you were just helping him out as a bud? What about when you saved my neighborhood from being demolished?" The man folded his arms.

"It was purely out of personal interest," Denloy said quickly. "Really, it was. Ashton just called in a favor. The neighborhood was worthless- I had no other reason to save it." *Please, Arlyn*, he mentally begged, *don't smell the blood money. Believe me. Don't sense my guilt.*

The artists burst into laughter, which startled Denloy out of his thoughts. "You don't have to guard your words so closely," the woman set a kind hand on his shoulder. "There's no cops around here, kid."

"I wondered whose idea that was," the young man chuckled. He then looked to River and Arlyn. "So are *you* running a youth program now too, or are these ones yours?"

Arlyn answered for him. "Close enough! I'm Arlyn, his niece, and . . ." she glanced at River. She had never actually considered their relational status, the boys being 'lawfully' adopted and all. "Would you technically be his nephew?"

"Let's just say I am," River shrugged. "I'm River, by the way."

"Uncle Will is showing us around Belhaven, we've never been here before," Arlyn beamed. "What's all here to see, anyway?"

The two artists listed the top spots in the city, but Denloy couldn't hear them. He was stuck on Arlyn's words. How quickly she had said them. *I'm his niece. Uncle Will.* She said them as if she had done so every day for her entire life. No hesitation at all. A second realization hit him just as quickly. She had meant them. He had become well-versed in picking up people's demeanor. He had seen Arlyn lie before, like at the party when she had pretended everything was normal. When she lied, she spoke slowly. Confidently but intentionally leaving gaps in her speech to allow outside input, she workshopped her every word. She was an excellent liar.

I'm Arlyn, his niece. That had not been a lie.

He snapped back into reality just as his niece and apparent nephew (*that* was a question for later) said their goodbyes to the artists and continued down the alley, glancing back every few seconds to check that he was still there. "Come on, Uncle Will!" River said brightly, his voice cracking in the way a teenage boy's voice does. "We've got lots of places to see!"

Will Freely answered his nephew's call. "First," he smiled, watching Arlyn's bright eyes shining, "I have something to show you."

The man sighed, leaning back in his chair and stretching his aching back. His blond beard, short and gruff, was like sandpaper against his hand as he rubbed his chin in thought.

"Is it going well?"

A woman, brown curls tugged back away from her freckled face, approached, resting a hand on the man's head and planting a kiss in his hair.

"Well enough." The man glanced up at his wife, his smile fading as he caught the direction her eyes were looking.

"Stop," he said gently, reaching out and tipping down the photograph her gaze was locked on. "It does no good."

"It reminds us what we've sacrificed." His wife's voice was soft and sad. He nodded.

"And why we have to keep going," he said.

18

"This," Denloy declared, spreading his arms wide, "Is Belhaven's Inventor's Bazaar."

It had been a short walk to their destination, and now the three were standing in front of a huge open air market. It sprawled out in every direction, including up. In fact, the more Arlyn looked, the more she realized that *most* of the market was above them, stands held up by balloons or poles, and connected with stairs, bridges, and ladders.

"A whole market, just for inventors?" Arlyn asked in awe.

"That's right," Denloy smiled. There were so many memories stored among the bridges and lights above them. Some good, some bad, but none equal to the joy his niece was showing. "I thought you might like it, and you could buy the rest of the parts for the typewriters."

"That is a *great* idea!" Arlyn called, already halfway up a ladder. "I hope you have money on you!"

Denloy smiled and nodded. He did, and for once he was glad of it.

"Ohhhhhh," Arlyn giggled, nearly tap-dancing on a platform as Denloy and River climbed off the ladder. "This is so epic." Arlyn took River's hand and dragged him over a bridge, aiming for a stand which seemed to sell random junk. Arlyn rarely had as tough a time with her inner clock as her cousin might, but that night, hurrying from stall to stall, she could not have said how long they were in the market for the life of her. Everywhere she turned was a new wonder, a new distraction, a new stand selling something she had never seen before. It wasn't long before the three were laden with cloth bags, holding not only the required typewriter parts but also several other random items including chains made of a new metal alloy, a cool glove that was completely heatproof, several pairs of welding goggles, and leather pouch full of delicate metal hair clips shaped like stars.

"These are *so cool*," Arlyn beamed, holding up both her braids which were now fully bedecked with astronomical bodies. "I might need to go back and buy more- wait, what's that?"

Denloy gave River a laughing look, which he returned with a wink, mostly because they'd been dealing with this particularly distractible version of Arlyn for the last two hours.

The stand which had so recently caught the young Freely's attention was one of the large ones, held up with cloth balloons much like the *Freelander's*. Not only was the circular stand lined with orange and yellow neon tubes, it also seemed to sell them.

"Uncle Will!" Arlyn bounced, waving her arms. "Imagine how cool that stuff will look running along our message lines!"

"It certainly would be a statement," Denloy chuckled. River laughed.

"Excuse me," Arlyn began, bounding up to the stand, three bags swinging from her arm along with her satchel. "Excuse me, but how much would it be for fifteen feet of this stuff?" She touched some lengths of clear glass tubing. The salesman raised a bushy eyebrow at her, setting down a beautiful mechanical butterfly. The man had a gray beard that almost touched the table he was selling from, and his kind eyes were circled by copper-rimmed glasses, though one lens was cracked.

"Well hello little missy," the bearded man said. "Fifteen feet, you say? I can get you a deal, 20 for . . . for . . ." The salesman's eyes had drifted up, landing on Denloy as he walked up. The fellow didn't come across as an overly expressive person, so when his bushy eyebrows shot up and his hand came to scratch his beard, Arlyn knew she was seeing genuine shock. She spun around and saw a similar emotion etched onto her uncle's face.

"I . . . I'm sorry, miss." The man cleared his throat and shook his head. "Ahem, I just thought I saw someone." He turned around and rummaged in a bucket of tubing. "Now, for twenty feet it would be about ten bucks, neon included, plus if a free-"

"Ridge?" Denloy had stepped to the counter, still staring at the salesman. "Ridge Duncan?"

The bearded man straightened.

"Yeah, that's right," he said, wiping his glasses.

"It's me," Denloy said, searching Ridge Duncan's face. "It's Will Freely."

Ridge went a little pale behind his beard. He blinked and shook his head, a small chuckle in his throat.

"No, no, see, Will Freely died years ago."

"I didn't," Denloy said quietly.

"Um, not to interrupt or anything," Arlyn butted in, very much interrupting, "but if you two are just gonna keep staring at each other without explanation, River and I are gonna head out."

"I'm sorry Arlyn," Denloy shook his head, beginning to smile. "This is Ridge Duncan. He was a great friend to your dads and I." Denloy watched as Ridge's eyes traveled to his niece, smiling all the while. *Ridge doesn't know much*, he reminded himself. *Nothing I couldn't explain away, at least. Arlyn is safe.*

"Arlyn Freely?" Ridge was saying, hurrying out of the stand, clutching Arlyn and Denloy into a huge bear hug. "I don't understand at all how you survived, but I'm so glad you did."

"Am I related to you?" Arlyn asked tightly, lungs ever so slightly crushed.

"No no . . . well . . . no. My daughter dated one of your uncles for a bit, but it never came to anything."

"Sick," Arlyn nodded. Ridge smiled at the two Freelys, entirely ignoring River, who really didn't mind because he was thinking about how many legs butterflies had. Six seemed excessive, considering they spent most of their time flying. Here he was, walking all his life, and he only had two. It hardly seemed fair.

"Wait a second," Ridge cried, spreading his arms wide. "What am I doing? We need to get you home! You have to meet Loren, and Della-Oh, she'll be thrilled to see you, William."

"I'm afraid it's not William anymore," Denloy said kindly, but looking away all the same. *Don't make the connection*, he begged Ridge in his mind. *Please don't understand why I had to change my name.*

"Will, then? Willy?" Ridge asked with a grin, stepping back.

"Wilmot. Wilmot Denloy," the businessman said. Ridge stood the same, but a curtain seemed to fall over him for just a second as he tilted up his head.

"Ah," he said. "I see." His eyes scanned Denloy before brightening again. "Well come on, what's all this standing around about?" He said with a laugh, reaching behind the counter of his shop. He pulled out the case of neon supplies he'd packed for Arlyn and stuffed a jar of money and a coat inside before pulling a string which let down curtains around the whole stall.

"What are we waiting for? Follow me!"

This, Graylin thought, *is very nice*. She and Teddy had stayed at the club for several more acts, each just as good as the last, until about 10:00, when all the bands became so intoxicated that their playing was no longer good. The music got increasingly discordant, until a boy who said his name was Donald tried to play a whole song with only a tambourine before being booed off the stage. At one point not long after, a fellow with long hair just started screaming into the microphone, and this the two crewmates took as their cue to leave.

Excluding the random shrieking, those few hours after their conversation would stick with Graylin as some of the best ever. Watching the musicians, standing next to Teddy, surrounded by the noise and the lights and the music, Graylin had been filled with adrenaline, grinning and cheering along with the crowd. Even better, she had felt comfortable in her own skin, despite the scores of eyes around her. Suffice to say, she understood now what Teddy loved about music, or at the very least his kind. It was wild, and sounded nice, and filled her with excitement and other emotions she couldn't quite pin down. Much like Teddy.

And now they sat together, on the roof of a building which also served as a stop on the boardwalk. Various strands of music, some soft and slow, some jazzy and bouncing, some loud and quick, all mingled in the air, twisting and braiding with the sounds of the city. Somewhere close by, a street car beeped its warning, and several men shouted. *Yes*, Graylin thought again. *This is very nice indeed.* Not only was the breeze nice, and the glittering of stars and lights nice, but Teddy was nice. Teddy *looked* nice, too. Graylin supposed he'd always had a dimple when he smiled, and bright shadowed eyes with wildness in them, and she simply hadn't noticed. But then again, that wasn't a huge surprise-over the last seven years, it seemed she hadn't noticed most of Teddy.

It was just then that Graylin was, not for the first time, eternally grateful that no one could hear her thoughts, but pushed such nonsense away anyhow. Arlyn tended to know what she was thinking, and these fantastical, poetic, embarrassing ideas she was having about Teddy were not thoughts she wanted her cousin to pick up on. Or anyone, for that matter.

"So, what did you think?" Teddy asked, kicking his feet into the empty air around the building.

"I think that you belong in those sorts of places," Graylin said, grinning. "And that I know why you like music so much now."

"You liked it?" He smiled.

"I loved it," she said emphatically, before glancing sidelong at the boy. "You should play for us sometime, or sing at least. I heard you humming along."

"Ah," Teddy looked out at the city. "No, no, I don't think that's a very good idea."

"It sounded good," Graylin told him earnestly.

"Shut up," he scoffed, pushing back some hair, but smiling all the same.

"Want to race to that sign down there?" Graylin asked.

"You're on," Teddy grinned.

"I seriously love these stars," Arlyn mused, admiring her braid as the four people made a trek away from the floating market.

"I like mine, too," River said, brushing the one Arlyn had let him pin in his hair, but which had totally been lost in the orange spiky mess which was his 'do'. "Now it's like a game, trying to find it." He rummaged around in his hair while Arlyn shook her head.

"Okay, but these bridges, man? Top tier awesome," she looked around. They were following Ridge across a hanging bridge, lit by little lights, which swung slightly. Above and below them hung dozens of more bridges, some straight and unbending, some loose. "It's like that hidden highway or whatever that Graylin loves so much back home, except better. You know that path through all those abandoned buildings?"

"Oh, yeah!" River skipped ahead. "It *is* like that."

"Can you believe all this?" Arlyn grinned, leaning over the edge of the bridge. The one they were on inclined upward steeply, and she could see stretches of brightly lit Belhaven blocks beneath them.

"That we randomly ran into a guy who knew your family?" River asked, glancing up at Ridge, talking animatedly to Denloy, who was responding with equal excitement. Arlyn was glad her uncle genuinely seemed to be happy to see Ridge. He was due for a bit of happiness.

"I mean, I guess that's pretty cool," Arlyn nodded, "but I was talking about *this*." Arlyn spread her arms out, looking down at the lines of lights beneath them, then the bridges around them, some stretching from balcony to balcony, other tilting all the way to the ground. Privately, she thought that there was *no way* any of this was up to code, but that did nothing to diminish her enthusiasm. "Belhaven! It's incredible!"

"And huge," River pointed out. "Speaking of which, don't you think we should try to find everyone else before we follow this guy to his house? They'll never find us, and let's not forget that Teddy and Graylin are alone out there."

"They'll be fine," Arlyn waved her hand and hopped across a sizable gap in the bridge (this one tilting down) where a board was missing. "At this point, one of three things has happened. Either they've fallen in love, they've killed each other, or they've been arrested. There's really no saying which."

"Funny that arrest is our best option." River grinned.

"And the most likely." Arlyn winked back. It was good to have some River time again. "Now come on, let's catch up before Denloy starts making jokes or something. Hopefully he doesn't have Leo's bad jokes gene."

"Well, since you have it too, I imagine it's hereditary," River teased.

Graylin tripped, the toes of her boots catching as she leapt to her feet. She was a devoted fan of races and figured beating Teddy in one would be a magnificent way to begin their new friendship. She sped for some stairs, almost tripping as she flew down them, just to see that Teddy had slid down a drainpipe. He dare use her fear of heights against her? Well, now Graylin *had* to win. She splashed in a puddle, the ripples disturbing the reflection of electric street lights, bright flames, and words made of neon lettering. The whole street was a scene of chaos, and would have been even if Graylin hadn't been running like a lunatic. She leapt to the cobblestones, and slipped between a fat man with an equally fat cigar, and a pencil like woman with an eye patch over both eyes. *Wait, how does that work?* Graylin thought suddenly, as the lady lifted the left patch to reveal a perfectly normal eye. *What the-?*

Graylin's inner musings were stopped short as she ran into someone. She bounced, stumbled, and shook her head, ready to shout at the buffoon that had just interrupted her very important thoughts on Ms. Double-Eyepatch. She had even opened her mouth, before she realized that the person she had so roughly bumped into was Lewis.

"Lew! What are you doing?" she asked, startled.

"Me? I'm not the one running like a hooligan through an extremely crowded street," Lewis retorted. "Where's Teddy?"

"Here! I'm here," Teddy gasped as he skidded to a stop, bending over and pushing hair out of his face.

"Ha! I win!" Graylin cried, bouncing on her heels. "In your face Teddy, in your pretty little face."

"What was that?" Lewis asked, smirking.

"Um, nothing," Graylin said, suddenly keen to change the topic. "Anyway, what have you two been up to?"

"Getting food supplies, like we were supposed to," Enland said, looking at the two suspiciously. "Why? What were *you* guys doing?"

"Having teenage criseses. Crisi? Whichever," Graylin said. "And listening to some pretty sick music."

"Have you guys seen River and Arlyn anywhere?" Lewis asked. Graylin shook her head.

"Nope. You?"

"No. I wonder where they've got to." Lewis glanced around.

"Let's go find them, then," Enland suggested, and the other three nodded their agreement. Graylin had only taken a few steps before she noticed a crunching beneath her feet. Mildly hoping that it wasn't the boardwalk snapping, she glanced down and saw a flier covered in several muddy footprints.

"Inventing Match? What's this?" She flipped it over. "Every morning, midnight to five, live betting, must be twenty-one to participate, bla bla bla. Sounds like Partsy."

"What does?" Lewis asked, who had just doubled back upon realizing that Graylin wasn't with them.

"This Inventor's Match," Graylin looked up eagerly, and Lewis could practically see the chaos light up in her eyes. "We need to find my cousin."

19

RIDGE DUNCAN'S HOUSE WAS a quaint little two-story wedged between two larger buildings on the ground. The only way to the front door, which was on the second floor for some reason, was via a shabby-looking lift lined with neon pipes. The boards looked as if they hadn't been painted in a decade, some of them half broken off.

"Is this an . . . an elator?" Arlyn asked her uncle as they stepped inside. Denloy smiled at her. The walk to the house had been good for him. Yes, there had been a small bit of anxiety wrestling in his brain of Ridge's knowledge of his brothers, but as they talked, Denloy realized that Duncan knew nothing about Mike and Ben's true task or intentions. It actually had been rather nice, talking to an adult who looked, smelled, and talked like the life Denloy had left behind eight years ago, and yet still thought highly of him and his brothers. It had filled him with a sort of warmth, and it seeped into the smile he gave Arlyn.

"This is an elevator, yes. A primitive one," Denloy gave Ridge an apologetic nod, to which the bearded man grinned, "but one all the same."

"I want one," Arlyn beamed, a manic gleam in her eye as the lift began to move. She smiled at Ridge. "Denloy helped Graylin and I build a message system on our ship, and designed our button set up like, like an eeeelebator's." She was really struggling with that word, and she wasn't sure why.

"Graylin?" Ridge asked as the platform came to a stop. "You mean-"

"Yes," Denloy smiled. "She's alive too, and they're both as smart and as chaotic as you might expect."

"Well, I'll be," Ridge shook his head. "It's a miracle." He smiled at the two Freelys plus River, and then opened his front door. "Don't worry about your shoes," he said. "Del and I have been looking for an excuse to replace the floor. In fact, rub the mud in if you have any."

Arlyn, who truly hadn't thought about the state of her boots until that moment, did as instructed. She glanced around the small mudroom they were in, trying to find something to compliment. Every time she entered a new house, Lily's voice echoed in her head. "Find something nice to say so they don't think Leo raised you."

The floor was off the list of compliment-able things, so Arlyn looked to the walls. To her left was a collection of blurry photos in brass frames. She recognized Ridge in four of them, including a family portrait with Ridge and a woman Arlyn presumed to be his wife. In between them there were four people, three of whom she didn't recognize. But the *fourth* . . . the fourth was Lily. Arlyn had to do multiple double-takes, trying to comprehend what her eyes were seeing. Her mind was telling her there was no way she'd found a picture of her former adoptive co-parent figure in this random house, but the more she studied the face, the more she realized there was no denying it. The woman in the picture was Lily. Her and Graylin's Lily. *Leo's* Lily.

"WHAT?!" She stopped in her tracks, spinning on her heel to confront Denloy and Ridge. "Lily?!" she spluttered. "*Lily* is the daughter one of my uncles dated?" She stared at Ridge, hands on hips. He hesitated, glancing at Denloy.

"It's normal to be scared when she does this," River patted the old man's shoulder reassuringly.

"I," Ridge was stammering, "I didn't know you knew Lily. How do you know her? Have you heard from her? Is she alright?"

"Alright?" Arlyn cried. "She's great! Okay, maybe a little less than great because Uncle Leo recently died and we sort of ran out of the house on her, but up to that point she was just brilliant." She glanced at Ridge hesitantly. "Why? Haven't you heard from her?"

"Lily . . . Lily was a bit of a wild thing," Ridge said, hooking his thumbs into his suspenders. "Let's just say she didn't appreciate Del and I's method of parenting. Thought we were a bit too controlling." He hung his coat on a hook and sighed. "After the disaster, we tried to reach out. She responded once, about a week after it happened, and said she wanted to be left alone. We haven't spoken since." In one motion, Ridge took off his glasses, cleaned them, wiped his eyes, and replaced his spectacles.

"But enough of this. This is a joyous day- and there will be plenty of time for dwelling on the past later. Della!" Ridge called into the quiet foyer, his deep, chesty voice echoing through the whole building. "Della dear, you'll never believe who I met today!" He started up the stairs, followed by River and the Freelys.

"Uncle Leo and Lily dating?" Arlyn muttered to Denloy. "You knew about this?"

"You didn't?" he teased. Arlyn didn't know where this lighthearted Denloy had come from, but she thought she enjoyed it.

The stairs brought the four to a homey space. To the right was a living area, and to the left a kitchen, where a kindly older lady was working. Directly across from them sat a set of stairs leading further up, probably to bedrooms, Arlyn assumed.

"Sorry, love!" Mrs. Duncan was a rather large woman, chestnut curls piled up on top of her head to form a bun. She wore a plain green apron, faded from years of use and covered in stains. "Dinner is a bit late tonight, but I-" She turned around, ready to greet her husband, but halted mid-sentence.

"My word, is that William Freely?" she gasped. "Oh, you poor boy, Ridge, get him in the living room. You look horrid, what happened to you? Who let you grow that beard?"

Denloy, trying not to smile, caught Arlyn's eye, and she grinned. This drew Mrs. Duncan's attention to the two teens, and she looked curiously at her husband. "And who might these two be?"

"Don't worry dear, everything will be explained." Ridge put a hand on her shoulder. "This is Arlyn Freely, and her friend, whose name I didn't catch."

River stepped forward, extending a friendly hand. "I'm River."

"Arlyn?" Mrs. Duncan asked, eyes wide. "Really?"

"Boy. Ouch," River muttered. "Now I know what it feels like to *not* be a famous person."

"Yes, it's Arlyn, Della dear, and I'm sure they would love to meet Loren," Ridge said, amused. Mrs. Duncan clapped her hands to her face.

"Oh! Oh, Loren! Yes, yes he would *love* to meet them, hang on." She hurried to the stairs and sped up them, Ridge laughing affectionately.

"She is not usually this excitable," he said, leading the three to a couch. "I'm afraid it's been a hard few months for us, and you have just brought us a great joy. It's been a while since we've had a good surprise."

"Surely not near as good a surprise as you've given us," Denloy said sincerely. Ridge just laughed and clapped a hand on Denloy's back.

"Who's Loren?" Arlyn asked, looking around the living room at the fraying rug and leaking window. She loved it here already. The living area seemed to melt into the kitchen, and it smelled of tea and heat. The lights were bright and golden, shedding a warm glow across everything.

"Loren? He's our grandson. He's been living with us for nearly five months now." Ridge smiled, handing out cups of coffee. "He's . . . well, you'll see. He'll be very excited to meet you."

Graylin loved her cousin, she really did. But after half an hour of searching, with no evidence of either Arlyn, her red-haired companion, or a certain uncle of theirs, she was starting to feel both slightly irritated and impatient. Thus, when the four broke into an open market, floating up above the buildings below, Graylin abandoned all thoughts of her cousin with ease.

"Shoot," she said in awe. The entire market, a series of stalls held up by various balloons and engines and fans, was interconnected by bridges. In each stall, Graylin could pick out distinct features that told her this was an inventor's market.

“Oh, this is just perfect,” she breathed, and hurried to the nearest stall, ignoring the shouts and calls of her crewmates.

Above the stall, a tent lit by golden lamps and lanterns, was a sign that read AMPS. Having gotten a full review on precisely what these were by Teddy just hours before at the Treble Club, Graylin was eager to see the products up close. Inside the tent was an older man, with long coily salt-and-pepper hair held back with a headband, and a curly mustache of the same coloring.

“Eh, welcome to my tent,” said the man jovially. He was tall, even taller than Teddy, and as thin as the wire Graylin used to hack her cousin's toaster. In other words, really thin.

“My name is Giuseppe. Do you want some amplifiers? No? Perhaps a quiche? They are fresh out of the oven.” The man, Giuseppe, was holding out a circular tart in a shiny tin, his hands covered in oven mitts. He had a lilting accent, and Graylin instantly liked him.

“Ah, no, I'm good on the quiche,” Graylin said, a little awkwardly. “Could I look at your amps, though?”

“Oh, please! Go right ahead, and just call if you need anything.” Graylin bent down and studied the box. It was fairly basic, just a wooden cube, the outside coated in thin metal sheets, with a rounded interior that spread out into the wide open front. Teddy had told her it used to be that all guitars were made with the amplifier built in, a hole under the strings opening into the hollow interior. But once Race became popular, people started making guitars without that hole, letting the vibrations inside the hollow guitar body travel down the tubing and into the new amplifiers, for extra noise. There was a panel at the top of this one, which she surreptitiously removed.

“Hello! How do you do? Quiche?” Graylin heard Guiseppe's greeting and turned to see who had entered. Teddy.

“Teddy! Come here, and tell me what you think of this.” Graylin beckoned to him, and he watched her carefully as she explained her plan. “We could get one of these and hook it up to your guitar. Then you could play music for us, real stuff, like we saw earlier!” she said eagerly. Teddy laughed.

"You would probably be the only one to enjoy that," he said. "Besides, my guitar already has an amp built in, it's acoustic. Amplifiers, they're built to make the noise bounce in a certain way so that it can exit the box louder than when it entered it." Teddy settled back and sat cross-legged on the floor next to the amp. "And I'm only one person. I can only play one instrument at a time, and pretty poorly at that. I won't be able to sound like those bands we heard earlier."

"But what if, and hang with me here, we could somehow, I don't know, *capture* the sound waves," Graylin said. "And then play them back, over top of each other."

"Ah, you two know each other?" Giuseppe asked. Graylin hadn't heard him come up, but he was right behind them.

"Yeah, we-" Graylin started, unsure how to finish. Were they friends now? Still just crewmates? She wasn't sure.

"We're friends," Teddy smiled, and Graylin suddenly felt all warm. She had a new friend, and this was a win. Arlyn could no longer claim she was unsociable. Yes, she had technically known this new friend for going on six years, but she felt it still counted.

"Ah, I should have known. Now, what is this I hear about your musical pursuits?"

"Oh, that's all Teddy," Graylin said proudly.

"I love music," Teddy told him. He wasn't shy, like Graylin expected him to be. He said it confidently and happily.

"Ah I see, and all you have is a guitar?"

"Yes," Teddy said.

"And *listening* to music? How do you do it?" Giuseppe asked, turning his back and hurrying behind his front table.

"Well, I see any live shows I find, I guess," Teddy said. "Where we live, in Odios, Race is still very underground, but I go to shows when I can." Not only was Graylin surprised to hear that Teddy had a life outside the Freely crew, she was also curious to hear there was a way to listen to music beyond live shows. Giuseppe shook his head in mock disappointment.

"A music lover with no knowledge of the greatest musical advancement. Now that is truly sad." He lifted out a box, big and wooden, with a large twisting metallic cone coming out of the top. "This, my friend, is a gramophone."

"It can play music?" Teddy asked, curious.

"Yes yes yes, look, look!" Giuseppe lifted a wax cylinder from behind the counter, and lifted the lid of the player, revealing a complicated-looking contraption. He placed the cylinder in its spot and gently shut the top. Music instantly began to crackle from the cone. Graylin recognized it as a song Lily hummed often.

"Wow," Teddy breathed.

"Can we buy one of these things?" Graylin asked excitedly. "How does it work? Is it-"

"One question at a time. Yes, you can buy one, and no, I don't know how it works. I make amps, not gramophones."

"I don't have any money on me," Teddy said. "And I doubt I'd have enough, anyway. I'm not paid as the pilot, *and* I am a jobless loafer. My only source of income was-"

"Leo," Graylin finished. "Tell me about it. I'm in the same boat, brother."

"He is your brother?" Guiseppe asked, raising an eyebrow.

"Oh, no no no, it's just," Graylin hurriedly assured him, "just a figure of speech."

"Good," Guiseppe said quietly, turning away with a smile. "I should hope a girl doesn't look at her brother that way, and vice versa."

All the things that his words implied made Graylin feel a little funny, and she was lost for words. Thankfully, Guiseppe turned back from the counter.

"How about you come back for one, ey?" he asked, smiling again. "Perhaps we can lower the price for such devoted customers." He pulled out a pad of paper with a wink. "Give me a name, and I can hold one for you. I have a very limited stock."

"Theodore," Teddy told him.

"Last name?"

"Er . . ." Teddy looked slightly awkward. "I-"

"We can use Freely," Graylin said. Guiseppe wrote that down and smiled at them.

"I'd be pleased to see you again."

"What *is* your last name?" Graylin asked suddenly, as they left the shop.

"I don't really know," Teddy said thoughtfully. "I don't know if I've thought about it for a while, and certainly not since Leo took us in. That orphanage was shifty, man, and I wouldn't be surprised if they'd lost my paperwork."

"But if Uncle Leo adopted you . . ." Graylin wondered.

"You're asking if I am, technically, a Freely?" Teddy asked, smiling. Graylin thought, again, that it would do the world much good if Teddy were to smile more.

"Well, yeah. Maybe you are," Graylin shrugged.

"I can't be certain," Teddy said, "but I don't think he adopted us, really. Not formally, anyway. No one would have let him. A single, twenty-something man, with a semi-stable income and two young wards? No way he would have been allowed to adopt three more kids." He took a big breath, and let it out heavily, watching the market around them with shining eyes. "Besides, I couldn't be a real Freely," he grinned at Graylin. "I'm not as smart as you guys are, nor funny, either, and I really don't understand how the Freelander works, no matter how hard I try."

"Well, that's a load of rubbish," Graylin scoffed. "Not as smart? You're smarter than me any day. Not last night I spent an hour trying to remember where I put my shoes, before remembering I had them on, and that was after Lewis told me not to track mud through the kitchen *twice*. And I've heard you talking with River and Enland, and as far as I'm concerned you're miles ahead of them. You think differently than they do."

"It's not very hard to think differently than River. I mean, the guy's brain works like a drunk bird. His thoughts just float along, carried by the breeze until it runs into something resembling a good idea," Teddy said, rubbing his nose. Graylin snorted.

"See? You're funny too," she said, trying to wipe away the snot she'd just loosened without letting Teddy see.

"I'm not funny. I'm just a bit sad," Teddy said, smiling a little. "Which is actually lucky, because I'm quite certain most of my personality would be gone if I wasn't."

"Sad?"

"Yes."

"About what?" Graylin asked. Teddy stopped and shook his head.

"I'm not entirely sure. And maybe it's not sadness so much as fear, I guess, that I'm just going to hate my life. Like everything is great now, but I'm just going to keep getting older, and we can't just do this whole 'wild teen crew' thing forever, you know? Someday we are going to have to be adults, and I'm afraid that I'm going to hate being an adult. Afraid and sad, because it's inevitable."

"And you always feel like this?" Graylin asked, startled. No wonder the boy was quiet, and distant, and shy. She saw it now; he was sad and afraid, all the time. Teddy nodded, but then smiled at her.

"Not always, but often. And less, after tonight. Less sad," he said.

"Truthfully?" Graylin asked. She had an inexplicably deep desire to help, spurred on by a strong sense that she knew sort of what Teddy was getting at.

"Yes," Teddy said. "Truthfully."

"I don't want you to be sad," Graylin said seriously as they started to walk again. Teddy's mouth was pulled into a grin by his dimple.

"You make me less sad." He seemed to fully register his own words and then hurried to correct them. "And by 'you', I mean the crew in general, not just you specifically because that would be weird and probably uncomfortable. You do, but not like *just* you."

"That seems unlikely," Graylin said, "but okay. Now we really should start looking for my gosh darn cousin, I want to head to that Inventor's Match."

It took the two over another hour to find Lewis and Enland in the maze of the market, and another to finally spot River's precise shade of red hair, entering one of the simpler houses below them. Once they saw River, they spotted Arlyn and Denloy right next to him.

"What the heck are they doing down there?" Graylin asked, disgruntled. "And whose house is that?" She was leaning on the edge of a bridge, watching the crowds below them.

"Maybe they're being kidnapped," Enland suggested, always the faithful pessimist.

"Nah, they would have been given back by now," Graylin told him seriously, which sent Teddy into a fit or snorts. "Come on, let's get down there."

It didn't take long for the crewmates to arrive at the simple house, though simple, perhaps, was an understatement. The building's stability wasn't entirely certain, and Graylin could easily tell that at least three of four load-bearing walls were bearing no weight.

"I'm not even sure if I *want* to know what my cousin is doing here," Graylin said, examining the neon-lined platform in front of them. "And what is *this* magnificent creation?"

"It's a lift, like an unfancy elevator, so hurry up and get on it. It is far past our bedtimes anyway," Lewis said, ushering them onto the pulley controlled platform.

"Thanks *mum*," Graylin muttered, only loud enough for Teddy to hear, before complying with Lewis's orders. This only set him off again, and she was forced to drag him along with her lest he be left behind. *We can't have that*, Graylin thought, *I've just told him all my secrets.*

"You, Graylin Freely, could use a bit more parenting," Lewis said pointedly, and flicked the switch to start the lift. It jerked and rose. Click, click, click, the chains thunked into place, and the platform swung idly as it reached the height of its ascent. Graylin reached out and hammered on the door.

"Grandpa Ridge?" A boy's voice called from the stairwell followed by the distinct thump of someone running down stairs. "Grandma said there was a surprise. Did I get in?"

Arlyn stared at the stairwell as a boy, probably sixteen or seventeen, appeared at the bottom, eyes shining behind rectangular glasses. His blond hair hung down in a tumbled mess, almost reaching his chin. "Did I finally get in?" he asked, his smile sparkling. "The university, did they send me a letter?"

Ridge shook his head. "Slow down, kiddo. We have guests." He looked over at Arlyn, Denloy, and River. Loren looked at them, not blinking, eyes widening. Arlyn briefly wondered how many wide eyes she would end up facing in this city.

Loren knew these people, or two of them at least. The man with the blond beard and the *very* pretty girl next to him. He'd never met them, of course, but he'd seen so many photographs he couldn't question their identities. Besides, there was no mistaking the upturned eyes and the look behind them, as if gears were running at the speed of light.

"You're Freelys," he breathed. He glanced at his grandpa, who nodded, a huge smile on his face. "You're Freelys," he repeated.

"I'm Arlyn," the girl stood, and held out her hand. "It's nice to meet you." The boy shook it, stunned.

"Yes. Yes I know." Then he blushed and looked at the ground. "I mean, I know you're Arlyn, not that it's nice to meet me, that's kind of weird, I . . ." His eyes moved to Denloy, and his eyes narrowed. Not in an angry way, or a suspicious way, but in a thoughtful one, like he was sorting through a thousand ideas in his head.

"You're Wilmot Denloy," the boy said, his eyes moving from Denloy to Arlyn and back again. Denloy nodded, and the boy began to grin. "I was right."

"I'm sorry?" Arlyn asked.

"I was right!" He laughed a little, looking at his Grandpa Ridge, who shrugged.

"And I was wrong."

"I'm confused," River whispered to Arlyn.

"Loren, why don't you take Arlyn and her friend upstairs and show them your work?" Della said kindly, holding her husband's arm. "We'll take care of Willy."

"Actually, dear, he likes to go by Wilmo-" Ridge began, but Denloy laid a hand on his arm.

"It's alright. I can be Willy for tonight." He nodded to Arlyn. "I'll catch up with Ridge and Della, why don't you two go upstairs?"

Loren seemed to shrink completely. He suddenly realized that the girl in front of him and her red-haired friend weren't just pictures, just stories of the amazing Freelys, they were people. Even worse, they were kids his age.

He swallowed and looked at his grandma, trying to show her how much he didn't want this. This wasn't where he was comfortable.

"Work you said?" Arlyn asked curiously. "What work?" Loren gave her a small smile, shoulders sagging.

"I can show you. Follow me." They went up the stairs, past the portraits and drawings, and Arlyn marveled at the general coziness of the house. "My room is just here," Loren said, opening the door just enough for them to get through. As Arlyn stepped inside, there were three things she noticed. First off, the suitcases hastily shoved under the bed, which was odd, as the rest of the room looked as if he'd lived there for months. Second, a note written in light blue ink.

Remember to take a break from studying sometimes! Maybe go down to the markets and try to make some friends!

Arlyn could feel something in her chest falling, but ignored it in favor of the third thing she saw. Completely covering much of the wall were scribbled notes, drawings of airships that clearly resembled the *Freelander*, and pictures of people who she thought she knew, connected by brightly colored strings and various documents with words so small she couldn't read them. She saw photos of herself and Graylin, and of their parents. There were faces she recognized and names she didn't. A puzzle of her life at eight years old.

"Dude . . ." River beamed as he looked around. "This is so sick!"

Loren smiled sheepishly. "You think so?"

"Are you kidding? This is amazing!" River turned to the braided girl in the middle of the room. "Arlyn?"

She was silent.

She hates it. Loren thought. *She thinks I'm weird. I knew it. I knew this would happen. Why am I so stupid?*

Arlyn turned around. "You did all of this yourself?" She stared at the blonde boy in front of her, a grin spreading across her face. "This is incredible! How long did it take? Did you draw it all yourself? Where did you get all of this stuff? This is amazing!"

"Really?" Loren brightened slightly. "You don't think it's . . ."

"Think it's what?"

"That it's weird?"

"Well, of course it is, but it's also *epic*! Not everyone has a giant conspiracy board in their room." Loren didn't smile, and Arlyn realized that he may have meant the fact that it was her family, *not* the fact that it was an epic conspiracy board. "And the part about it being my, uh . . . family is totally cool, man." Arlyn hadn't really intended to use the word 'family'. She'd intentionally not thought of the dead that way since the Disaster, choosing to push some of the grief away, and she wasn't sure why the word had come out now. In any case, she wanted to reduce any of Loren's anxieties, so she smiled at him. "Apparently there're *loads* of conspiracies about the Freelys out there," she said, "putting them on a board is just efficient! And incredible!"

"Oh, but Graylin isn't dead," River chimed in. "Sorry to say." Arlyn snorted at his remark.

Loren quickly pinned a "NOT DEAD" note next to Graylin as well. He looked all over the board again, then turned back to them. "Graylin is alive? Where is she?"

Before either could speak, they heard a loud knock at the door.

"You've summoned her," Arlyn grinned, before flying down the stairs.

20

THE DOOR IN FRONT of Graylin swung open. The person behind it was not at all what she was expecting; though who she *was* expecting, she wasn't sure. It was a man, older, with cracked spectacles and a very long, wizard-like beard, gray like his hair. He stared at the four, looking surprised.

"Why, hello! What's this?" As soon as the words hit her ears, Graylin remembered she *hated* knocking on doors, and that she should probably drag Lewis in to speak before she messed something up.

"I'm looking for my cousin," Graylin said weakly, looking past the man inside. There was a woman there too, watching the conversation curiously. "I believe she is-"

"Graylin! You're here?" Arlyn's ever-present shout rang from further inside. Graylin saw her cousin skip down some stairs, trailed by River and another boy about the same age. Good! Her cousin *was* here. The awkwardness was gone.

"Oh yes, cousin mine, I'm here. Now why are *you* here?" Graylin asked her, standing on her tiptoes to shout over the man.

"Because there are important things to be learned, and I am faithfully learning them," Arlyn said. "Now get in here." She grabbed her cousin and Lewis's sleeve and yanked them inside.

"Is that-?" The new boy asked, watching Graylin with wide eyes.

"The unfortunately not-dead Graylin Freely." River nodded, pushing the crew toward the living room. "Those two fools over there are my brothers. The one with the dark circles and weird hair is Teddy, and the grumpy one who resembles a camel is Enland." He glanced at Lewis, already scowling at him. "And that's Enland's chick, Lewis."

Lewis raised a threatening hand before handing Loren a business card of her own making.

"It's nice to meet you," she said pleasantly.

"And the lovely people whose house we've just invaded are the Duncans," Arlyn said, rocking on her heels as the crew was sat in chairs and plied with snacks. "Mr. Ridge and Mrs. Della are Lily's parents."

"I'm sorry, what?" Graylin choked, spraying the tea Della had just pushed into hands everywhere while Lewis practically melted from embarrassment.

"You know, Lily. Our not-aunt. Leo's Lily. These are her parents," Arlyn said, privately thinking that if Lily had been present, she probably would have slapped Graylin for her horrendous manners.

"You . . ." Graylin looked from Ridge to Della and back again before leaning to her cousin. "You're sure? *Our* Lily?"

"*Yes* cousin, the very one," Arlyn answered, practically vibrating with excitement. "But that aside, you've *got* to see what Loren has." She paused and turned to him, "If that's alright." He glanced at his grandparents, who smiled encouragingly, and then nodded.

So Loren was this new boy's name. Graylin searched his face, trying to find evidence of his relation to Lily. She thought she could see it in his eyes, the sparkling blue ones which kept glancing away shyly. Graylin nodded, turning her examination on her cousin. Arlyn certainly seemed to have taken a shine to him, looking back for his reaction to every word she said. Graylin gave Teddy a glance and grinned. This was going to be fun.

In the time introductions had taken, Della had tugged many of Graylin's drawings down from the walls and was showing them excitedly to her. "Do you remember these? I've kept them up all this time! Do you still draw?"

"Uhhh you have all my drawings . . . ?" Graylin tried to smile at Della. "That's great. Not creepy at all." She leaned toward Teddy. "First Denloy, and now her? I'm starting to feel like I'm the only one *without* a collection of my childhood drawings."

"A drawback of being a Freely, I guess," Teddy smiled.

"No kidding." Graylin folded her arms. This whole 'running into people who knew her and her parents but whom she didn't remember' thing was quite a strange experience.

"You were such a talented little thing," Della sighed, reminiscing. "You and Arlyn both."

"Shame we've grown out of it," Graylin commented. Della laughed and tapped Graylin's knee.

"But I've kept you kids long enough," the older woman said happily. "This old fart and I should get back to your uncle in the kitchen." She winked at Graylin and Teddy, and took her husband by the elbow to lead him away. "Besides, I think your cousin wants you."

This was an understatement. Arlyn Freely was buzzing, hopping from one foot to another, waiting for Graylin by the stairs leading up.

"Come *on*, cousin, hurry up! You've got to see what Loren's made!" she said, swinging her arms. Next to her, the blond bespectacled boy blushed.

"Alright alright, let's see it then." Graylin stood up, and Arlyn whisked the crew upstairs.

After being led down a hall and past several doors, the six crew members, plus Loren, entered a small bedroom. There was, as one might expect, a bed inside, as well as a desk, a window, several suitcases, and a huge board covered in paper, string, and pictures. Graylin glanced at her cousin, who was beaming, and nodded appreciatively. Unlike the bed, this board was *very* unexpected, so much so that Teddy took one look at the board and cursed out of both admiration and surprise. Enland's eyes followed each string and piece of the puzzle, adding increasingly more complicated compliments under his breath as he did so. Lewis simply added a very wide eye to the collection of surprise.

"What's this?" Graylin asked in awe, stepping forward to the board. She didn't really expect an answer, and she didn't get one. Every eye was on the collection on the wall. It was like a web, a Freely web, complicated and sticky and intricate. There were drawings Graylin recognized as her mother's, and blueprints she remembered to be her dads. There were photographs of people she knew innately belonged to her, but whom she could remember nothing about. Strings connected it all, colorful threads stretching from page to page. Loren's notes enshrouded the board, pinned and taped and tacked.

Graylin felt a rush of overwhelming *youngness* wash over her, coating those strings in her head, as if she was really seeing her family for the first time in years. For a fleeting moment, she was eight years old again, hugging her grandfather's knees, messing with the folds in her aunt's new skirt, and listening to some older cousins painstakingly explain the rules to a new board game they'd invented for the seventh time. It wasn't until she saw a picture of herself with her parents that Graylin remembered she was no longer a long-haired, wide-eyed, normal little eight-year-old. She reached out to tap a particularly faded photograph featuring her and Arlyn together.

"This is wicked," Teddy said, turning to the board's curator. "Where'd you find all this?"

"Here and there," Loren said absently. "Some of it is my parents' stuff, some I found myself." After a moment he added, "the records are public, if you were wondering."

Arlyn, knowing she wouldn't be able to make heads or tails of it, settled on the section that seemed to encapsulate her new-not-new Uncle Will. She found that the names "William" and "Wilmot" were used interchangeably; Loren had clearly suspected the identity coverup, as Leo had. She found lines to his various companies, charities, and other organizations where notes claimed that he "remained anonymous". In the middle of this was another note with the names Oskar and Felix written above "IMPORTANT RESOURCE." Arlyn immediately liked the sound of these people. One string, however, caught her attention. A long piece of twine stretching from the board to a bookshelf, and carefully attached to the cover of a weathered copy of *Huey's Journey*. Stuck to the corner was a note. *Arlyn's favorite, insp. For Pekin Industries?*

It was *for me*. The thought rang like a bell. Quiet. Then louder, and louder, and louder until she could feel the vibrations of the words shaking her heart and bringing glistening tears to her eyes. *He loved me.*

All this time. She felt incredibly empty and incredibly full at the same time, and all warm inside.

"Not to be rude or anything," Graylin considered the board, "but as cool as this collection looks, I have no idea what it means."

"It means the Freelander Disaster was all a setup," Enland said solemnly. His gaze flicked to Loren. "It was intentional. Not an accident."

"That's what I think, at least," Loren nodded. He pushed up his glasses and turned to the board. "It *has* to have been. The Freelys didn't just blow up their whole family by accident, they were smarter than that. They had a plan, I'm sure of it, and then something just went wrong. Maybe they meant to create a tragedy, I really don't know." He looked at his board, eyes roving, as if hoping new information would suddenly appear. "Every step was planned out," Loren continued quietly, "I'm certain. Ships don't just blow up like that. There's something we don't know."

"Well, what do you know," Graylin looked to her cousin a little desperately, "it wasn't even manslaughter. It was murder." *It couldn't be, surely.* Graylin gnawed at her lip. It was a terrible thought, but had that not been what their letter had implied? Her parents had clearly claimed fault for the Disaster. So why, even in the face of Graylin's growing uncertainty in her parental memories, did the realization feel so *wrong*?

There was a rustle as Lewis shifted in her seat, and Enland put an arm around her shoulders. Graylin clicked her tongue, chewing on the inside of her cheek, and Teddy rubbed his nose.

"Add that to the list of things to mention when we find them," Arlyn said finally, voice serious. "Below the meatball recipe, but above why they never wrote or came to look for us."

"Find them?" Loren's eyes were suddenly very wide. "Are you saying that-?"

"Yes, they're alive," Graylin folded her arms. "We think. But my cousin and I have concocted this wonderfully detailed and glorious plan to find them, which so far has involved finding our long-lost uncle and subsequently going to Belhaven and ignoring them entirely. Ah, and speaking of ignoring our problems," Graylin rummaged around in her pocket, "I found something that might interest you, cousin." She handed Arlyn the extremely crumpled flyer for the inventor's match. Arlyn shook her head; her cousin tended to have this effect on paper.

"What's the prize for this thing?" she asked, trying to smooth out the wrinkles.

"Don't know, don't care," Graylin leaned close to her cousin's ear. "And getting the Freely name back out there is sure to impress your little conspiracy theorist."

"Rude!" Arlyn shoved her cousin away. Could she go a single moment without mentioning Arlyn's boy-attracting habits?

"Anyway, we haven't made anything in days, and we're due for a bit of trouble," Graylin grinned. Arlyn started to smile too.

"Yeah," she flipped the flyer over. "'Must be twenty-one to enter,' it says here. We don't exactly look twenty-one."

"It's a backstreet club for inventors with illegal betting. I doubt they care if we're underage," Graylin said. "So come *on*, I'll tell you about the music we listened to on the way there. And you can bring your darling if you like." With that, Graylin yanked the poster from Arlyn's hands and skipped from the room, followed by Teddy, River, and Enland.

Arlyn, choosing to ignore her cousin's second comment about Loren, shrugged and smiled at him.

"Welcome to the Freelys. After you."

21

THE CREW SAID A genuinely heartfelt goodbye to the Duncan's, promising to return soon to pick up Denloy, who had promised to stay there and eat some food, and therefore satisfy Della's worried comments about how skinny he was.

"And have Loren back by three!" Della called at their retreating backs as they clunked down the lift. As it was currently 11:00 P.M., Arlyn waved and promised, thinking that four hours ought to be perfectly enough time for them to ruin their family name with a nice round of illegal inventing.

The entrance to the match's place of conduct was a dark, narrow, rather dingy alley, filled with everything from stray leaves and old newspapers to several crates and boxes.

River was looking uncertainly around. "Guys, I don't know about this. This place is kinda shifty."

Graylin raised her eyebrows. "What's wrong, River? Feeling nervous?" She stomped on some glass and kicked a bottle away.

"Well, come on then, let's not be shy. We have some inventors to beat," Arlyn said. The cousins knocked, and the little slide at the top flew open, revealing two shifty, bleary eyes.

"What 'choo 'ere for?" the voice slurred.

"To win." Arlyn held up the flyer, which the eyes glared at.

"What'chore name?" he asked.

"Arlyn," she said. "Freely." The man laughed dizzily.

"Did you say-"

"Yep, that's right." Arlyn rolled her eyes, almost expecting the question now. "Freely. That's us."

The door swung open.

The place smelled. Badly. Stale drink, cigarette smoke, and burning metal wafted in the cave-like room, tangible and thick, so much so that Graylin could see it swirling about the ceiling. *The ceiling*. Half of it was regular concrete, and half was glass and metal, with dark ocean water pressing down on top of it. Graylin remembered seeing the inky water below them occasionally while she and Teddy had explored the market, but she hadn't really thought about it until now.

Lighting the room were more neon strands, which shed colors over the many people inside, people with spiked hair and tattooed arms, clenching cards and tossing poker chips around. Shadows danced around everything, under chairs, in corners, behind the bar. Slivers of moonlight shone through the water above creating a rippling spotlight on the center ring, the moon's beams mixing with the golden gleams of the lightbulbs above the table in the center.

Conversation paused in the bar as the crew walked in, or, more specifically, as *Lewis* stepped in. Arlyn knew her friend was rich, her family powerful, and that the faces of the Maynewins were known around Odios. But she had not been aware that their prestige extended just as strongly throughout the rest of Osden, and to the capital city, no less. Or perhaps it was purely her beauty which caused the silence.

"Lewis? Lewis Maynewin?" A voice, a male voice. Stepping from the far corner of the room was a man. He had warm brown skin and black hair twisted into coils. Damien Maynewin, Lewis's brother, smiled at his sister.

"Damien?!" Lewis beamed and hurried to him, throwing her arms around his neck.

"What are you doing here?" Lewis asked her brother, smiling.

"Ah, you know, this and that. I commentate sometimes," Damien grinned back. "Oh, by the way, everyone here thinks the Freelys are dead? I've tried to tell them I've seen them with my own eyes, the girls and Leo, but no one believes me." He looked over at the girls and waved.

"She's a *Maynewin*?" Loren asked Arlyn, a little squeakily. Were all of these teenagers famous?

"Oh yeah," Arlyn said. "They have a house in Odios where they stay most of the year, but don't tell anyone I said that. It's supposed to be a secret, keeps the press away. Damien left a few years ago, though. I never really wondered where he'd ended up. Guess this is it." Arlyn smiled at Loren, watching his surprised face. "I'll be honest, I was a little surprised when you didn't recognize the name earlier."

"Well, I was a little surprised to find a dead person at my doorstep," Loren defended himself. "And I guess I never would have expected-"

"Never expected a Maynewin to be hanging with the grungy likes of us?" Arlyn patted him on the shoulder. "Same, dude. I'm surprised every day."

"Cousin, you'd better come see this," Graylin's tone was serious. "Get a load of these guys." She watched as the opening match began. Two older men were slapping together as many pieces as they could find with sweat running down their faces.

"Is that our competition?" Arlyn had to stop herself from snorting. The buzzer sounded, and the match had ended. Both men had a pile of smoking metal at their feet. Within a minute, both contraptions exploded, leaving both the contestants with blackened features and a large amount of booing from the crowd.

"Please tell me that was satire," Arlyn said disapprovingly to a heavily tattooed man beside her.

"You're quick to catch on," he huffed. "Here to bet on the matches, are ya?"

"Here to win them, more like," Arlyn said confidently as the man laughed beside her.

"You're funny. I ain't seen you around here before. What's your name, kid?"

"Arlyn."

"No inventor ever went by just a first name."

"Arlyn Freely," she said, holding out a hand. "That's my cousin Graylin over there. You are?"

"Barry," the man said. "Barry Saks. See kid, I can have nicknames too."

"Right." Graylin turned her cousin away from 'Barry Saks', moving her own attention back to the ring.

Thankfully, Arlyn was somewhat correct when it came to the competition. The first round was a rookie's match, intended for inventors that hadn't played their hand in a while. The current match was a fierce battle between a younger woman with short brown hair, and a man close to the same age, spiky black hair matching his torn jacket. Brown Hair was working her hands around a chain, fitting it onto a crank. A crank for what, Graylin could not be sure, but it was thrilling to watch. Black Spikes shielded his eyes from the spark of two gas chambers connecting with each other, watching his opponent diligently, his eyes flicking from her invention to his own. The crowds, however, did not seem very interested as Brown Hair attached a small fan blade to her crank. A few people in the back switched bags of coins and muttered.

"So, this a king-of-the-mountain sort of thing?" Graylin asked, turning back to 'Barry'.

"Like I said, you two are quick to catch on. Real quick." He nodded towards the match, which was ending. Brown Hair had won, and she stayed at the table, while a new contestant, an old lady who legitimately could be a mad scientist, took Black Spike's spot. "Whoever wins the match stays, and the loser leaves and has to go to the bottom of the list."

"So, what are the rules on teams?" Graylin asked.

Barry shrugged. "No problem with them. Don't see how it'd work, though."

"Oh, my cousin and I practically have one mind," Graylin assured him. "Sometimes we even finish each other's-"

"Sentences!" Arlyn put in cheerfully.

"Don't interrupt me," Graylin said scornfully. "Like I said, we work great together."

"Well, good luck then," Barry shrugged and turned away. Graylin turned to her cousin.

"Finish each other's *sentences*? That's not what I was going for at all. Who are we, fairytale characters?"

"Well, what did you want me to say?" Arlyn asked as they hurried to add their names to the register.

"Inventions! We finish each other's *inventions*. When have we ever finished each other's sentences?" Graylin asked, grinning. Arlyn considered this.

"Fine, fine. Now come on, let's get on that list."

They spent the next half an hour casually watching the other contestants, mildly interested in the goings on. However, both cousins, for once, were more interested in two specific people than the machines being built and deconstructed in front of them.

Arlyn was watching Loren, who seemed to be shrinking with shyness by the second. Arlyn was half-concerned he'd just up and disappear within the hour. Graylin, on the other hand, was trying to stop herself from staring at Teddy. Their conversation had transformed Teddy from the shy little twig of a pilot to a dreaming, lazily wild musician. And he looked . . . Graylin wasn't sure what. Handsome? Yes, but not in a chiseled way, more of a rebellious way. Pretty? Yes, but not in a feminine way, more a dimpled smile and bright eyes sort of way. Or perhaps, Graylin thought, she was just seeing him, really seeing him for the first time.

Little did Graylin know that Teddy, indeed, *had* changed that night. He *was* different. Over the past few years, he'd been becoming more himself around his brothers, but around the whole crew he had been determinedly hidden. However, the two's conversation from a few hours previously had driven a spike straight into the thick wall he'd built around himself and began to knock it down. It wasn't all gone, but it would be, eventually.

"Up next, going against the reigning champ, Charlet Cedric, are-" The loudspeaker crackled, and Graylin thought for a second it had broken, but no, the announcer was laughing mockingly. "Well folks, it seems we have been *honored* with the presence of two Freelys tonight! Isn't that great? I thought they were all dead, but no! Never had ghosts participate before, now have we?" The room was ringing with laughter.

"Arlyn and Graylin Freely up next folks, oh boy, I can't wait to see this." Graylin's hand was twitching.

"Let me punch him, cousin, let me at him," she growled, looking towards the man who'd been speaking over the system. He was in the corner, on a tall stool, looking smug. He had brown hair, eyes of an undefinable color, and, in Graylin's opinion, a very breakable nose.

"No," Arlyn said, grabbing her cousin's arm.

"But look at his stupid, smug face. See how he likes being punched by a 'ghost.'"

"I said no, Graylin. Do you want to be thrown out of here for starting a fight? We haven't even got to compete yet," Arlyn said, mentally thinking of ways to ruin the man's night in an unsuspicious way. She wouldn't let her cousin physically attack him, but if, say, a bolt miraculously flew from her workstation and hit him in the face . . . well, he had it coming.

"Anyone willing to bet on the Freelys? Think these two can manage a win here in the world of the living?" The man was speaking again, and Arlyn signaled to River and Teddy to come closer, just in case they were needed to hold Graylin back. "No one? No one thinks this new pair can beat Mr. Charlet?"

"I promise we'll make it worth your money!" Arlyn called from the back. Heads turned their way, but instead of focusing on the two cousins seemed to assume River or Teddy had said the words.

"I just can't believe Charlet is a man," Graylin muttered.

"Right, well, would the *Freelys* please take the table? Calling the Freelys to the table," the man continued, smirking,

"Good luck," Teddy said, smiling at Graylin. Graylin grinned back.

"I don't need luck Teddy. I've got my cousin on my side."

The two hurried to the table and adjusted all their equipment to be accessed easily. Graylin tucked the one strand of hair that was always falling into her eyes behind her ear, and Arlyn flipped her braids over her shoulder. In front of them was a pile of scraps, but somewhere in the thick of it she spotted a lighter, a can of gasoline and some styrofoam. A nice flammable substance.

Graylin too was scanning the pile, as was Mr. Charlotte, or Charlet, or whatever. She could pick out a chain, a round spool that would work as a pulley, and a small switchboard.

"What're you thinking?" she muttered under her breath to her cousin. Arlyn squinted at the pile.

"Some sort of . . . bomb," she murmured.

Graylin nodded. "I see a chain, and a spool," she said. "Remember Mr. Hooper's crane?" They looked at each other and knew they both had the same idea.

"On your marks," the announcer's voice sparked from the speaker next to them. "Get set . . ."

"Ready?" Arlyn asked.

"Of course cousin mine."

"GO!" With a nimbleness that only years of Partsy could give a person, the cousins, side by side, snatched up the parts they needed. Arlyn had snapped some goggles over her eyes, and was using a lighter she'd found to weld two small sheets of rounded metal together.

Graylin was staring avidly at the little chain on the table in front of her, trying to remember exactly what the crane had looked like while mentally switching parts around to adapt to her needs. She snatched a metal bar, attached the spool to it, and slipped on three gears. With a chink, Graylin pushed the chain into place.

Arlyn flipped her goggles up, and glanced at her cousin, intent upon her work, and smiled a little. She knew what Graylin was up to, adapting the crane idea to throw something, probably the very bomb she herself was making.

Smart. Very smart, she thought, before flicking her goggles back down and grabbing the vial of gasoline. She uncorked it, and poured a little into the casing she'd made for it, and then snatched at the styrofoam.

The crowds were paying a little more attention now. The two supposed Freelys weren't floundering as they had thought they would. In fact, they were working with a level of speed and creativity that the little room of engineers had never seen. When Arlyn scanned the watching faces, all were shining with interest. All except a man with graying hair, a ragged face, and extremely bitter eyes. He was simply glaring at her and Graylin, one hand on his drink, the other hand tapping the table.

Arlyn glanced back at her work, at the metal casing, her eyes widening as she saw what had happened to the styrofoam. She had planned to just set it in there, coating it in gasoline for quick ignition, but to her surprise, it had transformed into a gooey substance. Under pressure, she grabbed a small metal rod and dipped it in the unknown substance, tapping her cousin on the shoulder, who on instinct handed her a lighter.

Arlyn held the flame to the mystery substance, and almost immediately it took light. "Agh!" She dropped the flaming rod on the ground; the fire was scalding hot. She looked at Graylin and cracked the biggest grin she had in a long time. The substance didn't explode on its own, but the shotgun shell she'd spotted in the jumble of junk certainly would.

Graylin watched the burning rod as she constructed her "crane-a-pult". The fire wasn't going out. She glanced at her cousin, who was puncturing the bottoms of shotgun shells, dumping the black powder into a cloth sack, tied to a very flammable string.

"One minute!" The man on the loudspeaker sounded shocked. *Good.* Graylin thought. Her creation was almost complete. Two metal rods for arms, reinforced with thin bands she welded to it, stuck out from the base, to which she had attached the small switchboard she'd found. The chain was connected to a pulley, so that when she pulled the arms back, it would go farther than a normal catapult and could launch its ammunition with greater speed and accuracy.

The switchboard, which had been a mangled mess, was the only thing left to repair. In fact, it *still* was a mangled mess, but now it was a mangled mess that worked. Graylin cranked back a lever, loosening the chain, and pulled the arm back. It clicked into place, and the small hook on the end dangled, ready for munition. Graylin studied it. It needed something else, something . . .

She spotted a ragged pile of cloth still on the table, not yet used by either her cousin or their opponent. Arlyn still had a bit of gasoline left, and the lighter lay by Graylin's Crane-a-pult. Hadn't Arlyn made a hot-air balloon last time they'd played Partsy?

Tying and ripping feverishly, Graylin snatched up the parts, and began to hurriedly make four round balloons, then grabbed a near empty glass flask from a man next to her, ignoring his protests. She dumped out the drink, which smelled oddly like rubbing alcohol, and poured in the extra gasoline. Click, click, tie, tie, bang, bang.

"Ten! Nine! Eight!-" The man was announcing.

"Hurry cousin!" Arlyn urged, still looking at her smoking creation. Graylin began to smile, and clicked the last lighter into place. The machine slowly rose, about a foot off the table, because why not make it float?

"Three!" The whole crowd was chanting now, including the crew. "Two!"

"Attach it cousin!" Graylin stepped back to let her cousin hook her steaming ball of death to the hook on the crane.

"ONE!" The word rang in the room, everyone cheering and gasping and pointing. Graylin and Arlyn just high-fived, grinning, hands and foreheads sweaty with adrenaline, nerves, and the heat of the crowded room. There appeared to be at least three times as many people now as when the crew had first arrived, and everyone was staring at them.

Charlet went first. Around his arm was a band of fabric with a coil of rope attached. On the end of the rope were the parts of several mousetraps. "Behold!" he said, aiming his contraption at an empty bottle sitting on a somehow empty table. He pulled a trigger on his contraption, and the coil of rope shot out towards the bottle, the mousetrap parts getting threateningly close to Teddy's face before hitting the bottle and clasping around it. Within a second the empty bottle was sitting at Charlet's feet.

"So, he made a bottle grabber?" Graylin scoffed as the crowd cheered.

"The reigning champion has done it again!" The announcer cheered. "And now, onto our spectral friends, the Freelys!"

Arlyn flicked the lighter on, raising it up so the crowd could see it. She nodded to Graylin, who readied the crane-a-pult for fire.

"I'd stand back if I were you, folks!" Arlyn announced in her loudest voice. "And cover your ears!"

She lit the cloth on fire, jumping back behind her cousin, who released the handle of the machine, sending the metal ball flying into the air, a trail of smoke coming from the cloth. It hit the ground with a soft *tink!* and rolled slightly to the left.

Deafening silence, then, BOOM!!!

Both cousins went flying back, Arlyn grunting as Graylin landed on top of her. Her ears were ringing; all she'd seen was a flash of light, then, looking over her cousin, the bright orange glow of fire. When the ringing faded, she could hear cheers erupting from the crowd.

Graylin's eyes widened as the fire in front of her continued to burn. Her ears still slightly ringing, she stumbled up, just in time to be captured in a hug from Teddy. "That was awesome!" He grinned, nearly laughing. Too surprised to protest at this open display of friendship, Graylin laughed and hugged him back.

Arlyn rubbed her eyes. She could see River offering her a hand, Loren standing behind him, eyebrows worried, but a smile plastered on his face. "Awesome, right?" She beamed, taking River's hand and pulling herself up. Lewis and Enland nodded approvingly at the cousins as they too came down into the ring.

"That fire still hasn't gone out, Arlyn." Enland pointed to the flaming rod she had tossed aside earlier. "You may want to invent something to extinguish it soon."

Arlyn, however, was too excited to listen. "COUSIN DID YOU SEE THAT?!" she yelled over the crowd.

"HOW COULD I NOT SEE IT?" Graylin returned at the same volume. "WE NEARLY BLEW UP THE WHOLE PLACE! I LOVED IT!"

"That . . . that was amazing!" Loren stumbled over, eyes as wide as his smile. "What *was* that stuff?"

"No idea!" Arlyn laughed, giving him a high five. "But *wow* that was explosive!"

"You Freelys are incredible!" Loren cried, cheeks flushed.

"Freelys," scoffed a voice behind Arlyn. She spun around and saw a grayed beer drinker watching her with flashing eyes from the corner. "Always *blowing things up*." He said the words distinctly, heavily.

"I'm sorry-" Arlyn began, just to be tackled by River.

"That was so so so so cool!" River cheered, grabbing her hands and dancing a small jig. Distracted from the suspicious corner man and his suspicious comments, Arlyn laughed, the flecks of metal in her braid flashing as her hair swung.

"Well, well, folks!" the announcer shouted over the crowd. "It seems like our ghostly guests may live up to their name! Well done, Freelys!"

The cousins bowed in the shower of praise.

"Go on, give us a challenge!" Graylin called, drunk on adrenaline.

"Yeah, that was easy!" Arlyn chimed in. "You've got to have something better than that!"

"As you wish, your ghostliness!" The announcer said. "Ladies and gentlemen, please welcome our next challenger to the floor, Nepos Fellowman!"

Wild cheering filled the bar as a sweet-looking old man stepped into the ring. Even from her side of the table, Graylin could see his quick, intelligent eyes. The fire had been extinguished with a large tub of water, and Nepos now stood over the hazy ashes.

From the way everyone watched him, Graylin could tell he would prove a tougher opponent, though he stood with the demeanor of a sweet old grandpa. She felt an obligation to politely introduce herself, but fought it. This was a competition, not a convention.

"Now that our undead competitors have shown themselves capable of some quite ingenious inventing, not to mention mass destruction, let's amp up the bets, shall we? Anyone willing to put some money on these two? It's a gamble. Was their win was beginners' luck, or will it pay out?" Multiple people raised their hands and pushed some coins into the center of the table.

"Of course, if they win again, our competitors will get a share of the earnings! It'll be quite a win!" the announcer continued, urging those around him to toss stuff in.

"Well, this certainly looks entertaining." Arlyn said, scanning the new pile of parts as they showered down. There were more cogs, more machine-like parts. Graylin spotted a flint, a broken gun (likely from the same source as the bullets), multiple door knobs, and mounds upon mounds of wire.

Nepos sat, examining the pile with cautious eyes, watching every move of the cousins'. He knew what he was doing, Graylin thought. *Well, so do we.*

"I'm thinking . . . machine. Some sort of animal," Arlyn said under her breath to her cousin. "You?"

"Yeah, like a dragon," Graylin offered. Arlyn glanced at the smoking pile of ash that had been a table, recently destroyed by their last invention.

"Maybe *not* something that causes fire and destruction this time."

"A water breathing dragon then. Like a little sprinkler that walks around spraying people."

"I love it," Arlyn smiled, pleased with the idea. The final few bets were placed on the table- Nepos still had considerably more people backing him. The crowd had hushed to a dull murmur as the announcer began to talk again.

"Alright, round two for the Freelys. Can they pull off another spectacular win? We'll see . . . on your marks-" Nepos pulled down some glasses, with lots of flippy lenses. "Get set . . ." Graylin caught Teddy's eye, and he smiled at her. Likewise, Loren was watching Arlyn intently, though he had positioned himself intentionally out of her view. "GO!"

With the same idea in mind, both cousins scrambled for scraps. Graylin snatched up what she hoped would work for inner workings, and Arlyn started collecting pieces for the outside. Nepos, with surprising agility for a man his age, was snatching up pieces Graylin needed. Why couldn't he just be a nice old man? Must he have unnatural inventing abilities?

"Quick, cousin, your wrench." Graylin held out her hand, holding her multi tool up to a small wire. The wire grew hot suddenly, and her fingers burned. She had a sudden flashback to the moment, months ago, when she was fixing the *Freelander* fan, and she and her cousin had shared a wrench. Graylin had just burnt her fingers then, too. Leo had been alive, they had no secret uncles, and their parents were, to their knowledge, dead. Everything had changed now. But, Graylin thought as she saw Loren and Teddy in the crowd, change wasn't always a bad thing.

Arlyn was trying to create the shell of the dragon, attaching every panel with hinges so it could move with the mechanical beast. If she had hours to spend on this project, she would make it pretty, cutting individual scales. As of now, however, she only had (she glanced up at the huge stopwatch on the wall, pieces of paper flipping down with every second) nine minutes, so the welding would have to be based purely on functionality.

Graylin breathed a sigh of relief, and brushed sweat out of her eyes. She had found a nearly perfect motor in the pile of junk, and she was certain that if she had not, their dragon wouldn't have even a chance of being finished on time.

There was a large leather jug in the center- perfect. Graylin needed something to hold the water. The motor, with a little gasoline added, would work just fine to propel the sprinkler system and move the dragon. Graylin wanted this thing to walk.

Graylin had already built the legs, and pulled on the wires attached. The legs bent, working just like tendons in a live animal.

"How's it coming, cousin?" Arlyn asked casually, pulling down her goggles and using the laser to attach a few parts.

"Just brilliantly. You?"

Arlyn looked up. "That depends. Does this dragon of ours have ears?"

"Well, it won't respond to our voices, if that's what you're asking. We've only got ten minutes."

"I mean aesthetically. Do ears or no ears look more pleasing to the eye?"

"Uh," Graylin bent over the gear panel and inserted a miniature gear into its place with tweezers she'd pulled from her belt. "Yeah, let's say ears."

"Grand."

"Five minutes left!" The announcer bellowed.

"Five whole minutes? Great, now maybe I can get his eyes to blink," Arlyn said to the side, intentionally loud enough for the crowds, and Nepos, to hear. "I think I'll name him . . . Herbert."

As Graylin finished the mechanical frame of the dragon, with the large water tank in the middle, Arlyn attached the motor her cousin had repaired, and started adding the shell of armor.

"FIVE!" Arlyn's heart leapt as the crowd counted down, and she twisted in the screws with energy so far unmatched that night.

"FOUR!" Graylin yelped and rushed away, pushing the barman out of the way and shoving a barrel under the pipe, and twisting the cap so that it gushed out.

"THREE!" It splashed as she poured it into the tank, causing white billows of steam to hiss to life as the water hit the sparks Arlyn was creating.

"TWO!"

Arlyn inserted two marbles she'd found, a blue one and a white one, as eyes, and clicked her eyelids into place. Graylin added a few knife blades for claws, and-

"ONE!" the announcer cried. "STEP BACK!" The cousins did so. The crowd was more than surprised. They were shocked, but certainly not into silence. The noise was phenomenal. Laughs and cheers and shouts rose from those who had bet on the cousins, with groans and cries of astonishment from those who hadn't. Arlyn wasn't quite sure why-Nepos's invention wasn't so bad. It appeared to be . . .

"A lock box, disguised as a book!" Nepo announced. It *was* very well disguised. In fact, he had just taken a book from the pile, carved it out, and built from there. "But it's more than that. It also can extend-" he flicked a button, "so it can hold more. Also, do you see this lock?" He held up the box again. "No thief could pick this lock."

"Bet I could," Graylin said boldly. Nepo sneered, no longer a nice old grandpa.

"Yes, with what tool?"

"I call it a hammer. It's very handy for smashing locks until they're useless," she shot back. Laughter and cat calls rippled through the crowd, causing Nepo to look even more irritable.

"Well, that would make you a scoundrel, wouldn't it?"

"Oh, we never denied that," Arlyn said.

"At least I'm not a sleaze," Graylin shot back. The old man looked so hurt that Graylin actually felt bad. *No Graylin! You can be nice to Teddy, but not your competition.*

"Woah woah woah, hold back the unsportsmanlike conduct there!" the announcer crackled. "Disguised box, very impressive. Let's see if the Freelys can beat it!"

"This-" Arlyn said, stepping forward and pointing to the dragon. "Is the world's first . . ." She caught her cousin's eye and grinned. "*Water* breathing dragon." The crowd murmured; money changed hands.

Graylin stepped up and pressed a button just behind the dragon's left ear. It cranked to life, its eyes blinking mechanically. Then it began to walk, thunking down the table over the collection of bets, going all the way to Nepos before it began spewing water like a friendly, mechanical watering can. The water sprayed everywhere; on Nepos, his invention, and everyone backing him.

"Whoops!" Graylin called cheerfully from the other end of the table. "He's really got a mind of his own, can't control him."

"So incorrigible," Arlyn agreed. Everyone in the club, excluding a drenched Nepos, started up a round of wild clapping, and the Freelys both took bows, cheeks flushed.

"Impressive!" the announcer said, trying to hold back his laughter as a soaking wet Nepos left the ring. "Who'd like to take the next round against these unexpected champions?"

The bar went quiet.

"Any takers?"

Silence.

"Anybody at all?"

A single hand raised above the crowd. Loren stepped into the ring.

"Well then! Another young one throwing their hat in, bravo to you, young man!" The announcer congratulated him. "May I ask your name?"

"M-my name, my name is Loren," he said as loud as he could muster.

"Louder, son! What's your name?" the announcer's loud voice made Loren wince.

"My name is Loren!" he said more confidently. "Loren Rainey!"

Arlyn stood in shock. "Does he even know what he's doing?" she asked quietly enough that only Graylin could hear.

"We'll see," Graylin said.

"Are you sure you want to do this, Loren?" Arlyn asked from across the ring. "You saw our last two rounds. I trust your abilities, but we aren't going easy on you."

"Actually-" Loren started, but his face was obscured by the pile of parts dropped on the table in front of them.

Okay Loren, you can do this, you spent four years studying the Freelys! he told himself as he watched parts fly off of the table. *You know how they invent! You know how a few things work! All you've gotta do is go at it!*

He reached for a coil of hose and found it being tugged back from the other side. "Could I use this?" he asked, trying to see over the table who was on the other end.

"How about no?" Arlyn's voice came from the other side. "Graylin wants it for something and I'm closer, sorry!" She yanked it from his hands, the length on Loren's side snaking backwards through the junk pile. Arlyn handed her cousin the hose, who in turn gave her a length of necklace chain with a clasp.

Graylin fitted the hose securely into a long-necked bottle, scanning the pile for anything she could use as a body. Without a word, Arlyn shoved a trigger-activated mechanism toward her, welded to a haphazardly built body, and a pair of handcuffs acting as holders for the bottle.

Loren's gaze was fixed on a piece of paper that lay in front of him, his fingers moving quick as light over it, folding this way and that. Between his fingers, he stretched out a rubber band, which he figured would make a good launch mechanism. He pulled a cord, and a puff of air flew into his face, causing some dust to fly into his nose.

"A-a-achoo!" he tried to cover it with his sleeve, but the sneeze only sent more dust flying.

"Gesundheit!" Arlyn said from over the pile, which was growing smaller by the minute. "How's it coming along?"

"Great!" Loren said, proudly setting the last piece of his machine in place. He glanced at the clock. *Five minutes*? That was not enough time, not when he was certain there was still a flaw in his invention. "Um, actually, not great anymore."

"Stop the chatter and hand me that bottle of paint, we don't have much in terms of munitions here!" Graylin shot at her cousin. "Thank you." She dumped the sludgy substance into the bottle, then dropped in a smaller amount of water, taken from somebody's drink.

"So, who do you think is gonna win?" River asked the remaining crew outside of the ring.

"Oh, Arlyn and Graylin for sure. No matter how much Loren knows, he's never played a game of Partsy in his life to my knowledge. Why do you think the girls are so good?" Lewis said, tossing a coin she found wedged between the table boards into the betting pile.

"He's got skill, no doubt, but he's no Freely," Enland added, watching both sides of the battle intently.

"Alrighty folks! We've got two minutes on the clock and it looks as if the Freelys are about to do it again! But hold on, Loren here's got something. We'll just have to wait and see." The announcer was just as captivated as the audience, barely remembering to say anything at the one minute mark.

"Would you mind decorating this, cousin?" Graylin asked, handing Arlyn their invention. The bottle of paint was hooked to a firing system that Graylin had quickly tested under the table. Her shoes didn't look great with green splotches, but it proved the contraption worked. Arlyn snatched it up and started to add small things, lights turned on by a lever, a broken magnifying glass slapped on to make a scope, and the necklace chain, which now served to keep the bottle's seal from going flying.

"How's this?" Arlyn asked, shooting Loren an apologetic glance. Graylin swept the machine away from her, clipped on a shoulder strap, and began to fiddle with the trigger.

"Thirty seconds!" The announcer called. Arlyn glanced left, at her cousin composedly taking off a side panel from the shooter and messing with the gears inside. Then she glanced right, at the poor, shy, scholar of a boy trying to make an airplane launcher like she would. At this moment, she decided his need was greater than her cousin's.

She thrust her piece, a spring to counteract the paint gun's kickback, into her cousin's occupied arms, and ran around the table to Loren.

"What is this? Arlyn Freely is *helping* her opponent? Well we've never seen anything like this folks!" The announcer shouted gleefully over the din.

"Bloody traitor, Graylin muttered, but she was grinning. It was fun, watching her cousin act like a fool for this boy without even realizing she was. Besides, she was practically done, and they still had-

"Ten seconds!"

"Here, take this pulley, and loop the rubber band on it," Arlyn said, working feverishly next to Loren. He was just looking at her. *Arlyn Freely*, the *Arlyn Freely is helping me build an invention*? He stared at her, watching her dark green eyes flick between parts, snatching and stretching and tying. Braids swinging with every movement, Arlyn's face was shining with excitement. She looked at him, and grinned. "Come on Loren, I'm here to help, not take over." He snapped out of his reverie and got to work.

"Five!" Arlyn, in her rush to attach something, nearly knocked over the boy next to her, and hurried to grab his arm and haul him upright.

"Four!" Loren stumbled, and grabbed onto her. Suddenly they were standing very close, Arlyn staring at Loren's bright eyes.

"Three!"

"Get a room!" Graylin called.

"Two!" The two stepped back and grabbed for the invention.

"ONE! Step back from your inventions please!" Both teams did so. Arlyn gave Loren a smile, and then dashed back to her cousin, who was shaking her head.

"What?" Arlyn asked defensively.

"You, cousin, are pathetic."

"Well well well folks, here we have it, our tenth round of the night, and for any newcomers in the room, the last two rounds have been won by two Freelys!" Arlyn and Graylin raised their hands and waved to the crowd. "I think it's fair to say that, while streaks *have* been longer, never has such skill been witnessed in this building. Which is why, when another brand new contestant offered to face these engineering magicians, we were all amazed. May I introduce the brave competitor of our Freely duo, Loren Rainey!" The crowds clapped politely, Arlyn and Graylin joining in, Arlyn with shouts and woo-hoos. The boy blushed with embarrassment and pleasure.

"Now, what have you built, Loren Rainey?" Loren held up his paper airplane shooter, and showed it to the room. It *did* look pretty impressive. Crisp white paper folded into a shape that would fly, and a steady wooden base.

"I built an exploding paper airplane launcher," he said, raising up what looked like a normal paper airplane, but something was off in the folds. The cousins watched intently.

He loaded the airplane into the launcher, twisting the rubber band around and around. He glanced back at Arlyn, who gave him a thumbs up. He pulled downward on the airplane, and then released.

The paper airplane went flying into the air, but wait, now there were two of them, four, nine, sixteen! The airplane had split into multitudes of itself, so many that half the bar was now holding one. Applause erupted from the crowd, Graylin could barely see the shape of her cousin's hand.

"Bravo Loren Rainey!" The announcer joined the applause, holding his own airplane. "That was quite the show! Let's see if the Freelys can even compete!"

Sorry Loren! Arlyn mouthed across the table, handing their invention to her cousin. She really *did* feel bad, even though she knew that the boy had never had a chance.

"Ladies and gentleman!" Graylin raised up the weapon. "Would a few of you take the courtesy of tossing some of your airplanes into the air?"

The crowd laughed, and a few people tossed their planes up. Graylin's gaze locked onto three, and held the gun casually, the other hand stuck in her pocket. She squinted, paused- and fired. A stream of paint hit one of the planes, sending it barreling down to the ground, now covered in light-green paint. She shot down another, then another, the crowd tossing more and more in as she did.

"My cousin and I are thrilled to present to you the paint gun!" Arlyn took a bow, dodging a shot of paint from the gun.

The crowd cheered wildly, paper airplanes were everywhere, even the announcer was clapping for them. "Would you look at that folks! This is a tough round to judge, and I've been doing this for eleven years! If you all will be so kind as to give me a minute, many thanks to all the inventors who participated tonight!"

"What do you think, about his invention?" Arlyn asked her cousin.

"I think, cousin," Graylin rolled her eyes, "That Loren over there doesn't stand much of a chance."

"Well, I was impressed." Arlyn folded her arms.

"I'm sure you were, cousin," Graylin said. She turned around, but her cousin was gone, shaking hands with Loren. Graylin grinned; Arlyn was not often one to trail after a boy, and it was even more amusing to experience than she could have predicted.

"I'll admit, I didn't see that coming. Good show, sir, good show indeed." Arlyn shook Loren's hand.

"Uh, thanks!" Loren was shaking, flushed bright red. Arlyn Freely was congratulating him. *The* Arlyn Freely! He caught River's approving nod and thumbs up from outside the ring, and he'd been right, going into the ring had been an excellent idea.

"Good dream then?" Arlyn asked.

"Amazing dream," Loren smiled. "You've no idea how many times I've imagined this."

"Er . . ." Arlyn glanced at the ceiling, trying not to dive too deep into that statement, while Loren suddenly realized what he'd said.

"Oh man." He hung his head, pushing up his glasses and rubbing his eyes. "I . . . that's not what I meant, I just," he glanced up as Arlyn began to laugh, "I just meant, you know, that I've thought how cool it would be to invent with a Freely, not that I'd imagine hanging out with you specifically, not that you're not great, you *are*, I just don't want you to think I've been fantasizing about ghosts or something, and I'm just gonna stop now because I keep putting my foot in my mouth."

Arlyn was personally finding Loren's flustered nature quite endearing, and patted his hand.

"Hey, I live with Graylin, the literal queen of mouth-footing. Don't worry about it," she grinned.

"I'm pretty sure you and Graylin are going to win," he said, still flushed, not realizing he was still holding onto her hand. "Your paint gun was amazing! And I sort of cheated, by using you."

Arlyn shook her head. "No way, all I did was toss you a few parts, the idea was totally yours! I'll be honest, I was a bit confused when you came in, but bravo! Now, let's go see who came out on top."

The announcer cleared his throat, the sound crackling across the bar and silencing the crowd. "After a tough decision, I've come to a decision." The whole room held its breath. "Mr. Rainey, while you did better than expected, the win still must be awarded to the Freelys!"

Wild cheering erupted from the crowd. Without warning, Arlyn grabbed Loren's hand and raised it into the air. "Let's hear it for Loren!" she yelled. A whole new level of noise came from the crowd.

River stood up, motioning for Enland, Lewis, and Teddy to get up with him. "Loren! Loren! Loren!" He chanted. Soon the chant spread around the entire bar.

"Loren! Loren! Loren!" The cousins chanted, their new friend a bright red mess beside them.

"Lovely folks, just lovely!" The announcer clapped his hands. "But let's get on to the next round. Now, we've had these two Freelys fighting together most of the night, but I think we're all dying to see how they'll do on their own! Freelys, are you ready?"

Arlyn walked Loren out of the ring, running back down to greet her cousin. "Let's dance, cousin mine," she said, tapping her foot on the old wooden floor.

"We're ready!" Graylin called, tucking her hair behind her ears.

A mound of junk was dumped onto the table, both cousins watching it, searching and scanning the pile for anything that might be useful.

"On your marks . . ." The announcer said, Graylin grinned at her cousin on the other side of the table, who returned the gesture with a thumbs up.

"Get set . . . "

The crew leaned back in their seats. This would be a game of Partsy to remember. Loren was leaning over the railing, eyes flicking between both cousins.

"GO!"

There wasn't a word spoken as the cousins tore through the pile, snatching this and that, their hands were nothing but a blur, with the occasional spark coming off of the quickly dwindling supply of metal.

Arlyn's mind was devoid of any form of plan. Sometimes Partsy was about letting your hands take over for you, a trick both she and Graylin had learned after years of playing each other. Gears, switches, clocks, birdcages, anything and everything flying before her eyes. She trusted her hands well enough to craft something useful, instead using her eyes to watch Graylin's every move.

As for Graylin, she was staring at her hands as well, trying to do what she sucked at and visualize the invention she wanted to make. It wasn't going very well.

The rounds flew by, the announcer counting down again and again and again. The first round, Graylin made a small flying contraption whose blades consisted of knives, while Arlyn constructed a delicate, mechanical dragonfly.

"This is too easy!" Graylin had called after that round, despite the fact that Arlyn had scratched a win. "Change the time limit to five minutes!" The crowd gasped, but the announcer complied.

The five rounds after that were manically fast. Over and over, the cousins would whip together machines, deconstruct them, and switch them around in a matter of seconds. Their plans seemed to change constantly; first it would seem that Arlyn was making a hat, but then it was a small man, before finally landing on an electrically amplified music box. Graylin switched from micro goggles to a jetpack with thirty seconds of the clock, making the crowd gasp and cheer.

Graylin won two rounds, Arlyn three, and then they tied. Both girls were sweaty and tired and yet the cousins were having the times of their lives. Despite the fact that it was growing very close to 2:00, which was only an hour to the allotted curfew of 3:00, Graylin and Arlyn both clamored for one more round, gulping down two cups of straight, cold coffee and shaking their heads.

"Those two are going to kill themselves someday," Lewis muttered. No one was listening, they were watching the preparations for what would surely be the final match.

"Alright folks, wow, what a night it has been!" The announcer called. He sounded exhausted, but excited. "Come on, let's see those bets pile in!"

The betting wasn't like normal betting, where the betters got twice the amount of money if they bet on the right person. More, they sort of donated money to the center, like a poker game, and whoever won got it all. If they bet on the right person, they got nothing, besides intense bragging rights. But over the last few hours, the things used as bets had been getting odder and odder, everyone having spent all their real money. The last round, Arlyn had actually won a crate of vegetables, which she had plopped in Lewis's lap. There had been invention parts, food, drinks, a few articles of clothing that would never fit, and a solid gold ingot. But that was nothing to this round.

People were rushing up, throwing things on the table, pushing them into place around the pile of scraps. There was a large collection of dried flowers, a huge clock with weird looking numbers, and a cactus? Arlyn hoped, for her cousin's sake, that Graylin didn't win this round. The girl could hardly keep herself alive, let alone a plant, even if the plant was one of the easiest to care for.

"Ladies and gentleman, I have an announcement to make." The announcer tapped his microphone, which made a high-pitched sound Graylin *very* much disliked, getting everyone's attention. "Thanks to the astounding showing from the Freelys, we have an old champion returning to the ring!"

Younger members around the bar could be heard asking questions, while the older patrons were elbowing each other and cheering wildly. The gray man, the one who had thrown out comments about the Maynewins and Freelys blowing things up, stood from his table in the corner, straightening. He held up a hand to greet the praise, eyes flashing. The cousins glanced at each other. Who *was* this guy?

"Ladies and gentlemen," The announcer boomed to the crowd. "May I present to you . . . Gregson LeMay!"

The man stepped into the light, and Arlyn saw that he was more than just gray. He was a grizzled man, with broad shoulders and a crowd-pleasing smile on his face. He slicked back his wild, silver hair as he nodded to various patrons, saving his particularly icy gaze for the Freelys.

Both cousins looked around at the wildly cheering crowd, thoroughly confused. Even Barry Saks, who'd been silently applauding them, looked directly at Graylin, making a throat cutting motion with his finger. Whoever LeMay was, he was obviously notorious, but for his skills or personality the girls weren't sure.

Loren's eyes had gone wide, again. Honestly, Arlyn was close to deciding that his blue gaze was always adorably surprised. He motioned to her, as if wanting to tell her something, but people were already pushing the competitors to the table. Arlyn waved to him apologetically. *Sorry! Tell me later*? She mouthed. As LeMay stepped into the ring, his sly expression flicked from one cousin to the other in the three-way competition. He stood straighter and held out his hand.

"Congratulations on the exciting night. It's been a while since I've seen inventing like this," he said, smiling icily.

"Thank you," Arlyn returned with a chilly grin.

"I especially liked that explosive substance you made earlier," LeMay said stiffly. "What do you call it?"

"Nothing, we've never made it before. Bit of a spur-of-the-moment discovery," Arlyn grinned.

"Another bomb, another Freely," he said wryly as he turned away. "Same stuff, too."

"Sorry, what?" Graylin asked, but he didn't respond. Whether he even heard or not, the cousins weren't sure. They looked at each other, immensely confused, when the announcer's crackle broke through their thoughts.

"Competitors, are you ready?" he asked. LeMay pulled a large pair of goggles from a supply bucket, wiped the lenses, and pulled them over his eyes. Arlyn glanced at her cousin, nodding. *We'll talk about it later*, she tried to say, *just focus on this last round*. Graylin nodded back.

More bets were placed on the table; everyone was out of money by this point, and were tossing whatever they had. Several people were being scolded for moving their bets, while others were still shoving entire piles of random objects towards the center.

"On your marks," cried the announcer, "Get set . . . GO!"

Parts went flying around the table, scraps of metal, pieces of wood, even a string of lights, which Arlyn promptly snatched from the pile.

Against Graylin, letting her mind wander was just fine, as she knew her cousin was just as distracted, but this man meant business. She spotted a rusted jack-in-the-box, quickly testing it and adding it to her pile.

LeMay had amassed his own pile of junk, carefully examining each piece and part, not even looking at the cousins. His hands were a calculated machine, moving in precise patterns as he amassed more junk. He had clearly done this before.

Graylin's eager gaze had not moved from LeMay; if his idea was that he was going to beat her, he was sorely wrong. Her own hands reached for anything she could find, slats of wood, sheets of cloth, bobbins of twine. Everything was fair game.

Arlyn hung the lights in a decorative border around her contraption. She had gone for solely function the past three rounds, and it was time she made something pretty. She took an aluminum tin and jabbed some holes in the side, tying some stray guitar strings to each hole then attaching them to the top part of her invention. She set a candle in the tin and continued to work on the underside of the can.

"You have exactly two and a half minutes, contestants, it's anybody's game here!" The announcer said from the box.

Don't rush, don't rush, don't rush. Graylin repeated to herself. Rushing could ruin a perfectly good invention, and she wasn't about to lose to some guy who gave her a death stare and said odd things about the *Freelys* and *bombs*. She squinted her eyes as she welded a part together, deciding that glaring back at the competition was unsportsmanlike unless she disguised it.

"One minute!" The announcer called. The crowd was dead silent, watching the competition with wide eyes. Graylin only had one part left she needed, but she saw her cousin eyeing it. She dashed for it, throwing herself halfway across the table to grab it, snatching it just before Arlyn did.

Arlyn watched her cousin flash back to her invention, and hurried to finish her own, trying not to dwell too long on LeMay and his weird comments. *Once this round is over*, she thought again, *just finish this round.*

"Ten seconds!" The new announcer cried. Graylin wiped her brow. She didn't know why she had felt so compelled to make this, but as soon as the idea had entered her mind, she couldn't get it out.

Arlyn on the other hand barely even knew what she had just built. It looked good enough, but given that she'd put zero thought into it, it felt strange, watching her hands build it. She just wanted to know what LeMay had *meant*.

"THREE!" The room was buzzing as LeMay and Graylin struggled to finish, and Arlyn tried to pull herself into the competition.

"TWO!" Arlyn spotted something she could add and hurried to replace the part.

"ONE!" Arlyn glanced up- LeMay was trying his hardest to add just a few more things to his invention. It looked like-

"STEP AWAY!" Called the announcer. Arlyn leapt away from her table.

"Wow wow *wow* folks what an evening, what an evening indeed! Would you look at that, our three best competitors faced off in one epic battle, and with such amazing results! Now *that*'s what I call a night to remember ladies and gentlemen!" The announcer jumped off the stool and was coming closer to the table. "It appears that familiar face Gregson LeMay has made an astonishing-"

"Airplane!" called LeMay, holding it up proudly. He flicked a button, and the little flying machine's propeller began to spin. LeMay drew his arm back and threw the machine. It chunked, clicked, and glided past Arlyn's head. The crowd whooped and hollered- it was truly impressive. It swooped all the way to the crew, and River stood up to catch it.

"Now, I'll be honest with you," LeMay played to the crowd, smiling. "I got the idea from Mr. Rainey earlier. Also, this thing doesn't have a real motor in it. It flies off the power of the throw, but hey, you find me someone else who can build such a heavy machine that's still able to glide." The crowd laughed, and he bowed. He was certain he was going to win.

"Arlyn Freely, what have you built?" boomed the announcer a little too enthusiastically. Arlyn winced and rubbed her ears, before looking down at her machine. It had started out being a box that, when cranked, would release a big glowing orb that you could use like a lamp. In the end, the glowing orb idea had been switched out for something more like a bundle of string lights. But it was close enough.

"This, honored guests and minor criminals, is a lamp-in-the box!" She held up the seemingly ordinary cube and cranked the handle on the side. The ball rose out, slow enough that it seemed almost celestial. Everyone began to clap loudly, including Graylin and LeMay, both watching Arlyn's invention with envious eyes.

"Ah! I give up!" LeMay threw up his hands jovially. "I can't beat a Freely." He said it mockingly, jokingly, and the crowd laughed. He was playing them with ease, as if he'd done it a million times.

"Well well I think it's fair to say that Arlyn might be in line for yet another win!" called the announcer over the din. "But let's see what Graylin has to say about that."

Graylin grinned. She was standing in front of her invention, to keep it hidden. At the speaker's words however she stepped aside, and the crowd gasped. Even Arlyn's jaw dropped.

Graylin had built the *Freelander*. Perfect in every outward detail, it hovered, clunking slightly, above the table. Arlyn gaped. How had her cousin completed such a feat in only five minutes? The ropes, the rudder, every propeller . . . was perfect.

"Now, I too have a disclaimer," Graylin announced. "The real ship, which I modeled this after, once had one thousand balloons, and now has three hundred and fifty. I'm afraid my model has only around fifteen."

"*Fifteen balloons*, did you hear that folks?" The commentator practically screamed. "Impressed is beyond how we all feel, I am sure." Everyone continued to goggle and gasp at the machine, as if checking to see if it was about to fall. But it remained in the air, bobbing gently up and down. Murmurs ran through the crowds like . . . well, like a murmur through a crowd.

"Well, it's a tough decision, believe me," said the announcer finally. "Hasn't tonight just been incredible folks? But, I think, for our final, champion round, I'll have to go with . . . Graylin Freely as the winner!"

Arlyn and the crew whooped and surrounded Graylin. Enland and River patted her on the back, Lewis hugged her, Arlyn punched her, and Teddy smiled a dimpled smile and kissed her on top of the forehead. Perhaps it was the adrenaline, or the light nature of the kiss, or the overwhelming rush filling Graylin from head to toe, but she did not object. She simply beamed as she and her cousin were cheered on. Everyone was laughing, crying, and shouting. It was a medley of joyous chaos.

"Hey Graylin! Come look at what you won!" River called from the table, and the crowd pushed Arlyn's cousin forward. The two cousins stared at the pile with wide eyes, laughing in awe.

"Look at that!" Arlyn cried, reaching for a small stuffed animal kitten resting next to the cactus. It was well-loved to say the least, with orange and black patches on its mostly white fur, and reminded Graylin very forcibly of a stuffed animal she'd had as a child, Flepe. She thought the puppy was still on the ship somewhere; she'd find it when they got back. Perhaps the two stuffed creatures could keep each other company.

"Here cousin," Arlyn handed Graylin the very floppy cat. "What're you gonna name it?" She teased.

"Oh, probably nothing," Graylin muttered, embarrassed, sticking the animal in her pocket.

"Stuffed animals are dumb," River said, holding tightly to a finger he'd poked on the cactus.

"You're dumb," Graylin shot back, patting her pocket as someone tugged on her sleeve. "My kitten's name is Pasta and she doesn't like you."

"Is it over?" Loren asked aimlessly, hoping Arlyn heard him. He turned around, seeing the remnants of many rounds worth of inventions, including the fire from the first round. The thick jelly Arlyn had created was still burning, bright and hot. *Still?* Loren turned back to tell Arlyn, but she was nowhere in sight. He turned back to the crew, but only saw the trove Graylin had won being admired by various crew members. “Arlyn? River, where’s Arlyn?”

River looked around, but couldn’t find her. “Dunno. Probably lost in the crowd somewhere. Get used to that, the Freely girls kinda do their own thing all the time. I wouldn’t let it get to you.”

22

ARLYN LED AS THE two cousins pushed their way through the crowd, searching for LeMay. In the chaos of the victory, the girls had completely lost track of him, and Arlyn didn't intend to let him get away that easily. They had questions for him. *Another bomb, another Freely. Same stuff too.* What in the world had he meant?

"Ah, if it isn't the ghoulish girls themselves." The grizzled man raised his head as the girls approached. "Congratulations on that last match." He had seated himself at his small table in the corner, out of sight. As they walked up, Graylin got the feeling he was in the particular chair often; the way he settled in the seat, maybe, or how he seemed to match his surroundings. Everyone's eyes, which had been so focused on LeMay just minutes before during the match, now slid over him. He was now nothing more than part of the environment.

"Thank you," Arlyn said, sitting down. She was trying to decide between making small talk or interrogating him. However, Gregson LeMay continued before she could make a choice.

"That was some fine inventing out there. Rarely seen better."

"Thank you," Arlyn said again. Okay, interrogation. "Listen, before the match, we heard you talking about our parents? And a bomb? Could you like, maybe, explain that?"

"You two are really committed to the bit, huh?" The man took a sip of his drink. "Listen kid, I was close to the Freelys. No matter how impressive your inventing abilities are, I know you're not one of them. You can drop the act with me."

"Oh no, cousin." Graylin rolled her eyes. "He's seen right through us."

"You knew the Freelys?" Arlyn asked. Yes, his airplane had been good, but she never would have guessed that this worn, gray man had known her parents.

"Yeah, I knew them. Knew them well. Worked together, for a bit," he said.

"On what?" Graylin asked, sitting down at the table. He gave the girls a long, appraising look, before shrugging and taking another drink from his bottle.

"Not supposed to talk about it, confidentiality, and all that." He gave them a ragged grin, and took another bottle from a passing waiter. "But on the other hand, those precious, *genius* Freelys really screwed me over. Don't see why I should keep their secret any longer." He popped the top off his bottle. "Especially not from their children."

"That's the spirit." Graylin smiled sarcastically, wrinkling her nose at the smell of the alcohol.

"You must keep this quiet, mind," LeMay said lazily. "Don't think the Prime Minister will be pleased if he hears I've been spreading his secrets."

"We have a prime minister?" Graylin muttered to her cousin. Arlyn batted her cousin and her abysmal political knowledge away.

"Don't worry, we'll keep it to ourselves," she told LeMay. She mimed zipping her mouth and throwing away the key, which LeMay didn't seem to understand, but ignored all the same.

"The Freelys and I were hired, by Osden, to make a weapon." LeMay gestured to the still smoking mess of black goo the girls had made, the one which had caused such an explosion. "That, to be precise."

"Our parents were paid to make that specific load of gunk?" Graylin asked. "Why?"

"Dunno," LeMay said, scratching his chin. "They never told me. It's very reactive, very flammable, fairly dangerous. I knew Benson and Michaelangelo from school, so when they were bestowed this almighty job from Osden, they came to me for help. All I was told was that we needed to make a weapon, a powerful one. We experimented, we researched. The girls were the real masterminds, with all their chemical knowledge. Eventually, after a few years, we came up with that." He pointed again to the gooey black substance, still burning. "Called it pyrogleminine. It's highly explosive and can burn for hours, days even. Ours was a bit more complex than your mixture of gasoline and styrofoam, but the recipe is close enough in basics."

"And then?" Arlyn asked. LeMay chuckled humorously.

"You know, you're inquisitive enough to be a Freely. Would've said you were one, if they weren't all dead." He looked off into the distance dramatically . . . or so it seemed, until Graylin saw his gaze was actually latched back on the waiter, and what he was carrying. She shook her head; this guy had a real problem. With the amount of alcohol he was consuming, Graylin wondered how he had even kept his hands steady enough to make that airplane.

"And then it all fell to crap. We had just made the breakthrough, presented our ideas to Osden's weapons department. I was *sure* I was going to be let in on the secret, to be told what it all was for, and be rewarded for all the work I'd put in. And then . . ." LeMay shook his head, expression contorting into a sneer. "And then the Freelys disappeared, along with all our work. Poof, and they were gone. A few weeks later, I was told they were dead."

"They never told you what they were doing?" Graylin asked. "What a bunch of jerks." She may or may not have gotten a bit involved with the story, and forgotten it was about her parents.

"You can say that again." LeMay clicked his tongue. "So then, of course, the weapons department came after me, wanting to know where their precious weapon and those who made it had been going. I told them over and over I didn't know, but they didn't believe me. So, they took away everything I had. Kicked me out of the program, swore me to secrecy, and told me I'd never get another job again." He tossed his third empty bottle to the side, ignoring the swearing of the lady he'd hit. "So here I am, watching as people claiming to be the children of my backstabbing friends beat me at an illegal inventing match."

"So you have no idea why they left?" Arlyn asked. "None at all?"

LeMay stared into the faces of the remaining Freelys and sneered.

"None at all."

Graylin was about to ask more questions, like "how much alcohol is in your blood right now" and "where might my parents have gone, if, say, they were alive" when a blond, shaking figure pushed through the crowd.

"Arlyn?" Loren's studious gaze had been replaced with an anxious one, his eyes latching on the dark-haired Freely cousin.

"Loren!" Arlyn stood up quickly, chair scraping on the ground with a screech. "Loren, what's wrong? What happened? Who needs to be yelled at?"

"I . . ." Loren glanced around, taking in LeMay and Graylin sitting across from him. "I couldn't find you and then I couldn't find Graylin and, and then I went to find you but couldn't find everyone else and I just . . . were you talking with Gregson LeMay?"

"Yeah, but you need to slow down," Arlyn said gently, tapping his arm to get his attention. "Everything's fine. LeMay here was just telling us how he used to work with our parents."

"Your parents? Gregson LeMay?" Loren asked, shocked.

"Maybe you two *are* Freelys," LeMay said sarcastically. "Five minutes in, and you've already broken your promises." He glanced up at Arlyn, squinting with one eye. "Keep it confidential, remember?"

"Ahh, sorry." Arlyn winced. "I'll tell you later," she whispered to Loren.

"I'd be careful if I were you, missy." LeMay said. "Going about, making friends. You may not be a Freely, but you sure are talented. People like to use folks like us, get us to do things and leave us in the dust." He nodded to the rest of the crew. "Even your friends."

"Well, we've had ours for a while now, and I must say I've grown a little attached to them," Arlyn said. "Anyway, it was good to meet you. You put up quite the competition with the airplane." She held out her hand as Graylin stood. LeMay did not accept it.

"Likewise, Miss Freely," the man said snidely. The cousins began to walk away, but her conscience pulled Arlyn back. "Hey, LeMay?" Arlyn said, "I really am sorry for what my parents did to you. That wasn't cool, and if it makes you feel better, they sort of abandoned us, too."

"Girl," LeMay glanced up, "If I thought you really were a Freely, that would mean a lot."

Arlyn nodded to him and turned away. It was time to go.

Across town, seated at the Duncan's little kitchen table, Denloy was playing *King In The Corner*. Della had plied him with cake after cookie after tea as they had chatted about everything. Denloy was relieved that the girls hadn't been there for that. It had been a real challenge, that bit, keeping up the act, trying to figure out how much the Duncans knew, struggling to build up a story of the last eight years that didn't include the guilt and the pain and the hallucinations and the lies. It had been tricky, to be sure. Thank *goodness* he'd had so much practice.

It must be said that the Duncans had been very respectful. "It's your business, of course," Ridge had said, holding up his hands. "You're a grown man."

Just like a teenager being begged to tell the truth, Denloy had felt this strange compulsion to spill everything and say it all. Della's warm smile and Ridge's cheerful claps had come close to breaking his shell, but something about the night's events, maybe that memory of Arlyn's voice saying *Uncle Will*, had strengthened him. He had resisted.

And now? Well, now the hard part was over. Now he could simply enjoy the evening, playing a children's card game with two people whom he'd admired and respected for so long.

The lies, he decided, could wait.

23

THE CREW LEFT THE bar laden with things the girls had won, but practically floating with the adrenaline of the night. They all agreed that, although it had been fun, they probably wouldn't be coming back for a while. The sky had been clear and sparkling with stars when they entered the club, but a strange dull rumbling had Graylin checking the sky for lightning.

"What *is* that sound?" she asked, spinning around in several circles, scanning the sky. "Sounds like thunder."

"Oh, my bad," River patted his stomach. "I'm starving."

"Well, let's get some food then." Arlyn hooked her arm in Lewis's. "Come on, Uncle Denloy and I spotted a place earlier, and we've got some time before Loren needs to be home."

"This Loren guy is working wonders already," Graylin muttered to Teddy as the seven set off. "Like Arlyn's ever worried about curfews before."

"You can say that again," River laughed, skipping up behind them. "But then, she's not the only one acting weird tonight."

"Yeah, I know. Enland sat in that club for a whole three hours without falling asleep." Graylin nodded.

River chuckled. "I meant *you*, G. You're less than six inches from Teddy, and you're not squirming."

"I'm sorry," Graylin turned to gape at River, mouth falling open, "What did you just call me?"

"G. You know, like Graylin? G for Graylin?"

"Eugh." Graylin really *did* squirm now. "That is terrible. Never call me that again."

"Whatever you say, G."

"River I swear I will-"

"Oh, shut up, you three." Arlyn reached back and snatched at her cousin's shirt, yanking her forward to walk with her, Lewis, Loren, and Enland. "You stop that piddling, cousin, we're trying to make good impressions here," she muttered in Graylin's ear.

"Oh come on, Loren's got a whole wall devoted to us and our eccentricities." Graylin smirked, hooking her elbow with her cousin's. "If anything, our weird personalities and bad jokes are probably making him swoon for you."

"Shut up," Arlyn sang, slapping Graylin in the back of the head. "Anyway, we're here."

'Here' turned out to be a general convenience store with a few benches outside and a picnic table that seemed to be made entirely out of splinters. The aroma floating around the building was surprisingly quite delicious, but this turned out to be coming from a man standing next to the store with a fryer and a cardboard sign labeled "EATS". Nonetheless, he charged a cheap price for a bit of fried food and a bottle of juice and was quite friendly despite his shady appearance. They all purchased various food-stuffs and sat down, sprawling on the splinter benches, on the ground, and against the walls. Enland had gone out on a limb and bought a deep fried ball of sauerkraut, which looked, smelled, and most certainly tasted disgusting. Enland simply couldn't admit it had been a poor investment however, so he sat down next to Lewis with a look of very forced hunger plastered on his face.

"Ugh, Enland, please," Lewis wrinkled her nose, scooching deliberately away from the map man. "Get that disgusting thing away from me."

"Lewis wants you to move, River," Graylin said seriously. Arlyn and Teddy both snorted in laughter as River opened his mouth to deliver a fiery comeback.

"Well . . . well . . . fine," he said finally, holding his head high. "Come on Loren. These guys are a bunch of bozos."

"Arlyn and Graylin aren't anything like I thought they'd be," Loren said as he set down his paper cone full of fried strips of chicken, taking a seat on a bench next to River. The bench looked out over the city, and the view was almost magical, with the sparkling lights and wonderful collection of sounds. "All my info was eight years old, I guess."

River shrugged and took a sip of his juice. "If there's one thing you can always count on those two for, it's a surprise. Also being late, they have terrible time management skills."

Loren laughed, the peal floating into the night sky. River grinned.

"The cousins *do* change a lot, but in some ways they're very . . . very solid. Like some things about them just never change, and probably never will. Like Graylin, she's *always* been in her own head, and there's never been a time when Arlyn wasn't trying her best to help everyone else." He smiled, watching as Arlyn moved to sit by her cousin.

"If it weren't for Arlyn Freely, there's a good chance I wouldn't even be alive today," he said, taking one of Loren's chicken strips and popping it in his mouth. It was such a simple action, but it somehow made Loren understand even more clearly the sort of relationship the crew shared. It seemed very nice. "The day Arlyn and I met," River continued, "I was mid-way through chucking rocks at windows on a building that gave me bad vibes. I got caught, and the police were holding guns to me."

He chuckled. "I was a stupid kid, and to tell you the truth, I probably would have been put in the ground with the way I fought back. Then from behind the cops I heard these gunshots, and I looked over just in time to see Arlyn, ten years old, holding a gun up into the air. It gave me time to get away, and eventually the cops forgot about me. But Arlyn didn't. She found out where I was and came to see if I was okay. She's got to be one of the most caring people I know. It was just a coincidence that Leo picked me as one of the kids to take in after that. He didn't know I'd met Arlyn already."

"Wow . . ." Loren watched as Arlyn tossed a scrap of food at Enland, who hit it away angrily. "What *isn't* she good at?" It wasn't really a question, but River answered anyway.

"Showing her feelings," River answered without looking away from Loren's food. "Especially when the going gets tough. She doesn't allow herself to get emotional when it's hard, so utterly determined to be a light in the darkness that she'll hide her emotions so she can help somebody else. I've only ever seen her cry twice, and even then she's insisted she's alright, and two minutes later she's back to her normal self. It scares me sometimes, her ability to be strong like that."

"And Graylin? What's her thing?" Loren asked, watching River with mesmerized eyes. He wanted to learn as much about the Freelys, *proper* stuff, not just theories, as possible.

"Well, in my professional opinion, her biggest problem is her fear," River said wisely, nodding. He really had become a master at reading people. "She hates it when people make fun of her, or tease her, and she can't stand to look silly, because she's afraid of what they'll think. Especially if she's by herself. I think that deep down she's afraid people won't like her if she does something weird. But that's where Arlyn changes Graylin. Graylin will dance like a mad fool and make horrible jokes when it's just her and her cousin. The same with Arlyn actually- she doesn't put on a front with Graylin. Not like she does with us."

"Wow . . ." Loren said again, glancing admiringly at the two cousins. Arlyn was laughing with Lewis over something, while Graylin appeared to be tossing fried pickles into Teddy's mouth, but intentionally over-shooting some of her throws so that they hit Enland in the face.

"You know," River began, watching the group as well. "I think you have a pretty good chance with her." Loren choked on the fried chunk of mysterious chicken he'd been chewing, but not because the source of the chicken was, indeed, unknown.

"What?" he coughed, looking at River with watery eyes. River grinned.

"With Arlyn. You've interested and impressed her, at the very least, and trust me, that's more than I could ever say."

"But you've known her for so long, like you said," Loren said, trying to smile. "It seems to me that if anyone would have a chance, it would be you."

River laughed. “Oh, it’s not like that anymore. Arlyn Freely has had a line of star-struck boys after her since she was twelve, and I was only in that trail for a few months. I discovered pretty quick that I would rather remain best friends with Arlyn than ever even try to date her.” He gave Loren a grin. “Between you and me, whenever she *does* fall for someone, that boy will have a real time of it. He’ll be lucky as all get out, but I have a feeling that dating a Freely cousin is not for the faint of heart.”

Loren just sighed and watched Arlyn yawn and stretch before she stood and walked towards them.

“River, my friend, the rest of the fellas were talking about heading out and finding some sort of problem to cause, and they have respectfully requested that you join them,” Arlyn said, also stealing some of Loren’s fried chicken. River grinned and bounded away, eager to make some brotherly mischief. Arlyn smiled, sticking her hands in her pockets.

“Lewis offered to take care of Graylin for the night,” she said to Loren. “Best of luck to her, honestly. But I guess that means you’re stuck with me.” She looked out at the sprawling city. The convenience store was on the third floor of a large building, connected to the market by a large boardwalk acting as pavement, as if it was simply on ground level. From up here, Arlyn could see a whole new angle of Belhaven, and she loved it. “What’s your favorite place around?”

Loren stood up, bouncing the back of his heel on the ground. “I’m not really sure,” he said. He stepped to the edge of the boardwalk with Aryn and looked out. “To be completely honest, I haven’t seen much of Belhaven yet.”

“Let’s just walk then,” Arlyn said, eyes drifting across the bright maze of lights. Loren tucked his hair back and looked away; he’d never been good at the whole ‘interacting with people his own age’ thing. To him, hanging out with large groups, such as the crew, had always seemed the worst possible situation.

But this? One on one time with another teenager, let alone a girl, *let alone one like Arlyn Freely*? This was far, far worse.

“So you really don’t know what they’re up to?” Loren asked, watching the brothers run off, a wide grin of trouble on all their faces.

“Nope!” Arlyn beamed. “I gave up trying to find out a long time ago. It’s a brother thing, and I am, for all intents and purposes, an only child. I mean, you know that already, but I have *remained* an only child for the past eight years. To the extent of my knowledge, I guess.”

“You’re really not weirded out by it?” Loren asked, quieter this time.

“Weirded out by what?”

“My . . .” Loren hesitated, trying to think of any name to make it sound less humiliating. “Conspiracy wall?”

“No? Should I be?” she asked. “I mean, you thought we were all dead. Seems reasonable, from where I sit.”

Loren shrugged. “I don’t know. I guess I don’t know how I’d feel about my family being dissected under the microscope by some random teenager.”

“But you’re not some random teenager, you’re Loren Rainey.” Arlyn put a reassuring hand on his shoulder. “And we’re friends. Besides, they’re not really family so much as just people that were a part of my life when I was eight. Lily always says I’ve just blocked out all of it, but it’s not something I can dwell on forever. At least, that was my excuse when taking care of Graylin for the first four years. Eventually she realized I was putting my hurt aside to care for her, and she started to feel guilty, so she tamped her hurt down too. She cares a lot more than she lets on, disguises her sadness with wit and temper, that kind of thing.”

“What do you disguise yours with?” Loren asked.

Arlyn thought for a moment, playing with her braids. “I don’t. But it’s,” she chuckled, “braided into every part of me. I make friends with everyone, I talk constantly and make jokes all the time. I figure out what everyone is struggling with within two minutes of entering a room so that I can fix it. I talk about losing my entire family like it was just a regular Wednesday afternoon.” She paused and looked at Loren. “Was it a Wednesday?”

“Friday,” he answered.

"Like it was a regular Friday afternoon," Arlyn corrected. "But anyway, I just mean that's how it's always been. I can't really set it aside. And I know it's important and all and being a Freely is a big thing, but like, it's just my last name, you know?"

"I guess so," Loren said. "No Rainey has ever done anything worth talking about."

"I beg to differ," she turned them around a street corner. "That menagerie of string and ink is certainly something to write home about. Or to write about in general. It's seriously impressive."

"It was my parents that did most of it, really," he brushed it off. "I just tied together some strings, is all."

"And they let you bring it all along when you came to Belhaven? That was nice of them!" Arlyn beamed. If Loren was this interesting, she couldn't even *imagine* what his parents were like.

"Well, I sort of just took it," he said. "It was all that I had . . . all that was left." His pace picked up.

To say that Arlyn's heart dropped was an understatement. It crashed, nearly taking her down with it. "I'm sorry, Loren," she put a hand on his back, and he slowed again. "When did they-? If you don't mind me asking."

"Almost six months ago now," he said blankly.

"Oh. I'm so sorry." She wanted to say many things, things she would have given anything to hear six months after her own parents died, but she couldn't form the words.

"There was a house fire," Loren continued to the air around them. "It was arson, I swear it. It couldn't have been anything else. I was in the basement writing, and it got hotter and hotter and-" Unknowingly his nails dug into his arm. "And there was nothing flammable in the house, they had made *sure* of it because everything was too important to lose! It wasn't their fault at all and I-"

"Loren." Arlyn's voice was forceful, but not sharp. She had his wrist in her hand, holding it away from his arm.

He looked at her with tears in his eyes. "I'm sorry, I didn't mean to-"

"You're okay." Her voice was soft now. "It's okay. You don't need to be sorry. Let's sit down a minute, my legs are tired." Arlyn's legs were not tired at all, but she needed a reason for Loren to be alright sitting down. She was an expert in navigating a dead weight complex.

She spotted a bench overlooking a night market and set her feet up on the bottom railing as she sat down next to Loren. He was crying quietly, not able to stop the tears and apologies. "I'm sorry, I didn't mean to, I'm sorry, I shouldn't have said anything."

"Loren, it's okay. I'm the one who asked. You have nothing to be sorry for." She set a gentle but present hand on his shoulder. "I believe you."

"I should go home," Loren said, standing up suddenly.

Arlyn held his hand tight. "Loren, trust me, home is the last place you need to be right now. Let's you and me walk around a while, do something fun, have conversations, hm? Going home just puts you right back in that box you just worked so hard to get out of. The first few steps outside of it are the hardest, I promise."

Loren considered this for a long time. "Okay."

"Excellent!" Keeping his hand in hers, she started off in the first direction that caught her eye. "I've been dying to get into some trouble."

Denloy smiled at Della while she catered him with his third slice of cake. It had been a long time since anyone had doted on him in such a way, and to be completely honest, he was enjoying it. Of course, thinking about lies had reminded him of the one he hadn't yet constructed, and while eating a slice of berry pie, he had made up his mind. As soon as they got back to the *Freelander*, he would begin inventing a story, a proper one, one which would keep his nieces from happily ever finding their parents.

But for now . . . well, he could enjoy tonight, loosen up, per se. He could laugh and chat and reminisce with the Duncans, talking about past victories and celebrations. Living as Wilmot Denloy for so long, he'd almost forgotten the *good* parts of William Freely, the ones that enjoyed parties and people, the parts which would have laughed their heads off if they had seen the formal, uptight, black-tie affairs which Denloy had grown so accustomed to. What a stark difference between those events and the warm, aromatic Duncan kitchen.

"So, Will," Ridge said, folding his hands together. "Do people still call you that?"

"Occasionally," Denloy lied, smiling genially. *Pretend.* It was so familiar, pretending, and ironic, really. For the past eight years he'd pretended to be an upstanding, friendly businessman, just a touch lonely, who was perfectly healthy in the head and didn't see visions of the family he'd killed. Now he was pretending to be the upstanding, friendly Freely brother, perhaps the loneliest out of the four, who was perfectly healthy in the head and wasn't hiding the truth from everyone he loved.

Incredible, he mused absently, how similar both of his masks were, and how neither were truly him.

"Well, Will, I must tell you I owe my grandson a huge apology," Ridge chuckled, sipping his coffee. "You see, he's been saying for almost a year now that William Freely survived the Freelander Disaster, and then became Wilmot Denloy."

"Did he now?" Denloy raised his eyebrows, stomach flopping just a little. If that boy, Loren, had figured out his true identity, did that mean others had? *Relax*, his brain whispered, *just enjoy this. Stop working yourself up.* He took a deep breath and gulped down the floral dregs of his tea to wash away his thoughts.

"Oh yes. Nobody believed him, mind." Ridge raised his eyebrows. Then he shook his head and took another drink. "That kid is a genius, so you'd have thought we'd have learned to listen to him by now."

"A genius, you say?" Denloy asked.

"Oh yeah. Truly gifted." Ridge smiled. "A little awkward at times, but his mind is just on a completely different level than the rest of ours. I mean, after all, who else would make that connection?"

"Who indeed," Denloy chuckled, inwardly breathing a sigh of relief. "To tell you the truth, Arlyn and Graylin are a bit like that. Just incredible."

"*You* were like that," Ridge grinned. "All of you Freelys."

"We tried our best," Denloy shrugged, grinning. "Bit of a hard reputation to live up to, I'll admit. But we sure did try."

"You didn't even need to try." Ridge shook his head, long beard swinging as he beamed. "You were amazing."

Arlyn's eyes seemed to glow a soft amber as she looked into a weathered lamp under the canopy she and Loren had found shelter under. There had been a brief rain, which Loren explained was common, being so close to the ocean and all. She watched as soft-winged insects swarmed around it, small eyes blinded by the beautiful sun within arm's reach. Arlyn wondered how the city must look to someone so small. How grand it must be. The lights, the trolleys, the buildings, *the university!* She had been meaning to ask Loren about that.

"Say," she said, pointing to the very academic looking spires of a building in the distance. "Isn't that the university you were excited to get into?"

Loren, also wildly bemused by the flittery bugs, turned his attention to the distant structure. "Oh, I suppose. Grandma and Grandpa were really excited when I applied."

"Were you?" she asked.

"I . . ." he hesitated, "I mean yes, I was, I am, but . . ." He sighed. "It was their idea. They thought it would get me to stop looking into the Freelys. Because they think I'm crazy. And it's not like I don't want to go, I've always wanted to be a professor or an author or something, but if they're just putting me in time out, what's the point?"

"Well, you're not crazy, that's for sure," Arlyn said. "Crazy would be having very little evidence and then going on a cross-country adventure to find people who may not even really be alive. Imagine *those* weirdos." She grinned. "Besides, you have your whole life ahead of you to go to university and be a professor and all that. My grandma was getting her third degree when the ship went down. You've got plenty of time."

Loren sighed. "Do you know what you're going to do with your life?"

Arlyn thought for a moment, looking up at the moths. "I think I'd like a garden. Maybe a little pond full of ducks. Oh, and I'd love to learn to cook someday. Like really cook. Make food people enjoy and not have to bury pots and pans in the yard. That kind of life sounds nice."

Loren looked at her, this girl, Arlyn Freely. He had just met her, yet known her for so long. *Not her*, he thought, *your idealized imaginary version of her*. No, the Arlyn in front of him wasn't the one he'd imagined, because she was real. She was kind and caring and smart and her eyes sparkled when she spoke and she didn't think he was strange at all. She watched moths dance in street lamps with endless enchantment; she talked about the world as if it were her friend, not just somewhere she lived. What he wouldn't have given in that moment for the courage to ask her to stay, just for a little while.

"Pyrogleminine," Arlyn said suddenly, eyes snapping down from the lepidopteran world above. "That's it! That's why the Freelander went down, why it burned, why they hid it. It was pyrogleminine!"

"Pyrogleminine?" Loren repeated. "What are you talking about?"

She grabbed his shoulders. "LeMay, at the bar, told us he made a weapon with Graylin and I's parents. Pyrogleminine, that weird goo I made in the bar, the one you were talking about earlier! Our parents made it for Osden during the war- and it's just like you said earlier- when the pyrogleminine disappeared, the war ended. And what big event coincides with the end of the war *and* involves our parents?"

"The Freelander Disaster," Loren said, eyes going wide. "Oh. *Oh*. The pyrogleminine was on the Freelander. That's what they were carrying on it! That's why it burned for so long after going down! It was pyrogleminine!"

Arlyn was practically dancing under the streetlight, grabbing Loren's hands and glowing with their discovery.

"We've got to tell Graylin!"

Graylin drew in a deep, deep breath. The air was cool and fresh, thanks to the brief curtain of rain which had drifted over Belhaven within the last hour. Lewis had instantly ducked under an awning, of course, but Graylin had blatantly refused- the rain was so clean and free, and made the whole world seem bright. Also, she had been due for a shower. Now the two girls were sitting on a dock, jutting out over the inky water lapping at Belhaven's edge, their feet dangling in the cool water. It was very peaceful.

"COUSIN!" Arlyn Freely, followed by one Loren Rainey, pounded around a corner, feet landing so heavily the entire dock shook. "COUSIN YOU WILL NOT BELIEVE WHAT LOREN AND I FIGURED OUT."

Graylin leapt to her feet, mostly so she could stop her cousin before she just barrelled off the dock. Graylin seriously doubted that Arlyn's discovery-fueled frenzy had brakes.

"Arlyn Freely, what have I told you about screaming your head off near houses in the middle of the night?" Lewis also stood, putting her hands on her hips. "We've discussed this."

"You said, directly, that in matters of great importance, the screaming of heads off was acceptable." Arlyn skidded to a stop, doubling over to catch her breath. "Boy howdy, I need to work out more."

"And is this a matter of great importance?" Graylin asked, grinning as her cousin wheezed.

"Yes, major importance, in fact," Arlyn beamed, standing up straight. "Remember pyrogleminine, that gooey-burny-sticky stuff?"

"Cousin, I may have memory issues but I'm not *that* bad. That was like an hour ago," Graylin said.

"Right right right. Well, remember how Loren told us earlier that after the Freelander went down, the war between Osden and Nalvern ended?" Arlyn bounced. Graylin raised her eyebrow, but Arlyn waved it away. "Yeah yeah right, it was only a few hours ago. Anyway, now we know our parents *invented* pyrogleminine, and that they, according to LeMay, took all their work with them when they left him."

"Yes . . . and?" Graylin asked, searching desperately for the connection.

"Cousin, try to keep up!" Arlyn clapped her hands with excitement. "The pyrogleminine was *on the Freelander*. That's why the ship blew up, that's why it burned for so long, and that's why the war ended! All the pyrogleminine was gone!"

"But why wouldn't our parents just get rid of the pyrogleminine another way? Why kill our whole family in the process?" Graylin asked, holding her hands behind her back speculatively. "Cousin, I know it's been a while since we saw our parents, and I know Loren's board says they blew it up intentionally," she nodded respectively to Loren, "But I don't know . . . it just doesn't feel right."

"I don't know for sure." Arlyn said, still buzzing with the discovery. "So we need to get back to that board. Where the heck are the boys?"

The three brothers were found far more easily than Graylin expected, considering they were in a massive city. All they had to do was follow the sounds of poor choices and likely danger and boom, there they were. It was not long at all before the seven teens were knocking on the Duncan's door, some of them quite hungry, some of them extremely excited, all of them excessively tired.

"Oh my dears, do you have any idea what time it is?" Della cried as she threw the door open. "Get in here." She pulled them all in one by one, tapping them on the shoulders and head. "Five, six, seven. How many of them are there supposed to be?"

"Six of mine," Denloy called from the kitchen table, "one of yours."

"Perfect." Della shut the door behind the teens and spun around. "Now you can *all* hear my chewing out."

"Oh, leave them alone, Del," Ridge said, sitting across from Denloy, holding some cards. "We knew they were gonna be late, they're Freelys for goodness' sake."

"Boy, I wish that excuse would have worked on Leo," Graylin muttered.

"It really is late, Della. The city will be waking up soon," Denloy said, setting down his cards. "We ought to get out of your hair."

"Absolutely not!" Della cried, waving her arms. "You all are staying here tonight, it's four in the morning!"

"No no, we have a ship," Denloy protested. "We've far overstayed our welcome, my nieces kept your grandson out too late, and I really think we've caused enough damage-"

"William Freely, you stop that wittering." Della motioned with her hand. "There is no chance I am letting you guys leave this house without a good night of sleep and one full meal." She continued talking, dragging out blankets and pillows from random closets, moving with almost unbelievable speed. "You'll take Loren's room," she called to Denloy, voice muffled by the vast pile of pillow cases she was carrying. "The three girls can have the guest room, of course, and the boys the living room." She was now beginning to lie out beds, stuffing pillows in cases and fluffing comforters.

"Ah," Denloy said quietly to Arlyn, "I didn't separate the boys and the girls when you stayed at my house. Should I have?"

"Puh-leese," Arlyn rolled her eyes. "You've met us. As a collective, the only normal teenage hormones we've got are those of frustration, sadness, and general irritation. Graylin and River did come pretty close to a fistfight, but beyond that, we were fine."

"Oh, I've got a better idea!" Della clapped her hands to her face. "William, you can have *Ridge and I*'s room, and then-"

"Mrs. Duncan Lily's mom, lady?" Graylin interrupted hesitantly. "Us girls are fine on the floor in here, Loren can keep his own room, and the boys can share the guest room with Denloy. I'm sure he wouldn't mind that."

"I wouldn't mind at all," Denloy nodded. "That will be perfect."

"Are you sure, really, Ridge and I can-" Della began, before her husband cleared his throat. She seemed to catch the message he was trying to convey and resigned.

"Alright alright, you can have the guest room. But if you want anything, you just have to let me know, and-"

"Come on Del, let them go to bed in peace." Ridge gently took his wife's arm. "They're all responsible kids, and they will keep in mind how late it is and respond accordingly." He glanced through his glasses at the crew, gaze pointed and laughing.

"Oh, alright." Della gave Arlyn one last pat on the cheek before pulling her grandson in for a hug. "Goodnight Loren dearest, sleep well."

"I will Grandma," he said, patting her back awkwardly, feeling the eyes of the rest of the crew on him. Denloy too made a round of 'good nights', before following the Duncans upstairs. As soon as she heard the thumps of the bedroom doors, Arlyn rubbed her hands together.

"Okay, quick run down. Boys, sit. Not you Loren, you're important and know things."

"Um, woah." River grinned, plopping on the couch. "Rude."

It took Arlyn and Loren, with brief and unsubstantial help from Graylin, about ten minutes to outline and review all the information they had learned that night. When they discussed Loren's theories about their parents' intentional blowing up of the *Freelander*, Enland took off his glasses and rubbed his eyes. When they detailed LeMay's story about pyrogleminine and the parents' betrayal, River sighed and spiked his hair. When they concluded with the idea that pyrogleminine had been what the Nalvernian War had been about, and what had caused the Freelander Disaster, Teddy glanced at Graylin, hoping she was okay.

"And that's about it," Arlyn finished. "That's all we know."

"Not quite," Loren piped up. All eyes turned to him, and he cleaned his glasses nervously. "There have been multiple reports of explosions, very similar to pyrogleminine, within Osden itself, and whispers that they are being conducted by Freelys." He realized how that sounded, like he had been withholding information, and hurried to elaborate. "They are all rumors, of course, and not very credible. In fact, when I first heard of them, I didn't even bother to dig deeper. It just seemed so unlikely that someone claiming to be a Freely would really be testing pyrogleminine. But now that I know they're alive, that you're looking for them, *and* that they're the ones who invented the pyrogleminine? Well . . ."

"Well, it's a place to start," Arlyn said stoutly.

"It might be nothing," Loren quickly added. "I wouldn't get your hopes up."

"I wouldn't exactly describe them as hopes," Graylin said. "In today alone we've learned that our parents probably planned the disaster which killed our whole family, invented a massive lethal chemical weapon, betrayed their business partner, and were responsible for *your* parents' deaths in a turnabout way. Their reputation really isn't looking too good." And yet, even as she said this, the inner workings of her chest gave a mighty flutter. Not the cute, romantic kind, the 'I feel a bit sick' kind. Sick with excitement, and sick with fear. They had a plan, a lead to her parents, and it was terrifying.

"We need to go to bed," Enland sighed, elbowing a deeply snoozing River, who had fallen asleep roughly three times despite, or perhaps because of, the seriousness of their conversation. "Help me Ted."

Together, the two lifted River by the armpits, heaving and struggling to flop his arms over their shoulders.

"Wouldn't it be easier just to wake him up?" Loren asked hesitantly.

"Not when it's River," Graylin said seriously. "Night, guys."

"Night," Teddy smiled. Graylin shot him a finger gun, which he happily returned, before following Loren upstairs.

"I promise he isn't usually this loud," the girls heard Enland tell Loren as River gave a mighty snore, his feet dragging on the steps.

"I can smother him with a pillow if you want," Teddy offered.

"No, I really don't think that's necessary," Loren said nervously. He had such a hard time differentiating between humor and seriousness.

"Please," Teddy said, "it would be my pleasure."

24

LOREN AWOKE WITH A start, the greatest dream in months of nightmares slowly fading from his mind. The Freely cousins alive, new friends, and people who believed him! He held a hand to his excited chest, trying to quell his racing heart to stop it from jumping out of him. "It wasn't real," he whispered to himself. "It wasn't real." He said it until his heart was left hanging from its strings, weighty and lumbering as normal. *Emotions are too strong*, he thought. *Why can't they ever just be normal*? And as if reading his thoughts, River entered, far too loud for the morning hour.

"You awake, mate?" he asked, not whispering at all.

Loren fell back on the bed, both hands trying to keep his heart inside of him. "It wasn't a dream."

"Well, I wouldn't exactly call Enland a dreamboat, but I'm sure he'll be glad you think so." River came and sat on the edge of the bed as if he had always done it. "So, since I was off partaking in my own activities last night, I didn't get much chance to really know you."

Loren stifled a small chuckle. "There isn't really much 'me' to know."

"Oh sure there is." River motioned to the hallway outside. "You're a cello player, that's something to know." He pointed to the strings on the board, "either your favorite color is green, or green is a cheap color of string, and I know it isn't because Enland likes to try crocheting and complains about it every time he goes to the market. You clearly like to write because nobody puts that much time into their handwriting unless they have to look at it all the time."

"How did you notice all that?" Loren asked, realizing River was right on every account.

"None of my friends have made a habit of expressing their feelings or entire personalities in any way except context clues, so like a sloth in the snow, I had to adapt," he said proudly. "I'm basically a native snow-sloth. And also a bat, picking out details using screaming and stuff."

This time Loren did laugh, so hard that he nearly fell off of the bed. River pulled him back up by the arm, saying, "Bats scream, don't they? Got really good ears for that? I'm like that, but with eyes for miniscule details."

"Like a hawk," Loren offered. "They have good eyesight."

"Oh, but hawks are dangerous," River said, almost instinctively looking up as if one would be circling the ceiling above them. "I'm nice and fun and easygoing, like if a hawk was those that would be me."

"Are you now?" Loren asked. "I didn't get to really know you yesterday, either."

"Well, consider me met." he stuck out his hand for Loren to take. "River Freely, resident funny guy and haver of friends."

"You seem self aware."

River shrugged. "If I can simplify myself down to a few traits, I'm easier to like and from there, like the glorious virus I am, I will spread and rise to my full form: a friend!

Loren smiled. "You guys really are a good crew, aren't you? Is that what you call each other? You're the crew?"

"Generally, yeah," River chuckled. "We get into some sticky situations now and then, but with just enough intelligence to run a ship or open a can of olives."

"You guys run a ship?" Loren *had* wondered how they had all gotten here, and while slightly skeptical of them individually, he figured the crew was capable of doing such a thing as running a ship as a collective, After all, they had Freelys.

"Yeah, the Freelander two point *zee-ro*." River emphasized the name, and could nearly sense Graylin twitching in her sleep from the mispronunciation. "Rebuilt to a lovely third of the original size, and fitted with every useless invention known to man. I take that back. *Some* are useful, but most are just modified clocks that do an unnecessary amount of things to tell you the time. Arlyn was in a phase about them for a while."

"That sounds . . ."

"Amazing?" River grinned. "It loses a bit of its shine after the fifth time you've been chased around it with a spatula, but when you're *not* trying to hide from Lewis it's just fine."

"Is she really that dangerous?" Loren said, thinking about the very serious and proper girl who had directed the bar so flawlessly the night before.

"More than you know," River said gravely. "But there're a few empty rooms to hide in. We really could use a bigger crew. Just one or two more people and we would be a full ship." River glanced at Loren from the side, being far less smooth than he thought. "What benefits do you think we could offer besides housing, delicious meals, and lifelong friendship and paid vacation time?"

"Is that different from regular time?"

"No, but really, if you think about it, it's all a vacation."

Loren thought for a moment, "Do you have healthcare?"

"Well, you won't die or be grievously injured." River paused. "Maybe. Probably not anyway. I haven't died yet, so if that's anything to go by, I think you'd be pretty safe."

"It seems like a pretty good ship to be on," Loren said.

River sighed, "Okay, what I'm asking is-"

"River! There you are." Enland poked his head in Loren's door, Teddy's face appearing beneath Enland's as he wriggled his way in between his brother and the door. "Ugh, Teddy, get out of my way."

"Your way? You, Lando, are in *my* way." Teddy managed to put his hand on the doorway as Enland squashed him, and he groaned. "How many fried pickles did you eat last night?"

"I dunno, a lot?" Enland said defensively, trying to see over Teddy's head. "Lewis said I need more meat on my bones."

"She lied," Teddy said, finally getting a good shove in, pushing Enland hard enough that he could force his way into the room.

"Would you two quiet down? It's like super early," River said, rolling his eyes at Loren. "Can you believe I *live* with these guys?"

Teddy smacked River in the back of his head before spinning away quickly, just missing Enland's physical rebuttal he knew was coming.

"You guys are interrupting my 'get to know Loren' time," River said, shooing his brothers away. They refused to be shooed, but Loren didn't mind. He was watching the three boys, thinking about what their growing-up years must have been like.

"So Leo adopted all three of you?" he asked curiously. Teddy had set himself in Loren's spinning desk chair, and was rotating idly. Enland, meanwhile, had been examining the conspiracy board, and he turned to face Loren at the question.

"Yeah," he said simply. "Well, probably. We don't know for sure."

"He *definitely* did," River said.

"Seems unlikely to me," Teddy said, still spinning slowly.

"We. Don't. Know. For. Sure." Enland said pointedly, his tone such that Loren was certain they'd had this conversation before. "But it doesn't really matter," the cartographer continued, "Leo was like a dad to us anyway, legal or not. Or at the very least a far older brother."

"Wow." Loren shook his head in awe. "What was that like, being raised by him with the girls?"

"Imagine," Teddy began, gesturing with a pencil, "A carnival. Now imagine that carnival is on fire."

All four boys laughed, before Enland reminded them the rest of the house was asleep.

"Did you guys know each other before Leo took you in?" Loren asked. He knew about the Freely adoption tradition, of course, but he had never really thought about what it must have been like for those lucky kids chosen.

"Nope," River grinned. "We were all at the same orphanage, but we each arrived at different times, and there were enough of us there that we didn't really come in contact much. I'd been at the orphanage pretty much since birth. My parents both died when I was tiny. Yellow fever."

"How many times have I told you not to grin when you talk about your parents' deaths?" Teddy shook his head. "It makes you look demented."

"Arlyn does it," River said.

"Arlyn occasionally looks demented," Teddy muttered.

"What about you?" Loren asked him. Teddy began spinning again.

"My parents weren't . . . uh . . . married? My mom raised me by herself for a while, until I was four or something like that, but without . . . well, you get the point. I know my mom died not long after she gave me up, and my dad too, but I don't know anything else."

"And Enland? Your parents? Did they give you up too?" Loren asked, before seeing the frantic '*no*' motions Teddy and River were making. He shrunk, embarrassed. "Oh, I'm sorry. I understand if that's too forward of a question."

"It's alright," Enland said, giving Loren a small smile. "No, they didn't give me up. They wanted to keep me . . . Social Services did *not* want them to." He caught Loren's horrified, wide-eyed expression and hurried to elaborate. "Oh, don't get me wrong. It was totally warranted. They were *not* good people."

"But they just took you from them?" Loren asked sadly. "And you were old enough to remember?"

"I was eight," Enland said. "I never heard them called anything but Mommy and Daddy, so finding out what happened to them was pretty difficult. Leo and the Maynewins were happy to help, though, and I found out they died in a car accident when I was twelve."

"As you can imagine, these wonderful origin stories gave us all some attitude issues." Teddy said, spinning faster. "Our first time meeting was when the headmaster of the orphanage gathered us to tell us he was kicking us all out for our misbehavior, unless we wanted to be adopted by a guy named Leo. Naturally, we all chose Leo."

"He was just gonna kick you guys out? How old were you?" Loren kicked off his blankets, dangling his pajama-panted legs off the side of his bed.

"Teddy and I were both ten, Enland was eleven," River said. "But-"

"Boys!" a voice, Della's, shouted up the stairs. "Breakfast!"

"Well, boy howdy." River bounced off the bed and flew out the door.

"And that is River in a nutshell." Teddy spun once more before standing up. "Food over tragic backstory any day."

When the boys arrived at the kitchen table, they found the girls and Denloy already dogging into the sprawling meal Della had whipped up. The tiny little circular kitchen table was covered in platters of bacon, eggs, muffins, and thick slices of toast. Golden butter dripped off the bread and muffins, and the bacon glistened. Graylin glanced up as the boys tripped down the stairs, and raised her eyebrows.

"You look like you've been hit by a train," she told Teddy as he sat down next to her. His hair was sticking up at odd angles, bags rimmed his eyes, and his shirt hung in weird folds.

"Yeah, well, let's just say River's snoring didn't tone down last night," Teddy said, raising his eyebrows. "If anything, it got worse."

"At least you weren't down here." Graylin glanced at Arlyn. "Someone, cough cough, my cousin, cough cough, wouldn't shut up about her new friend and his conspiracies."

"Meanwhile, *you* kept regaling us with stories of your and Teddy's little escapade," Arlyn said, leaning over, a fried egg stuck on her fork.

"Please, I could hardly get a word in edge wise with Lewis telling us to be quiet." Graylin said, her arm bumping into Teddy's repeatedly, and this bothering her far less than it would have in the past.

"Did any of you sleep at *all* last night?" Denloy asked, eyeing the teens.

"Not really," Arlyn said, shoving the egg into her mouth.

"You didn't tell me you guys came here on *the* Freelander!" Loren said excitedly, taking a seat next to her at the table, which was getting quite crowded. "I thought River was being sarcastic!"

"River doesn't really *do* sarcasm," Graylin said through a mouthful of muffin. "He is disgustingly genuine all the time."

"We *did* fly here on the Freelander!" Arlyn grinned, watching as Della piled Loren's plate with food. "It's not the original, of course, it would be far too big for us if it was. Also, you know, the original was sort of destroyed."

"No kidding," Loren smiled. "The first one was designed to be operated by your Grandpa Charles and his cousins, and there were like twenty of them."

"There *is* still extra space, though," Arlyn said, an idea hitting her. "If you, you know, want to join us." She looked away from the boy, feeling oddly embarrassed by how much she wanted him to say yes. "You could fulfill some of your theories, and I guarantee you'd be a tremendous help."

Loren blinked at her, eyes confused behind his glasses. "You're inviting me to go with you?"

"Yeah!" Arlyn grinned. "I mean, if you want to, of course. I know you have plans here, with university and stuff, but . . . well, just think about it, okay?"

"I will," Loren said softly, mind already racing. "I will."

After their breakfast was thoroughly scarfed down, the crew busied themselves by folding and tidying the sleeping amenities they'd used the night before, mostly at Lewis's urging. Denloy chatted with the Duncans, laughing occasionally, and watching his nieces happily. The house thrummed with vibrance and life.

Loren stood in his room, the drawn shades keeping the space in dim darkness, staring at the suitcases under his bed. It wouldn't be very difficult to go with the Freelys. He was already practically packed, save his conspiracy board. He could leave right now, and go on the sort of adventure his parents had always dreamed of. With the Freelys and their crew, he would travel the country, searching for answers to fill his board. He could get to know Arlyn better.

And then his eyes landed on the only picture on his desk in a frame. It was very recent, this photograph, and held the faces of he and his grandparents. Della was beaming, her arms around Loren's shoulders, her face lit in a way it hadn't been since Loren's parents had died. Ridge too was smiling, standing solidly behind his wife and grandson. Loren looked into the weathered, lined faces, and thought about the kindness his grandma and grandpa had shown him over the last five months. He thought about the deep sadness he caught in Della's face when she thought he wasn't watching, or the tears Ridge let roll down his cheeks when he stared too long at pictures of his two daughters, both now lost to time in different ways. Loren took a deep breath, and began to pull papers off his wall.

"Goodbye, my dear," Ridge said, pulling Arlyn into a hug. "It has been such a joy, seeing you. A miracle, really."

"You wanna talk about miracles?" Arlyn grinned. "Take a look at your grandson."

"You come back soon, you hear?" Della said, stealing the black-haired Freely from her husband and squeezing her tight. "We've missed you for the last eight years, so I reckon we've got pretty good at it, but that doesn't mean it won't be hard."

"Oh, we'll visit, don't worry." Arlyn smiled. "I don't know if River will survive very long without your muffins." She glanced at her friend, already carrying a huge paper sack full of breakfast leftovers.

As Graylin suffered through the Duncan's affectionate farewells, Arlyn turned to Loren. The boy was standing next to his grandparents, watching the crew with solemn eyes.

"I'm sorry, Arlyn," he said quietly as she approached. "I would love to come with you, but I can't leave my grandparents like this. I mean, they just lost my mom, and then finding out that *you* guys are alive . . . well-"

"Hey," Arlyn put a hand on his arm. "Hey, look at me." Her eyes maintained contact with Loren's face until he met her gaze. "It's okay," Arlyn said simply, smiling. "Family is important. I may not be overly attached to my parents, but you can bet your butt that I would have given anything for Leo, or for Graylin. I understand."

"You do?" Loren's whole face relaxed. "Oh thank you, I-"

"Now shush," Arlyn pulled Loren into a hug, holding him tight. "I don't like goodbyes and I don't feel like crying in front of everyone."

"Here," Loren sniffed, and pulled a collection of papers from his pocket, holding them out with shivering hands. "This is everything I have on Mackson's Bay. Reports, newspaper clippings, letters . . ."

"Thank you, Loren," Arlyn said, eyes glowing with the bittersweet sparkle of farewell.

"I hope it helps," Loren said. His eyes locked on her and remained there as the crew began their trek back to the *Freelander.*

25

WILMOT DENLOY WAS SITTING in a chair in the *Freelander* meeting area, trying to concentrate on the book he was reading, and having a very hard time of it. The arrival of his two nieces did not help him pay attention. He had to smile as they approached, both using the couch in ways it was not intended to be used. Graylin perched herself on the back, hugging a pillow to her lap, and Arlyn stretched out on the rest of it, propping her head up with an elbow. An onlooker may have noticed, in that moment, the similarities all three Freelys shared, in habit and looks. One would have seen the brightness in every Freely eye, all of which tilted up at the corners. A very astute watcher might have seen the similar shapes of the three's noses, or the way all of their hair, different though it may be in texture, parted in the exact same spot: off center, to the left.

However, as they sat down, anyone could have seen that Arlyn Freely had something to say.

"We met someone last night," she told her uncle. He smiled, sticking his thumb in his book to hold his spot.

"Is that so?" he asked. "Who?"

"This dude called LeMay," Arlyn said. Denloy choked on the tea he'd been sipping.

"LeMay? Gregson LeMay?" he coughed.

"That's the one!" Arlyn grinned. "We met him at this illegal inventing competition. That's where we went the other night, with Loren, and where Graylin picked up that ratty cat she keeps carrying around like she's a child."

"I am *not* acting like a child," Graylin said irritably, shoving the little Pasta further into her pocket. "I just like it."

"I'd been meaning to ask about that." Denloy smiled, setting his teacup down. Only he and Lewis used the tea cups, everyone else preferred mugs. "Not about the cat, but where you guys were. How is LeMay? What's he up to?"

"Honestly, I don't think much, but he did give us some great info." Arlyn leaned against the arm of the couch. She was eager, no, excited, no, *thrilled* to share their discovery with her uncle. He would be ecstatic, would he not? That they found a piece of the puzzle? "LeMay worked with our parents on this secret weapon called pyrogleminine. Have you heard of it?"

Denloy's heart dropped. No, he thought, *no no no no*. They weren't supposed to find out. Not at all, but especially not like this.

"Pyrogleminine? No," he said, wincing inside. All he wanted was to protect them, but even in pursuit of shielding his nieces the lie felt terrible. Arlyn's eyes were glowing with excitement.

"LeMay didn't know why, but Osden's weapon's department hired our parents to make it, and they asked him to help. And we made it, Graylin and I! We didn't even try, just threw together some styrofoam and gasoline during one of our rounds, and there we had it!" Arlyn grinned, pleased to present her uncle with so much information. Denloy tried to put on a smile. What was he going to do? *Lie*, his mind whispered, *it's for their own good. Lie.*

Denloy wasn't prepared for this. He hadn't had time to invent a sufficient story to distract Arlyn and Graylin from the pursuit of their parents yet. He needed to be quick. *LeMay, LeMay, LeMay*, he needed a story for LeMay.

"Gregson LeMay," he said finally, "Well, he was a smart man, when I knew him. He was young, and brilliant, and maybe a little . . . over-excited, to be working with my brothers." He sighed, pretending to button his cuff, mind racing as he tried to piece together the next bit of lie. "In the beginning he was okay- a little absentminded, but smart. But as time went on . . . well, he became a fanatic of sorts. Obsessive. I heard that a few months before the Freelander crashed, Mike and Ben had to kick him out of the project. They just couldn't work with him around. He hero-worshiped my brothers, idolized them. At some point it turned from normal to creepy. He started following them, taking their things, watching them."

"Really?" Graylin asked, big eyes wounding Denloy to the core as he tried to ignore the trust there.

"Yes, I'm sorry to say," he nodded. "Ben had this theory that Gregson was working on projects of his own, ones involving mercury. LeMay'd always been interested in the stuff, and was constantly trying to slip in into the group's plans. Of course, we know now . . ."

"Mercury is poisonous," Graylin said, realizing what her uncle meant. "It was making him go insane."

"Exactly, or at least, that was the idea," Denloy smiled sadly. "Personally, I think it was just his drinking habit, finally getting to him." The girls nodded. They had noticed LeMay's fondness for alcohol.

"Wow," Arlyn said quietly. "So it was all a lie? All that stuff about pyrogleminine and the weapons department?"

"I'm afraid so," Denloy nodded. An idea hit him, and he snatched at it, adding to the tale. "What I think is that you stumbled upon a sad man, who's been used by the world in a very rough way. I think he saw two people, who shared a name with his idols, walk into a bar and perform some fantastic inventing, and thought that you were . . . disrespecting them, somehow, or copying them, and that he fed you lies as punishment. As for the pyrogleminine stuff, if I'm being honest, I think that he could have chosen anything you invented that night- the gunk just happened to be what he settled on. He gave it a funny name, and voila- he had a story."

"But pyrogleminine is real," Arlyn said softly. "Loren's board is covered in reports about it."

Denloy swallowed, his heart dropping. "Oh yes," he said, voice only barely breaking. He cleared his throat. "Yes, actually, now that you mention it I *do* remember Mike and Ben mentioning it at some point. I wouldn't be surprised if they were consulted about pyrogleminine at some point, but I highly doubt they invented it, and I doubt it was anything close to what you girls made." He took as deep a breath as he could, trying not to let the girls into his head. All of this was pure rot, of course. He knew his brothers invented pyrogleminine. He'd been there, after all, and it did sound as if the girls had come very close to recreating a form of it. Hands shaking just slightly with the weight of his lies, Denloy continued. "It does make more sense that LeMay chose the name of an already existing weapon, and then assigned it to your parents. The LeMay I remember was rarely sober enough to invent such a story all on his own."

Arlyn was quiet for a second. She had been so certain that they had been on the right track with this, sure it had brought them closer to the truth. It made so much sense, and Loren had agreed that pyrogleminine had been on the *Freelander* when it crashed.

"Well, I'm going to go get myself a snack," Denloy said finally, standing up and rubbing his low back in a very Leo way. "I *am* sorry," he added. *If only you knew how much.* "I'm sure it felt great to feel you'd made some progress." The girls nodded to him, and he turned away.

"Wait," Arlyn said, and he froze. *They know it's a lie.* "We're going to stop in Mackson's Bay next. Loren found some clues pointing there. Most of them involve pyrogleminine, so maybe they're worthless after all, but I suppose it's the closest thing to a lead that we have. Have you ever been there? Any recommendations of places to see?"

Heart pounding, trying to calm his nerves, Denloy smiled. "Oh, yes. There is a phenomenal candy shop there your dads and I were quite fond of, which we should definitely stop by," he said. Graylin hopped down from her seat and grinned.

"Ooh yes!" She gave her uncle a fist bump and hurried away. Denloy stared after her before looking hopelessly at Arlyn.

"Told you she'd warm up," Arlyn laughed. "All it took was a few months and the suggestion of sweets." She stood as well and smiled a little sadly at her uncle. Denloy realized her smiles hadn't been quite as genuine since they'd left Belhaven, and he had a sneaking suspicion that the lack of a blond, bright-eyed scholar boy by the name of Loren was the cause.

"Thanks for your help," Arlyn said. "I know you're trying to help us. We both do."

Denloy smiled at his niece, his heart breaking. Yes, he was trying to help, but he wasn't sure if they'd see it that way.

"Don't thank me," he smiled, tucking his book under his arm. "I want to know the truth just as much as you." *But I don't.*

"We know, Uncle Will," Arlyn grinned, before skipping away.

It was nearly a week later when the crew was called to assemble in the meeting room. When Graylin skipped in, Arlyn was already there, holding a very long stick.

"Cousin! You have finally arrived!" she announced grandly.

"Indeed, I have!" Graylin declared. "Now where the heck is everyone else?"

"Right here G!" River called, skipping into the room.

"If you continue to call me that, I will not hesitate to eat your breakfast," Graylin told him. "And don't think for a single second that Lewis won't help me."

"Denloy says he'll be here in a minute," Arlyn said, standing at the little message system box on the left-hand wall. The typewriter parts purchased in Belhaven had been quickly installed, and the system was now in full-fledged use. Arlyn typed a quick message back, looking up as Enland, Teddy, and Lewis arrived. "Ah! People!"

She straightened her overall strap, popped a paperclip in her mouth, and clapped to get everyone's attention.

"Alright friends and foes," Arlyn announced, "our next stop on this great big adventure of ours will be Mackson's Bay, about two weeks from here. However, in the meantime, there has been a disturbing occurrence upon this ship which I feel needs to be discussed." The crew exchanged glances, all thinking of separate things. River and Teddy, who had spent the last three nights sewing bells on the ends of Enland's house slippers (a joke in themselves), tried not to look at each other. Lewis went red, thinking of the long walk she and the cartographer had snuck off the ship to take, and Graylin cleared her throat, thinking of the cookie she'd sent Teddy through the message system tubes (food transport had been strictly prohibited by Lewis).

"Er, what would that occurrence be?" River asked guiltily, hoping that Teddy was inventing an alibi for them.

"The *disturbing* lack of drama on this ship!" Arlyn cried, stepping onto the low table in front of the couch. "How long has it been since we performed a play? Ages, ages I say! And Uncle Denloy is a rich man who's been to many a play. Think of the advice he could give us!"

"You're right. I don't think we've had one since our last camping trip." Lewis nodded, silently rejoicing that Arlyn had not brought up her and Enland's moonlit wanderings.

"Are we even the Freelander crew anymore?" Arlyn cried, getting into her soliloquy stride. "Where's the drama? The theatrics? Not one play has crossed the decks of our great airship in nearly four months and that is a tragedy in and of itself!"

"So it's settled." Graylin hopped onto the table next to her cousin, mostly to nip the dramatic shouting in the bud. "We'll put on a play."

"A play?" Denloy smiled at his nieces, walking down the hall towards the crew. "What's this I hear?"

"There he is, the man himself!" Arlyn jumped from the table. "We want to put on the best production this side of Belhaven, and you, sir, are to be our director."

Wilmot Denloy laughed at his niece's enthusiasm and shook his head. "Me? A director?"

"You're an adult. Don't you know how to boss people around?" Graylin asked. She just assumed when people turned twenty or so they gained the magical ability to tell people what to do and see results.

"I won't deny that I do a lot of instructing," Denloy smiled, "but I have never been involved in a play of any sort, save the ones your fathers and I used to put on."

"Do you remember any of them?" Arlyn asked, interest piqued. "We should do one of those! Saves us writing time."

Denloy looked around at the six young, shining faces staring at him. He hadn't realized he could become so attached to anyone so fully, so quickly. He *loved* these kids . . . and he could have cried at that moment, purely because he hadn't known he could do that anymore. Love.

Or maybe these kids were just special. Leo had loved them, too. Maybe this crew of six simply had the ability to melt the sad Freely brothers' hearts. He saw in them the joy, dreams, and ambitions of his childhood, and he *needed* to save that.

"Alright," he nodded finally, smiling. "I'll direct this production. Get me some paper and some assistance, and we'll write the script."

There was a brief vote and debate, ending with a strict gavel smack from Lewis, which decided that River, Arlyn, Graylin, and Teddy would all be on Denloy's writing team. The five sat down in the meeting area, all holding papers and pencils, ready to jot down their script.

"So, our favorite play to perform," Denloy smiled, cleaning his glasses, "was actually a romance."

"A romance?" Graylin wrinkled her nose. "Ew. Gross."

"Well, the humor came into play when you considered we were all brothers," Denloy grinned. "Now, the basic premise is that our main character, a beautiful young lady, embarks on a quest, which she cannot finish, or receive the rewards from, until her closest companion dies. We changed the . . . genre, if you will, of the play many times. We tried soldiers, nurses, regular folks, treasure hunters, criminals . . . the settings are endless."

"Have you ever tried pirates?" Arlyn asked, sitting up straighter. Denloy considered this.

"Ah, no actually, I don't think we did," he said.

"Well, let's roll with that! Our beautiful young lady is an epic pirate lady captain, and her close companion shall be her best mate!" Arlyn beamed. "And then the love interest will be a fellow crewmate."

"How about Enland and Lewis play the lovers?" River suggested.

"Well *duh*," Graylin muttered. "Who else is gonna do it, me and Teddy? You and Arlyn? I think not."

"I can play the guitar for backing music," Teddy offered quietly. Graylin smiled- she *still* had never heard the boy play, and was excited to. She wasn't sure why exactly, but the thought of listening to him do what he loved made her happy. Sort of like watching Arlyn build a complex machine, or Lewis decorate a cake, or River . . . well, River didn't really have any talents, but the point was across.

"You don't want to act?" Denloy asked. "There's a part I think would be perfect for you. We always had one rebel in the play, and for a pirate ship setting we could really play that up. You can be the rabble rouser. That was Leo's favorite part."

"Rebel? Rabble rouser? *Teddy*?" Arlyn scoffed. "I think you've got the wrong man. Teddy's not like that at all."

"What do you mean?" Denloy asked, looking around at the group, genuinely confused, and feeling instantly embarrassed. "He is, isn't he?" Denloy had seen that look in Teddy's eye, heard the whispered comments and held in laughter. He could have *sworn* the pilot had a touch of rebellion in him, the kind that he'd seen in some of his friends long ago. He'd *sensed* it. Was he really so out of touch with his younger self, he couldn't even read basic teenage personalities?

The thought made Denloy sad, and he looked apologetically at the boy.

"I'm sorry," he said, not sure how to take back what he'd said.

"It's okay," Teddy said, feeling very much like it was not Denloy but Leo watching him. His adoptive father *had* always been able to see more of Teddy than the boy had wished. "I can play the music."

The four crewmates quickly moved on, writing what dialogue Denloy could remember, and scheming roles for different people. Eventually, Lewis was called in to give her costume expertise, and the group was generally lighthearted and cheerful. And all the while, Denloy watched.

He'd thought for several hours the night before, tapping his pencil as he sat at his desk. He had been *such* a fool. He'd known it as soon as

Arlyn had mentioned Gregson LeMay. His nieces were smart, intuitive, and quick. Had he *really* thought he could simply wait for a plan to come to him? That a solution, one which would keep his nieces from ever finding their parents, would just fall into his lap? It had been nonsensical, this idea, and he was ashamed he'd ever had it. So, he had thought, and thought, and thought and thought. How to stop them, and protect them, and protect himself?

He had spent the whole night musing, and still couldn't come up with a solution beyond simply telling them the truth, which was out of the question. Perhaps, in Mackson's Bay . . . the girls were sharp, yes, but not above distraction. He could easily find something there, but it wouldn't be indefinite. It would only buy him time. What other quest could he send them on, and would it ever be enough to keep them from their long-term goal? He doubted it. Maybe he could talk more about Leo. They had obviously loved him. He could use that.

He'd nodded to himself and had gone to sleep with a peaceful mind.

"Tilt that curtain a little towards me!" Denloy called to River as the crew set up their stage. The red-haired boy did so, and Denloy gave him the thumbs up.

"Hey Uncle Denloy! Is this good?" Arlyn asked, stepping from behind the large rolling curtain and spinning around, dressed in full, if not historically accurate, pirate regalia.

"It's perfect!" he told her, grinning. "Your Lewis is quite the skilled costume designer."

"You can say that again," Arlyn agreed, tugging at her scarlet waistcoat and lacy ascot.

"Lewis! I hate you! You're the worst costume designer ever!" Graylin ran out from below decks, bedecked in many shawls, beads, and her curls tied back with a headband.

"Oh, come on. It's a scarf around your head, not the end of the world." Lewis entered the top deck behind Arlyn's cousin, looking very piratey, and irritated.

"Cousin, it touches my neck. It touches my neck!" Graylin screeched, wriggling like someone had dropped ice down her shirt. Arlyn now saw that the tied beaded ends of the headband scarf were dangling against Graylin's neck.

"Here." Arlyn tucked the ends up, using a clip to secure them. "Better?"

"Now it looks silly," Lewis sighed. "If you could just be a little less sensitive G-"

"Did you just call me G?!" Graylin took off her borrowed sandal and chucked it at Lewis's head. "Don't ever call me G!"

"It wouldn't be a Freelander Theatre Production without Graylin intentionally hurting someone," Arlyn sighed.

"Leo used to be like that. Michelangelo too, but not as much," Denloy chuckled.

"Inherently violent?" Arlyn raised her eyebrows.

"Prone to annoyance." Denloy corrected. "And reacting in comically exaggerated ways."

"Okay, yeah, that sounds like Graylin," Arlyn agreed. Then she laughed, thinking of Leo, and how he totally had *not* been like that when they knew him. "You said Uncle Leo was like that?"

"Definitely. He was the youngest, of course, so if he wanted to be heard, he had to make some noise," her uncle said. Arlyn nodded, because that made sense, and then smiled at a few particular memories of Graylin and Leo's shouting matches. At the time they had been terrible to witness, but looking back on it, she supposed she could see what Denloy was saying.

"Hey! Uncle Denloy man!" River came charging up, half of his hair spiked with a cornstarch and water mixture, half of it limp. "I need to ask you something!"

"By all means, ask away," the businessman smiled, as his two nieces ran off.

"Have you ever been in love?" River asked, plopping himself onto a crate. Denloy raised his eyebrows.

"In love?"

"Yeah!" River pulled out a pad of paper. "Enland and Teddy think my character should have a bit of a thing for Arlyn's character, just as a side plot, and Teddy's never been in love, and Enland won't talk about it, so I need your help."

Denloy thought for a second and then smiled. "Well, I guess I have been in love. A long time ago."

"Tell me everything." River exclaimed. Denloy nodded, thinking.

"Her name was Joanna, and she was . . . amazing. She was kind, and sweet. We dated for maybe a year, and I- well, I was going to marry her. I had almost picked out a ring."

"Well, what happened?" River asked.

Denloy shrugged. "We just sort of ended. I don't know, really. I guess . . ." Denloy thought back to before the Freelander Disaster. He had been so carefree then. "Well, my brothers and I started having problems with one another. Then they died. I didn't have much choice but to restart, and restarting meant leaving Joanna behind." He sighed, and then smiled. "Besides, we hadn't talked to each other for at least a month before the disaster. We'd sort of . . . fallen out of love."

"Wow," River said, eyes wide. "That's so tragic. I don't think I can write that in. It's too sad." He flipped the page. "So that's just how it ended? Just like that?"

"Just like that," Denloy said. "It's amazing how a relationship you relied on for so long can disappear so quickly." He watched as Graylin spitefully pulled a curl out of the ponytail Lewis had tied it into, over on the stage. "I checked up on her a few years ago. She's married now, with two little kids. She's happy."

"Are you?" River asked. Denloy stared at the boy. He didn't know. Was he? For a long time, for the past eight years, really, he would honestly have said no. He hadn't been happy.

"Yes," he said, feeling relieved that it was true. "Yes, I *am* happy."

"Good," River said, turning back to his open notebook. "I don't like it when other people aren't happy. Teddy's not very happy sometimes, and I don't know that Graylin is either."

"You shouldn't hold yourself responsible for everyone else's happiness," Denloy said seriously. River scrawled a few notes.

"Oh, I know. But that's what Arlyn does, and ever since I first met her, she's been . . . my role model, I guess. Everyone loves her. She's smart, she's kind, and she's also happy. I know she's not *really* happy all the time, but at least she acts like it, which in turn keeps up everyone else's spirits. And if I am always happy too, there's less for her to do, right?"

"I think both you and Arlyn should relieve yourselves of that burden," Denloy said.

"That's what Uncle Leo would have said," River smiled.

"I honestly don't know how he managed those two for so many years," Denloy chuckled, as Graylin and Arlyn tag-teamed, grabbing Enland around the waist, lifting the shouting boy into the air. He flailed, smacked Graylin in the head, and reached frantically for the top bar of the curtain as Arlyn and Graylin teetered. The second his hands closed around the bar, the cousins let him go, and he hung there, kicking wildly, calling for Lewis.

"They are fifty percent amusement, fifty percent a headache," Denloy sighed, rubbing the bridge of his nose. "That's the Freely cousins for you. Very extreme. The same day they broke their three-month silence, they found a secret message, gathered the crew together, snuck into the Maynewin's, crashed a ball, and confronted you," River grinned.

"Yes, I see what you mean," Denloy said, watching the girls from across the deck. Arlyn was now literally tossing ideas to Graylin, who unfolded the pages and tossed new ideas back. Every so often, one of them would leap up and enact whatever idea they'd read, much to the joy of the other. Graylin was currently falling dramatically to the floor.

Denloy smiled as River rushed away. Oh, how he *wished* he was simply on this trip for enjoyment. He wished he didn't have a secret to keep, or an agenda to play. He thought about how Leo must have seen the crew. Like his own children, he was certain. He sighed. Joanna had always talked about kids.

26

"LADIES AND GENTLEMAN!" RIVER cried to their audience of one. "May I present to you the Freelander Acting Troupe's original production and performance of 'My Love Lies in the Sea'."

The first scene was set, the open winds of the sea imitated by the surrounding sky. Arlyn walked onto the 'stage', followed by Lewis.

"Captain, o Captain!" Arlyn called out to the sky. "Look upon the golden sea below us, and see its beauty.

"Beauty, you say," mused Lewis. "Yes." Lewis had pulled back her hair and wrapped it in a scarf. Her eye patch, which she always wore, added to the pirate effect. "Tis' a fair maiden, the sea; but her hunger is ravenous, much like that second mate, Samuel."

"You always pick on him, Captain. For what more has the fellow done to you but stolen a few bits of scrap from the table after the meal?" Arlyn said, folding her arms at Lewis. "Samuel is a hearty man, with strong arms that pull the ropes of this ship with ease, so what are a few of his faults to all of ours?"

Lewis sighed dramatically. "I suppose you are right, Ev'lyn. But my mind only thinks of what goods we may find at our destination. Treasure is bound to be waiting for us, my dear."

"Captain!" Enland rushed onto the stage in all his theatrical glory, hair braided back and finished with a velvet ribbon. "The island is in sight!" He paused and nodded to Arlyn. "Evelyn."

"Ollen," she nodded back to him. "Will you please tell Samuel the sails need adjusting? Don't worry, he'll know which way they go."

"Can do."

Lewis and Arlyn stepped off of the stage as River entered as Samuel.

"Ho, Samuel," Enland greeted him.

"Ho, Ollen," River replied.

"Evelyn says the sails need to be adjusted, and said you were the one to come to." He nodded to the fake sail they had set up earlier.

"She did, did she?" River mused. "What a fine request from a fair lady."

"Aye," Enland nodded. "But, alas, it seems she'll let nobody ask for her hand."

"What a shame, too. She's got a fine demeanor as well as her features." River sucked in his laughter while Arlyn cackled offstage.

"There's no pride in sticking to nothing," Enland said. "Now, go hoist those sails."

Their audience of one clapped as Enland and River left the stage, and the next set was quickly assembled.

"Land ho!" Lewis cried, leaping off of a crate and onto the set, decorated like an island. "Alright mateys, let's find us some treasure!"

"The bounty says that on this island is the final resting place of Captain Omar Blackheart!" Arlyn kicked the 'sand' out of her shoes and ran to Lewis. "Tis' a familiar name to me, though I couldn't tell you why, Captain. Have you any idea where we would recognize him from?"

"Not a clue, Ev'lyn." Lewis said, taking a shovel from Enland and sticking it into a pile of small boxes, clearly lying.

"You aren't even going to check for Blackheart's bones? He'd have buried his treasure near them, I'm sure," River said.

"Silence to ye, Samuel!" Lewis spat. "I've known the sea for far too long to doubt my senses."

There was a harsh sound, metal against metal, and Lewis smirked. "Well, would ye look at that?"

Using the shovel to throw the boxes aside, Lewis revealed a chest buried under the pile. "Ollen, help me hoist this out!" she called to the first mate, who nodded and quickly pulled the chest out towards the group.

From the side of the stage, Teddy's guitar rhythm rose faster and faster.

Suddenly, Graylin burst out from behind the boxes, a sinister grin on her face as the crew screamed. She was dressed in peasant's clothes, with Lewis's colors around her eyes and her hair tied up similarly to the cook's.

"My daughter comes at last!" she yelled. "But ho! She comes to defile her father's grave for dirty coin."

Lewis's eye went wide, but she said nothing. River, on the other hand . . .

"A g-g-ghost!" he leapt from his spot and ran offstage, screaming. The audience laughed as he ran.

"You have fallen far my daughter," Graylin said, standing taller. "And for that, I curse you. Your father loved you, and you now shall be denied the ability to love! Not until the one you care for most comes to harm at your own hand!"

Lewis scoffed, "Care? I care for no one but my best friend."

"Thank you, madam," Arlyn said graciously, bowing.

"Don't take it too far, it's mostly for political reasons. But I shall never love, nor desire to love anyone. This curse, witch, will not affect me," she said, pulling out her sword and holding it at Graylin's throat.

"Witch? Be careful thine words, daughter. You may come to regret them." Graylin said, a look of perfect, graceful disdain on her face. Teddy, apparently caught up in the play (or Graylin's acting), faltered a moment in his playing, and Graylin shot him a look before throwing the smoke bomb at the ground. By the time it cleared, she was gone. River poked his head around the curtain.

"And I thought I had family problems. Your parents were a creepy sea captain and a witch?" he asked, stepping out aways.

Graylin chucked a fairly heavy bead at his head from off stage. "I'M NOT A WITCH." This was not in the script, but Lewis covered it beautifully with a mocking laugh.

"Yes indeed. I believe my mother's curses to be entirely false, however. She has no magic- otherwise, why would the troubles and trials that separated my family ever have happened?" Lewis lowered her sword and stabbed it straight into the lock. With a bit of engineering magic that had taken Graylin and Arlyn several snacks to construct the top flipped open, revealing a trove of treasures. Gold, rings, and gems, and glittering in the light; all, in reality, made of sugar. Teddy and River had gone through a pound throughout the various practices.

"Ah! Such treasure!" Lewis exclaimed, and bent down. "Evelyn, look and see! Are there any greater treasures in the world?"

"I can think of one," Enland said, watching Lewis with loving drama. The one man crowd gasped dramatically. It was becoming clearer and clearer that the first mate had held more than respect for his captain. Lewis, however, acted oblivious.

"Ah Ollen! Best of first mates! Come and claim your treasure!" she called. Enland stepped forward with a nod and studied the gold. Then, he picked up but one ring, one obviously meant for engagement.

"An interesting choice," Arlyn said with a wink, standing slightly too close to Enland. Her hair, matted and tangled, blew around wildly in the wind. "Who, may I ask, is it for?"

"That is my secret, and will remain so," Enland said, slipping it into his pocket.

Enland exited the stage, and Lewis turned to Arlyn.

"You are becoming obvious, my friend. Your pursuit of Ollen is all too clear," she said. Arlyn laughed.

"What can I say? My charm comes naturally." They also exited the stage, leaving the set to be changed.

The next fifteen minutes went by, Lewis and Arlyn both becoming increasingly more interested in Enland, and Enland letting his stares linger longer and longer on Lewis. Furthermore, Arlyn and Lewis's squabbles were becoming more and more frequent; in the previous scene they'd been on the verge of a sword fight. Now it was Enland and Lewis's second biggest scene- the confession.

"I cannot hide it any longer," Enland was pronouncing, holding Lewis's hand. The sun was just setting, making the mood very romantic. Lewis had been very smart about the timing of the play. "My love for you soars like the birds in the air, leading me to land." He kissed her hand.

"Ollen! My dear Ollen! How long have I dreamed of these words! You cannot know!" Lewis said, looking full to the brim with joy. She was simply radiant. "I love you so, and I know I will never be happy without you." They leaned in to kiss, but BAM! Teddy beat a huge drum they'd found below decks. Enland instantly fell to the ground, as if struck ill.

"Ollen! My darling!" Lewis cried, bending over him in alarm. He shook, convulsed, and cried.

"The curse!" he yelled in pain before going limp. Just then, Arlyn entered from the side.

"You fiend!" She cried, addressing Lewis. "You monster! You would let my beloved Ollen die?"

"*Your* Ollen?" Lewis screeched, seeming to grow taller. "He is not yours! He is mine!"

"Yours? Ha! You cannot even be with him. You are so selfish as to love him, even though it kills him?" Arlyn cried, mocking.

Lewis was quick to react. She pulled out her sword in a flash.

"Don't you dare speak to me in that way, Evelyn. I am your captain, and you will address me as such!"

"You are nothing but a heartless witch!" Arlyn screamed, and she started her attack. Arlyn and Graylin had choreographed the battle, and it was beautiful, filled with steps, spins, swings, strikes. Then, with a cry, Arlyn collapsed to the ground. Lewis had punctured the small bag of wine hidden in her jacket, and the 'blood' seeped everywhere as she huddled on the floor.

"My captain," she murmured faintly. "My . . . friend. I'm sorry." Lewis, who could cry on command, began to sob. Arlyn went limp. Another smoke bomb went off, and Graylin appeared.

"Well," she said, hand on hips. "I honestly didn't expect you to kill her. But a deal is a deal. You may now be with your lover." She whisked herself away. Lewis stayed huddled in a ball, crying, until Enland touched her shoulder. She turned to him, and he hugged her as she cried over the death of her friend.

The play ended with a moonlit kiss between Enland and Lewis, and an enormous round of applause, considering it came from just one person.

"Bravo! Bravo!" Denloy said, applauding as the cast took a bow. "That was glorious! I've never seen that story performed so well!"

The crew was ecstatic. The sun was gone, and Graylin had inconspicuously lit various lanterns and hung them up for the last scene of the play, so that the golden light shone off the glossy boards of the deck. All six crew members were gathered in a circle, engaged in a simple game of duck, duck goose with some very Freely alterations (these included a spray bottle, a bar of soap, and a lemon).

Denloy watched as they all laughed and played. For so long, he'd seen them act like semi-adults, but now, in this moment, they were children.

Graylin glanced over at her uncle. Running in circles, it was a bit hard to catch his expression, but it looked happy. That was good. Graylin felt unbelievably happy in this moment, and it would be a real damper if everyone else didn't.

Distracted by her musings, Graylin tripped, falling into Teddy, whom she'd been chasing and knocking him over, falling on top of him and Lewis. She let out a shriek of laughter that was so un-Graylin like that Teddy began to laugh too, loud and bright. This shocked everyone else into fits of giggles, and they were still a little delirious with laughter when Enland drug up armloads of pillows and blankets. It was a delightful night; a cool breeze flowed over the deck, just cold enough that it felt good to burrow under the covers. None of the crew could bear the thought of sleeping in their stuffy, cluttered cabins when the wide deck was an option, and everyone simply tossed the blankets into a pile and jumped in.

How can I keep lying to them? Denloy thought, watching the mass of laughing teenagers. *I just got them to like me!* There was a nagging in his head, similar to the feeling of guilt, tugging and pulling at his brain. He would tell them upfront, he decided in a flash. Now. While they were in a good mood. He would bring up Leo, tell them it's what he would want, and just get it over with.

"Arlyn," he said as his niece ran past to get food.

"Yeah?" She stopped and looked at him, her eyes sparkling. He couldn't tell her. He just couldn't be the one to make that sparkle disappear.

Denloy was quiet, then smiled. "You did great."

"Thanks, Uncle Will!" she said, continuing towards the kitchen.

Denloy tried so very hard to smile.

27

"Hey, Uncle Will, check this out!" Arlyn ran to her uncle, holding a deck of cards in her hand. She took four from the deck and fit them between her fingers. She opened her hand and all four went flying into the wall, and stuck there.

"Bravo, Arlyn!" Denloy clapped as she took her cards out of the wood. "That's a good deck too. Where'd you get it?"

"My friend Finnigan," she answered, poorly shuffling them between her hands. "He's still in Odios, but I'd throw cards against him pretty often. He was never any good until I told him we could go somewhere if he won against me. It was actually pretty impressive."

"How was Odios, and growing up with Leo?" Denloy asked. "He always told me he never wanted kids, ever, said they would hold him down. But it seems like you three were amazing together."

"Oh, it was fun," Arlyn said, thinking about how she could tell Denloy about her childhood without sounding like a maniac. "Graylin and I got into a little trouble, but it was never that bad." Okay, so maybe Graylin had gotten lost an average of once a week for the first few years, and then been forced to sleep in some very shady abandoned buildings, but Arlyn had always covered *beautifully*, and Leo had never known the difference. Graylin turned out ok, right? "I'm surprised Uncle Leo didn't try to find a school to send us to after the first year," she added.

"You sound just like your dad, you know that?" Denloy smiled.

"That's what Uncle Leo used to say whenever Graylin and I suggested we go to the city." Arlyn skipped into the empty meeting room, her uncle in tow. "Said our dads were always impulsive, and he was glad our moms showed up to act as voices of reason."

"Have you thought of going back to Odios? Leo obviously thought it was a good place for you," Denloy said. An idea struck him, a perfect, wonderful idea. *I can sow doubt.* He brushed off his shirt. "Pardon my asking, but aren't you even a little angry with your mom and dad? I mean, they left you. They left *us*. Why go find them if they never even tried to come back for you?"

"Are *you* angry at them?" Arlyn asked, sitting in a chair. Denloy couldn't answer. Truthfully, yes he was, but as he couldn't tell Arlyn why so he just shrugged.

"A little, maybe."

"Angry enough that, given the opportunity to see them again, you would refuse it?" Arlyn asked seriously. "Leaving us behind was rough, but definitely not enough to warrant rejection. Especially because I know now that they had a plan to get us off the ship."

Denloy had no response, because his niece was right.

"At first I just wanted to see them again," Arlyn said, fiddling with a card, "And I still do, but now . . . well after hearing all that stuff from Loren, and meeting LeMay, now I also want to know what they had been doing before the disaster, and how it was their fault, and what they've been doing all these years."

Denloy felt that tugging again, the one whispering that he would need to change his niece's direction soon. Maybe even before Mackson's Bay. It was as if there was a clock in his head, ticking, ticking, ticking, ticking. He didn't have much time left.

"And if we can't find them?" Denloy asked quietly. "If, over the last eight years, something has happened to them, or they've left the country? What then?"

Arlyn was silent. "I'd never thought of that," she said quietly. She dropped the card she'd been fiddling with and bent to pick it up quickly. "Don't mention that to Graylin, please," she said hurriedly. "I don't want her to have that in her head. She needs to have something to hope for." She looked out at the clouds around them. "If we don't find them . . . then I guess we just learn to live with the questions. Go home, I guess. We could live with you!" She beamed at the thought.

"You'd want to?" Denloy asked, surprised.

"Of course! You'll have to share responsibility with Lily, who we owe a lot to considering we just up and left her, but I'm sure she'll be happy to share us."

"That would be wonderful," Denloy said earnestly. Arlyn grinned and bounced away. As she left the room, her space was filled with Denloy's nagging worries, very much resembling the eyes of his past he'd grown so accustomed to before he'd found his nieces. They'd been missing for the past few weeks, and he'd almost forgotten about them, but here they were back again, blinking and staring and watching.

With the return of his worries came the resurgence of his guilt, the one that had been devouring him for the last eight years. It was so heavy, he actually started to walk slightly hunched. He should have been there, all those years, for Leo and his nieces. He should have saved them. He had known Michaelangelo and Benson's plan, and in some ways he had encouraged it. Yes, he had backed out in the end, but that was part of the issue. He *should* have stayed, if not to stop his brothers, then to protect their children, and the rest of his family. But he had fled, and pouted.

"Hey Uncle Denloy," Graylin said, tapping his door as she passed. He glanced up at her, smiling quickly. This wasn't hard; every time Graylin greeted him, it was like a ray of warmth.

"Hey. Where are you off to?" he asked.

She leaned against the doorway, playing with her length of chain. "I'm not sure, actually." She said. "I *was* looking for Teddy, and then Lewis said Enland was hanging out with him, and then I was going to find Enland and I saw a jar on the counter and remembered I was thirsty . . . but now I'm not actually sure why I'm right here."

Denloy nodded. He himself tended to be absentminded. Back home, he'd had a very specific written note system to keep himself on task with all his duties, but that had mostly fallen to the side on the ship.

"You have that chain a lot," he blurted. "Why?"

"Oh." Graylin looked down, saw the chain, and quickly stowed it in her pocket. "I don't know. I guess I just like moving something. And it feels nice, it's all cool and heavy." She grinned. "It drove Lily crazy. She couldn't stand it when I fiddled while she was trying to talk to me. Most of the time, I didn't even realize I was doing it until she yelled at me to stop pacing or something."

"I hear you there," Denloy smiled, and then grinned inside as he mentally saw his colleagues' reactions to the way he was talking. Unintentionally, he'd picked up some of the crew's phrases recently. Graylin grinned and left the doorway before returning quickly.

"By the way, I think you were right about Teddy. What you said about him while we were setting up the play? Arlyn just doesn't know him very well."

"He reminds me of some people I used to know." Denloy nodded. "I suppose every generation has its rebels, doesn't it? They're all fighting against something else. For my friends . . . the fight got to them all." He watched Graylin closely for a second before deciding to speak. "You should watch Teddy, I think. Make sure the fight doesn't get to him, too."

"If only I knew what he was fighting," Graylin said, sighing. "Well, I've got to go find my cousin." With that, she hurried away. Denloy sagged in his chair, the load of holding back all his secrets felt like an actual pain in his mid back, the weight pressing down on his spine. It ached in his bones, his heart, and his head. He didn't know how much longer he could do this.

"Do you guys feel like Denloy seems sad the past few days?" River asked his brothers as the three sat gathered around the pilot's chair.

"Sad?" Teddy asked. "I wasn't aware he was anything *but* sad."

"He told me he was happy when we were doing the play," River mused.

"Ever heard of a lie?" Teddy muttered, stopped by a smack from Enland.

“And how did you get this information, anyway?” Teddy added, ignoring Enland’s physical rebuke. “Did he just say ‘hey River guess what I’m happy’? Because that seems unlikely.”

“No, I asked him.”

“River,” Enland said accusingly, “You can’t just ask someone if they’re happy.”

“And why not?” River asked defensively. “It’s vital info, which I want to know. And it’s easy. satch. Enland, are you happy?”

“I would be happier if you acted like less of a buffoon,” Enland said.

“Teddy? Are *you* happy?”

“At this moment? Sure. With you? Not in the slightest,” Teddy answered, flicking a few switches and pressing a button quickly.

“As sorry as I am to say it, though,” Enland added, messing with a braided bracelet around his wrist, “I do agree with River that Denloy has seemed especially subdued over the last few days. I think something’s bothering him.”

“It’s probably River and his callous questions,” Teddy said.

“Is *not*,” River argued.

“We have to remember, Denloy is a Freely too,” Enland said, ignoring the bickering. “I think we’ve been missing out by not seeing him like we do Arlyn and Graylin. He has some of the same habits as they do, which could mean he also has their tells.”

“Like when Arlyn chews on a piece of string or Graylin almost suffocates her hand with a strip of leather?” River raised his eyebrows, not quite perfecting the single raise yet. “Those are pretty specific.”

“It’s a chain, not a piece of leather.” Teddy said, simply looking for a fight now.

“What the heck is the difference?” River asked.

“One sounds wicked, one does not,” Teddy said, standing up a little to look at a gauge.

“You are so weird,” River scoffed, as Enland rolled his eyes.

“Would both of you shut up? And no, I didn’t mean those kinds of things. I was thinking more like . . . like how Graylin acts when she is really trying to hide something. That kind of tell.”

"I see what you mean," River said, shifting his seat on his box.

"You think he's hiding something," Teddy said, glancing at Enland. He shrugged.

"Not necessarily. Maybe. I'm just saying that he's a Freely, and we should think of him as such," he said, as the spoke of gentleman entered the top deck. The three brothers glanced away from each other, their conversation ending with River poking Teddy, and Teddy kicking him back.

Downstairs in the kitchen, Lewis and Arlyn were leaned up against the counter, chatting. When they got really into conversation, the topic was always a mystery, and often they didn't even remember what had got them started.

"Hey, remember that really ugly vase we took from my house before we left?" Lewis asked. "Where is that? I've been waiting to throw it off the ship for over a month now."

"I haven't the slightest recollection of what you're talking about," Arlyn admitted. "But speaking of your house, how do you think your parents are feeling about this whole 'I'm going on an adventure for months on end' thing?"

"I think they're worrying themselves frantic when not otherwise occupied, but that overall they will be just fine." She said, "I posted a letter when we stopped in Belhaven, so at least they know I'm alive."

"Really?" Arlyn was impressed. "Man, now I feel bad. I should have sent one to Lily."

"She's strong. She'll be okay," Lewis assured her.

"Possibly."

"And speaking of Lily . . ." Lewis grinned. "Are we not going to talk about how she and Leo totally dated?"

"I still can't believe we were right!" Arlyn exclaimed. "And now we know her parents! And they're super nice!"

"And they have a cute nephew," Lewis added.

"Don't tell me you like him!" Arlyn said, actually stunned. What a tragedy *that* would be.

"What? No, of course not. But you *totally* do." Lewis elbowed her. "And I had my money on Finn, so this is a shock to me."

"You were making bets on who I'd get together with?" Arlyn scowled. "I would've expected better of you, Lewis. It's not like I fall in love with every boy I see!"

"But they fall in love with you," she reminded her.

"I've spent the last three years pretending that wasn't true, and I don't intend to stop now," Arlyn said. "But, out of curiosity, who does everyone else have their bets on?"

"Graylin and I have our money on Finn, but it turns out Graylin isn't very good at this whole bet thing, because she kept interrupting you two every time Finn was about to ask you out. Intentionally, I might add, she just doesn't like him, or the idea of someone taking her cousin," Lewis said. "River thought maybe that one kid from that first gang you accidentally joined had a chance, but then pretty quickly changed his money over to Loren once we met him. Enland refused to participate at first but eventually revealed that he thought you and that Issac kid from the higher districts looked nice together."

"Issac?!" Arlyn choked on the chocolate milk she'd just poured herself. "Holy cow, I haven't seen him in years! Yeah, he was the one who got us access to the upper district places so we could etch random initials into that city official's house! Did Teddy have any comment on all of this?"

"Actually, he bet his money on himself, and I'm pretty sure is still working up a way to convince you to go out on a date with him so he can have everyone's money."

"That's actually pretty smart," Arlyn said, amused by her crewmate's creativity. "If he says he'll split the profit, maybe I'll help him. Plus it'll make Graylin go crazy."

"Absolutely!" Lewis laughed. "And speaking of that cousin of yours and Teddy, who could've expected *that* to be our ship's romance?"

"Not me, that's for sure," Arlyn grabbed a deck of cards from the counter and began flicking them at the wall. "I *almost* feel lonely, what with those two and you and Enland."

"Well, I highly doubt Graylin will allow anything like affection to be felt for a boy before you get yourself someone," Lewis noted, "and Enland and I are nothing new."

"I wish you two would just get married, to get it over with," Arlyn said. "I don't like all this beating about the bush, and I'm sure Uncle Will is rich enough to officiate marriages."

"About your uncle." Lewis raised her spatula in warning to River, who had just come in to a plate of cookies on the table. "Do you-"

Just then Teddy popped into the room, grabbed an apple, and left with equal speed. Arlyn completely missed the end of Lewis's sentence, finishing her milk in a gulp. "I'll be right back," she said quickly, and dashed from the room.

"Hey, Teddy!" Arlyn sprinted down the hall, spotting just the bottom of Teddy's faded cloth shoes as he ascended the stairs.

"Hm?" He paused, ducking down to squint at the speaker.

"I've heard some rumors going around that you have money on yourself to be my first date," she said, with a mischievous glint in her eye.

"Crap, who told you?" he asked.

"Lewis, but here's my idea. If you split the profits with me, I'll do it. Next time we stop somewhere, even."

Teddy smiled. Arlyn suddenly wondered if she'd ever seen Teddy smile before, and then decided that she definitely had, and was simply forgetting about it.

"River is going to murder me. I'm in," he said.

"Even better, Graylin will be livid," Arlyn laughed. "But don't worry, she's all yours when we're finished, deal?"

"To the extent she is yours to give away, deal."

Graylin nearly bumped into Denloy on the stairs. His head was bowed, and his hands were in his pockets. Graylin *had* been heading to the lower bowels of the ship, having finally decided to search for her lost stuffed animal Flepe (Something about seeing Pasta sitting all alone on her bed made Graylin feel very lonely) but some element of her uncle's posture made her pause.

"Hey Uncle Denloy. What's up?"

Denloy's gaze shot up, "Oh. Nothing. Nothing at all."

"You obviously haven't learned that *I'm* the liar on this ship, and only one is allowed. So spit it out, what's wrong?" Graylin said, hands on hips. Denloy was forcibly reminded of Graylin's mother, the last time he had seen her. He smiled just a little, seeing his brother and their wives for just a moment, rather than the small, thin girl in front of him.

"How well do you remember your parents, Graylin?" he asked finally, quietly. Graylin was taken aback.

"I don't know, I mean, as well as can be expected, I guess. Why?" She folded her arms. Wilmot Denloy watched his fiery, vulnerable niece. Should he tell her? Should he reveal everything to her and Arlyn, and let them deal with the painful knowledge?

Seeing Graylin's pursed, down-turned lips, and big eyes, and the chain around her fingers, he was reminded once again that they *couldn't* deal with it. Denloy could not bring himself to ruin his nieces' views of their parents, just as he couldn't let them find their parents. They'd already lost them once, and then Leo too. The weakness, the fragility he saw in his nieces . . . well, he wasn't sure if they could survive the truth now. As much as it was torturing him to keep the information to himself, surely it was his duty to deal with it. For his nieces.

Right?

28

DENLOY SAT AT HIS desk, rolling a heavy metal marble between his fingers. It was cool, and solid, and gave him something to focus on besides his thoughts. Of course, there were many things which could do this: tapping a pencil, hand, or foot, folding a paper, bouncing a ball. But over his nearly 10 years of business meetings, he'd settled on the marble. It was unobtrusive, silent, and small enough to fit in his pocket at all times. Graylin and Arlyn, he'd noticed, were fiddlers too, constantly tapping or tugging and wrapping or bouncing. He should give them his spare marbles and see if his nieces liked them as much as he did.

His nieces. Denloy's marble rolled just a little faster, and now his foot bounced too. *His nieces.* What was he going to do about his nieces? Every day both made him more sure that he could not let them find their parents, and brought him closer to the reality that if he didn't do something soon, they would. Every day, his secrets hurt him a little worse. He was beginning to recognize landmarks, like the mechanical stone bridge in Dartwin, or the rusty cliffs near Nellsburn he had once scaled with Mike. They were getting close to their "base".

He thought back to when he was younger, to how stupid and naïve he'd been. Even as a toddler, he would've followed his brothers to the ends of the earth, even towards death itself. They were all so close back then. Michaelangelo and Benson were the best older brothers someone could have, always supportive and willing to help with a project. Often the four would all go out on trips together, talking and inventing and all that. Leo, even if he was the youngest, always wanted to hang out with his older brothers and made waves in his own right. They were a perfect team. The inventors, the businessman, and the prodigy.

But everything had changed once Osden approached Michaelangelo and Benson to lead the government's newest program. Even before they married, Benson's wife Delilah had made a name for herself there, heading Osden's up-and-coming chemical engineering program. Then she had met Benson, Michaelangelo, and Mike's wife Juliet. The two women had hit it off instantly, both loving and flourishing in technical, type A, hard-working environments. Perhaps that's why Denloy had never really taken to them.

Both twins had married, and the two couples had started their never-ending, government-run, weapons-centered double date. Day in, day out, the four inventors had put their brilliant minds together, and produced things beyond imagination. After a few years, the twins grew apart from their younger brothers, especially Leo. The nature of their work both drove him away and encouraged his brothers to push him back, hiding as much as they could, revealing only enough so that Leo knew he didn't want to be involved. But they still came to Will, asking for help with what seemed to be plans to better the world. Osden was running out of the ,materials to make gasoline, it seemed, its natural stores running dry. At first, they had simply been trying to invent a new fuel source, and machines which could run on it, using Delilah and Juliet's chemical knowledge and the twins's mechanical smarts. Eventually, Osden had slowly pushed the Freelys away from these alternative plans; things, they said, may just not work out regarding the alternative fuel source. However, their neighbors, Nalvern, the country of romance, riches, and riots, was sitting on a figurative gold mine of gasoline. Soon, the two couples were experimenting with weapons, bombs, and a special goopy substance they called pyrogleminine, anything to 'convince' Nalvern to sell Osden some of its precious gas. Things got bigger and bigger, and motives more and more convoluted, and Denloy had finally ducked out. He couldn't do it anymore.

Denloy glanced up at his wall where he'd hung a bulletin board stretched with pictures and sketches. Up there was the last picture he'd taken with his brothers, just a few weeks before their fight. He was in the middle, Leo to his left, Michelangelo to the right. In Mike's arms was Graylin, hugging her dad around the neck and beaming, Juliet's hand on her back. To Leo's left was Benson, holding Arlyn like a bride. Arlyn was stretched out, grinning from ear to ear, her braids hanging down while her mother tickled her feet.

Denloy switched his marble to the other hand and dropped his head to the desk. He didn't want to do what had to be done. Arlyn and Graylin would despise him for shielding them from the truth. But what else could be done? Whatever good intentions his brothers had started with were long gone now and perhaps had been for a long time. *That* they proved by putting all of their pyrogleminine in the *Freelander* while it was laden with their family, the most precious of cargo, knowing full well that something could go wrong, and that if it did, well . . . it would be a disaster.

But that wasn't their idea, now was it? No, it hadn't been. *He* had been the one to suggest they leave Osden's program behind and take the pyrogleminine with them. *He* had been the one who thought they should use the family reunion to disguise their betrayal. Yes, he had quickly realized the dangers and backed out, but it *had* been his idea. His brothers had simply agreed with the plan, and then set up precautions which Denloy had been too angry to learn about. And at the girls' expense as well.

The girls whom he was supposed to save, but didn't. The girls who only lived because of his little brother Leo, the best, the kindest of the four brothers. The girls who were good, and bright, and who had suffered too much loss for their young years, too much disappointment, too much sadness. Meeting their parents would only bring more.

Denloy lifted his head, fingers fiddling with the marble, leg back to bouncing. Here he was again, back at the girls. He didn't know this, but his thoughts often circled much like Graylin's, jumping from topic to topic, running rings in his head until they looped several ideas twice.

And when there was a thought he particularly didn't want to think, it always showed up more.

He would have to talk to the cousins, to tell them. Lie even, if need be. As long as Arlyn and Graylin didn't find their parents. A sudden memory flashed before him, of the play the crew had performed, or more specifically, the beaming smiles afterward. How the girls had laughed and teased each other, seeming almost to read each other's minds at times, bouncing ideas of the other's brilliant brains. They were so much like their fathers . . .

And suddenly a fresh fear hit Denloy. The girls were very much like the Freely side of the family, their dads especially. Their minds worked similarly, their personalities different but not drastically so. If he let the girls get to their parents, what would keep the cousins from being dragged down the same capricious path? What would keep Arlyn and Graylin from finding a purpose and interest in whatever his brothers had been doing all these years? Would they abandon their friends, like Michaelangelo and Benson had, in favor of work contributing to 'the greater good'? Would they too be sucked down into the cesspit that was governmental and political agendas, swirled around until their morals were weak and their friendships nonexistent?

Wilmot didn't know what his brothers had been doing these past eight years, but he knew he couldn't let his nieces get involved. For certain now. He couldn't deal with the weight any longer. He would have to talk to them.

Arlyn hopped up the stairs to the top deck two by two and spotted her target instantly. Graylin was sitting by the railing, crisscross, resting against the carved wooden poles. The chilled breeze was blowing her curls everywhere, and Arlyn suddenly wondered for the first time how her fairly touch-sensitive cousin dealt with so much hair.

"What're you doing, cousin?" she asked as she strolled up. She needn't have asked, really. Graylin was sitting outside, staring at nothing in particular. She was barefoot, holding a little device they had made which emitted clicky sounds whenever the numerous switches and buttons were pressed. Clearly, Graylin was in full thinking mode, but what she was trying to work through, Arlyn didn't know.

"Do you really think they know we're alive?" Graylin asked, leaning her head against a rail and looking down. The landscape below them was completely invisible, thanks to the ship's height and the blanket of fog stretching from the ground up to the *Freelander*. The hazy white mist was a little cold, and Graylin's hair, face, and shirt (an old thin button up of Leo's) were all damp.

"'They' meaning our parents?" Arlyn asked, though, again, the answer was obvious.

"No cousin, Gladius and his cronies," Graylin said sarcastically, giving her cousin a look. Ah, thought Arlyn. So Graylin was in *this* sort of mood. "Yes, I mean our parents."

"No, I don't think they know we're alive," Arlyn said, sitting down too. She didn't want to say what she really thought- that either her parents *were* alive, and didn't care, or that had made it off the *Freelander* and fled the country, never to be found again. "Honestly, I half expected this trip to go like a story, where we, the *obvious* heroes, learn more and more about our quest as we go on." Arlyn sighed. "But all we have are more questions."

"Like how is it their fault the *Freelander* burned?" Graylin offered.

"And why did Uncle Will argue with them?" Arlyn added.

"And what were they doing for Osden's government?"

"And how does pyrogleminine tie into all this?"

"And what have they been doing all these years?"

"And-"

"And how did they know it was time to eat?" A voice asked from behind them, cutting Arlyn off. Lewis stepped forward and took a seat as well. "Dinner will be done soon."

Further away on the deck, Teddy and River were engaged in an intense ninja game where they had to lash out at each other's limbs with their own, and when hit, no longer use the 'wounded' arm or leg.

River was currently hopping around on one leg, trying to outrun Teddy, who seemed to have lost the use of both his arms.

The dinner bell clanged from below deck. All heads turned to the doors leading down. Teddy got in one last kick at his brother, River stood from where he'd been bent over catching his breath, and Denloy straightened, hands still on the rail where he'd been looking out at the fog.

"That'll be Enland, telling us it's done." Lewis said, as the girls got to their feet. And sure enough, a miffed Enland arrived as they headed for the door, his arms folded in impatience.

"It's time to *eat*," he said pointedly. "Did *no one* get my message to the pilot's chair?"

Teddy slid into his chair and checked the control panel system, pulling out a paper from the receiving tube.

"Would that be this one here?" he asked. He scanned it, crumpled the page, and then tossed it at River's head.

"Ha ha," Enland said dourly. Lewis just smiled, put an arm around his waist, and led him and his brothers to the stairs.

"Arlyn, Graylin, wait." Denloy tapped his nieces on the shoulder, wishing beyond reason he didn't have to do this. He didn't *want* to do this. "Can I speak with you two for a moment?"

"As long as we don't miss dinner." Arlyn said, smiling at him, and stopping. Her smile didn't fade, but the happiness behind it did as she saw the expression on her uncle's face.

"So, what is it?" Graylin asked, shoving her hands in her pockets. She was cold, and there was a strange, high-pitched squeaking sound coming from below deck that was drilling inside her head, making her irritable. She'd need to check that. Besides, the wind was picking up, and her curls kept blowing in her eyes. She was not in the mood for this.

Denloy was quiet for a moment, then sighed. "Listen, girls . . . I don't think you've really thought about what it might mean to find your parents." He was trying to find a way to say what needed to be said without giving something away that might hurt his nieces further.

"What I mean to say is . . . I can't let you find them. For your own sakes, I just can't."

Arlyn and Graylin glanced at each other, startled. Not find their parents? Pursuing them was the focus of this entire trip. The statement, well, the whole *concept* really, threw both cousins for a loop, and filled them both with the feeling that something was off. They were missing something here.

"Listen . . ." Arlyn said, "Uncle Will . . . can we talk about this later? I think maybe you need some sleep. I mean. These are our *parents* we're talking about. If they're out there, we're going to find them." Arlyn had seen too many people traveling through Odios, too many stragglers and homeless folks, not to recognize desperation when she saw it. And right now, her uncle Will looked desperate.

"No, girls, you don't understand. I can't let you find them. I *won't*," Denloy said, reaching out to put hands on both of their arms. His hair was wild with the wind, and his eyes watering with both cold and emotion. In his nieces' faces, he saw the same defiance he'd seen in Michaelangelo and Benson's. The look that said, *Tell us what to do again. We dare you. Go on, try it, you sad excuse of a man, you lying, cowardly-* Denloy squeezed his eyes shut, trying to block out their voices. There was a very high-pitched sound somewhere that seemed to invade his thoughts, putting him on edge. He gritted his teeth, trying to push it away, trying not to get angry. "I just can't let you," he said again, a little more firmly.

"And who gave you the golden scepter and crown, and said you could tell us what to do?" Graylin said irritably. "All hail King Denloy." Graylin shoved his hand off; she didn't want him touching her. She wanted *nothing* touching her, and she backed up, just to prove the point.

Arlyn groaned as her cousin stepped back rebelliously. Graylin was getting angry, she could tell. Denloy was even worse, eyes turning from sad to shocked to bitter in the face of Graylin's mockery. How unfortunate that he'd never seen this side of his niece before, this side which Arlyn knew on instinct mirrored Denloy himself.

"Why *shouldn't* we find our parents?" Arlyn asked, trying to be reasonable. The anger radiating from her two family members made her nervous. She could tell something was about to happen, and Graylin was prone to snap in these situations.

"Because they are murderers! They are corrupt!" Denloy suddenly exploded in anger. He stepped forward, grabbing their arms again. "You don't know half the story, yet you insist on contradicting me, just as they always did! Do you think they didn't *know* the dangers of bringing the weapon on the ship?" No! *You weren't supposed to mention it!* Denloy's inner voice screamed. *Now Arlyn and Graylin will know, and you'll hurt them, just like you do everyone. Now they won't trust you!*

"Weapon?" Graylin asked, whole body filled with her racing heartbeat. She could feel in it her head and her fingers and her toes. "And what 'weapon' would this be?" *Murderers*? Echoed in her head.

"The weapon, the weapon! Pyrogleminine, the one they created, the one they cared about more than they ever cared for you or I!" Denloy cried, trying to shut out the voices and the wind and the memories and his nieces' innocent, hurt faces, all at once. "They knew what they were doing when they invented a chemical weapon capable of destroying entire countries in a single blow. They *knew* what they were doing when they refused to give it to either country. They knew that everyone on the Freelander could die when they organized the reunion, because I told them, I warned them, and they still went through with it. They knew it could happen, all that death. They are murderers, and you'll go that way too!"

"You're saying that we're destined to be murderers?" Graylin shot back, anger taking her over. She had stiffened, her hands bared into fists. Arlyn knew why, a knowledge which no one else possessed. She knew that for months after their parents' deaths, eight-year-old Graylin had cried herself to sleep every night. That she wanted to see her parents so badly, it felt like a disease. And that what was really making Graylin mad were these accusations and attacks against her parents that she couldn't defend against.

"Even if that *is* true," Arlyn said, "it hardly seems fair to assume we'll turn out the same way." She said it shakily, but calmly, attempting to diffuse the situation. "Besides, Uncle Will, you're not making sense. Countries? Weapons?" Denloy felt something inside him break with fear at Arlyn's questions, the very ones he didn't want her to ask. And as he faltered, for just that second, Graylin saw herself in him and knew what was off. *He's hiding something*. What wasn't he telling them?

"You know what doesn't seem *fair* to me?" Denloy blustered, knowing that it was the fear inside him making his words so sharp. And yet, as he continued, he suddenly *was* furious, the anger burning fierce. He didn't have to search for his next words, they were just there, ready to be flung at the girls. "How could you even *want* to see them after they abandoned you on the Freelander?" He pointed a finger at them. "After they found out I wasn't on board, what do you think they did? They still went through with it! They didn't even *try* to save you! They deceived you!" His hands were flexing, and Arlyn had the urge to shrink back.

By now, the rest of the crew had gathered on the top deck, watching the battle, drawn by the shouts.

"Oh, really?" Graylin stood tall, nearly yelling. "And what? The same can be said for you! We asked you about this fuel, about pyrogleminine, after we met LeMay, and you said it was all fake! You lied to us!"

"I did what I-" Denloy began, pulling angrily on his shirt, but Graylin cut him off.

"And what about on the Freelander?" she asked loudly. "You left us too! *You* were supposed to be there! But you weren't!" Graylin's voice was breaking. "You weren't, and now Uncle Leo is dead because of it. Why weren't you there?" Her words were mere echoes of Denloy's constant thoughts, and hearing them aloud felt like being shoved. "I was young, and angry, and stupid!" He tried to defend himself. "I didn't know they were actually going to go through with the plan!"

"Plan? You mean you knew about it?!" Graylin shrieked. "You knew they were going to put the pyrogleminine on the Freelander?!"

"It was my idea!" Denloy roared desperately, his anger inexplicably fueled by his guilt. "I told them to escape with it, and use the reunion as a cover. But then I left, and told them it was a bad idea, and I didn't know they were going to do it because I didn't know what was in the letter! I'm so sorry, because I loved you guys! I love you now! And I can't let you turn out like my brothers. Murderers!" *This is all wrong*, he thought, *this isn't how this is supposed to go*. And yet he couldn't stop the flood now, couldn't hold back the rushing rage that was filling him.

"Our parents weren't murderers!" Graylin shouted, tears of frustration forming in her eyes. "And it's not their fault- it's yours! It's all your fault! You're the murderer, not our parents!"

"It's not," Denloy was shaking, his niece shifting into his own conscience before his very eyes. "I'm not, it's not my fault. *They* are the murderers!" His instincts, his terrible, loathsome, self-serving instincts were rising, screaming at him to defend himself. He had to defend himself.

"It was my idea, but I backed out, I swear I did! I did! They are the murderers!" Denloy shouted with terrifying force, making even Graylin back in fear. Graylin hated feeling fear. Even more, she hated feeling weak, but trembling and shaking she felt so, and being fearful and fragile filled her with defiance. She would *not* be weak.

"You want to stop us. You really do?" she cried, wiping at a tear angrily. "Then tell us the truth! What did our parents do, with the fuel and the countries and *you*?" She said 'you' so bitterly, so hatefully, that now it was Denloy who looked startled. *They hate me*, he thought, his heart breaking. *They despise me.*

"I can't tell you," he said quietly. His quiet speech let the voices back in, *they hate you Will, you do nothing but hurt people, don't tell them what really happened*, and most hurtful of all, *it was your idea.*

"I'm sorry?" Graylin asked incredulously.

"I said I can't tell you!" Denloy bellowed. "Please, just trust me."

"Trust you?" Graylin shrieked, actually crying now. Her nose was red with the cold, her eyes and fingers mirroring the shade as she clenched her fists. The wind was so strong, and that propeller sound so high pitched, and her thoughts moving so fast. *Why are you like this?* they screamed at her. *Just calm down. Why do you have to push away everyone who cares about you?* But then there were the raging thoughts, the seething ones. *I could never trust him. He lied to us, and he killed Uncle Leo. He killed our whole family. It's his fault.*

"Yes, trust me!" *Why should they trust me?* Denloy's hands moved like he wanted to throw something, or hit something, but couldn't find an object. "Trust me when I say that your parents killed everyone aboard the Freelander. They were obsessed with their project, thinking of nothing but the greater good, even if it meant their family's deaths! They are murderers!"

"Just because they were doesn't mean we will be!" Arlyn's anger was slow to rise, it always was, but when it rose, she was terrifying. The cousins stood next to one another, trying their best to stand their ground against their uncle, every Freely eye flashing with malice.

"You can't guarantee that's who we're going to be!" Graylin shouted. "So what if our parents *are* evil? I still want answers, and you can't stop us from getting them!"

"YES I CAN!" Denloy roared, anger flaring to boiling point.

The cousins leapt back in shock, silenced. The roar echoed dully around the darkening deck, sinking into the fog surrounding the hull.

"Girls . . . I, I'm sorry I just . . ." Denloy said, stepping closer. Both girls backed up, staring at their uncle. Graylin was stunned, but her cousin was not. Where the outburst had frozen Graylin, it had released Arlyn from her peacemaking hesitations, and her anger was building dangerously.

Her eyes were cold. "No. Don't you ever, *ever*, talk to my cousin that way again. Understand?" Denloy didn't answer. "UNDERSTAND?!" Still he didn't speak, just shut his eyes for a few moments, breathing heard.

Arlyn stepped towards him, and this time Denloy backed up. "Listen, Arlyn-"

"I SAID DO YOU UNDERSTAND?!" she repeated, stepping further, Denloy getting closer to the railing. He was cornered, and like an animal in the same situation, began to fight back.

"We're going to find our parents, and you *will not* stop us," Graylin said, her voice breaking with collapsed emotions. They had been held up on the tide of her momentum and anger, but now that had dropped, filling her with too many thoughts, too many voices.

They aren't listening, Denloy's mind voice said. *They are mocking you. They challenged your authority, your love, and now they are mocking you.* **No, no they're not!** Denloy's other voice cried. **They are hurting, and they are-** *They are MOCKING YOU! You can't let them do this, they'll only get hurt worse. You must stop them.*

"I won't stop you?" Denloy asked coldly. *Whatever it takes to stop them.*

"That's right," Arlyn said, standing as tall as she could in the presence of such fury. Denloy's face contorted. His arm came back, his eyes flashed . . . and he slapped her. The force was enough to knock her back, and she stumbled. The crew gasped and Arlyn backed up, tears springing to her eyes, the surprise of being hit worse than the actual pain. She had never been hurt out of malice before.

Graylin was shaking with anger, the floor swayed beneath her as her vision went blurry. Arlyn was holding her cheek, tears flooding her cheeks, and suddenly Graylin couldn't think, she couldn't stop herself. *No one* hurt her cousin.

She charged at Denloy, no thought on her mind but the desire to *do* something. She held out her arms, but whether to defend herself or cause harm, she wasn't sure. Until she reached Denloy . . . and shoved him with all her might. He stumbled only once, face freezing in terror, before he disappeared over the edge of the railing.

Time itself slowed down as Denloy fell into the endless fog. The white folded under him and then wove back together as he tumbled through. It flowed back together seamlessly, as if nothing had happened. But something had. Now the *Freelander* didn't hold seven, but six.

There was no sound except for Graylin's quick beating heart. She blinked, once, and then twice, but there was no denying what was now settling so heavy in her chest; Wilmot Denloy was gone. And it was Graylin's fault.

"Graylin . . ." Arlyn whispered, frozen in place. She felt a hand on her shoulder. She didn't need to look, or care to. She could hear the stunned breathing around her, and knew the crew had stepped up behind.

"He's . . ." River trailed off, for once unable to speak.

"Gone." Arlyn finished the sentence for him. She swallowed. *Oh, cousin*, she thought. *That wasn't how this was supposed to end.*

Graylin stared over the edge of the railing, the ship still cutting through the fog. He was gone.

She turned around and started for her room in dead silence. None of the crew spoke, and there was only one thought in Graylin's mind.

Murderer.

29

GRAYLIN SAT IN HER cabin. Alone. Silent.

He had been right all along, Uncle Will. She *was* a murderer. All that evil he claimed was inside her parents was inside her, and it has just revealed itself as a monster willing to push her uncle to his death.

Arlyn leaned up against the wall outside her cousin's room. She hadn't stopped Graylin. She hadn't wanted to. She could have, but she didn't. *Murderer*, she thought to herself. Outwardly, she seemed alright compared to Graylin. She'd talked with the rest of the crew, and kept her cool even as her heart was racing under their stares and her hand twitching with fear. She needed to keep calm for her cousin.

Arlyn sighed, her breath shaky as she did. Graylin had never taken guilt easily. When she'd done something truly horrible, and she knew it was her fault, she often wouldn't speak for hours to anyone but Arlyn. Those silent stretches were suddenly feeling like nothing compared to Graylin's state now. None of the crew had even seen Graylin since the incident, and all attempts to reach out had been promptly rejected. Arlyn rubbed her forehead, reached for the doorknob, and silently padded into her cousin's room. She sat herself firmly in the desk chair, facing the bed where Graylin had her face in her hands.

"I did something bad," Graylin whispered as Arlyn sat down. "Something really, *really* bad." Arlyn couldn't see her cousin's face, but her hands were rough and red from rubbing her eyes.

"Yeah. Yeah, you did. And there's not much of an excuse for it," Arlyn said, her tone soft. "But I didn't stop you either, so it's not all on you."

"I *killed* him, Arlyn." Graylin's voice turned icy. "He's dead, and I was the one who caused it. I'm just what he said. I-I'm a murderer." She began to cry. The only thing she could see was her uncle falling over and over. And herself watching him.

"You are, and I'm your accomplice." Arlyn sat back in the chair, green eyes studying her cousin in detail. "You were angry, I was angry, and we did something wrong. And it's going to feel like this. Isn't it?"

It wasn't advice. It was a question. As much as Graylin relied on her cousin, Arlyn needed Graylin just as much to tell her the truth, to tell her things were real. Since the accident, everything felt muted, gray, and empty. Every emotion she was supposed to have was absent from her. She didn't feel happy, but she didn't feel sad, or angry either. Just . . . blank.

"It is," Graylin said. "He's dead. That's our only family left in this world. Gone."

"We still have-"

"No! We don't have our parents!" That dangerous, deadly anger was boiling in Graylin again. "They're murderers, and so am I! And even if we do find them, what's stopping us from doing exactly what Uncle Will said, hm?" She finally looked up at her cousin, who took a deep breath. "We're going to turn out just like them. I already have."

"We still have Lily," Arlyn said after a moment of silence. "We still have Lily, and Lewis, and Teddy and River and Enland. That's our family, Graylin. And it has been for eight years."

"We haven't seen Lily in *weeks*," Graylin said, frustrated. "And I feel like murdering a man will probably affect whatever relationship I had with the crew." She tried to swallow the lump in her throat. "I don't get it."

"Don't get what?"

"I tried so hard to be nice, to be friends with everyone. I thought I was doing so good! And then, and then I killed him!" Graylin broke down again. "Why am I like this?" she sobbed into her hands. "Why do I hurt everyone I care about? I annoyed my parents into leaving me, and I never said goodbye to Leo. He never knew I loved him. And you . . . I've made you bear so much, because I'm too weak to. And, and . . . him. I killed him!" Her voice broke as her heart did. "I've hurt everyone who's ever loved me!"

"Damn it, Graylin!" Arlyn stood up, kicking the chair into the desk. "You know that isn't true! And don't even try to say it is! Yeah, we messed up, and yeah, it was bad, but you can't lie and say you're simply horrible and chalk it up to that!"

Graylin was silent.

"Plus, there's one person I promise you haven't hurt."

"Who's that?"

"Me."

In the meeting room, a few days later, the rest of the crew were talking. Without the Freelys present, all the life seemed to have been sucked from the ship. Clocks ticked. Footsteps thudded. Voices exchanged short phrases- and that was it.

"Arlyn doesn't seem to be doing too bad," River said, folding some paper idly. He'd been doing this almost compulsively for the last hour, and had a stack of little triangles around him.

"Well, she's never been one for falling apart at stuff like this anyway," Enland said helpfully, sketching out a new map from memory, this one featuring Denloy's estate. As hard as they tried not to think of him, William Freely was on everyone's mind.

"Leave it to Arlyn Freely to make Graylin actually talk," Teddy said dully from the corner of the room. He was sitting, knees to chest, on the ground, writing something he refused to let anyone see.

"Oh, shut up Teddy," River snapped. "Arlyn is practically the only family Graylin has left now. Just because you're friends now doesn't mean you're her tell-all."

"I just don't want her to think we hate her!" Teddy raised his voice, dropping his pencil. "And she will."

"I know it's hard," Lewis said, setting down her knitting. "Yes, you three have known them for a while, but I met the Freelys who'd just survived a tragic airship crash that killed practically all of their family. Even then, Arlyn was a pretender, acting like things weren't bothering her when they were. But Graylin, she takes big things slowly, and needs some space. So that's what we're going to give her."

River stood up, glanced out the window, and sat back down, the room going quiet for a while. The background of scribbling pens and a slightly off-time clock in the hall were still there, but nothing else. This is, until a large metallic clanging sound rang up from below decks. Teddy's head shot up, looking around almost anxiously as Lewis stood.

"Dear me, don't tell me that as something breaking," she said seriously. "Of all the times . . ."

"I'll fetch Arlyn," River said, thrilled to move, but he was stopped.

"No." All heads turned to look down the hall, where Graylin was stepping from her room. "I'll go."

And just like that, she was gone.

By the time Graylin had dropped into the dark bowels of the *Freelander*, she was finding it very difficult to hold herself together. Every breath made her feel like she was suffocating, every step like she was about to pass out. She wished she would, just to get out of it. Before she could yearn for numbness for even one more second, however, Graylin's cousin appeared.

"Oh. Hi," Arlyn said. The two stared at each other, standing several feet apart, silent. They hadn't seen each other since their first conversation several days previously. Never before had there been a barrier between the two cousins and now there was this. The surprise, the awkwardness in Arlyn's expression whispered to Graylin all she needed to know. She and her cousin had been inseparable before, practically the same person . . . and now Graylin scared Arlyn, disgusted her. Now, Graylin was a murderer, and her cousin was not. And that could not be fixed.

"What was it?" Graylin asked finally, referencing the breaking sound that had beckoned her down here.

"The left boiler door. It flew right off, banged up the caliper of the bottom engine as well," Arlyn said. "I think it's what made that whining sound the other day. Did you hear it? I noticed it when . . ."

When they were arguing with Denloy. When they had been unconscious of true consequences. When they had killed their uncle.

"I heard it," Graylin said gruffly. "You find the door?"

"Yes."

"Okay." Graylin pushed past her cousin and dropped her tool belt to the ground by the correct boiler. She glanced at Arlyn once before she turned away. Arlyn pulled down on a small chain from the ceiling, clicking on the lightbulb closest, and felt her heart break. Her cousin looked terrible; she hadn't noticed the other day. Graylin's eyes were red, the bags around them purple and dark and bruised. Her nose was florid, like her raw, tear-stained cheeks, her hair a cloud of smoke curling around her face. Tremors shook her lip, the threat of sobs hanging behind the lines beside her mouth. She stood, slightly bent under the low ceiling, like a tree sapling in the middle of a hurricane. Thin, spindly, and very close to giving up and letting herself be blown away.

"Hand me a wrench, please," Graylin croaked, holding out a hand. Arlyn did so and then knelt down to help. The cousins slowly fixed the damaged parts, where the door had dug into parallel mechanics. They re-tightened bolts, feeling slowly along the dark ground for them and placing them where they were supposed to be. Once that was finished, Graylin held up the heavy door as Arlyn inserted the bolts which had kept it on, slid into the hinges, all in silence. Graylin's arms shook, and Arlyn used a mallet to smack one bolt into place.

"Oh," she said suddenly, "I think I found our problem." She glanced around, seeing nothing. "We're missing a bolt for the hinge."

Graylin let the door hang lopsided and searched around for it as well, helping her cousin. They shone lights, looked under machines, and even pulled out a large magnet on a stick, but found nothing.

"We'll have to stop for a new one," Arlyn said. Graylin nodded. Something about Arlyn's expression as they searched for the bolt, the way she had concentrated with her brows furrowed, reminded Graylin painfully of Denloy. In a flash, it was all happening again; Arlyn had been slapped, Denloy was boiling with anger, and Graylin was rushing forward, shoving . . . her uncle was falling, and falling, and falling . . .

"Hey. Graylin, are you okay?" Arlyn's voice broke in. She searched her cousin's face and Graylin began to sob. "Hey, come here. You clearly need a hug."

Graylin didn't fight it. She slumped into her cousin's embrace, shaking with tears. She had no fight left. The last time she'd fought, she'd killed someone.

"Don't try to comfort me," Graylin said, voice muffled. "I don't deserve it. And there's nothing words can do. There's nothing anything can do. He's dead."

"You didn't mean it. He yelled at you, he hurt me and you just . . . reacted."

"But that's the problem, Arlyn. I just *reacted*, and it resulted in death. Gone. Forever." Graylin sobbed. "What am I supposed to do?" she gasped, needing air, tears rocking her. "*What am I supposed to do?*"

"If you hadn't gone at him," Arlyn said, "I would have. We would have been in the same spot either way."

"Better you than me," Graylin whispered. "You're stronger than me." Arlyn suddenly realized just how bad their situation was. When would her cousin ever have admitted that?

"Listen," Arlyn said, standing up straighter. "You can't stay like this forever. You'll waste away, and we can't have that. I saw Denloy's eyes, Graylin. He was angry too. And he could have just as easily hit you, just as he did me. It was . . . sort of like self defense."

"Really?" Graylin asked, sniffing. "Was it, *really*? Because from where I'm standing, it doesn't feel much like self defense." It wasn't self defense, and they both knew it. Arlyn kept petting Graylin's head as the girl sniffed and rubbed her nose, trying to hold on to her cousin's words, using them to float just above her lake of despair.

"Come on," Arlyn said finally. "We need to tell the rest of them that we need to stop for that part. Also, it's almost dinnertime, and you're eating with us."

30

WHILE DINNER ONLY HELPED *a little*, it did still help. As it turns out, talking to people does wonders for one's mental health.

As Graylin climbed slowly up from the engine room, Teddy was the first to step forward. Mouth pressed into a worried line, eyebrows drawn in sympathy so a little crease formed between them, he reached out and took her hand. After a brief hesitation, he pulled her into a hug.

"I know what you mean now," Graylin whispered over his shoulder, "about being sad, all the time. Always."

"I'm sorry," Teddy whispered back, holding her tight. "I wish you didn't." Graylin sniffed, drowning in the hug and needing it. Running a hand over her hair, Teddy pushed a small object into Graylin's grasp. A stuffed animal puppy. It was small, brown, and curly haired, with little embroidered eyes hidden by fur.

"I heard you talking about this a few days ago," he said quietly, pressing her hands around the animal. "I found it in the storage room. I thought it might bring you some comfort."

"Thank you," Graylin whispered, voice hardly audible. Here he was at last, her little Flepe. The animal which had helped her through the death of her parents, resurfaced again to soak up her grief. Only this time, she wasn't eight. This time, she was to blame.

And yet, even as she petted the familiar head and hugged the little shape, she did feel a small bit of her terror and emptiness melt away. But perhaps that was just Teddy and his hug.

Teddy let her go, and the crew all sat at the table, every eye watching Graylin anxiously. She sat down and began to eat with small, practiced, forced bites. Her head was bent, her shoulders slumped.

Glances circled the table, worried stares from every eye. Graylin had never been so . . . cowed before. The fight, the anger, was all gone.

Everyone else pretended to eat for a few minutes, but all gazes remained on Graylin, whose own eyes stayed on her plate.

"It's alright," Graylin croaked suddenly, glancing up. "I won't kill any of you guys. I promise."

The words might have been teasing, or joking, particularly coming from Graylin. But no one laughed, especially when Graylin suddenly burst out crying.

River and Enland stayed in their seats, stunned; Graylin Freely, crying? But the rest snapped into action. Lewis was first to the saddened cousin, yanking her into a hug. Teddy arrived next, pulling Graylin in gently. Arlyn joined them, then River and Enland, who finally got over their shock. Arlyn was willing to bet that no one on that ship had ever foreseen *this* happening, a large group hug in the middle of dinner with a sobbing Graylin in the center.

Despite being unexpected, it worked wonders. When Graylin started sniffing her tears away, everyone backed up.

"I hope you know," Teddy said softly, "that all of us still care about you." Graylin wiped her nose, and Teddy smiled. "Even Enland," he said.

"It's true," Enland said dejectedly. Everyone laughed a little, even Graylin, wiping away the last of the tears.

After dinner they all talked and smiled (laughter seemed too distant a goal), and went to bed in fairly average spirits. Both cousins were sound asleep by nine, utterly exhausted. Graylin had a dream that night, which, being human, she often did. But she remembered this one for quite a long time. *That* was something unusual.

She had been alone, cold, and exhausted at the edge of a cliff. Or on the railing of the *Freelander*. Her dream self wasn't sure. Either way, the edge was slippery, and below her was a swirling mass of fog and cloud. Then a dark, swirling mass appeared behind her and stalked closer and closer. Graylin became so afraid, she froze. She had nowhere to run. Her fears would catch her.

Just as the first tendrils of black smoke reached her, smoke which smelled distinctly like the burning *Freelander*, she slipped and fell over the edge. She fell wildly, spinning and tumbling through the white mass, when she halted. Not hitting the ground, as she suspected, but caught by invisible arms. And then suddenly, those arms *weren't* invisible, but belonged to Leo. Arlyn. Teddy. Lewis, River, Enland, Lily. Her friends. Her family. They had saved her, and Graylin knew they would do it again. No matter how many times she messed up.

She woke with a start, the sound of banging metal coming from the next room over. She put her pillow over her head, hugged both Flepe and Pasta to herself, and fell back asleep. She did much of that over the next week. She got a hug from Lewis once an hour, and Arlyn once a day, which Graylin disliked so thoroughly she resolved to grow stronger just so she could escape them. Teddy's occasional hugs, however, miraculously didn't seem to bother her nearly as much. Slowly, day by day, the strings in her head that had snapped braided themselves back together, with help from the crew, her family, who loved her.

One morning, nearly a week later, as the *Freelander* neared the long awaited Mackson's Bay, all six crewmembers were gathered around the kitchen table, a chorus of fork clinks and chewing the only sound. Lewis had been making only Graylin's favorite foods, in an attempt to rid her friend of the thin, sickly look which hung around her nowadays, so breakfast was a collection of Nalvernian toast and fresh blueberries. Graylin had been making an admirable attempt to eat more, if only to appease Lewis, and while she'd put back on her lost pounds, she still looked smaller, thinner, and younger than normal. Arlyn sighed as she watched her cousin eat her food, eyes glued to her plate. Graylin was too young to deal with this, just as she was too young to help. Sixteen-almost-seventeen was not generally thought of as a super responsible age, and here they were, on a flying airship, alone, the sole witnesses to a murder which they committed.

Arlyn would usually have tried to block this line of thinking, especially when around her friends, but today she just couldn't help it. She'd had a nightmare the night before, and somehow knew that she wasn't the only one, and that the person who had visited her dreams had slipped into other's as well.

"I saw him, last night," Graylin said suddenly. She swallowed and looked up. "Denloy. In a dream."

Arlyn was right then. She wasn't the only one.

"I have too," Teddy said quietly. "Nearly every night this week."

The silverware tinged and scraped against dishes. River took a drink of water.

"We stop in Mackson's Bay tomorrow," Arlyn said finally, setting her fork down. She hated the silence, the barrier that seemed to shut everyone off from one another. She'd felt it with her cousin first, and now she felt with everyone else too, like the force field around a magnet, pushing them away from one another.

No one spoke. No one met her gaze.

"Listen," Arlyn said suddenly, pushing her plate away. "We've been through a lot, us six. Together. But Graylin and I won't blame you if you want to get out of this."

Silence.

"Tomorrow might be your last chance," Arlyn continued. "I don't know how many more times we'll stop, and who knows what will happen once we find our parents . . . *if* we find our parents. But . . ." Arlyn looked away, unsure how to say it. "Well, if you decide to leave, just know that no matter what happens, we won't . . ."

"You won't be implicated as murderers, if we're ever caught," Graylin finished. River blinked, and Lewis took a breath. The six teenagers suddenly, for the first time, realized the seriousness of their situation. Accident or not, what the cousins had done was manslaughter, and more than being morally wrong, it was illegal. Sooner or later, someone would find out about Denloy's death. He was a very rich businessman, after all. Influential. A socialite. There would be newspaper articles, search parties, investigations. The crew would be questioned. What would they say? That they didn't know? That he'd disappeared?

That they'd killed him?

When they went back to Odios, *if* they went back, there would undoubtedly be consequences for the incident. And Arlyn wanted to make sure that their friends knew they could get out of it. None of it had been their fault, after all. They had simply been dragged along in the deadly current which was the Freely family, which the cousins were starting to suspect had already claimed many lives.

"Anyway," Arlyn continued finally, "that was the speech I saved for you guys."

Somewhere else on the ship a machine made a sound, but only Graylin looked towards it. Everyone else was watching their plates.

"We're sticking with you," Lewis said suddenly, looking directly at Arlyn. "Of course we are. We're in this together."

"Lewis," Graylin said, almost begging, "Please, think about this. This will mar the *rest of our lives*. There is no escaping this. At some point, it will come back. At some point, they'll find out."

"They? Who is they?" Lewis asked, standing up. "The police? When Damien ran away from home, my parents hired everyone imaginable to find him. You've met my mom and dad, and trust me when I say that they pulled every string. And where was he? He was in Belhaven, of all places, the biggest city in Osden, and yet no one ever found him. It will take them years to search all of Osden, and even then Denloy could have fled to a different country. Think about your parents! They've been out there for years, *years*, and no one's found them."

"What if they find a body?" Graylin asked solemnly. Lewis shook her head.

"They won't. We were in the middle of nowhere. They'll never find him."

"They will if we tell them," Graylin said quietly. The ship groaned.

"What do you mean?" Lewis asked.

"I mean we go to the police in Mackson's Bay. Turn me in."

"It was an *accident, Graylin*," Lewis said fiercely.

"An accident which killed our uncle!" Graylin shouted, standing up too. "Maybe it takes months, maybe it takes years, but someday someone will find the truth, and they'll come after us. *Me*. And how will it look, Lewis, if after who knows how many years the police show up at my doorstep, with my fingerprints or something on Denloy's body, and I tell them it was an accident? No one will believe me, because we kept it a secret! I'll be charged as guilty because I *am*."

"Then we'll make ourselves a story," Lewis commanded loudly. Everyone stared at her. "I know it sounds terrible, but what choice do we have?" She took a shaky breath, and looked at her hands. "He left us when we landed outside of Belhaven. We'd had a fight. He went for a walk and never came back. We flew on to look for him, and ask around in the next town, but we couldn't find anything. We'd hoped he'd be at your parents' place, but he wasn't. That's all we know."

Graylin swallowed, her heart racing. Lewis looked them all in the eyes.

"Listen, I know it's terrible, I know. But it's all we can do. We are on this trip to find your parents, and we can't quit now."

"If we don't stop at murder," Graylin asked quietly, trying not to cry, "where *do* we stop?"

"We stop when we find the truth," Arlyn said. "Before Denloy died, he said some stuff about our parents. What if he was right? We need to know."

"Maybe I don't want to know, Arlyn," Graylin cried. "I don't know why Osden hired our parents, or why pyrogleminine was made. Uncle Will said that pyrogleminine was on the Freelander, and I don't know if it was there to protect the people, or if the people were there to protect it, and I *don't want to*. I want to go home. I want none of this to have happened."

"But it *did* happen," River said. "And we have to keep going."

Graylin looked around the table, desperate for a friend and fellow thinker. And she found it in Teddy, watching her with his bright eyed, sweet brown gaze. In his expression she could feel the same hopelessness and fear now filling her, that sense of pure, heartbreaking, devastating terror that they could never escape what was now hanging over their heads. Graylin wanted to believe that this was all a nightmare, and that she could just wake herself up.

But the cold sweat on her back and the pain in her chest felt very, very real.

"We have to stop tomorrow," Arlyn continued finally. "We need gas again, and a hinge for the lower engine door. Besides that, we'll do some digging, and see if we can't find the source of all that pyrogleminine testing Loren told us about, and hope that it's our parents and not someone else."

"We'll keep a low profile," Lewis said. "We won't throw your name around this time. It'll be okay."

"Will it?" Graylin asked dully.

"Yes," Lewis said. "It will."

Graylin pushed her chair back and left the table. Everyone watched her go, Teddy's eyes lingering the longest.

"I wish I could help her," he said quietly as she left the room.

"We all do, Teddy." Enland said. "We just need to give her some time."

"What if she needs something?" Teddy asked, looking around at the crew. "What if it gets too much, and she drowns in this? Do you honestly think she'll ask us for help, because I don't. She'll just keep sinking and sinking and sinking until she's gone."

"We'll keep an eye on her," Arlyn said.

"And if she's hiding it?" Teddy asked. "If she's pretending to be okay, when she's not?"

"What are you suggesting we do, Teddy?" River asked. "Stay with her at all hours of the day?"

"I don't know!" Teddy said emphatically. "I don't know. I just want to help."

The five crewmates, all varying degrees of late teen, looked around at each other, feeling for the first time how very young, how very alone and unprepared they were.

"I'd wanted to talk about what Denloy said, about our parents," Arlyn said, standing up to pour herself a glass of chocolate milk, "but I think maybe we should hold off on that now."

"What do you mean? What did Denloy say?" River asked.

Arlyn, for maybe the hundredth time that week, thought back to that final fight. "He said our parents were murderers, and that they put pyrogleminine on the ship during the reunion. If I had to guess, I would say that is what went wrong. Remember how explosive it was when we made it in Belhaven? Surely it just caught fire, and then- boom."

"Loren thought your parents *set* the fire, maybe to protect the pyrogleminine, remember?" Lewis added.

"But would your parents have done that, knowing that it would explode and hurt your family?" River asked, eyes wide.

"And why put it on the Freelander in the first place?" Enland asked. "What were they doing with it? Trying to move it to where Osden wanted it?"

"Which begs the question of *what* exactly Osden wanted it for," Lewis added. "Maybe we were trying to coax something out of a different country." She paused. "Or maybe we were going to give someone else pyrogleminine, as a gift."

"Teddy?" Arlyn asked. The boy was still sitting at the table, looking out the window behind him. "What do you think? Teddy?"

"Hm?" He looked up at them, thoughts anywhere but at that table because that's where Graylin wasn't. Arlyn sighed.

"I need to go think."

She left the kitchen, walking a little slower than normal, dragging with the weight of their secret. She wanted peace, and quiet, and answers. She wanted to talk to Loren, who had inexplicably made her feel better, with his quiet intelligence and calm presence. Instead, she let her feet guide her, and walked up the stairs and down the small hall to her uncle's room. Both of her uncles, actually. It used to be Leo's room, then it was Denloy's. Now it was no one's.

She pushed open the door, grimacing as it creaked loudly. The room was fatally, painfully alive, suitcases still strewn about, papers half-written and laying on the bedside table. The desk lamp was still on, and only now did Arlyn notice those plastic tubes they had seen in Belhaven powered it. The rest of the desk was completely empty, save a piece of paper and an inkwell that sat under the lamp. She picked it up, reading it silently.

The last will and testament of William Denloy Freely

Whenever it happens that I perish, I want the remainder of my wealth and all properties I own to go to my nieces, Arlyn Versaie Freely and Graylin Lenore Freely. I would like $10,000 set aside for all of those who worked under me before my passing, and I would like it split evenly between them.

My card collection I would like to be given to Arlyn, and all of the books in my library to be given to Graylin. To Arlyn specially I would like to gift my copy of Huey's Journey, and Graylin should be specifically given all drawings done in her hand. To both shall be given my collection of marbles- may they give them something new to fiddle with, beyond random machine parts. My kitchen and all that is within it is to be given to Lilian Eloise Duncan, in memory of my late brother, Leonardo Colin Freely. Any other living relatives of mine shall receive nothing.

Signed: William D. Freely

September twenty-sixth

Arlyn swallowed and set the paper down. She wasn't sure why she'd felt drawn to the room, but part of her wished she hadn't entered. Just when they were struggling most with the weight of their uncle's death, she had to find proof of his affection for them.

"At least we know," she whispered to herself.

"Know what?" a voice behind her asked.

Arlyn whipped around, caught off guard. It was Enland. She heaved a sigh of relief; her tired mind had almost let her believe it was her uncle.

"I found Uncle Denloy's will," Arlyn said, holding up the paper.

Enland read over the will. "It's dated last Tuesday,"

"He must have written it that morning," Arlyn said, heart sinking. "It's almost as if he knew."

"He can't have," Enland said softly. "It was just a coincidence."

There was silence as the two glanced around the room. Then Enland made a jab at taking Arlyn's place, adding in the comedy.

"So, what will you do with this plethora of riches he's left you?"

Arlyn shrugged, trying not to think of it as blood money. "Well, I'm not sure. Maybe we'll spice up the Freelander a bit, give it a new set of decorations. Some of those lights from Belhaven, balloon replacements, stuff like that."

Enland shook his head. "You could do a lot more than that. Lewis gave me an estimate of how rich he was once. You and Graylin are, at least according to the will, millionaires."

"Maybe it doesn't really matter," Arlyn said after a pause. "I don't think Graylin will ever be able to use it. And she'll never be able to go home."

"What do you mean?" Enland asked, looking concerned. "Why not?"

"She wasn't wrong about the whole 'they'll find out eventually' thing," Arlyn shrugged. "It's only a matter of time, and if we go back to Odios, it feels like we'll just be giving her up. Besides, I don't think that, mentally, she'll ever be okay with going home. Odios is where we had the best years of our lives, and I don't know if she can handle heading back now."

She smiled sadly at Enland. "I *am* sorry that you guys have to be involved with all this. I'm sure you had hopes, plans . . . you and Lewis . . ."

"It can still happen," Enland said.

"Somehow I just can't imagine anything beyond the here and now," Arlyn sighed. "It's a little worrying, honestly. And I just feel so bad . . . I mean Teddy and River, I've never imagined futures for them. I'm sure they had plans, but I'd never thought about it. But you and Lewis, I mean, you two were going to get married. You were going to live happily ever after, the Freely family's very own fairytale. The heiress and the map guy. The rich girl and the boring man. Lewis Maynewin and the cartographer."

"That can still happen," Enland repeated encouragingly. "I don't love Lewis any less just because Denloy died."

"I know, but the *secret*, Enland," Arlyn said, suddenly trying not to cry. "It's going to infect everything. I'm so afraid that it will ruin *us*, the crew, and by extension, you two."

"Deep breaths," Enland said quietly, reaching out to touch her arm. How many times had Arlyn helped Enland through panic attacks, telling him to breathe? How many hours had she spent telling him jokes? And here he was, helping her calm down.

"This won't ruin everything," Enland assured her calmly. He smiled a little. "Lewis won't let it. You saw her earlier. Do you honestly think Lewis would let something like this ruin the future she wants?"

"No," Arlyn said nasally, wiping her nose. "I guess not."

"*Definitely* not," Enland smiled. "And it's not just us who can be happy. You can grow up too, settle down with Loren maybe."

"Oh, please." Arlyn shook her head, trying not to smile lest Enland think his cheering up attempts were working.

"I'm serious," Enland insisted.

"Enland, I have done all the growing up I'd like to do in the last few months. I don't know if I can handle much more." Arlyn *did* smile now.

"Then stay young *and* have a life," Enland suggested. "I can't really imagine you becoming a real adult anyway."

"What do you mean, 'a real adult'?" Arlyn asked, chuckling. "Look at that fellow over there, he's a *fake* adult. It's all a ruse."

"I mean . . . like Leo wasn't a real adult. He was old enough to be, sure, and he even acted like one sometimes, but deep down I think he was still a kid. Like the opposite of an old soul," Enland said.

"I think you're right," Arlyn nodded. She sighed and set down a bolt she'd been fiddling with. "I think I'm gonna go get a snack. Want to come?"

"No thanks. I need to go find Teddy," Enland sighed. Arlyn shrugged and headed downstairs to the kitchen, where Lewis was stress baking.

"Do you think I'm terrible, Arlyn?" the cook asked as Arlyn entered the room. Lewis was standing at the counter, kneading bread frantically, the puffs of flour in her hair making it look like a partially powdered wig.

"Terrible?" Arlyn asked, poking her finger into the dough. "At baking? If I say yes, do I get to eat all of this . . . whatever you're making?"

"No, I mean in general." Lewis punched the dough and flipped it over. "I feel like maybe I am. What sort of psycho suggests we invent a lie to hide the murder of your uncle . . . and believes it's a good idea? Because I do. Honestly I do. I feel like rubbish, but I *do* think it's a good option." She stretched the dough out and folded it in half. "Actually, I think it's our *only* option."

"I know what you mean," Arlyn nodded. "But I also agree with you."

"You do?" Lewis looked up in relief. "Oh, thank goodness. Ever since breakfast I've just been feeling like a total . . . like a heartless . . . I don't know, I guess. I just feel dirty, because keeping this a secret was my idea."

"But it wasn't, really. Graylin suggested turning herself in, and we were all shocked. We never even considered anything beyond keeping it to ourselves," Arlyn said.

"I know," Lewis sighed, shoulders sagging, scooping up the dough and dropping it into a bread pan. Arlyn put an arm around her, and Lewis leaned against her friend.

"Look at us," Lewis said, smiling sadly. "We used to be so much fun."

"Excuse you, I still am." Arlyn skipped away. "I am the epitome of hilarity. I'm a joker in a world of fools. I'm the definition of a real knee-slapper."

"You can't laugh off everything, Arlyn," Lewis whispered. "I'm just not sure if you and Graylin will be able to joke your way out of this one."

"We can always try," Arlyn said. "Now come on, let's go talk about something nice until this bread is done."

31

GRAYLIN AWOKE WITH A start, faint stomping echoing from the hall outside. She rolled over, hugging blankets around her tightly. They were here, Mackson's Bay. She wasn't entirely sure if she was ready for it. In fact, she was fairly certain that she wasn't. Graylin didn't want to get out of bed and address her past deeds and her parents' transgressions. After all, they were here because it was the next stop. The next level. Pyrogleminine. Weapons. Osden. Her parents. LeMay. Denloy.

Graylin buried her head in her blankets as the thoughts chased each other. The tips of her fingers, which were still above the blankets, told her that her cabin was colder than usual. It was getting colder; every day, darkness sct in a little earlier at night and stretched longer into the morning. She groaned. She just wanted to sleep, sleep, and sleep and sleep, until it was all gone.

"Hey, Graylin? Wake up, we're landing soon." Lewis knocked on her door.

"It's too cold," Graylin said, voice muffled, pretending like the chilly air was the worst of her problems.

"Well, you brought cool weather clothes, didn't you?" Lewis called.

Graylin thought about this for a second. "Um, no?"

"Graylin," Lewis sighed disappointedly. "Listen, would you just open the door? I feel like my mother."

Graylin flopped to the end of her bed and opened the door. Flepe tumbled off her bed and onto the floor, and Lewis stepped daintily around him.

"Hmm," Lewis moved to Graylin's dresser, wading through the puddles of clothes overflowing onto the ground. "Graylin, honestly, your room is a disaster. I don't know how you live like this."

"Let me just reach into my pocket and find how many craps I give." Graylin rolled over, fished around in her pretend pocket, and then pulled out an empty hand. "Oh look. There's none."

"Well, it really looks like you neglected to pack any warm clothes," Lewis sighed, completely ignoring her. "I mean, the best you have is your regular thin shirt and trousers. A waistcoat will help, I suppose, but with this breeze . . ." She glanced at Graylin, still buried in blankets. "You know what? I'll be right back. Let me grab you something of mine."

Graylin had just finally left the warm comfort of her bed when her friend returned holding a long sleeve, tightly knit shirt.

"Ew," Graylin sighed, "rich person clothes."

"Really, Graylin, this is your own fault for not thinking ahead," she said, handing it over. "And, please, let me fix your hair one of these days, goodness."

"My hair is fine," Graylin huffed, pulling the shirt over her head, re-donning her button up, and yanking her suspenders over her shoulders and socks over her feet up to the rolled cuffs of her pants.

"It's not. You have curly hair, Graylin, you need to take care of it," Lewis said, fiddling with a strand. How funny, Graylin thought, that she was here, preparing to step out into the world for the first time since killing a man, readying herself to beat the next task on the journey that was finding her parents, and Lewis was chastising her over her hair.

Perhaps it was Lewis's way of maintaining normalcy in their lives. Maybe it was something for her to hold on to as waves of surprises and losses bashed the crew repeatedly over these last few months.

"Thank you, Lewis," Graylin said finally, untwisting one of her suspenders.

"Next time, pack your own clothes," she said, brushing off one sleeve. "Now come on, we'll be landing soon."

Graylin followed Lewis up to the top deck, where everyone was hurrying about, nearly running into Arlyn, who was bearing the telltale marks of someone who had just checked on the engines and had been forced to wash their hands as a result. This included wet sleeves, some oil stains on her fresh pair of pants, and a disgusted look on her face.

"My hands are so *dry* now," Arlyn lamented, rubbing them on her shirt. "Why are they so *dry*?"

"You too!" Lewis cried, poking Arlyn's bare, goosebump ridden arm. "Where are your autumn clothes? Am I honestly the only one who remembered that seasons exist when packing for this trip?"

"Oh definitely. Is that a surprise to you? Everyone knows you're the smart one," Arlyn nodded. She too was quickly forced into some of Lewis's clothes (for her, this was a long, thick skirt with a large slit, and an epic plaid scarf). Arlyn also found a bowler hat in their collection of Leo's old clothes below decks and donned it with pride.

"Dang, do I look good," she proclaimed.

"That you do, cousin," Graylin agreed solemnly.

"You look great!" River cried.

"Not really my type," Teddy shrugged with a cheeky smile.

"Fine way to treat your one and only date, Teddy," Arlyn said. "How do you feel about doing that today, by the way? It'll have to be quick, because besides learning just who's behind that pyrogleminine testing, we also need to buy a hinge for the lower left engine door."

"By date, you mean . . . ?" Teddy rustled his hair, raising an eyebrow.

"Our date Teddy boy. You bet you would be my first date, and I accepted like the thrifty friend I am."

"Now I remember," Teddy nodded. "Speaking of thrifty, I hope you have cheap tastes, because I am destitute and broke, and want all my gambling rewards to buy a gramophone."

Arlyn held up a hand. "Never fear, I've got some spare cash hidden somewhere nobody can find it that we'll use to fund this outing of ours." She moved her hat on her head, tugging on a braid. "In fact, let's head out now, before Graylin finds out."

Scrambling down the ladder, Arlyn leapt off the last rung and hit the ground running, beckoning for Teddy to follow her. "We'll be back!" she called to Lewis, eyes set on the brick town rising before them.

The buildings looked old and weathered, beaten by the crisp sea air. The roads were winding and maze-like, outlined with ivy and the first fallen leaves of pale green and yellow. A chill bit the air, but it was a sort of cold that Arlyn knew would fade to warmth as the sun rose. She had no difficulty believing that her parents had been here at some point, for who wouldn't want to visit? The umbrella'd restaurant patios and glowing lanterns and merry window boxes gave off a very fresh, welcoming impression. Grass gave way to bricks beneath their feet as the two made a beeline for the first landmark they could see, which was a giant statue of an anchor.

"Okay . . . okay, okay," Arlyn gasped, trying to catch her breath. "Now how realistic of a date do we have to make this? Because I'm not gonna kiss you or anything." She looked up at Teddy, who was already scaling the anchor. He was so like her cousin.

"Kissing was never on the table, to be honest," Teddy said. "If I thought it was, I never would have offered the date idea."

"Um, rude," Arlyn folded her arms. "You're telling me you don't want to kiss this pretty face?"

"Respectfully, heck no," Teddy said, swinging his legs. "You couldn't pay me enough. You just have this . . . this River vibe, and honestly it kind of puts me off." Arlyn grinned, amused by the obvious joke.

"Alright, so my vibe is not appealing. What if I had my cousin's vibe and or face? Would your heck no become a heck yeah?" she teased.

"It would become a shut up," Teddy scoffed, sliding down the statue. Arlyn turned to him and studied the boy. His tired eyes were gleaming, smiling just a little, eyebrows raised. Alright, so *maybe* she could tell what her cousin saw in him . . . but only a little.

"Come on music boy, let's find something to do," she said, turning and skipping ahead. "You did a good job with that guitar part for our play, by the way."

"Thank you," Teddy shoved his hands in his pockets. He paused to glance at a poster for some annoying thing or another. "*Like leaves and flowers, sunny sunny showers, so is my life.*" He read, looking disgusted, and pointed to it. "Does anybody understand this stuff?"

"I thought you were a poetry guy," Arlyn smirked.

"Said who?"

"River."

"River is a filthy liar," Teddy said as they kept walking. "I do like *good* poetry, though. That? That is not good. That's not even okay. That's just a bunch of nice words squished together." He pulled something out of his pocket, a scrap of paper, Arlyn thought, and dropped it in a nearby trash can.

"So what does *good* poetry sound like?" she asked. Teddy smiled. Arlyn suddenly realized that, several months ago, she wouldn't have been able to claim ever seeing Teddy's smile. But now, despite the worries and the struggles the crew was dealing with, he seemed to be smiling more and more. This made Arlyn feel better, as one of her major concerns about Teddy and Graylin's hypothetical eventual relationship was that they would feed off one another's sadness.

"You're trying to trick me into saying some of my stuff, which I won't do," he said. "But I can tell you that the good stuff, the poetry I like, is the stuff people write on walls, or typewriters. I like poetry that's funny, or that sounds good to say, but also tells a good story. The musical sort. I'm not down for the 'my life sucks and everything is bad and no one likes me' stuff, either. Poetry isn't meant to make you feel worse, it's meant to make you feel better, or inspired, or thoughtful. But not depressed."

"And do you write that sort of stuff? The kind that makes you feel better?" Arlyn asked.

"I try."

"Is that why you're so tired?" Arlyn asked, thinking of his shadowed eyes and worn expression. "Are you kept up by the feels of your poetry?" Okay, so maybe she was teasing him, but if Teddy was going to someday become romantically involved with Graylin, he'd need to get used to it.

"Ah, no," Teddy said. "I've been kept from sleep by . . . *different* feels lately."

"Like my cousin feels?"

"More like 'we murdered a man' feels. Like 'we are completely alone' feels," Teddy clarified, smiling sadly. "Like 'how are we ever going to be okay' feels."

Arlyn nodded. Those particular feels had been making the rounds around the ship lately.

Across the city, Graylin and Lewis were just departing the *Freelander*, mostly because Lewis told Graylin she wouldn't get dessert for a week if she didn't come with her. Come *where* exactly, Lewis hadn't been very forthcoming about, but as dessert was Graylin's favorite meal of the day, she complied. They strolled around sprawling farmer's markets where striped canvas stands lined the streets, each one marketing something different. From the rafters of a stall with a patched green tarp for a roof hung every vegetable known to man, and across from them, a colorful display of hats, ranging from stovepipes to berets. All Graylin could do was stand close to Lewis, hoping beyond hope that not an eye would land on her. She wanted, no, *needed* to be invisible. Eyes could tell more than many other senses; one look at her, and everyone would know. She was lost. She was dirty. She was a murderer.

"We're getting close, I can feel it," Lewis said, squeezing herself through a dense crowd centered around a stand with live fish.

"Getting close to where?" Graylin asked, silently wishing she'd simply dealt with no dessert and stayed home. "Is this going to take long?"

"Oh, hush, and quit your whining!" Lewis stepped gracefully over a fence and dragged Graylin through a shady-looking alley. "We're almost there!"

"Almost where, exactly?" Graylin asked again as they pushed through a low-hanging line of clothes out of the alley.

"Here!" Lewis announced, beaming with pride. She had, after all, spent nearly an hour trying to decide where to take Graylin as a distraction. As Graylin's eyes adjusted to the sudden light, a rust-colored brick building with four eight-paned windows rose into view, towering on the corner of two streets. Above the copper-toned double doors, a red and white striped awning bore the words, **HORACE & SONS SWEET CO.**

"Is this . . ." Graylin looked through the display window at a stretching and squeaking taffy machine. Next to it was a mixer with golden-brown caramel dripping from the paddle. "Is this the place Uncle . . . Uncle Denloy told us about?" She shrunk a little at the words. She hoped not. The idea made her feel nauseous.

"No, but it *is* a candy store. I'm not sure which store Mr. Denloy and your dad used to go to, but I know that this one just opened within the last few years." Lewis dragged her to the front doors. "Now come on. You like sugar, remember?"

Yes, Graylin liked sugar. Sugar made her feel happy. She didn't *want* to feel happy yet. She didn't deserve to feel happy yet. Graylin suddenly wished she had worn a coat or a cape of some sort, not because she was cold, but because she didn't want to be seen. The strings in her head began to fray; she was going to break down. She could sense it, any second they would all snap. The last time she'd felt the strings break like this, she'd had Teddy there, both making the problem worse and, in the end, fixing it. But Teddy wasn't here. Arlyn wasn't here.

"Hey, come on." Lewis took Graylin's arm gently. They made a funny pair, the two: elegant Lewis, with her leather gloves and perfectly done waves of curls, hanging loose around her shoulders today, holding onto scraggly, scrawny, frizzy, curly-haired Graylin, wearing a raggedy shirt and scuffed boots. "You'll be alright," Lewis said comfortingly.

"What if they know?" Graylin whispered, staring at the doors. "What if they know what I did?"

"What if they learned that you, Graylin Freely, were human? That you've had bad things happen to you, that you've been put in tough situations and responded fallibly? Everyone's done that, Graylin." She took Graylin's hand and squeezed her fingers. "You've been through a lot. You have to recognize that."

"Been through a lot? Yeah, sure." Graylin shook her head. "I haven't been through much at all, Lewis. My parents aren't dead, so I'm not an orphan. Two uncles died, but everyone loses people, and one was killed at my own hand, the other because he saved me. I have *done* a lot. I haven't been *through* a lot."

"You *have* been through a lot. You have, and we're helping you through it. We're here for you," Lewis said earnestly. Graylin wrinkled her nose.

"You sound like a greeting card."

"I sound like your trusted friend of many years, which I am. Now come on, and enjoy the day. You have a whole life of healing ahead of you, Graylin, and it'll be hard, but it starts now. Might as well start off on the right foot." She hugged her arm closer. "Besides, they have no way of knowing even your name, let alone your past week."

As they stepped into the shop, the scent of sweets and baked goods filled their noses. A checker-patterned floor spread beneath them, reflective as a mirror. In the center, a thin, winding spiral staircase, and on it, a set of heavily tanned, coal-haired boys, about their age, looking down at them. Graylin watched them skeptically. Their hair did not curl. It was straight as a ruler, hanging limply down their heads in the heat of the building.

"Is that-?" one of them asked.

"I think it is," the other finished.

"I can hear you, you know!" Lewis shouted up the staircase. "Three years and you can't even greet your own cousin politely?"

"Lewis!" the two shouted at the same time. As they sprinted down the staircase, Graylin realized they were a lot taller than her, almost as tall as Teddy. Thicker though, more muscly, and slightly stocky, too.

"About time you came and visited us!" One of them said, he was wearing a white shirt with a blue vest. His brother was wearing the same regalia but with a green vest, the fabric embroidered with many gold highlights and sequins.

Lewis hugged one, the fellow in the blue, and gave an exaggerated sigh. "It's good to see you, Paul. Still horribly out of touch with basic fashion, I see." She pushed him away and moved to hug the one in green. "You too, Liam."

"What can I say? It's the uniform of the trade, and I think I pull it off wonderfully," the green-vested boy grinned. "We weren't expecting a visit from our rich cousin. What brings you this far from home?"

"Just a small adventure with a few friends." Lewis waved away the question nonchalantly. "And, since we were in Mackson's Bay, I thought I should bring Graylin here."

"Graylin, is it then?" Paul offered her a handshake, which she took hesitantly. "It's about time Lewis brings some of her friends to come visit us."

"And so, the great Graylin Freely, Lewis's friend, has finally come to Mackson's Bay!" Liam announced dramatically, getting down on one knee and bowing. "Tis' an honor to have you here, madam."

"Erm, thanks," Graylin said uncomfortably, trying not to pull her hand away when Liam kissed it elegantly, her heart beginning to race. They knew her last name. How did they know her last name? Lewis must have told them about her and Arlyn before. If they knew she was a Freely, what else did they know? Their eyes were locked on her. Graylin's palms grew sweaty, her heart racing. Surely, *surely* they must know the truth about the secret she and Lewis held between each other. Trying not to panic, Graylin glanced around at the shop. Everything was bright and gaudy, filled with sparkling wrappings and silk wallpaper. There were small tracks hanging from the ceiling, with small trains and cars running on them, dropping little wrapper butterscotches to the ground. A clunking machine in the window was whistling, bouncing slightly as it churned out dozens of hard candies, spilling like gems into a bowl.

"Lewis, you must come say hello to Mama and Papa, they'll be thrilled to see you," Paul said. Graylin looked away from the chandelier she'd been studying, alarmed. Lewis, leave? Leave her alone, with the winking boy in the green vest and the weight of their secret? No, thank you.

"I think I'll stay with Graylin, if that's okay," Lewis said politely, seeing Graylin's pallid features. "We don't have long here, and I want to make sure we hit the highlights of the store."

"Well then, right this way ladies!" Liam exclaimed, sliding across the reflective floor on bright red leather shoes. "We'll start over here. Tell me, Graylin, what's your favorite kind of candy?"

Arlyn and Teddy sat outside the ice cream parlor they'd found, slowly licking down the discount desserts they got for cheap since Mackson's Bay was out of season. Arlyn had *almost* registered for the rewards program (every tenth ice cream cone was free), before Teddy had reminded her she wasn't supposed to be gallivanting about as a Freely. So, much to the distress of her cheapskate soul, she had been forced to skip the rewards and simply had to settle for the off-season sale. Frozen treats in hand, the two had selected seats on the shop patio and sat watching the crowd in relative silence. That is, until a girl around Arlyn's age, with her long dark hair in tons of minuscule braids, approached them to compliment Arlyn's hat. The two had struck it off and chatted for several minutes, talking about everything from hair to the weather, while Teddy leaned on his hand and yawned, trying to keep his eyes open. Arlyn made a mental note to make the guy get more sleep.

"Well, that was fun," she said with a sigh, drinking her now melted strawberry ice cream out of her cone.

"Did you ask her about the Freelys?" Teddy asked, opening his eyes. Arlyn shook her head.

"Of course not, we're trying not to draw suspicion."

"Right, right," Teddy rubbed his eyes, yawning again. Arlyn was struck with the thought that if Graylin had been there to witness Teddy's yawns, she would have found them adorable.

"Teddy, we're not actually on a date, right," Arlyn said suddenly, "but that doesn't mean the concept doesn't still apply. Think about what dates are for."

"Spending time with the person you find attractive?" Teddy asked, raising his eyebrows.

"Um, no. Well, sometimes, I guess," Arlyn waved her hand. "That's irrelevant. What dates are *often* for is getting to know your prospective significant other."

The phrase 'insignificant other' popped into Teddy's head, as did a picture of River, and he smiled, nodding to Arlyn. "Okay, I'm picking up what you're putting down."

"Well, what if we took that same sort of idea, but did it for friends?" Arlyn asked. "I mean, we're friends, right? But we don't really know each other. What if we just bounce questions back and forth off of each other until we get a feel for each other's vibe?"

"Just play catch with some vibes," Teddy nodded, smiling. "Alright."

Arms loaded with sweets, Graylin and Lewis left the candy shop, heading out into the shining sun dimmed by the cold, the light of which cut through the frosty morning air enough to make life enjoyable again. Graylin took a deep breath, blinked a little in the face of the autumn breeze, and pushed back her hair, the air feeling extra cold against her clammy skin. The whole time they were in the shop, Graylin had felt on edge, jumping at the slightest sounds, her heart racing.

"So what do you think?" Lewis asked, grinning, as they set off down the road. "Of my cousins?"

"Mine's better," Graylin said honestly, popping a small yellow hard candy into her mouth.

"Well, Liam was certainly interested in you," Lewis chuckled, fishing in her own bag of candy. "I'm glad now I didn't bring Arlyn, or things would've been much worse. Liam, as I'm sure you've noticed, is quite the determined flirt."

"That was *flirting*?" Graylin asked, scrunching her nose, thinking of the awkward winks and unnerving side glances and random lies disguised as compliments. "I hated it."

"I wondered if you might," Lewis laughed, pulling out a sweet. "Here, try this. It's Spruce Gum." She pulled out a small pink square wrapped in wax paper, and held it out. "My cousins have sent me some before, and it's quite good."

"What's it taste like?" Graylin asked, her boots clicking on the cobble streets.

"Well . . . I don't know exactly," Lewis said thoughtfully. "It tastes . . . pink."

Deciding that eating 'pink' would make a sufficient remedy for the emptiness in her stomach, Graylin popped it in mouth. At first the square was hard, and difficult to chew, but the more she chomped, it got stretchier and stretchier.

"What do I do with it now?" Graylin asked, sticking the wad in her cheek.

"You chew it. It's chewing gum," Lewis said. "I got enough for everyone, because I thought Arlyn would like it."

"Speaking of Arlyn, where the heck is she?" Graylin asked, stretching the gum smooth in her mouth.

"She and Teddy headed out about a bit before we did. I think she mentioned something about a date," Lewis said, smiling with benign mischief.

"A date?" Graylin dropped her bag of candy. Her cousin was on a date? *Teddy* was on a date?

"Oh yes," Lewis nodded her head.

"Oh," Graylin said weakly. Was this a thing? Was Teddy interested in her cousin? It wouldn't be a surprise, really. Who wasn't, after all? Maybe she simply hadn't noticed. Maybe she had been too preoccupied with herself to notice her friend Teddy's feelings for her cousin. And her cousin . . . did Arlyn like Teddy back?

"Hey," Lewis laughed, picking up Graylin's bag, "don't get in a fuss. Remember those bets we had, on who Arlyn would go on a date with first? Well, Teddy bet on himself. And as Arlyn would never actually go out with him, he had to ask her, just for the money."

Graylin rearranged her sweets and walked on in silence. She felt very empty, and somehow knew deep down that it was because *Teddy* was on a date, not that Arlyn was, but she couldn't say why. She liked him as a person, she knew that, but, well, he was just her friend. Sure, she enjoyed Teddy differently than she did Arlyn, but that was to be expected when one was your cousin, surely. She and Arlyn were practically the same person; it was hardly a fair comparison.

As Graylin and Lewis passed a sandy stretch of beach, they were surprised to catch sight of a few familiar heads of hair, specifically a dark blonde one and one of brilliant orange.

"Enland?" Lewis called incredulously, waving back when the cartographer greeted her. The two girls hurried down to them, stripping off their socks, shoes, and outer shirts, as the sun had really warmed up the air.

"What's going on here?" Lewis asked, smiling at Enland's drenched shirt.

"River is being a nuisance," Enland sighed, "as always. I had to get him off the ship, and now look what he's done." He held up several papers, one so wet that half of it actually fell to the ground as he spoke.

"Oh, I'm sorry," Lewis said sympathetically, hiding her smile. "Have you guys seen Teddy and Arlyn yet?"

"No, where are they?" River asked, hiding guiltily wet hands behind his back.

"On a date," Lewis told him casually.

As River spluttered and choked and Graylin continued to feel as if her stomach was falling several feet a minute, the causers of such distress, Arlyn and Teddy, continued on quite unbothered. They'd left the ice cream joint and wandered through several maze-like streets, 'playing catch with some vibes'. As they walked, Arlyn realized how funny Teddy was. Their questions for each other became more and more random, starting with 'what's your favorite color' and shifting all the way to 'what do you think is the best way to become famous?'.

"Learn to play golf real well," was Teddy's answer, as he grinned. "That's what *real* famous people do."

"I disagree. Everyone knows that poker is the ideal rich man's sport," Arlyn grinned.

"How would you feel if River grew a mustache in the future?" Teddy asked. Arlyn gagged.

"I would feel better wearing a blindfold at all times than see that," she said. "River? With a mustache? Disgusto."

She glanced sidelong at Teddy and took a stab at a question she'd been waiting for since they started the game. "What are your thoughts on my cousin?"

Teddy smiled and scrunched his nose. "I'm going to have to skip this question." He stuck his hands in his pockets. "For both of our sakes."

"Oh come on Teddy, there's no reason to be embarrassed. I honestly want to know what you think of her. Do you want to kiss her? Do you want to hug her? Do you want to run your fingers through her luscious curls?" Arlyn teased. "Though that last one might be a bit hard, to be honest, she doesn't really brush her hair consistently."

"I mean, she does have nice hair," Teddy said, thankful for the multiple options and that he didn't have to consider all of them. He wasn't quite sure what conclusion he would come to, but he *was* sure he didn't want to know.

"Oooh, someone's in loooove!" Arlyn sang.

"I am not in love. Not yet, anyway," Teddy said.

"I mean, if the whole accidental murder thing didn't turn you off, I feel like it's only a matter of time," Arlyn grinned.

"You are *excessively* lighthearted," Teddy shook his head. "You're like River, he's such an innocent, optimistic little twit."

"Hey, you need to be a bit more like that if you ever want a chance with my cousin," Arlyn said. "As her only living and or reliable family member, I am now the one dealing out the blessings, got it?"

"You want me to be happier, for Graylin?" Teddy smiled.

"Well, yeah."

"Luckily, I happen to be getting better at being happy, and Graylin's definitely been a help." Teddy said. "She makes me happier, and makes me want to be."

"Aw, that's so cute!" Arlyn skipped ahead. "I can just imagine you two someday, with little kids running around. Do you want kids?"

"I don't know," Teddy sighed. "Yes, I think so. A few years ago I would have said absolutely not. Part of it was because I was young, part of it was that I just . . . almost every kid I knew didn't have parents, and Lewis's sucked, and being an adult in general just seemed scary and sad, and kids were part of being an adult."

"And now?" Arlyn asked.

"Well, things change a bit as you age, I guess. And I'm older now, not as jaded in that particular way."

"Ugh," Arlyn laughed, "I'm sorry I asked. I don't want to hear that."

Teddy started laughing too, shutting his eyes and almost wincing. "I know. That felt cheesy to even say."

"Well, the good news is that you are not the only one experiencing cheesy feelings on our ship, and I don't think you'll be the last." Arlyn grinned. "And I am glad that you're opening up, Teddy boy."

"I didn't mean to," Teddy sighed. "You and Graylin are both dangerous, just sort of making me spill my flipping guts all the time."

"I have that effect on people," Arlyn assured him. "Though Graylin is a surprise. She generally makes people share less, while I am a magical therapist who draws the deepest secrets out of even the most stubborn, traumatized teenage boy. Just look at Enland."

At the section of beach, while Lewis stood next to Enland down by the water, Graylin kept glancing behind herself toward the road, trying not to become anxious about Arlyn and Teddy's continued absence. She couldn't stop checking every few seconds. It was like a nervous twitch, repeatedly looking over her shoulder.

"Graylin!" Lewis called from the water. "Hey, Enland has some money in his satchel up there. Could you run and grab us some lunch?"

"Sure," Graylin waved back, thankful for something to do. She grabbed the cash and hurried up to the road, stepping onto the pavement and walking several blocks before being pulled up short. It was as if someone had grabbed a handful of the strings in her head and just yanked them, filling her with fear and bringing her to a stop. She looked around- she had no idea where she was, but it was very busy. There was a shop to her left selling what appeared to be only effeminate scarves, and on her right was a small stand filled with vegetables. Panicking, Graylin briefly considered buying said veg and offering it as a lunch option. Thankfully, the image of Lewis's disappointed glance if she brought back only carrots was enough to drive away such cowardice, and Graylin plowed on. She swallowed, clutching the money tighter in her hands, feeling extremely self-conscious. She needed to get a grip.

Graylin started off again, taking a turn here, pausing now and then when the crowds became too condensed to squeeze through. The longer she wandered, the sweatier her hands became, and the more uncertain her steps. She didn't know where she was going, and her sense of direction was frankly abysmal. Even in Odios she got lost occasionally, and she had lived there for eight years. *Just ask someone, cousin*, reprimanded Arlyn's voice in her head. *Fat chance*, Graylin thought back. Just wander up to some stranger and ask for directions to a restaurant? The very idea made Graylin feel a little queasy, though part of that was how hungry she was.

Looking helplessly around the street, Graylin reluctantly began to search for someone who looked nice. There was a man to her left wearing a very outdated hat who looked nice enough, but he was eating the corn on the cob in his hand vertically rather than horizontally, and Graylin decided she didn't trust him. To her right there was a woman carrying three children in her arms, but she looked exhausted and Graylin didn't want to interrupt. Finally the lonesome, slightly lost Freely cousin decided she would simply ask one of the friendly police officers chatting outside a shop a ways down the road. They, at least, would be accustomed to strangers asking them questions.

"Um," Graylin approached the two officers, holding onto her money so tightly that, had it been alive, it would have died of strangulation. "Sorry, but could you tell me a good place to get food?" The men turned around.

And Graylin realized her mistake. What was she *doing*? Here she was, a murderer, a runaway, and an unaccompanied minor, asking a policeman for directions. Admittedly, not all of her transgressions were equal with one another, but in that instant the weight of all, and the secrets they entailed, fell upon her shoulders like a load of rocks. She was so *stupid*. Of all the people to ask, she had to go and choose the only ones who were trained to spot people like her. In a crowd of innocents, these two men's entire job was to find the guilty one. And *she* was the guilty one.

"Are you alright, miss?" One of the policemen asked kindly. He was older, with twinkly eyes and a graying beard. "You're looking a bit peaky."

"I'm . . ." Graylin was suddenly shaking, and she held her hands behind her back, lest their trembling reveal her guilt. Her guilt which was, at that very moment, urging her to spill every secret weighing her down. *I'm only sixteen*, she wanted to sob. *I don't know what I'm doing, I have no parental figure, I left my home with zero thought about what it would entail, and the only adult I had left, I killed.*

"I'm just hungry," she finished out loud, voice weak.

"Well, if it's food you need," the policeman smiled, "There's a lovely little soup shop just down the way. You'll take a turn at that sign up there, and then it's just a few feet away."

"Thank you," Graylin said quickly. She paused, and then continued. "Could you tell me how to get back to the beach once I leave the soup shop?"

"Ah, o'course love," the other policemen smiled. He was younger, with a light red mustache. He told her, in very good detail, the route back to her friend's section of beach, smiling encouragingly all the time. She stowed every word as firmly in her brain as possible, repeating the directions to herself as she thanked them and hurried away, heart pounding.

Straight down the brick road, she thought, *then a left, then an alley, then another left.*

The soup shop, it turned out, was less of a shop, and more of a stand. You didn't go inside, you simply ordered from the window under a cloth awning. Hanging from the side of the stand was a sign reading You've Been Souped, along with a picture of a man with a curly mustache and a comically raised eyebrow. Graylin quickly got into line, just behind two men who looked very much like one another. There was a chalkboard sign by the window reading 'October special: Potato'. Graylin hadn't realized it *was* October already, and looked around anxiously until she saw the date on a stray newspaper. *October third.* Well, at least only a bit of the month had passed; there was nothing quite as disorienting as realizing it was much later in the year than one thought.

"Always love a good soup," one of the men in front of her said. *Straight down the brick road, then a left, then an alley, then another left.*

"I think I'll bring some home for J. I'll put it in that insulator, and we'll see if it's still warm by the time we get home. You think it'll keep the warmth in for seven days?" The other asked. Graylin absently thought that they must be brothers, both sporting similar voices and nearly identical blond beards. Their backs were facing her, but when they turned, she caught glimpses of their very straight noses.

"It might, especially if we try out that shortcut, flying over that forest the wife loves instead of around it. She likes the colors this time of year, you know. It just gets so foggy."

Straight down the brick road, then a left, then an alley, then another left. Graylin was rocking on her feet, looking anxiously around, waiting for the two policemen to charge up and haul her away. How long before they realized why that strange girl asking for directions had looked so nervous?

"Hey," one brother said, "did you hear the news?"

"News? What news?" The other brother asked, pulling out a lighter and fiddling with it. "You and the lady aren't pregnant, are you? You know we all agreed to never do that again."

"What? No, of course not." The first brother shook his head. "And you *still* don't smoke, give me that." *Brick road, left, alley, left.* "No, I mean from Wilson. Sounds like the head macho is all for starting up our automatic crafter." *Brick road, left, alley, left.*

"Oh, thank goodness," the second brother smiled. "I was gonna have to have a real talk with that man if he disagreed. The amount of extra work it would take to make all of it by hand . . ." He leaned around his brother to glance at the menu. "What sort of soup do you want?" he asked. "I was thinking maybe tomato . . ."

"Ew, gross, never suggest that again," his brother grimaced, flicking the confiscated lighter.

"Alright then, chicken-noodle?"

"Do I look like an ill little child to you? No thanks."

Brick road, left, alley, left . . . or was it left, left, alley? Graylin wondered, glancing around as a few fallen autumn leaves, the city's tumbleweeds, rustled past. *Or was the alley on the left?*

"Hey," someone said, tapping her shoulder. Graylin startled, heart jumping and freezing for a moment. But it was not, as she thought, one of the police. Instead, it was one of the brothers from in front of her, smiling down at her with kind, familiar eyes.

"Hey, do you want to go in front of us?" the man asked. "We haven't decided what we want yet."

"Um," Graylin swallowed, hands shaking again as her heart trembled with fear. "Yes, I mean, thank you."

She stepped forward to the counter, trying not to break down, struggling to take deep breaths. It was just her imagination. The man wasn't Denloy, and he wasn't Leo either. They were both dead. It was just a kind blond man with glasses and gray eyes. Those couldn't be *that* hard to come by, surely.

"I'll take six pints of the potato soup, please," Graylin told the soup seller shakily. The soup lady nodded and disappeared from the window. *Brick alley, left, road, left.* Graylin glanced over her shoulder. That man and his brother had much fuller beards than Denloy or Leo ever had. Denloy's had always been sparse and well trimmed, while Leo hadn't been capable of facial hair at all. It wasn't them. It wasn't them.

With a whispered thank you, Graylin took her two paper sacks of soup and the free oyster crackers offered with it and moved away. *Brick alley, left, road, left.* There was a brick alley to her right- that must be it. Refusing to look back at the brothers, now ordering their food, she headed down the alley.

"We really ought to find the rest of the crew." Arlyn said, slipping the large hinge she'd just bought into one of her pockets. "Or at least head back to the Freelander. Do you know what everyone else was planning on doing today?"

"Unlike River, I am not a snoop," Teddy said. "So no."

"You say that like snooping is a bad thing," Arlyn sighed. "Speaking of bad things, I'm bored."

"Best way to be," Teddy said. "But that's just one man's opinion."

"Try telling that to Graylin," Arlyn scoffed. "A bored Graylin is a crazy Graylin."

"Which is why it's the best way to be," Teddy grinned.

"Maybe we should vandalize a wall or something. I saw some dudes doing it in Belhaven and it was epic," Arlyn offered, beginning to dig around in her satchel for a snack. She was suddenly starving, a common side effect of Freely boredom.

"That's actually a shockingly good idea," Teddy considered. "Hey, is that food?"

"It's a sandwich I made a few days ago," Arlyn wrinkled her nose, unwrapping the brown paper outside to reveal several green splotches. "I think it's gone bad."

"Nonsense," Teddy said, plucking the sandwich from her hands and taking a large bite. "I'm hungry, and mold is good for you. You know, bacteria and all that." He chewed roughly twice before spitting the whole mess on the ground.

"Scratch all that stuff I just said," he gagged, pulling a very strange face. "Mold is not for eating."

"Even I could have told you that," Arlyn said, mentally adding Teddy to her list of idiotic friends, "and I eat paper as a pastime. Now, let's go find the crew."

Graylin sat herself on the curb, struggling to breathe. She'd followed the directions . . . she'd thought. She'd been repeating the phrase *brick alley, left, road, left* for so long, she actually couldn't remember if it was right. In fact, she had a sneaking suspicion it was not, because after following the brick alley, she'd arrived in a strange section of street where every house was covered in ivy. She'd taken a left, walked down the road for several blocks, and taken a second left, which had brought her here, to this extremely crowded thoroughfare. It was busy, loud, and bright, and certainly *not* the beach.

The fear trailing after her from talking to the police seemed to intensify, as did the shakiness in her legs from seeing those living reminders of Denloy, and Graylin had looked around desperately for a sign, a street, anything which would lead her back to her friends. When nothing presented itself, she set down the bags of soup on the side of the curb and pulled her legs up. She closed her eyes and rested her forehead on her knees. She wanted to cry, or sleep, or disappear. Anything would be better than this.

"Hey."

Once again, someone tapped her shoulder, and once again, Graylin jumped a mile. She leaped to her feet and took several steps backward before realizing, once again, it was not the police, or the men who resembled her dead uncles. It was her cousin, and someone with curly dark hair, bright brown eyes, and a dimple when he smiled was standing behind her.

"Teddy!" Graylin cried, relief flooding her. She wanted to hold his hands, to hug him . . . but then she remembered Teddy had just finished a date with Arlyn, and hung back. *Besides, you don't hug people, let alone your cousin's date.*

"Teddy? What do you mean, *Teddy*?" Arlyn asked, hands on her hips. "I, your great and awesome cousin, am right here."

"Hello cousin," Graylin said, heart slowly returning to its normal rhythm. She sniffed, trying not to let them see her red, dripping nose, and held up the sacks of food. "I got soup."

The three friends made their way through the city, heading towards the beach. Graylin's sense of direction had magically returned with the appearance of her cousin and Teddy, and she told them vaguely where she thought it was so that Arlyn could lead.

"You look like you're out of fuel," Teddy told her as they walked.

"What do you mean?" Graylin asked, still sniffing. Her nose refused to stop running.

"I mean you need some food," he said. "What kind of soup did you get?"

"Potato," Graylin said. "I *am* a little hungry, but mostly I'm just tired."

"Were you waiting for someone?" Teddy asked, gesturing back towards Graylin's curb. Graylin glanced at him, surprised.

"What? No, no, I guess I just got a little, a little lost."

"This place is huge," Teddy agreed.

"Speaking of which, what did you guys do?" Graylin asked, trying to sound as casual as possible. The trembling of her hands suitably negated this attempt. "You and Arlyn, I mean, on your date." As soon as she added the end, she regretted it. It was unnecessary, it sounded childish, and it brought that deep empty feeling back.

"We just wandered mostly, you know, got some ice cream. Vandalized a random wall. Ate some mold," Teddy said. "I tell you what, though, that was undoubtedly the worst date of my life."

"What?!" shrieked Arlyn, tossing back a random newspaper, which Teddy ducked to avoid. "Rude, Teddy! Keep talking like that, and we're gonna up your therapy rate from once a week to twice."

"How was it the worst?" Graylin asked, feeling strangely better seeing Teddy's smile.

"Your delightfully flamboyant and social cousin," Teddy said, "kept talking about boring things like therapy and my problems and how River loves me so much, he would die for me. Which like seriously man, please don't."

"She does that sort of thing," Graylin smiled.

"But the good news is that I totally have enough money for a gramophone now, since I won the bet on who Arlyn would go out with first," Teddy said.

"A gramophone?" Graylin asked.

"Yeah. You know, like the one we saw in Belhaven. I thought you might like one, especially if you aren't sleeping much. That's when I like music."

"That's why you went?" Graylin asked, a strange sensation filling her. "To get money to buy something . . . for me?"

"Yeah," Teddy looked at her. "You didn't think I liked Arlyn, did you?"

"What? No." Graylin assured him, despite the fact that she was thinking *exactly* that.

"Well, I don't," Teddy said. "It was purely monetary." Graylin smiled at him, the emptiness disappearing.

"Once again," Arlyn called back, "rude."

32

ARLYN LED THE THREE crewmates back to the beach with relative ease, and it wasn't long before they rejoined their friends frolicking in the sand. Being of a less socially awkward and nervous frame of mind than her cousin, Arlyn had not panicked and missed the obvious signage for the sought after beach.

When they had arrived, the long-cooled soup was passed out, and the crew drank it gratefully (Graylin had, in her nervousness, forgotten to grab the wooden spoons offered at the shop).

"While you three were off wasting time and getting lost," Lewis said, wiping away her soup mustache elegantly, "Enland and I did some digging."

"Where?" Graylin asked, looking around. She didn't see any holes in the sand, but she was happy to help. There was something very appealing about digging a pit on the beach, just to know how far you could go.

"Figurative digging, Graylin," Lewis sighed. This made Graylin feel frustratingly foolish, but for once in her life, she did not respond with anger. *That* Graylin, for better or for worse, had disappeared into the fog with Denloy. "We just headed up to the square and asked, inconspicuously, about any accidents or explosions happening lately." Lewis continued.

"And?" Arlyn asked, sipping her soup. "What did you find out?"

"From all we could gather," Enland said, "Loren wasn't exaggerating. It sounds like there has been an average of one major explosion a week for the last month and a half. Most of them are happening further out of town, in the countryside, where it only hurts a few cows."

"But recently there's been a few human fatalities too," Lewis added. "And the explosions fit everything we know about pyrogleminine. They are large, very damaging, and seem to leave a black goo on everything which burns for an extraordinarily long time."

"So it's true then," Graylin said. "Someone is testing pyrogleminine out here, *still*. Why?"

"Is it possible it's not your parents, and that someone else has just stumbled upon the recipe?" River asked.

"I guess," Arlyn said, "but it seems unlikely. We know that people going under the name Freely have been recorded in Mackson's Bay within the last year, and according to LeMay, it took our parents who are apparently geniuses years to create the formula for pyrogleminine."

"But you and Graylin made it accidentally in Belhaven," River argued. "Surely it can't be that hard."

"As gross as it is to say," Graylin said, wrinkling her nose, "River makes a good point."

"Yes, but you two are special. You aren't the average," Lewis said.

"Awww, thanks Lew," Arlyn grinned. "Not average, I mean, what better compliment could I ask for?"

"I agree with Arlyn, it seems highly implausible that a different group of inventors are the ones testing this new pyrogleminine, when we know your parents are alive, that people with their names have been here, and that they alone know the formula for it," Enland added.

Teddy, who had been drawing in the sand with a stick, looked up.

"So do we try to find them, then?" he asked. "Here?"

"As fun as sitting around and waiting for a deadly explosion sounds," Lewis rolled her eyes, "honestly I don't know if staying here for an extended amount of time is a great idea, especially considering how close we are to where Denloy died."

"Wow, way to rub salt in the wound, Lewis," Arlyn sighed. Graylin was silent, but not because she was thinking about Denloy. Rather, she was thinking of the blond bearded, kind-eyed man and his brother whom she'd met in the soup line. The one who had tapped her on the shoulder and let her go ahead.

The one, whom she was just realizing, was undeniably her dad.

"I'm so stupid," she said quietly. The ocean seemed to swell, the foam crawling up the beach towards them a little more with each wave.

"What?" Arlyn asked, looking anxiously at her cousin. Graylin was fragile right now, Arlyn knew, and she was afraid that the events of the day were only making things worse. She had never seen someone look so close to breaking as Graylin had sitting on the curb earlier. "Cousin?"

"I saw them. Our dads." Graylin looked up at the crew. "Today." Icy regret was coursing through her skin, the breeze rolling in from the ocean giving her goosebumps as her head swam. Of course. It all made sense. *Of course* they'd reminded her of Denloy . . . they were his older brothers. She'd been so preoccupied reminding herself that the men weren't her murdered uncle, that she'd never even considered the possibility one of them was her father. However, now that the thought had occurred to her, she knew, undeniably, that it was true. She had met Michaelangelo and Benson Freely that afternoon.

"They were ahead of me, in the soup line," Graylin said shakily, rubbing her face in a daze. "They were talking about . . . about my mom, and your mom, cousin. About getting soup for them, and a forest one of them liked. And they were talking about a new . . . a new assignment, from some commander, to make an automatic crafter."

"Crafter for what?" River asked. Arlyn stared at her cousin.

"Pyrogleminine. It has to be," she said, shocked. "So it *is* true. All of it. They're still making it, and they're still testing it. They're alive."

"Hang on, hang on, hang on," Lewis said quickly. "Back up, please. Graylin, if you were in line behind your dad, whom we've been looking for over the last three months, why the *hell* didn't you say something to them? Or us, for that matter?!" Lewis was getting progressively louder and louder.

"I didn't realize," Graylin said, shrinking back. "I was thinking about Denloy, and there were these police behind me and-"

"And you didn't recognize your own dad?" Lewis cried incredulously. Graylin could feel her lip tremble, and she folded her arms around herself and bit her lip to stop it. She hated being yelled at, but she wasn't the only one close to tears. Lewis's beautiful brown eye was shining.

"Don't you understand," Lewis said to Graylin, trying not to cry, "how important this is? I have spent almost every cent I had on this trip, and when I get home, you'd best believe I won't be getting more from my mom and dad, not after I disobeyed them outright by leaving! My freedom is over! And you- *you* can't even *go* home. I mean-" Lewis cut off, looking away, holding a hand to her mouth. "We've given up so much for this search, Graylin. And you found your dad, and you just didn't realize it?"

"I'm sorry," Graylin whispered.

"Sorry? Sorry doesn't cut it Graylin Freely!" Lewis cried. "We, all six of us, are done for!"

"You think I don't know that?" Graylin said loudly. "You think I don't know that I've royally screwed up? Because I do! I know. I just don't know how to fix it."

"How can you just not know?" Lewis shouted. "You need to know!"

"Lewis!" Arlyn and Teddy cut in simultaneously, Arlyn stepping towards the cook, Teddy towards Graylin.

"That's enough," Teddy said quietly. He couldn't let Lewis go on, not when Graylin was so close to shattering.

"You know this isn't fair, Lew," Enland said gently, taking the girl's hand and pulling her toward her seat. She sat down heavily, breathing hard. Her eye locked on Graylin, who was shrunk back on the sand with surprise.

"Graylin," she said softly, shoulders sagging, "I'm so sorry. I didn't mean it. I don't know what came over me."

Arlyn put a hand on Lewis's arm, watching her cousin's big, wounded eyes. Arlyn had been afraid of this, but she hadn't expected it to happen so soon. Already, the weight of their secret was seeping in between the crewmembers, expanding and pushing them away from each other, like water freezing in the cracks of rocks. Something solid, something dependable, which was now crumbling before her eyes.

"We need to calm down," River said. He waited until everyone was looking at him before continuing. "We're all under a lot of pressure here, and we need to keep that in mind." He turned to their cook, who now had silent tears of regret running down her cheek. "Lewis, we've put a lot on you especially. You've spent the last three months keeping us in line, feeding us, and generally making yourself extremely useful. Somehow it landed on you to be the calm on a whole ship of crazy, and that's not very fair."

Now he looked at Graylin, with her limp curls and red eyes. "And *you* are struggling. Anyone can see that. For some reason, all of us as a crew just decided that leaving you alone would be the best way to let you deal with things, and that's on us. We're sorry. Just because you don't like hugs, or don't like sharing your feelings, doesn't mean you don't need to." River sighed, the afternoon light dimmed by the clouds now covering the expansive sky. "And that's not to even mention the rest of us. What we all need to remember is this is the first time any of us have kept a murder secret. We're all good people, and it's going to be hard for everyone, so let's show each other a little grace."

"So what do we do?" Enland asked, rubbing Lewis's arm.

"Teddy and I will head back to that soup shop just to make sure the girls' parents didn't hang around. Enland and Lewis will head back to the ship, grab some blankets and food, and roll up the ladder so no one steals it. Losing the Freelander is the last thing we need now. Arlyn and Graylin will stay here and set up a campsite because we're taking the night off. We'll build a fire, tell stories, sleep under the stars, and take a breather, okay?" River looked pointedly at every crewmember. "*Okay*?" he asked again, arms folded. Everyone nodded, and he leaned back, satisfied.

"Great. Come on, Ted."

Teddy gave Graylin one last smile before standing and scrambling after his red-haired brother. Lewis stepped forward and knelt in front of Graylin.

"I'm so sorry," she whispered again. "I really didn't mean it."

"It's okay if you did," Graylin said softly. "You *should* mean it. It's all true."

"It's not true." Lewis shook her head. "You haven't seen your dad in eight years, and in that time your life has changed over and over. It's not surprising that you shouldn't recognize him in the few seconds you stood behind him in a line."

"If I had been thinking like I should have been," Graylin said seriously, "I should have recognized him. I *would* have. My head was in the clouds, and I wasn't paying attention, and I should have been."

"Perhaps," Lewis nodded, "but that doesn't mean it was okay for me to explode and blame all this on you. I *chose* to leave my parents, knowing full well what the consequences would be when I returned. I'm sorry."

"It's okay," Graylin said, looking away. Lewis squeezed her hand, and took Enland's arm, and walked up the beach, glancing back at the cousins.

Graylin ducked her head and began to gather any small twigs and dried leaves she could find under the trees nearby. Arlyn turned away to help, and a small brush pile had been assembled before anyone spoke.

"I heard him talk, cousin," Graylin said suddenly. She tossed a stick onto the pile. "My dad. Do you remember your dad's voice?"

"A little," Arlyn said. "Not really."

"Their voices . . . they're like Denloy's, but brighter. And your dad's is a little deeper," Graylin said.

"What do they look like now?" Arlyn asked, pulling a match from her pocket.

"Like they used to, but with beards. Scruffy ones." Graylin said. "I didn't see them much until my dad . . . he told me to go in front of them."

"He actually talked to you?" Arlyn asked weakly. Graylin nodded.

"I'm so sorry," she blurted, looking away. "I wish you had been there. It shouldn't have been me. If you had been there, cousin . . ." If Arlyn had been there, she would have remembered what they'd said more clearly. She would have gotten to hear her father's voice and see his face.

Arlyn also wouldn't have forgotten to grab spoons.

"No, no, that's not what I meant at all." Arlyn said quickly. "I meant your dad looked you straight in the face . . . and didn't realize it was you?"

"Well, yeah. I guess," Graylin said.

"It must be hereditary," Arlyn grinned. In all honesty, she was relieved that it was Graylin who had run into their dads, and not herself. And not only Graylin, but Graylin at her weakest. Normal Graylin perhaps would have reacted differently, and Arlyn certainly would have. She lit the match in her hand and dropped it onto the fire. "We *will* be okay, cousin. I promise you that."

Graylin stared at Arlyn, watching her cousin's face as if all her hopes were held there- because they were. She wanted, no, *needed* to believe her cousin.

And, slowly, she was starting to.

By the time all crewmates had returned to the beach, the sun had sunk behind the buildings to the east. Very, very briefly the sky had been lit a muted blush color, the shadows of the sand stretched like the candy at the store earlier in the day, just for the deep blues to melt into the darkness that fell. Lewis and Enland arrived first, arms full of blanketed bundles, various foodstuffs, and the crew's collection of camping pillows. These were basically just large, thick balloons with a quilt on top which could be blown up to the sleeper's desired squishiness. While they weren't the most comfortable thing to rest your head on, they were better than nothing. The fire was crackling happily when Teddy and River got back.

"Find anything?" Arlyn asked as they settled themselves by the fire. The sun had taken the unusual warmth with it, and the air was cold.

"Not much," River said. "We spent a long time just walking around looking for them, but no luck."

"Beans." Arlyn snapped another stick before tossing it on the fire.

"We asked around, though, thinking that two relatively identical dudes are fairly hard to miss. That was a bit more fruitful, but not much," River continued.

"People recognized the description, but we didn't get much asking for Freelys specifically," Teddy added.

"Funny that the one place we know your parents actually are is the one where they are least known," Enland said.

"There was one guy though," River said, "who said he knew them. He said they stop into his newspaper stand every few weeks and buy all the papers that they missed. The rumor is they're friendly, funny, but not super forthcoming. All he's ever gotten out of them is that they live west of here, but he doesn't know how far."

"It's a week's flight," Graylin said suddenly. She glanced at Lewis nervously, and then continued. "I heard them talking about that, too. That's when they mentioned the forest your mom likes, cousin. Your dad said they usually fly around it because it gets foggy, but they might try to go over it to make the trip quicker."

"You, cousin," Arlyn smiled, "are a wonder." Graylin shook her head but Lewis added her voice.

"She's right, Graylin. You can remember all that? Usually I can't even get you to remember what you had for breakfast, or where you put your shoes."

"It's not a skill," Graylin said. "My brain just decided to work, for once."

"Keep this compliment shield up," Teddy smiled, "and Arlyn's gonna threaten *you* with therapy, too."

"I don't have a compliment shield," Graylin said defensively. "I love compliments. It's a well-known fact that my love language is words of affirmation."

"No compliment shield cousin?" Arlyn asked, shaking her head. "Let's test this theory, then. We're gonna go around the circle, each saying something we usually think but don't say about Graylin. Enland, you start."

"You're smart," Enland said instantly.

"You're funny," River added.

"You're kind," Lewis added. Graylin raised her eyebrows incredulously. "You are kind, and sweet, and honest, even when you mess up. You're a good person."

"You're incredible," Teddy said simply. "And your mind, the way you talk and think, is beautiful." He'd hesitated before that last bit, but looking into Graylin's big, tear flooded gray eyes had told him now was no time for cowardice.

"Graylin," Arlyn said seriously, "No matter what, you are my favorite person. Ever. And you always will be."

"But you guys are all lying," Graylin choked, trying not to cry for like the billionth time that day. "Straight up, to my face. These are all lies."

"See, that's where you're wrong," Teddy said. "It's all true."

"No, it can't be," Graylin sniffed. "No one says anything nice until they're forced to, which means it *has* to be a lie."

"That's our problem, our fault. Not yours," River said.

"I'm gonna bring River in as a guest therapist," Arlyn grinned.

"What would it take to prove to you that what we said is true?" Lewis asked. Graylin stared at her and shook her head.

"I don't know."

"Well, I'll start showing my love by making dinner," Lewis said, reaching behind her and pulling out the food. Graylin sniffed and rubbed her nose, straightening and walking towards the water. Lewis, Enland and River all set about arranging the meal, though River was quickly kicked out of the operation because he kept eating the dough Lewis had quickly mixed up.

"Graylin?" The girl turned around from where she had been standing, watching the ocean. Teddy was walking towards her, regretting every step he took but not wanting to turn around.

"Oh. Hey," Graylin said, looking down at her toes. She had pulled off her boots and socks, and was standing at the water's edge, her feet becoming progressively colder and redder.

"Are you okay?" Teddy asked, before shaking his head and smiling sadly. "That was sort of a stupid question, because I'm pretty sure you're not."

"I wish I was," Graylin said, wiping her eyes, but turning her head so Teddy couldn't see. "I wish, more than anything, that I was still okay." She looked at her friend and took a deep breath, pushing back her hair and tucking it behind her ears. "But I think I can be okay, someday. I'm not sure when, but I think it will happen." She bent down and picked up a wilted white flower that had been washed up several minutes before. It was dripping wet and sad, but pretty all the same. She handed it awkwardly to Teddy, unsure of why.

"Here," she said, looking away. "Thank you. For trying to help me."

Teddy took the flower and held it.

"Thank you," he said. Graylin suddenly remembered the little white paper flower Teddy had given her that night over three months ago when they had attended Denloy's ball. She took a second deep breath, and let it out as she watched the white foam of the ocean tumble towards her.

"Do you know what I like most about you?" Teddy said suddenly. Graylin glanced at him.

"No."

"Your spirit," he said, looking at her for just a moment before examining the ocean again. Graylin didn't know why they kept watching the waves, since nothing interesting was happening out there. Just rolls of water, crashing dully into one another before sliding up the sand.

"Sometimes," Teddy continued, "it's like gasoline. The dangerous, the wild, the fiery gets close to you, and jumps to you. You spur it on, and make it better. Bigger. But sometimes it's more like . . . like nighttime. Quiet, and a little darker, but lit by so many of these beautiful lights, no one could possibly count them. And sometimes," he stopped looking at the ocean now, "it's just bright, and fun, like a nice day or a city full of parties. But it's *always* you."

"I don't think you know me very well, if you think that's true," Graylin said, giving him a smile but feeling a sinking in her stomach. She *wished* she was how Teddy described; that girl sounded wonderful. She sounded pretty and wild and smart and exciting and lovable. *In other words*, Graylin thought, *she sounds like my opposite.*

"Actually," Teddy said gently, "I'm not sure if *you* know you very well." He glanced down at the wilted flower in his hand. "When we started this trip, I was sad. Well, really, I was sad long before that. For as long as I can remember, I've just always felt trapped by . . . by me, I guess. I thought I knew who I was, and I sort of hated that person." He smiled and held the flower out, re-gifting it. Graylin took it gently. "But then I started becoming friends with you, and we talked in Belhaven, and suddenly I wondered if maybe I was wrong about you. If someone like you, who was obviously incredible, could think so poorly, and be filled with lies about herself . . . well, maybe there's a chance that part of what I think about *myself* is a lie too."

"Well, of course it is," Graylin said seriously. "You're wonderful."

"Let's make a deal then." Teddy said suddenly. He held out his hand, and assuming he wanted the flower back, Graylin passed it over. However, instead of receiving the gift once more, he took her hand and held it. "From now on," he said, "we're Truth Friends."

"That sounds dumb." Graylin wrinkled her nose.

"See? You're telling the truth already," Teddy smiled. "What I mean is, you lie to yourself, and I lie to myself, and because it's ourselves, we'll never be able to find the truth alone. So we'll work together from now on, and swear to tell each other the truth about the other." He smiled, his infectious one that, as always, made Graylin smile too. "And we'll change the name because you're right, Truth Friends *is* really stupid. Deal?"

"Okay." Graylin shook his hand. "Deal."

"Good," Teddy said. He released her hand, took the flower, and stuck it in his pocket. The waves climbed further up the beach, all the way past their bare feet, before retreating back to the ocean. Further up the sand their friends laughed, and someone, probably Enland, said something about a map.

"I can't come up with a better name than Truth Friends," Teddy said suddenly. Graylin laughed.

"But you can put anything into words," she said, thinking about what Teddy had said about her earlier. About being like fire, and night, and fun. How delightful it would be if his words were true! She felt like a small bit of her burden had been lifted away by Teddy's deal, and she wished it hadn't because it gave her what she saw as a false sense of relief, but she couldn't help it. She smiled anyway. "I wish I was more like you."

"I don't," Teddy laughed. "I've just said I can hardly handle having one of me around. Two Teddys? What a nightmare." He shook his head, while Graylin laughed. "I'm serious."

"Well, I think the world could use a great deal more Teddy, personally," Graylin smiled. Just think of how many Graylins there were out there, struggling and crying and carrying. If only they all had Teddys, and Arlyns, and Lewis and Enland and Rivers, to help them.

"Oh, sick! Look!" Graylin exclaimed suddenly, bending over. She picked up, and then held out, a very round blue-gray rock with dark spiderling lines. "It's so smooth."

"It's a perfect skipping rock," Teddy agreed.

"But it's so pretty," Graylin said. "I don't want to lose it." Teddy smiled.

"Alright, keep that one. Here." Teddy picked up an alternative rock, a little bigger, and just chucked it.

"That's not skipping," Graylin chuckled, as the rock splashed into the water.

"It's funner," Teddy, the so-called wordsmith, said wisely. "You try."

Graylin did so, throwing a rock as far as possible. It flew through the air, dove, and fell into the water.

"Bah, that could have been better," she said irritably. Teddy hurled a second one, as did she. Back and forth they went, choosing rocks and chucking them, unless they were pretty rocks, in which case they stuck them in their pockets. Eventually they started a competition, seeing who could throw the rocks the furthest, using running starts to assist the velocity. Teddy was generally better at this, but Graylin was confident she could win at least once.

So, she chose a specifically round rock, stepped away from the water, drew her arm back, ran forward, and flung the rock, lobbing it with as much effort as possible. She threw it so hard, in fact, that the momentum carried her and her very stretched arm forward into the water. With a mighty splash, she fell into the stygian waves. For just a split second, she was under the water, before bursting backwards out, spluttering and coughing, all while Teddy roared with laughter, bent over with his hands on his knees.

"Cold cold cold cold cold!" Graylin choked as Teddy most unhelpfully dropped to his knees, holding his stomach.

"Your face!" he wheezed. Graylin splashed the next wave to roll in entirely in his direction, splattering her new Truth Friend with icy salt water.

"Food's done!" Lewis called from up the beach, saving Teddy from an even wetter fate, and the two literally raced to the fire, eager to dry off and warm up.

Campfire food, smells, and sounds filled the rest of the night. As night fell deeper, the crew spent more and more time around the flames, needing the heat. When Teddy and River had been out searching for the Freely parents, they had stopped and bought the gramophone, and a wax cylinder for the inside bearing marks for one of Teddy's favorite songs. They wound up and played the song several times that night, eventually becoming sleepily delusional enough to dance like idiots for nearly an hour.

"Cousin!" Graylin clapped and cheered as Arlyn finished a clapping heavy routine with River, before Arlyn grabbed her cousin's sleeve and yanked her into the circle. It was an absolute riot, that night, and despite their exhaustion, it was the first time in over a week that the crew felt they could stand up straight.

It was late indeed when everyone blew up their pillows, grabbed their blankets, and bundled up on the sand. Arlyn was reminded of their deck-top sleepover held after their pirate play. Much like that night, the cool night air felt incredible once snuggled under the blankets, particularly next to the dying fire. Unlike *that* slumber party, everyone, even Graylin, bundled very close together. The crew needed each other, even if it was just to know their friends were nearby.

"What a night," Arlyn whispered to Lewis. The two girls were the last ones awake, sitting upright in their blankets, bundled up tight.

"Night? What a *day*. What a week, really." Lewis glanced at Graylin, snuggled fast asleep under her blankets, holding gently to an equally asleep Teddy's outstretched arm.

"I feel so guilty about yelling at her earlier," Lewis whispered finally, watching Graylin's blankets rise and fall slowly.

"She'll be okay," Arlyn murmured. "We all will."

"How was *your* day? With Teddy?" Lewis asked.

"Good," Arlyn grinned. "I give Graylin full leave to like him. She could do much worse."

"That she could," Lewis chuckled. Her mouth fell out of its smile into a worried line. "What about you? I feel like it would be hard, knowing your dad was in the same town as you, and that he met your cousin, but not you."

"Honestly, I'm relieved," Arlyn said as the waves brushed the sand. "Now at least I have some time to decide what I want to say to my mom and dad when we finally find them. A sudden sighting of the elusive parents would have been a bit too much, even for me."

"And now we have a direction," Lewis said, eye widening. "One week of traveling east, and we'll be there."

"Don't make me think about it," Arlyn groaned, burying her head in her blankets. Lewis laughed.

"Alright. Good night."

"Good night, Lew."

33

GRAYLIN AWOKE THE NEXT morning to someone shaking her shoulder. Or, rather, she slowly drifted out of her dream into awakeness, and in both her dream world and the real one, someone was touching her. Once her brain realized that the shoulder tapping was not just her imagination, her eyes flew open.

"Oh, I'm sorry," the policeman said kindly, bent over her. "Was that creepy? I feel like that was a little creepy." Graylin couldn't say anything. Her heart was racing as she tried to both wake up and process this man's presence.

"Graylin?" Lewis asked sleepily, raising her head. The sun had risen, but not very far, and the camp and ocean were both lit with stretched golden light which caught in both girls' hair.

"Oh, nothing to worry about," the policeman said quickly. "I'm sorry, I'm new if you can't tell. I would have shuffled up one of the boys, but I recognized you from yesterday, so I woke you." he nodded to Graylin. Graylin realized that, indeed, it was the younger red-haired man she'd met the day before.

"Wake us up for what?" Lewis asked, rubbing her eye as Teddy stirred and blinked himself awake.

"Ah," the policeman smiled a little sheepishly. "Well, it is my duty as an officer of the law to tell you, firstly, that you really aren't allowed to just sleep here on the beach. It's city property, so that's defined as loitering. Second, I got a noise report about you guys at roughly 12:12 AM, and I'm afraid Mackson's Bay has a music curfew, unless you have a permit, in which case you're fine."

"So why didn't you come to get us then, at midnight?" Lewis asked. The police shrugged.

"Honestly, the reporter is a known pain in the backside, so I figured he would have been out here already to give you a piece of his mind, and that you'd been punished enough. Unfortunately, I do have to hand you this handy dandy written warning," he produced a slip of paper, "just so I can say I did. And that for the loitering as well, you know, try not to do that." He smiled at the now awake crew and tipped his dark hat, the one that matched the navy blue of his suit. "Now, good day to the lot of you. I've got to dash, someone's parked a huge airship with like a million balloons illegally on the other side of town." He gave a formal bow and then strode away.

Graylin glanced at Teddy, caught his eye, and burst out laughing.

"Come on, you two, hurry!" Lewis called, gathering things up. "We've got to get back before he does." Everyone scrambled to their feet, kicking out the fire, bundling up blankets, and lifting the gramophone. It was a flurry of laughter as everyone helped one another lift their burdens.

"Come on, we haven't got all day," River called, halfway down the street ahead of everyone else as they set off. "We don't want a ticket now do we? Let's move those feet!" Urged on by Coach River, the crew set off running, sprinting several blocks and losing only a few random apples and one blanket which Enland had to go back for.

"Hang on," Arlyn gasped, panting, when they finally reached the *Freelander*. "Before we leave, I saw an awesome donut shop I want to hit up."

"Arlyn," Lewis called, already climbing the ladder. "Donuts? Now?"

"I'm in," Graylin said instantly, tossing her bundle to Teddy. "We'll bring back enough for everyone. Come on, Enland, toss me your purse."

"It's not a purse, it's a satchel. A manly satchel," Enland said.

"You just keep telling yourself that," Graylin smirked, as Enland handed it down from the ladder reluctantly.

"You lot just hover around here, and we'll meet you," Arlyn called reassuringly, as they skipped off.

"Stay safe!" Lewis shouted after them. "Please!" She shook her head at Enland as the two girls sprinted away. "I feel more and more sorry for Leo every day."

The cousins made their way through the sleepy streets, Arlyn in the lead lest Graylin lose the both of them. The sea air was salty and cool, and the warmth of the sun was just present enough to keep them from being cold. On the corner of a street, with whitewashed bricks and wooden shutters, was the bakery Arlyn was directing them toward. The smells wafting from it were intoxicating, and the Freelys made an instant beeline for the shop.

A bell tinkled as they pushed through the wooden door. On the back wall was a large brick oven, stretching halfway up the tall ceilings. There were two levels of benches, some that took ladders to get to, and some resting on the ground. In front of the checkout counter was an enormous glass case, filled with donuts of every shape and size.

"What can I do for you girls?" The woman behind the front counter asked. She had sharp eyes similar to Enland's, but her irises were a bright green. Arlyn thought, only for a moment, about another pair of bright green eyes she knew. Only, those were always seen behind a pair of glasses, and shone with a radiant light. Loren's light. This woman definitely *didn't* have that light.

"What are you thinking about, cousin?" Graylin asked. "You look like you're mid diarrhea."

"Thinking? I wasn't thinking," Arlyn said, pushing her cousin away, and turning to the counter lady, who looked slightly disgusted. "Uh, hello. We want two dozen of your best donuts."

"Flavors?" The woman asked.

"Caramel," said the cousins.

"We'll take four caramel donuts," Arlyn revised. "You choose the rest, if it's sweet we'll like it." The woman nodded and bustled off, filling the boxes deftly while giving the girls odd sidelong glances.

"Do you feel like this lady's watching us weird?" Graylin asked quietly. Arlyn glanced from her cousin to the donut lady and back again.

"I think it's your hair," she said sagely. "Could use some work."

"My hair?" Graylin asked, anxiously petting it down and doing absolutely nothing to help. "What's wrong with it?"

"Well," Arlyn considered, "let's just say that your unforeseen trip into the ocean last night didn't work well for you."

"Oh," Graylin said, tugging at a few very fluffy curls.

"Don't you worry your nice, if wildly unmanageable, head, cousin," Arlyn assured her. "I know for a fact that Teddy likes your hair."

"Please stop talking to me," Graylin said, trying to comb the curls with her fingers.

The donut lady returned, both boxes stacked and tied with a bow.

"Do you want a name with these?" she asked, setting them specifically down to the side so she could monitor the girls. "If you come back, you'll get two donuts for free, as per our regular deal." She pointed to a small sign which said 'thirteen out of twelve people love our baker's dozen deal! :)'

"Witty," Graylin gave her best attempt at a conversational smile, which turned out more like a grimace so Arlyn elbowed her to stop.

"We'd love the deal," Arlyn said. "I'm Arrr . . ." She suddenly realized she wasn't supposed to be using their real names, "uhhhh Armentinerly."

"What?" Graylin asked.

"What?" the donut lady asked.

"You heard me," Arlyn said, raising her chin. "Armentinerly. That's my name. Armentinerly Freely."

"Did you say Freely?" The donut salesman asked.

"*Did you say Freely*?" Graylin hissed.

"Freelys," said the donut lady. Those eyes Arlyn had noted earlier were suddenly very different from Loren's; they were dark and flashing, rather than bright and smart. "I knew I recognized you."

"Er," Arlyn thought frantically, realizing her mistake. "Recognize us? I mean, we're new here. We don't know any other Freelys."

"Then I recommend you change your name," the lady said sharply. "Freely means disaster around here. They show up for a few days and every time, something burns and someone dies." The woman scooped the money Graylin had paid off the counter and dumped it into the cash register, the coins showering everywhere. "Someone like my brother. I don't know how you're related to our Freelys or what you're doing here, but I want you to get out right now."

She shoved the boxes into their hands so hard, the flimsy sides bent.

"Right. Now."

"Cousin," Graylin said as they hurried from the store, "Did you actually just invent yourself an alias . . . for your first name? *Instead of the last?*"

"Uhh, maybe?" Arlyn winced.

"Freely, you said. *Freely*, cousin," Graylin groaned, shaking her head, and pulling out a glazed donut to eat out of stress. "Armentingingi ng Freely," she said through her mouthful of food. "That was the worst fake name ever, in every way possible."

"I'd prefer not to speak of that now," Arlyn waved her hand. "We need to get back to the ship."

Donuts were handed out quickly, and all six members of the crew gathered in the meeting area. A combination of donuts, a good night of sleep, and the bright room gave the group a very lighthearted aura. However, one Arlyn Freely was feeling very serious, watching as Graylin and Teddy split their third donut.

Their stop at the donut shop had brought her to a harsh reality, and it *wasn't* that she was terrible at inventing aliases. She had already known that people had died as a result of her parents' experiments. *I mean,* she thought, *they're making bombs, vastly and wildly uncontrollable pyrotechnic weapons, designed to cause mass destruction. Naturally, some people are going to die.* So why was Arlyn's stomach suddenly feeling like it had dropped several feet? Why did her head feel three times heavier than usual?

Perhaps, she decided, it was coming face to face with the sister of a man her parents had killed. Knowing of her parents' supposed moral ambiguity and rumored evil deeds was one thing; meeting a donut lady whose brother would never come back was another.

And then, as Teddy conspicuously stole half of Graylin's donut, Arlyn was suddenly confronted with a question. Did she even *want* to find her parents? Did she care what they were doing anymore? Even the day before, when she'd learned Graylin had seen their dads, she had felt nothing but relief that it had indeed been her cousin at that soup stand, and not herself. Thinking about her parents was making her feel sick, so she set her donut down and undid a braid.

They don't deserve us back. They don't deserve me *back*, she thought. *I don't want to know.*

"We need answers, cousin," Graylin said quietly. Arlyn winced as she realized everyone was looking at her, meaning she'd been thinking out loud again. Either that, or all her friends could read minds, which would be surprising and unfortunate.

"What would you have us do?" Lewis asked Arlyn gently. "Just give up? We've come so far and done so much . . . you know we can't do that."

"No, I don't want to give up." Arlyn stood up and began to pace, suddenly uncertain. "I know that, I just . . . I don't know what I want. I don't know *what* to do."

"I don't know what to do," Graylin agreed solemnly. "But I know what I can't do. I can't go back to being the person I was before this trip. I know I can't go home. And I *know* I can't just let all our questions go unanswered."

Arlyn swallowed. She closed her eyes and covered her face with her hands, just trying to get a few clear thoughts through. In her head, all of what they'd learned about her parents seemed to twist together, the angry words from the donut lady, LeMay, Uncle Will . . .

"You know what? You're right cousin," she said, raising her head.

"That's a first," Teddy smiled, resulting in a pillow to the face from Graylin.

"We *do* need answers." Arlyn tossed a braid over her shoulder. "Come on. We know which direction to go in, and we're ready." She stood up straight. "Let's go."

Two men, looking extremely similar with their trimmed blond hair and beards and twinkling gray eyes, hurried down a bright corridor. One, his glasses slightly fogged up, was sipping some steaming soup from a cup.

"This potato soup is where it's at," he said, brushing his soup mustache away to reveal his actual mustache.

"When eaten with a spoon," his twin brother said, "I agree. But honestly, I'm more impressed with our refrigeration system. It kept that soup legit all the way from Mackson's Bay to home, and then from home to here. That's nearly ten days of flying, and warmed up, it's as good as new."

"Sure makes you appreciate the soup, this weather," the other brother said, glancing at the rattling windows. "I swear fall was never this cold when we were kids."

"We didn't grow up in Munswel, now did we?" his twin pointed out. "Osden's got a milder climate."

"Mild?" a woman's voice asked. Coming down the corridor towards the brothers were two women. One had darker skin and a fine head of tight coils, tugged back into a bun, while the other, the speaker, had a very light complexion and loose, light brown curls, also pulled into a more manageable style.

"Mild?" the second woman repeated. "You better hope for mild, Michaelangelo Freely. You're a day late!"

"Ah, darling!" Michaelangelo cried, holding out his food. "But we brought soup!"

"Well, that *definitely* makes up for it then," The woman, Juliet, smiled, rolling her eyes at the other woman, who just so happened to be her closest friend and sister-in-law.

"We thought you'd been caught." The dark-haired Delilah said, planting a kiss on Benson Freely's cheek and subtly stealing the soup in his hands.

"Us? Caught? Never," Benson said, as the four started off down the corridor. "No, we traveled around Mackson's Bay like a couple of thieves. Ninjas. Superspies. No one suspected a thing."

"You better hope they didn't," Delilah said, sipping the soup herself. "Who knows what Osden would do to you, considering we've actively betrayed them and killed a few of their citizens."

"I love it when you talk business nonchalantly," Benson teased.

"Forget about the boys," Juliet smiled, hooking her arm in Michaelangelo's. "Think of what Old Commander Wilson would do to Del and I if you two didn't come back."

"Give you a widow's bonus?" Michelangelo raised his eyebrows.

"Oh, I'm sure," Juliet grinned. Benson puffed out his chest, stuck his jaw forward, and held his arms stiffly away from his body.

"I realize your husbands have recently perished," he mocked, stressing the 'sh' sound. "But I *really* don't care. You *ge*niuses better get back to work." He pretended to pull a cigar from his mouth. "This is all for the greater good, of course." The group laughed; Benson was doing an excellent imitation of Commander Tiberius Wilson. Tiberius Wilson, who was the group's primary contact in Munswel's government. Tiberius Wilson, who gave the four their orders straight from the Vater. His real name was rarely disclosed, and only to those most deserving, and the Freelys did not fit this bill.

Tiberius Wilson, who was strutting stiffly down the corridor toward them. His gray uniform, decorated with all the badges and medals a man who'd never actually been to war could have, was as crisp and starched as ever. The five adults stopped when they reached each other, all raising their right hands to their hearts, closing their hands into a fist, and thumping twice.

"For the Vater," Wilson growled.

"For the Vater," the four Freelys copied. In the beginning, this blatant groveling to the authority which was the Vater had rubbed several

Freelys the wrong way, particularly the two girls. They had put up with it, but only because Munswel had offered them the power, materials, and outcomes which the Freelys had sacrificed so much for. But now . . . well, now the four saw the Vater of Munswel for what he truly was: a visionary. A rescuer. A man blessed with eyes which could see the rest of the world for what it truly was, and who was unafraid to change what needed changing.

And things *certainly* needed changing.

"Freelys," Commander Wilson growled, dropping his hand from the salute. He always stressed the 'Fr' sound at the beginning of Freely. "I see you've returned."

"Yes, sir," Benson said, holding out his soup. "Care for any? It's potato."

"No." Wilson didn't even spare the steaming stew a glance. "Your fancy machine downstairs is acting up, and The Vater wants to start the first stages of our attack on Nalvern within the next month."

"Righto sir," Michaelangelo grinned. "We'll hop to it then."

"Hopping is entirely unnecessary. Just get it done." Wilson nodded his head stiffly. "Excuse me." With that, he strode away, the heels of his extremely glossy shoes clacking on the polished granite floors.

"What a phonetically aggressive man." Michelangelo shook his head. "I never knew the 'g' in 'get' could sound so sharp."

"Feels a bit surreal, the idea of attacking within the month," Benson considered, as the four Freelys resumed their walk down the long corridor. "We've been working at it for so long."

They were getting closer to the hub of activity where they'd spent most of the last few years. Men and women in suits and stiff hairstyles sped from here to there, dropping papers, examining war plans, and running errands. The rustle of parchment and tapping of typewriter keys mixed with the clacking of heels, and the large space echoed with the noise. They were now underground, but the bright white bulbs on the ceiling joined with the identical lamps on every desk, making the room bright, if not slightly sterile. The greenish walls had been painted to lighten the mood, but these had been so covered in plans and newspaper clippings that the effect was mostly ruined.

But the Freelys didn't notice, because this was *their* space. Every single person in the room was there to aid them in their search for a better world, and for the last eight years, this stark chamber had been their second home, particularly over the last month as they put the finishing touches on their masterpiece. Their masterpiece, their invention, the machine which had taken all four Freely minds to think up and put together, and which had soaked up nearly every moment of their lives since the Freelander Disaster.

The four strode across the busy worker-filled space to the opposite wall of reflective windows, the sort of thick ones which let all the workers see the Freelys when they were in the adjoining chamber, but showed the inventors only their reflections.

Michelangelo heaved open the heavy door, and the four entered the massive space behind it. Even the towering walls and vaulted ceilings weren't enough to diminish the size of the machine clunking away in the middle of the chamber. Running from the top of the invention was a large tube piping out a steady stream of unglamorous black goo, goo which the brothers had named pyrogleminine, and which was capable of mass destruction in the blink of an eye.

"What a beauty!" Benson clapped his hands together. "Just a few weeks, darling, and you'll be put to good use." He patted a large metal panel, while his wife shook her head in disappointment.

"Anyone else hear something funny?" Juliet asked mildly as she set her satchel by her work station. It was a wide surface, organized within an inch of its life, stacked with rolls of piping and several collections of unseemly chemicals. However, hidden behind a few maps and technical drawings, she could pick out her favorite sketches; the ones of her daughter. She had drawn Graylin many times before the disaster, but once she had lost her, it became Juliet's way of coping. She believed in Munswel's cause, and that sacrificing her daughter had ultimately been worth it . . . but this hadn't made losing her baby, her precious little eight-year-old with the big eyes and curly hair, any easier.

"Now that you mention it," Michaelangelo mused, "I think I hear something. Like a whining?"

"Right," Juliet agreed. "I bet it's that seal under the main tube, I think it's warped. It's been bothering us all week."

"It took the place of you, darling," Delilah teased Benson, poking him in the back as she pushed a huge rolling ladder towards the machine and climbing up.

"Are you saying I'm annoying? A pain in the backside?" asked Benson dramatically, scratching at his beard. "Are you suggesting that I am . . . whiny?"

"Your words, not mine," Delilah smiled, reaching deep in the satchel she preferred over a tool-belt. She leaned forward, resting one hand on the side of the machine and squinting into the darkness deep inside the machine.

"Juliet," she called back, "I don't suppose you can hand me a light?"

"Here," her sister-in-law held out a small tube with light streaming out one end- an electric torch, made with a light bulb and rechargeable wire, which the girls had invented several years prior. Delilah shone it into the machine, craning her neck to spot any sort of malfunction.

"I think you're right about the seal," she said finally. "It definitely looks loose."

Michelangelo, yawning and thinking fondly about his finished potato soup, moved to the massive control lever which turned the machine on and off so they could work safely. Several months previously Benson, sick of calling the towering mess of gears and tubing just 'the machine', had scrawled FAPC (Freely Automatic Pyrogleminine Crafter) across part of the control panel. However, his attempt to get this decidedly catchy name to take hold amongst the four was futile, and they continued to call it the machine. Because, after all, it was The Machine. The machine which Benson and Michaelangelo had sacrificed *everything* for, and which was the basis of Munswel's plans to change the world. The Machine.

"Shutting down!" Michaelangelo called, yanking the lever. He paused, waiting for the screech and groan of metal and large clunk that echoed through the chamber whenever The Machine stopped.

But it never came.

"You said you turned it off?" Benson called, voice echoing within the machine as he took his wife's place on the ladder.

"Er, yes, but-" Mike flipped the lever once more, just to make sure, and then glanced up at the exit tubing. Sure enough, it was still filled with a slow stream of pyrogleminine.

"Okay, removing the seal now!" Benson called.

"No, WAIT!-"

Across the building, on the third floor, Commander Tiberius Wilson grabbed at his desk as a tremendous **BOOM!** rattled the windows. With a crash, a wine glass fell to the carpet and shattered, the tinkling of glass in his room mixing with similar sounds around the compound. The red of the alcohol seeped slowly across the white rug.

"What is going on?" Wilson shoved his chair away and threw open his door. The hall was a storm of movement, with other high-ranking officials sticking their heads out to investigate the commotion as he was, each one of them coughing and waving away the dark, thick smoke filling the air.

"It's coming from downstairs sir!" A young man, dressed in a junior officer's uniform, hurried up to Wilson, holding a handkerchief in his hand.

"Give me that," Wilson snarled, plucking the sheet of cloth out of the man's grasp and instantly pressing it to his mouth. "Take me down there. I need to have a few words with our Freelys."

A group gathered behind Wilson as he hurried downstairs, everywhere a flurry of whispers and questions. As they neared the Freely's chamber, the one which held Munswel's most prized invention, a strong smell of burning filled the air.

Throwing the handkerchief to the side, Wilson burst into the space.

Black goo was everywhere, some of it smoking, some still on fire. It clung to the floor, walls, and ceiling, and coated the remains of the machine that had towered in the center of the room. It also covered all four human shapes sprawled on the floor, flames still flickering.

"Someone put them out," Wilson barked, gesturing to the figures, and stomping out some fire under his heavy boot.

"They're dead, sir," a young woman said, crouched next to one shape. The goo had spared this one's face, and the blond beard and gray eyes were easy to see. One of the brothers, then, but Wilson wasn't sure which. Even eight years hadn't been enough for him to learn to tell them apart. Eight years, in which these four geniuses had given Munswel so much, and pulled their cause so far, and who were now lying dead on the floor. They had been *so close*. With a shout of frustration, he kicked away a charred hunk of metal.

"Someone get me the Vater," Wilson growled, pushing people out of his way and shoving out the room. Everyone shrank back. "NOW!"

"It feels a bit surreal, doesn't it?" Arlyn asked. "Getting so close to our parents. We've been working at it for so long." She was standing on the top deck, watching the foggy forest slide past beneath them.

"I know what you mean," Graylin, next to her, nodded. "Almost like it's too good to be true, which is almost hilariously dumb because pretty much none of this is good."

"We left Mackson's Bay about a week ago," Arlyn said. "We should be there soon."

The wind whistled, and the ship groaned as the cousins watched the landscape. Graylin had her eyes fixed on an extensive set of cliffs in front of the ship, squinting at a section of rock.

"Cousin . . ." she said, stepping away from the railing and moving towards the front of the *Freelander*. Arlyn followed her, eyes widening as they neared the pilot's chair. Teddy stood, pushing back his hair.

Enland and River, who had been trying to coerce Lewis into making casserole for dinner, stopped and stared.

Jutting out from the side of the cliff was a structure, but describing it further seemed impossible. It didn't look like a home; it was far too majestic and imposing for that, with large arches and a dome of glass on one side. It also didn't look like a workshop or factory, thanks to the flourishes of metal and wood twisting around the windows and hanging from the eaves. And it *definitely* wasn't a secret base. It was the only building around, and even in the middle of a city would have drawn attention.

"It's beautiful," Lewis said in awe.

"It's really cool," River added.

"It's very conspicuous," Enland shrugged.

The cousins agreed with all this, but at that moment they could only glance at each other, yearning to know if the other thought it was their parents'.

For Arlyn, looking at the building was just like that moment when she'd seen Denloy for the first time, and she'd instantly known it was he for whom they'd been searching. The entire essence of the building, from the stream of smoke twirling from one of the chimneys to the eight years worth of vines covering a few windows, screamed Freely. This *was* her parent's place.

"Let's get the ship stopped," she said. Teddy nodded and got to work, so Arlyn turned to the rest of their crew, taking a deep breath.

"As for us . . . we prepare to head in."

Everyone nodded. Why they felt the need to prepare, no one could have said, but they all did. There was something about the building, or maybe about what the building held, that made Graylin button up her waistcoat, sling a large satchel around her shoulders, and splash water on her face. It made Lewis tie up her hair in a pretty scarf and lace up her boots all the way to the top. It encouraged Enland to put on a fresh shirt and stand in front of his brothers as they solemnly told him it looked good.

And it made Arlyn stand in front of the bathroom mirror, taking deep breaths as she tightened the straps of her suspenders, trying to imagine just what she would say. It was hard to think about. She wrote and rewrote a confrontation script in her head as the crew climbed down the ladder, dropping to the rough rocky path in front of her parent's building. The October wind seemed intentionally biting as they gathered on the gravel, boots scuffing and graying with dust. But, perhaps, it was the nerves making everyone shiver, or maybe it was the chillness of the barren rock surrounding them.

"Are you guys ready?" Arlyn asked finally, mentally scrapping the script. It wasn't working; they'd just have to wing it. She looked into Graylin's eyes, big and wide and very Freely, watching her. She'd asked the crew if they were ready, but really, she wanted to know if her cousin was ready. They were in this together.

Finally, Graylin nodded to her.

"Ready," she said. Arlyn took a deep breath, turned to the door, and reached for the handle.

"Here goes nothing."

34

THE DOOR DIDN'T CREAK. Graylin supposed it was used far too often for that. It simply swung open silently, spilling light into the dark room.

It was large, the secret hideout. Arlyn wasn't surprised. With eight years, an untouchable reputation, and no children to hold them back, she guessed they had put all their energy into the building and their still unknown evil plans. The ceiling was arched, and tall, with long chains hanging down. On the ends were small, dim bulbs, so numerous they looked like stars. To the left was a vast fireplace, after which was a large round tower made almost entirely of glass.

The crews' boots made hollow, echoing taps as they slowly walked in. It was silent, except for a dull machine whirring from under the floor.

"They must have a workshop down there," Graylin said, tapping her foot. No one else spoke, just nodded. It felt, to the rest of the crew, as if the silence was a barrier that it was the Freelys right to break, just as the parents were an obstacle it was the cousin's right to overcome.

Neither cousin would have been able to describe it if asked, but each step brought them both undeniable feelings of unease, though unease wasn't even quite the right word. More like dread. For Graylin it was familiar, this untraceable sense that something was going to go wrong, the one that didn't seem to have a beginning nor an end. She felt it all the time. But for Arlyn, it was new, and she was quickly learning that she didn't enjoy the sensation at all. It made both cousins feel itchy, like someone was watching them, and they needed to sprint away as quickly as possible.

"I don't know about you guys," River said finally, as they stopped at some large windows. Outside, the wind blew hard under the chilled gray sky. "But I don't think anyone has been here for a little while."

Graylin had never wished to disagree with River more. But, this one time, she knew he was right, because she felt it too. The emptiness. The coldness. It didn't feel sad and lonely, like an abandoned house. As they walked, it felt more like a space accustomed to people, to life, but was suddenly deprived, like a person who usually feasted but was now starving.

They had wandered several minutes before finding what felt like the origin of the emptiness. Two large frosted glass doors, just off the stairs leading down. Arlyn stared at it. This was the room. She knew, somehow, that this was where her parents had spent most of their time the last eight years. She pushed open the doors, revealing a large space with walnut floorboards that made a *thunk* when they were stepped on. The crew entered cautiously, all the while gazing around at the walls. The walls which were covered, top to bottom, in papers. Even the ceiling was bedecked, the creamy pages fluttering in the breeze the crew made by entering. Graylin had expected the area to smell like old books, but it didn't. It smelled of gas and burnt plastic.

Enland was the first to inspect the maps, tracing the lines made on them with his finger. "This is a map of Osden, and this one's a map of Nalvern, our neighbor to the east," he said finally.

Arlyn put a hand to her chin. "Nalvern, Nalvern . . . didn't Loren say something about a war between them and Osden?"

"A war your parents were involved in, by the looks of it," Enland said, pointing to the pinned notes on various points of the map labeled things like *Weak Point* or *Safe Route*.

Graylin inspected the map, noting the scatterings of little black dots spread across several maps. "What are these?" she asked aloud.

"Pyrogleminine tests," her cousin answered gravely, handing her a stack of papers and pointing to the key on the side of the map. Graylin skimmed over each paper, grimacing as the accounts became more and more detailed. One bomb had covered a man in flaming pyrogleminine, burning him alive, another left nothing but a smoldering pile of ash. At least fifteen of the accounts had been recent, and almost all of them had been tested in Mackson's Bay. So, then, it was all true.

"Why are they still testing these?" Graylin said, reading over the documents herself, "the war is long over. Is this all just for fun?" The thought was horrible. Had their parents really sunk so far as to kill crowds for the sake of amusement?

River was bent over a desk, shaking his head. "I don't think so." He held up an official-looking letter, with a vaguely familiar seal. "Someone is hiring your parents to wage war against Nalvern and Osden. Currently. Now."

"And whoever is behind it has pyrogleminine," Arlyn shuddered. "And all because of our parents."

"They would help destroy Osden?" Teddy asked, turning from the map of their country.

"I don't know," Graylin said softly.

Arlyn took a deep breath and blew it out. Then she tossed her papers to the floor, and turned to the crew.

"Come on, Graylin. We need to walk."

Graylin looked into her cousin's face, registered the pure hurt there, and obeyed. After all, as far as she knew, Arlyn was all she had left.

The two pushed from the room, followed only by the scent of the space and the eyes of their friends. Neither had a plan; they simply walked, swinging their arms in the same rhythm, matching each other's footsteps.

"Cousin," Arlyn said, as they entered the main floor, where the front doors were. "I don't like this place."

"Me either," Graylin sighed, looking around the space, at the dark green marble floors and the piles of papers. "I mean, it doesn't help that our parents are, like, massively and unaccountably disappointing."

"True that," Arlyn said. She felt like she needed to say something, to get something off her chest, but she could not figure out what.

There was silence as the two leaned against a towering window, looking out. The air leaking out from the edges was cold, and Arlyn shivered. Graylin brought her hand to her face, and dropped it.

"You know," she said quietly, "I always thought being a pessimist would save me from this kind of disappointment." She rubbed her eyes and then crossed her arms, refusing to look anywhere but at the gray, chilled skies through the window. "But it didn't."

"Deep down, I hoped they were all wrong," Arlyn agreed, tugging at her braid. "Uncle Will, LeMay, Loren, the donut lady . . . I thought they had to be wrong. That our parents didn't do all those things. That they aren't . . . bad people."

"You know as well as I do people aren't just good or bad," Graylin said, her voice so soft that it shifted to a whisper.

"Then what are they, Graylin?" Arlyn asked, almost teary. "What are my pare-"

The huge double doors at the front of the room swung up. Arlyn snatched at Graylin's sleeve and dragged her into the shadows, out of sight, behind a sofa. Neither cousin could hear much of anything besides the pounding of their hearts, so strong it could be felt in their heads, and fingers, and toes. *It's them*, Arlyn thought, *they're here*. The cousins crouched together, both hoping it was their parents who had just entered the base, and terrified that it was.

"Certainly did well for themselves, didn't they?" boomed a male voice. Arlyn winced. It was a firm voice, an authoritative one. A harsh one. The cousins glanced at each other before peering over the top of the couch.

There were three men silhouetted in the doorway. All were tall, burly, and wearing beige uniforms with black and white armbands. The man in the middle, the one with the harsh voice, stepped forward and looked around the room. Hearts freezing for a moment, the girls scrambled back under cover.

"Halson," barked the man. The cousins peeked again, watching one of the other men step forward stiffly.

"Sir."

"Halson, you are in charge of the top floor. We'll work our way down to ensure we miss nothing. We don't want any evidence of the Freely's involvement with us."

Us. Arlyn looked at her cousin, who shook her head. Who was *us*?

"Commander Wilson, sir?" Halson stepped up to his superior, swinging the rifle from his shoulder to his hands. "What's the plan now that the Freelys are dead?"

Dead. Arlyn felt rather than saw Graylin's head drop into her hands next to her. Dead. Her parents were dead.

The man in the center spun on his heel to face Halson, radiating irritation.

"I don't know, alright? I don't know. The Freelys were geniuses, and the chance of more landing in our laps seems a little unlikely, wouldn't you say?" The general started his stiff walk again.

"Yes sir, Commander Wilson," Halson was watching the ground, before lifting his head with a new bright idea. "But sir, why don't we look for more Freelys?"

"Are you even listening to yourself?" growled the commander. "All the Freelys are dead, everyone knows that. We had the last four in our employment, and now the name is truly extinct. Michaelangelo and his wife, Benson and *his*, well, they were the last of their kind. The Freelys are gone for good, and all the better for us. Let's imagine there were, in fact, a few Freelys left. Do you think they would be happy to learn that the smartest four died while working for us? Munswel would be blamed."

"But how would they know it was our fault, sir? No one knew about *Genius*, except us and the Freelys," Halson said brightly. "Besides, that explosion was an accident. It wasn't Munswel's doing."

"Enough!" Commander Wilson barked, the order ringing around the room. Halson stepped back, cowed. "This is all very enjoyable, this wild speculation, but it is all for nothing. The Freelys are dead, and we are wasting time. Now, Halson, *please* go to the top floor and make sure there is *nothing* that could suggest the Freelys were working for Munswel. Jones and I will take the floor just under you, and we'll work down." The commander grabbed the third man, who had so far been silent, by the shirtfront and dragged him to the left. Halson muttered a few things under his breath before following. Their steps receded, leaving much louder silence than had been there before their arrival.

"Dead," Arlyn said quietly. Graylin lifted her head from her hands.

"They're searching the whole house," she said hoarsely. "They'll take everything we need to learn what happened." Arlyn met her cousin's eyes, realizing what she meant. Their parents were gone, for good this time. And now those men, the soldiers from Munswel, were here to take away all that they had left to find the truth.

The girls leaped to their feet and tore off down the halls, skidding around corners, tripping down stairs, and flying through doorways. Neither could think of anything beyond the word *dead*. Dead. Dead.

The cousins burst into the map room, the papers on the walls fluttering with the gust of air. Teddy and Lewis both stood, seeing the looks on the girls' faces.

"We have to hide all of this," Arlyn said, rushing forward and beginning to yank papers from the walls. "Now, hurry, come on!"

"But-" River stood up too, moving like he was going to set a hand on Arlyn's shoulder, but she pushed him away.

"Not now." She shoved a handful of papers into his arms. Rushing from wall to wall, Graylin, too, was gathering papers, pulling them towards her frantically. Her hands were shaking, so badly, in fact, that she started to rip pages. Teddy grabbed her hand before she could destroy the bundle entirely. He wrapped her hand in his, waiting until she looked him in the eyes, before letting go of it and taking the papers down himself.

"They can't find these, or us. We need to collect as many of the papers from around the house as we can, and then we need to hide," Graylin said weakly. Teddy nodded and got to work.

Time was not on their side. But, then, when had it ever been? As they snatched and folded and rolled parchment, all the instances when the minutes had ticked faster than they were supposed to ran through Arlyn's head. Uncle Leo. Uncle Will. Loren's parents. *Her* parents. Everyone aboard the *Freelander*. Her parents, again. When had time *ever* been on their side?

Arlyn was just returning with an armful of papers from the main floor when she saw Lewis gesturing frantically to her, mouthing something. Arlyn glanced behind her and saw Graylin, sprinting with papers clutched in each hand down the stairs that led to the top floors.

"They're coming, cousin, they're coming," Graylin hissed. It was then that Arlyn registered the thunk of heavy footsteps descending the stairs. The girls slipped silently to Lewis, who led them quickly down a flight of stairs, into a small room that resembled an office. The desk was askew, the chair lying on the floor, every drawer both open and empty. Lewis opened a closet door to reveal the three boys and all the papers that they could save stashed inside.

The girls ducked in, shutting the door silently behind them. The dark was like the silence upstairs, only worse. Arlyn instantly moved towards Lewis and River, whom she wrapped her arms around, refusing to let go. But Graylin sat down, pushing herself into a corner, drawing her knees to her chest, and squeezing her eyes shut. It was overwhelming, the dark. The stillness. It let in all her thoughts and her feelings, which were so heavy and numerous, she felt like she was drowning in them.

Her parents, Michelangelo and Juliet Freely, were dead. All that hope and anticipation and fear, building and building and building for these last months like a pressure in her chest, had come to nothing. None of it mattered because they were dead now. They had been so close, her and Arlyn. They had been so close. Graylin drew in a shuddering breath as the thought that she had missed her parents by mere weeks, days even, hit her. Eight years she had believed her parents to be dead when they were actually living, and yet she and her cousin had *still* never seen them again.

A hand touched her shoulder, and she folded into the hug being offered to her. It was Teddy. Graylin had never before felt like she needed a hug so badly, because the tears now streaming down her cheeks were not only for her parents. They were not even *mostly* for her parents. They were for everyone, everyone that time had ticked too quickly for. They were for her aunts, and her uncles, and her grandparents, and her cousins and herself. Because nothing could go back to how it was before, and that scared Graylin beyond belief. All those years, living with Leo, she had secretly wished that something would change. That her parents would come back, and everything would be the way it had been before the disaster. But now, huddled in a dark closet, barely breathing for fear of detection, surrounded by pages detailing her parents' misdeeds, consumed by her own, and filled with the knowledge of their deaths, she felt like she had wasted those precious eight years. It seemed like they had been the best days of her life, and that nothing would ever be as good again.

Teddy held her for several minutes, patting her hair. The closet was silent, save for a few sniffs.

"They're dead?" he whispered to Graylin. As soon as the girls had burst into the map room, he had known it. Graylin simply nodded, her chin still on his shoulder.

"Cousin," Arlyn reached a hand out, and Graylin, letting Teddy go, took it. They had never held hands before, not once. But in the dark of the closet, they wrapped their fingers together and didn't let go, because all they had was each other.

Graylin took in a breath to speak, but Arlyn squeezed her hand. Outside, in the office, they heard a door open. Three heavy sets of boots, muffled by the heavy wooden door.

"Well, this is the last room," Commander Wilson said. There was the crunch of papers in his hands as he stepped further in. "For being all smart, these Freelys sure lived in a mess, eh?"

"You can say that again," Halson's voice faded and rose again, as if he were spinning slowly, taking in the room. "Don't seem to have much in here." There was a pause. "Do you think they have stuff in this closet?"

Graylin shivered, imagining the three armed men opening the door.

"Well, you never know with these intelligent types," the commander sighed. "Weird, the whole bunch of them." There was a chuckle, a deep, unsettling one. "The good news is, boys, that we've gotten a good deal of research in our hands here. If we can find even a few relatively brainy blokes back home, I'd say Operation Genius is still a-go." The chuckle turned into a sneer. "Nalvern won't know what hit them. And as soon as we have Nalvern-"

"We have Osden," Halson announced.

"That's right," the commander's footsteps thumped a few more times. "Well, pull the torches out, you know what to do."

"Torches, sir?"

That laugh again, so menacing that Arlyn shivered. "Our final thank you to the Freelys, as it were. Besides, we might have missed something. You wouldn't want Munswel incriminated, would you?"

Halson seemed to salute. "No, sir."

The commander's steps could be heard thunking to the doorway, and stopping.

"Then burn it."

Arlyn realized what was about to happen before Graylin did. She clutched at her cousin's hand as the light strip under the closet door turned a wild, blazing orange.

Graylin had hardly registered the change in light before heat began spilling from the crack as well, heat and smoke. All her muscles seemed to freeze as the smell hit her. The scent was of burning wood, and melting metal, and charred fabric. Within an instant she was eight years old, trembling in the map room aboard the *Freelander.* The floor was tilting, the desk sliding towards her from the other side. Any second now, Uncle Leo would open the door, letting light into the darkness, to rescue her and her cousin.

But it wasn't Leo who opened the door. It was Lewis, calm, even-headed Lewis, who pushed past the petrified cousins, wrapped her sleeve around the doorknob, and shoved it open.

The whole world was on fire. Everywhere Arlyn looked was bright and loud and hot. All the stimulation flooded her, and that familiar feeling of escape, like she *needed* to get to quiet, rose above her head like boiling water. She couldn't escape the noise or the sights, and all she felt was panic. It rolled and bubbled, threatening to overtake her;

but no, she couldn't let it. She *needed* to get out of the fire. She needed to rescue the papers, and herself, and her friends.

Graylin, coughing as tendrils of smoke tickled her lungs, scrambled for the papers they had saved so desperately. Next to her, all three boys had stripped off their outer shirts, tying them up and shoving pages into their makeshift bundles. The heat was overwhelming, choking Graylin as she snatched the last of the papers.

"Everyone hold hands, so we don't lose each other!" Lewis called from somewhere ahead. A chain was formed, Arlyn grabbing Graylin's hand just as they hurried from the room. If the crew had hoped that the rest of the hideout was still intact, they were sorely disappointed. A blast of pure heat and a creaking beam greeted the six as they stumbled out, clutching at the papers and each other. Graylin had just cleared the charred wooden support when it gave a mighty groan and crashed to the floor, spitting embers and sparks.

It was not until they were on the main floor, nearly to the front doors, when Graylin stopped. The flames cackled and laughed, jumping and dancing over the rugs and couches and bookshelves. Warm, stinging tears filled Graylin's eyes as she watched the fire. *We are the last of the Freelys*, Graylin thought. Somehow, it had never seemed so real before. But now . . . well, Leo was dead. Uncle Will was dead. Her parents were dead.

I could finish us off, a little voice in the back of Graylin's head whispered. *All I have to do is stand still. Let the fire come.* Why shouldn't she? She, unlike the rest of her family aboard the *Freelander*, deserved it. She was a murderer. She had killed her uncle.

The flames twisted and writhed, almost temptingly. *I could end the Freelys now. Get rid of us, once and for all.* And would that really be such a bad thing? The Freelys, who had invented and engineered and lied and caused more damage than Graylin yet knew the extent of. The Freelys, who had all disappeared, or died. The Freelys, who were revered and respected, but really were just a gaggle of adults who had gotten involved in what they shouldn't, and left her and her cousin to fix it alone.

No, Graylin, a louder voice retorted. *Not alone, not even close.* And when Graylin glanced up at her five crew members, her five best friends, all watching her anxiously, she burst out in tears because it was true. She wasn't alone, no matter how many times her twisted little mind tried to convince her otherwise. For better or worse, these people cared about her.

"Cousin?" Arlyn stepped forward as Graylin sobbed and felt her own tears surface. The fire raged and screamed. Arlyn could see the tortured look in her cousin's eyes, and her heart dropped as she realized what she'd been considering. She reached out and took Graylin's hand. She *would* rescue her cousin, because she had to. She *needed* her.

The *Freelander* had been parked next to the hideout, luckily, for otherwise both the Nalvern soldiers and the flames might have reached it. As it was, the crew hurried aboard, shoving all the papers into the meeting room as Teddy started up the ship desperately. The engine clunked and coughed, spitting out black smoke which matched the billowing clouds swirling from the hideout. All three hundred and fifty balloons bobbed as the airship rose into the air, moved by the rolling waves of heat from the burning building.

And Arlyn and Graylin Freely stood side by side on the deck, watching as the last of their hopes burned. Slowly, one by one, their friends stepped forward. First was Lewis, putting a hand on Arlyn's back and holding her close. Then there were River and Enland, one of which squeezed himself between the cousins and hugged them both, the other who stood solemnly behind them. Lastly came Teddy, who took Graylin's hand and held it tight, seeing her tears and feeling only slightly ashamed of his own. Maybe it was the smoke, or maybe it was the sadness, or maybe it was the loss, but every throat was dry and scratched, and every eye shone.

"What now?" Lewis asked softly. Arlyn glanced at her cousin. They had spent months trying to find their parents, only to learn that they were not only not at all who the girls had hoped they were, but also dead. Dead, and gone. Like Leo. Like Denloy. Like their aunts and uncles and cousins and grandparents who had been on the *Freelander* when it had burned.

But they had the papers. They had the knowledge and the ability to gain more. And, most important of all, Arlyn and Graylin still had each other. They *would* learn the truth, they *would* stay together, and they *would* fix this.

"Now," Arlyn said, watching her cousin's big gray eyes, and the flames reflected in them. "Now, we keep going."

Epilogue

WILLIAM FREELY TUMBLED THROUGH the air. Everything around him was a hauntingly opaque fog, swirling and twirling until he couldn't tell which way was up and which way was down. Nothing made sense, he couldn't see anything, his coat was tugging at him, pulling, when-

SPLASH! Suddenly he was underwater. He tried to open his eyes, to move, to do anything, but it was like his brain was stuck in the past. All he registered was the feeling of falling, and the inky coldness around him, and the weight of his clothes dragging him down. That is until his air suddenly ran out, and in a flash he couldn't breathe, he couldn't see, he couldn't move. He tried frantically to kick, to fight his way up, until finally, *finally*, his hcad broke the surface.

William gasped and choked, hardly able to keep himself afloat. His glasses were gone, of course, and all he could make out were the fuzzy shapes of trees in the distance, deep yellows and oranges, the leaves already turning color for the year. Shivering, he paddled towards what seemed to be the shore, the fog rolling in large, slow sheets. As he dragged himself from the lake, he tried to get a grip on his surroundings. He was by a body of water, in a forest, some small hills rising around him. His body was shaking from the shock of falling and hitting the icy water. The water . . . the *Freelander* must not have been as high as they'd thought, or he would have surely died upon hitting the lake.

The *Freelander*. He'd been on the *Freelander*, he'd been standing with Arlyn and Graylin, and then he had suddenly been tumbling through the air, a split second of flying before splashing into the water.

In a flash, William remembered the argument, the yelling, and the noise. He had shouted at the girls- they had shouted back. He had slapped Arlyn . . . how could he have done that? Hurt his beautiful, young, innocent niece, whom he'd yearned to protect. He had *hurt* her.

And now they were alone, his nieces. Arlyn and Graylin were alone, and they would find his brothers and learn the truth without him. And it would break them.

Frantically, William Freely scanned his surroundings, eyes catching a glimmer on the ground a few feet away. He bent down, felt around, and yes! His glasses. The frame was bent beyond repair, and one lens was cracked, the other smudged with mud, but Will cleaned them quickly and held them to his very Freely eyes. As the landscape became clear, he noticed a trail of hazy smoke twisting into the sky to the east, several in fact. Will could have cried with relief. He would find people, and then he would find his nieces. He could still help them.

William Freely was cold, injured, and determined as he dragged himself toward the smoke. He *had* to keep going.

Acknowledgements

Books are notoriously complex, made up of many parts and gears. Undoubtedly the most boorish of these is the acknowledgments, where the authors spew thanks to people the readers don't know. However, the fact remains that we could not have completed this tale of ours without the support of our friends, family, and many people in between. To start, our parents: Ben and Amanda Fust, and Mike and Jerra Fust. Their guidance, feedback, assistance and genuinely good parenting skills gave us what no one else ever could. Also, you know, they taught us how to read. Secondly, we would like to thank our Beta Readers: Julene Smith, Archana Venugopal, Abby Glann, Sadie Green, Jerra Fust, and Ben Fust, for their dedication to reading and analyzing fairly rough second drafts. We would also like to give special thanks to Ellary Carson and Wren(jamin) Carson for acknowledging how hilarious we are and helping us through tough days without snapping a neck. Our general community of people is unmatched, and without our people around us we would have been like a Freely without the *Freelander*. That is, unable to fly and distressingly uncreative.

About the authors

Emma enjoys many things, but as her interests tend to fall in the expectedly creative category, it might be best to list her dislikes. These include omelets, velvet, and a lack of semi-colons in modern literature. Emma hates roller coasters but adores storms, and would gladly become a tornado wrangler if this author thing doesn't work out. When not writing, drawing, listening to music, or thinking about doing any of those things, she can often be found in the company of her cousin and favorite person, Evelyn. This is her first book, and she intends to produce many more.

Evelyn would describe excessive comma usage less as a hobby and more of a lifestyle. When not trying to telepathically transmit her ideas into Google Docs via sitting ten feet away and looking at birds outside the window, Evelyn enjoys embroidery, making soup, collecting tea cups, and making herself laugh. When tired of her own sense of humor, she takes to finding comfort and comedy in her beloved cousin, Emma. This is her first of many novels to come, and her first foray into split authorship.

www.ingramcontent.com/pod-product-compliance
Lightning Source LLC
Chambersburg PA
CBHW030552310726
48979CB00011B/2122/J

* 9 7 8 1 7 3 4 1 7 2 9 2 8 *